Praise for *New York Times* bestselling author
Kat Martin

"[Kat] Martin is a terrific storyteller…"
—*Booklist* on *Season of Strangers*

"[Martin] dishes up romantic suspense, sizzling sex and international intrigue in healthy doses, and fans are going to be the winners."
—*RT Book Reviews* on *Against the Sun*, Top Pick

"Kat Martin is a fast gun when it comes to storytelling, and I love her books."
—#1 *New York Times* bestselling author
Linda Lael Miller

Praise for *USA TODAY* bestselling author
Delores Fossen

"Clear off space on your keeper shelf, Fossen has arrived."
—*New York Times* bestselling author Lori Wilde

"[*Savior in the Saddle*] takes off at full speed from the first page and doesn't surrender an iota of the chills until the end."
—*RT Book Reviews*

D1010327

Kat Martin is the *New York Times* bestselling author of sixty books. To date she has over sixteen million copies of her books in print in twenty-one countries, including Sweden, France, Russia, Spain, Japan, Argentina, Poland and Greece. Kat and her husband, author L. J. Martin, live on their ranch outside Missoula, Montana, and spend winters at their beach house in California. Kat invites you to visit her website at www.katmartin.com.

USA TODAY bestselling author **Delores Fossen** has had more than fifty novels published, with millions of copies of her books in print worldwide. She's received the Booksellers' Best Award, the RT Reviewers' Choice Best Book Award and was a finalist for a prestigious RITA® Award. In addition, she's had nearly a hundred short stories and articles published in national magazines. Married to an air force colonel, Delores is the mother of four children and has lived in England and all over the US. She's had a variety of careers and jobs: an air force captain, a special-ed teacher and a rehab counsellor. None was as fun or challenging as the time she spent as a stay-at-home mom. You can get updates about Delores's books or contact her through her website at www.deloresfossen.com.

New York Times **Bestselling Author**

KAT MARTIN

AGAINST THE WIND

◆**HARLEQUIN**®BESTSELLING AUTHOR COLLECTION

ISBN-13: 978-0-373-01041-7

Against the Wind

Copyright © 2016 by Harlequin Books S.A.

The publisher acknowledges the copyright holders of the individual works as follows:

Against the Wind
Copyright © 2011 by Kat Martin

Savior in the Saddle
Copyright © 2010 by Delores Fossen

Recycling programs for this product may not exist in your area.

H HARLEQUIN®
™ www.Harlequin.com

Printed in U.S.A.

CONTENTS

AGAINST THE WIND   7
Kat Martin

SAVIOR IN THE SADDLE   397
Delores Fossen

Also by Kat Martin

Season of Strangers
Scent of Roses
The Summit

The Raines of Wind Canyon

Against the Mark
Against the Edge
Against the Odds
Against the Sun
Against the Night
Against the Storm
Against the Law
Against the Fire
Against the Wind

The Bride Trilogy

Rule's Bride
Reese's Bride
Royal's Bride

The Heart Trilogy

Heart of Courage
Heart of Fire
Heart of Honor

The Necklace Trilogy

The Handmaiden's Necklace
The Devil's Necklace
The Bride's Necklace

AGAINST THE WIND

Kat Martin

For my husband, Larry, the love of my life.

Chapter 1

"Mommy, why do we have to leave?" Sarah Allen's six-year-old daughter, Holly, looked up at her with big blue, tear-filled eyes. "I like it here. I don't want to go."

Anxious to be on her way, Sarah reached down and lifted the little blonde girl into her arms. "Don't cry, sweetie. I promise you're going to love it. The mountains are beautiful and there are these rivers and big green forests, and you can have a puppy if you want." At least Sarah hoped so.

Surely the owners of the cottage she had rented wouldn't mind. The house was, after all, on a very large ranch, at least twelve thousand acres.

Holly sniffed back tears and looked up with interest. "A puppy? Can I really?"

"As soon as we get settled, we'll drive into town and you can adopt one from the pound." Sarah glanced nervously toward the door. The car was packed, the rest of their personal possessions boxed and shipped. She was leaving Los Angeles and she prayed she was leaving her troubles, as well.

The sooner they left town, the safer she would feel.

She set Holly back on her feet, took a last glance around the expensive Santa Monica apartment she had occupied with her late husband, surveyed the plush white carpet and chic furniture that was Andrew's taste, not hers. There was nothing homey, nothing the least bit geared toward a family. The condo was just for show—no substance beyond the surface beauty. Just like Andrew.

Sarah started for the door, but the phone rang before she could reach it. She considered just letting it ring, a hollow echo now that her things were gone, but she was afraid it might be important.

She lifted the receiver and pressed it against her ear. "Hello."

"Sarah, this is Martin Kozak." His raspy smoker's voice grated over the line. "We need to talk."

A shiver went down her spine. Marty Kozak was one of Andrew's business associates. A few weeks ago, Marty had started calling, trying to set up a meeting. Sarah didn't want to talk to him or any of Andrew's other shady business acquaintances.

"What do you want, Marty? I told you I don't know anything about Andrew's affairs. He never talked to me about business. We never discussed it."

He didn't think I was smart enough, or savvy enough about finances, or he just plain didn't want to.

And Andrew never did anything he didn't want to do.

"Like I told you before," Marty said, "Andrew had

something important I need. Did you find anything in his personal belongings? A list he might have been keeping? A flash drive, maybe, or a record book of some kind?"

"No. Before he died, we were barely speaking." That was an understatement. When they were together, Andrew did all the talking, mostly about himself. Sarah had been trying to leave him for years, but she had been afraid of what would happen if she did. "He didn't tell me anything, and he didn't give me anything."

"Maybe there was something in his personal effects."

"Not that I know of."

"I'd like to talk to you, Sarah."

"I'm sorry, Marty. I was just walking out the door. I've really got to go." By the time she hung up the phone, she was shaking. She had no idea what sort of trouble Andrew might have been in before he was killed, but she wasn't part of it and never had been.

Once you get out of town, she told herself, *everything is going to be all right.*

Things were bound to settle down. After her husband's murder, the police had questioned her extensively, but that had been months ago and they were certain his death was a result of his gambling debts or crooked business dealings. She figured Marty had waited for the police investigation to die down before he began to press her for whatever it was he wanted.

Sarah closed her eyes and dragged in a steadying breath. The past would fade, she told herself, and in time, even Andrew's associates would leave her alone.

Grabbing Holly's hand and the big leather purse that carried everything from bandages to emergency food—breakfast bars this morning—she took the private elevator down to the underground garage where her Mercedes, one of the few possessions Andrew had actually put in her name, was parked.

Everything else belonged solely to him and he managed to keep it that way with the prenuptial agreement she had signed. After he died, she was only mildly surprised to discover he owed more money than he had in his bank accounts and had mortgaged or sold all of the real estate he owned. He had even let his life insurance policy expire.

Sarah had been left with nothing. She had sold everything she could to raise enough money to move out of L.A., taken back her maiden name, changed Holly's name, and found a job over the internet in her home town of Wind Canyon, Wyoming. On a site for rental properties, she had happened upon a cottage on a ranch in the country not too far from town.

All she had to do was get there.

Still clutching Holly's hand, Sarah opened the rear car door, set her daughter in the booster seat and strapped her in, then rounded the vehicle and slid behind the wheel. It was a thousand-mile journey to Wyoming.

Sarah thought of Andrew, his extravagant lifestyle, his gambling and the crooked deals he made to keep the money rolling in. She thought of Marty Kozak and the rest of Andrew's so-called business associates.

She wouldn't feel safe until she got there.

Chapter 2

Jackson Raines tightened his hold on the steering wheel of his white Ford extended-cab pickup. The temperature outside was two below, the wind howling, the heavy snow blowing sideways. A Wyoming blizzard was nothing to sneeze at, even one this late in spring. Keeping his eyes carefully fixed on the road, he was surprised to see a pair of taillights up ahead, barely visible through the blowing snow, twin dots of red flashing in hazard mode, the car pulled off on the side of the road.

Jackson started slowing way before he reached the vehicle. He didn't want to slide into the damned thing, and on a road as icy as this one, it wouldn't be hard to do.

There was rarely any traffic on the narrow two lanes that led nowhere except to a couple of ranches in the area. He couldn't help wondering who would be driving out here in this kind of weather. Hell, he wouldn't be here himself if he hadn't been in town when the storm blew in, several hours earlier than expected. He should have known. In mountains like these, the weatherman was never right.

He slowed even more, downshifted until the pickup was moving at a crawl, then pulled in behind the stranded auto. California license plates. Through the blinding wall of white, he recognized the car as a newer Mercedes. *S500* gleamed in chrome on the left side of the trunk.

Jackson pulled on a pair of leather work gloves and climbed out of the pickup. He should have figured it would be some rich guy with more money than common sense.

Tugging his worn cowboy hat down over his forehead, he walked up to the car and rapped on the window. The driver flinched at the sound as if he'd been shot. He pressed the button and the window eased down, and Jackson frowned as he realized the driver was a woman. And in her lap, she was holding a little girl.

"Thank God you stopped," the woman said, her teeth chattering.

"What in blazes are you doing out here?"

"I thought we could get where we were going before the storm came in."

He could hardly argue with that since he had done the same thing.

"What's the problem?"

"Flat tire. My cell phone's out of range. I thought about trying to make it on the rim, but I was afraid I wouldn't get there and just ruin the wheel, then no one would be able to put on the spare."

He nodded. "You did the right thing."

"Can you help us?"

There was something familiar about the woman's voice. He leaned down, trying to get a better look at her, but she was wearing a fancy fur coat and she had the collar pulled up over her ears, hiding most of her face. "Open the trunk."

She pressed a button somewhere inside the car and the trunk popped open.

"Should I get out and help?" she asked.

His eyebrows went up. He hadn't expected her to be the type to put herself out, especially not in the middle of a snowstorm.

"Nothing much you can do." He looked at the little girl, blond hair and big blue eyes, and he could see she was frightened. "I'll do what I can. Roll the window back up before you freeze."

Jackson pulled up the collar of his heavy down jacket and crunched through the snow toward the back of the Mercedes, silver, he saw, now mostly covered by at least an inch of fresh powder. He pulled the jack out of the trunk, walked around and stuck it under the frame. As he shoved the handle into the slot and started cranking, he thought about the woman.

He could only see enough of her to know she had thick, chestnut-brown hair about the color of her fancy mink coat and eyes as blue as her daughter's. Her skin was smooth and he thought she had a nice straight nose but he couldn't really be sure.

Still, there was something about her....

Jackson pulled off the flat tire, got the spare out

from under the luggage in the trunk, eventually got it on and replaced the lug nuts. It was ball-freezing cold and he wanted to get back to the ranch before the storm got any worse. When he finished putting the jack away, he reloaded the luggage, closed the trunk and walked back to the window, which slid open with a soft electric hum.

The woman stuck out a slim hand encased in a brown kid glove holding a twenty-dollar bill. "Thank you so much. I really appreciate your help."

"Keep your money," he said, only slightly annoyed. Out here people helped each other because it was the right thing to do. "It was only a flat tire."

"Are you sure? You must be freezing. I wish I could pay you more, but—"

"Consider it a favor. Where are you headed?"

"Just down the road." She checked the map that lay open on the console. "It's just a couple more miles."

It had to be one of the ranches up ahead. There wasn't much else out here. "I'll follow you to the turn-off."

She nodded and fired up the engine. The Mercedes didn't have four-wheel drive, but it was a good, heavy auto, and if she took her time, she could make it to where she was going. As if she were still on the freeway back in California, she put on her left turn signal and pulled cautiously onto the road.

Jackson felt the tug of a smile as she navigated the big car carefully down the lane. Again, he wondered who she was and what had brought her twenty miles from Wind Canyon, the nearest town.

Back in his pickup, he cranked the engine and followed them at a safe distance until her turn signal went on again and she made a very slow turn onto the private road leading to the Whittaker Ranch. He watched until he was sure she was close enough to the ranch to make it, then gave her a wave she probably couldn't see and drove on down the road toward home. It was only a couple miles farther. Olivia would have a pot of coffee on the stove and if he was lucky, stew and biscuits for supper.

Jackson pressed down on the gas pedal, eager to get in out of the weather.

Sarah rounded a corner and saw the sign for the Whittaker Ranch. Biting back a swearword she couldn't say in front of Holly, she cautiously stepped on the brake.

"What's the matter, Mommy?"

"I turned too soon. This is the Whittaker Ranch. We're looking for the Raintree Ranch."

"Do we have to turn around?" Holly gazed worriedly out the window into the storm.

"We'll turn around as soon as I can find a wide enough spot in the road." She wasn't taking any chances. The next time she ran into trouble, her old classmate, Jackson Raines, wouldn't be there to help her.

Sarah released a shaky breath that turned white inside the car, even with the heater running full blast. Though he looked older, more rugged than he had when he was a senior at Wind Canyon High, she had known him instantly. She had kept her head down, hoping Jackson wouldn't recognize her, and she didn't think he had.

She knew he'd left town after high school. According to her friend, Nancy Marcus, he had gone to the

University of Wyoming on a boxing scholarship. Everyone in Wind Canyon had watched the Olympics the year Jackson had competed in the light heavyweight division, and though he hadn't won, everyone in Wyoming had been proud of the effort he had made.

Sarah had never heard any more about him.

She certainly didn't know he had returned to Wind Canyon. Maybe he was working as a hand on one of the local ranches. She remembered he had done that during the summers when he'd been in high school.

Driving carefully, she continued along the road and finally found a turnaround spot, her thoughts still on Jackson, the gangly teenager he had been and the lean, broad-shouldered, rugged-looking man he had become. With his high cheekbones, dark eyes and nearly black hair, he had been a good-looking boy. Now, at thirty-five—three years older than she—he was a man, with an air of confidence that made him even more attractive.

Focusing her attention on getting back to the main road, Sarah used the circular turnaround made for just that purpose. It was nice and wide and she was able to change direction without a problem, even with the building layer of snow.

She had taken Holly out of the backseat when the tire went flat so they could huddle together and stay warm. For the few miles left to their destination, the six-year-old was strapped into the passenger seat with the air bag turned off.

Sarah kept the car going slowly all the way to the entrance gate, then turned right, back onto the two-lane road. The next two miles felt like ten, with the car slipping on the ice beneath the snow and the wind making an eerie moaning sound.

Then she spotted the big sign, Raintree Ranch, hanging from a gate framed by huge pine logs. The name was different now, but the ranch had been there for as long as Sarah could remember. She had driven by a dozen times over the years but never actually been on the property—which was, after all, privately owned, and the no-trespassing policy had always been strictly enforced.

Sarah had left Wind Canyon two days after graduation. Having taken out a student loan, combined with the money she earned from a part-time job at a small café, she was able to attend UCLA. She had a cousin in Westwood named Betsy, who had offered her a bedroom, which Sarah gratefully accepted. She majored in literature with the goal of becoming a journalist, a goal that had never been reached.

Until now.

"Are we there yet, Mama?"

Sarah smiled. "Almost. It's only a little ways farther. Keep your eyes open for the ranch house."

Holly sat up straighter in the seat, trying to see through the heavy snowfall. In the distance, the main house came slowly into focus until it took the shape of a shadowy fortress, a big, rambling, two-story wooden structure with a balcony off the second floor. It was built sometime in the twenties, Sarah recalled, by the descendants of the ranch's original owners. There were a couple of lights on downstairs, but Sarah didn't stop.

It was after eight o'clock. When she sent in her rent deposit on the cottage, she had told the housekeeper, Olivia Jones, that she wasn't sure of the date or time of her arrival. The letter she received in return said it didn't matter, that she should just go directly to the cottage, which was another hundred yards down the road. There was a map, as well as the location of the key— beneath a flowerpot on the front porch next to the door.

The snow was getting worse. The main house sat some distance off the lane she was traveling, and as the Mercedes drove slowly past, no one seemed to notice. Though Sarah looked forward to meeting the woman who had been so kind to her when she had called about the rental, she was grateful for a quiet night to settle into her new home.

Sometime in the next few days, the rest of her meager possessions would arrive, not much since most of her things had been sold to raise money for the move from California. Thankfully, the cottage was furnished, so she didn't have to worry about that. Tonight she and Holly would eat the sandwiches she had picked up in Wind Canyon and go straight to bed.

Sarah smiled. She was back where she had been born, a town she had once wanted desperately to escape. But she was a grown woman now, not a schoolgirl. Wind Canyon was the perfect place to raise a child and she was incredibly glad to be home.

Still smiling, Sarah pulled the car up next to the little batten-board cottage and turned off the engine. But as she sat there working up the courage to climb out into the storm, the sweet feeling of homecoming began to fade. She had a lot of regrets about her life. One of the biggest was the way she had treated Jackson Raines.

Chapter 3

A brilliant Wyoming sun shone down on eight inches of fresh snow that blanketed the landscape. In the distance, the branches on the pine trees climbing the sides of the mountains drooped with their heavy burden of white. Already it was melting. It was mid-May, a little late in the year for a storm this size, though it wasn't that uncommon, either.

In the mountains, the weather was always unpredictable. It was one of the things Jackson liked best about living here, the fierce storms and wild winds, the sun so bright it hurt your eyes. As he walked toward the barn, pulling on his work gloves, he smiled. When he'd left Wind Canyon sixteen years ago, he wasn't sure he would ever return.

Now he was home and he was damned glad to be back.

He glanced ahead, his steps slowing as he spotted

the Mercedes with the flat tire he had worked on last night. What in blazes was the car doing parked at the cottage?

Jackson turned in that direction, each step leaving a deep boot print in the snow. He had almost reached the house when he heard his housekeeper, Olivia Jones, calling from behind him.

"Jackson, wait! Jackson!" She was breathing hard as she hurried toward him, a woman of sixty, broad-hipped, thick-waisted and gray-haired. She'd been a real beauty in her day, still had the dimples in her cheeks to prove it, and the same sweet smile she'd had when she worked at the ice-cream shop in town when he was a boy.

She wasn't smiling now. "Jackson!"

"Take it easy, Livvy. You'll give yourself a heart attack."

She cast him a look, then drew in a panting breath and slowly released it. "I forgot to tell you—I rented the cottage."

"You what?"

"We talked about it, remember? You said we ought to do something with the place instead of just letting it sit there and rot into the ground."

"I didn't say we should rent it. My brothers stay there whenever they come back to town."

"Which is almost never. They're too busy making money."

"Yes, but—"

"You said do something, so I did."

He lifted his cowboy hat, then settled it back down on his forehead. "All right, I guess that's fair." He looked over at the cottage. The gabled roof had just been replaced and the slight sag in the porch had been repaired, making it nice to sit outside where you could watch the small, rushing stream that passed by the house. "So what's that car doing parked there?"

"That's the new tenant."

"Tell me you didn't rent the place to some rich society woman from the city out here for the summer."

"Of course not."

"I changed the lady's tire last night and that's what she looked like to me."

"She's not *some society woman.* She used to live in Wind Canyon when she was a girl. She recently lost her husband. She wanted to come home and I thought this would be the perfect place for her to recover from her loss."

Jackson frowned. "What's her name?"

"Sarah Hollister."

"Doesn't sound familiar."

"She was Sarah Allen when she was a girl."

Jackson took the news like a sucker punch to the stomach. *Sarah Allen.* Damn, he had known her voice sounded familiar. Sarah had been two grades behind him in school, though he was three years older. He thought she was the prettiest, sweetest girl he had ever seen.

Man, had he been wrong.

Oh, she was pretty. From what little he could see last night, she still was. But even back then, Sarah was a social climber, a middle-class girl who wanted to be part of the in crowd, to socialize with the kids whose parents had money.

It had taken him weeks to work up the courage to talk to her. That first time, she had seemed almost shy. A few weeks passed while he madly saved his money. Like a lovesick fool, he had asked her to his senior prom.

Sarah hadn't just said no. When she realized some of her friends were watching, she had pointed at him as if he were something stuck on the bottom of her shoe, and started laughing.

"Jackson wants to take me to the prom!" She ignored his red face and the hands at his sides balled into fists. "How would we get there, Jackson? In that old, beat-up car of yours? Or maybe your brother could loan us his bicycle."

He had turned and walked away when he wanted to punch something, maybe hit the guy laughing even harder than she was, the school's pretty-boy quarter-back, Jeffrey Freedman. Jeff was the guy who gave him and his younger brothers, Gabe and Devlin, more grief than any of the other kids in school.

He and Freedman had gone at it once before and Freedman had come out the loser. Jackson might have hit him again except that by then he'd started team-boxing and his coach, Steve Whitelaw, had taught him that the street fighting he was so good at would only get him into more trouble. He was learning to channel the talent he had with his fists into a sport that eventually won him a scholarship.

Jackson glanced back at the cottage. He was no longer that same insecure boy who had left Wind Canyon sixteen years ago. But he would never forget the girl who had made him feel less than a man.

"You remember her, don't you?" Livvy asked, breaking into his thoughts. "She was real pretty, thick dark brown hair and big blue eyes. She was kind of shy back then."

"Shy? I'm afraid that isn't the Sarah I remember. And I don't want her here." He started toward the cottage, but Livvy caught his arm.

"What are you doing? I've already taken her money."

"Then give it back."

"She doesn't want it back. She wants a place to raise her little girl. I thought it would be nice to have a child around—and maybe some female company once in a while."

"Fine, but not here."

"Why not?"

"Because I said so. Go back to the house, Livvy. I'll take care of this."

"But…but…"

Jackson just ignored her and kept on walking. He tried to tell himself he wouldn't get the least satisfaction from throwing Sarah Allen off his land.

But he knew it wasn't the truth.

Sarah hummed as she worked in the quaint little cottage, unpacking her and Holly's things. She had tied a bandanna around her head to hold back her heavy dark hair and though the place was immaculately clean, busied herself lining drawers with the shelf paper she had found in one of the closets and generally taking inventory of what was in the house.

She glanced around the larger of two cozy bedrooms, one with twin beds, the other with a queen-size four-poster, each covered with what looked like handmade quilts. Surprisingly, considering the age of the cottage, there were also two bathrooms, which Sarah viewed as a major bonus.

She was on her way back into the living room— wide-planked wooden floors, a stone fireplace, a comfortable sofa and chairs—when she heard a brisk knock at the door. For an instant, fear gripped her. Living with Andrew had instilled a defense mechanism that set her adrenaline rushing in an instant.

She forced herself to relax. Assuming it must be Olivia Jones, the lady who had rented her the property, she hurried over, lifted the wrought-iron latch and pulled the door open.

Her eyes widened. It wasn't Olivia; it was Jackson Raines.

And he didn't look happy to see her.

"Hello, Sarah."

She wet her lips, which suddenly felt stiff as paper. "Hello, Jackson."

"You don't seem surprised to see me. I guess you recognized me last night."

"I…umm…figured it out."

"And you must have been headed here and not the Whittaker Ranch."

"I made the wrong turn." She tipped her head back a little farther to look at him. He was even taller than she remembered, somewhere around six foot three. He had certainly changed in sixteen years. Each of his features seemed more distinct, his dark brown eyes more intense, his cheekbones more sharply defined. She remembered the slight cleft in his chin, but now there was a faint scar along his temple and another bisected one of his nicely shaped eyebrows.

A little tremor of awareness went through her that

she was surprised to feel. It had been years since she had felt any sort of attraction to a man. After Andrew, she thought maybe she never would again.

"Do you...umm...work here on the ranch?" she asked.

The corner of his mouth edged up. "You might say that." He looked over her shoulder into the living room, surveyed the boxes on the sofa and the suitcases on the bed he could see through the open bedroom door. "I'm afraid we have a problem."

"We do? What is it?"

"Mrs. Jones made a mistake. The cottage is not for rent."

Her stomach tightened. "That...that can't be right. It was listed on the internet. The details have all been worked out."

"I'll see your money is returned. And I'll pay for any extra trouble this might have caused. Just tell me how much and I'll write you a check."

Her voice rose. "I don't want a check! This is going to be our home. Holly and I...we need this place. We love it here already." Tears welled in her eyes. She couldn't stand to think of being uprooted again, of searching for somewhere else to live, of disappointing Holly. Just then the little girl raced into the living room.

"Mommy—there's a nest of baby robins under the roof right outside my window! The mother bird is feeding them!" She slid to a stop just a few feet away from Jackson. "You're the man from last night."

"That's right."

"Holly, this is Mr. Raines. Jackson, this is my daughter, Holly."

"You saved us. Mommy said she didn't know what

we would have done if you hadn't come along. Maybe we would have frozen right out there on the road."

His lips twitched. "I don't think you would have frozen but I'm glad I could help."

"Please," Sarah pleaded, "isn't there any way you could speak to the owner, tell him how important it is for Holly and me to stay?"

His eyes drifted over her turtleneck sweater and jeans, the white sneakers she wore that would be worthless out in the snow. "Just how important is it?"

A lump began to swell in her throat. Being here meant everything. Since the moment she had walked through the door of the cottage, for the first time in years, she had felt as if she were home.

"I have a job in town, working for the *Wind Canyon News*. It's freelance, so it's only part-time and I'll be able to take care of Holly. I had to pull her out of school two weeks early but I figured it would be worth it. She's never lived anywhere but the city. I want her to know what it's like to live somewhere free and open—a place where there are trees and animals and birds, where the sky is blue and clear." She glanced away, afraid he would notice the glitter of tears in her eyes. "She just lost her father. She needs this, Jackson. Please... I need it."

He was frowning. He looked down at Holly, who was staring at him as if he were a real-life hero—which, to her, being a cowboy and their savior last night, he was.

He took a deep breath and slowly released it. "I suppose it wouldn't hurt if you stayed for a while. Just don't get too comfortable. If things don't work out, you'll have to find another place to live."

Relief hit her so hard her knees went weak. A bright smile broke over her face. "Things will work out. We won't be a problem, I promise."

He nodded.

"So you'll talk to the owner? You'll make sure it's okay for us to stay?"

He made a scoffing sound. "I'll take care of it." Then he turned and started walking away, out the door and across the porch, out into the snow.

Sarah ran after him. "I meant to ask…" she called out. "What's the name of the man who owns the ranch?"

He kept on walking, his boots crunching in the snow. Over his shoulder he called back to her. "Jackson Raines."

Sarah just stood there staring. Jackson Raines owned the ranch where she and Holly were going to live. Of course, after the way she had treated him all those years ago, no wonder he wanted her to leave! She dragged in a breath and slowly released it. Sooner or later, she would have to talk to him, apologize and try to explain why she had behaved so badly—not that there was any real excuse.

"He's a really nice man, Mama. I like him."

She managed a smile. "It was kind of him to let us stay." But clearly, it was only a temporary reprieve. He would be looking for a reason to get rid of them. He didn't want her here, and she couldn't really blame him.

Still, she wouldn't make it easy.

She intended to keep to herself, do her job in town and not cause any trouble.

Surely that wouldn't be a difficult thing to do.

Two days later, Jackson stood at the kitchen window, watching as a car hauler drove down the lane past the ranch house and rolled to a stop in front of the cottage. There was an old Toyota pickup on the flatbed, rusted and at least ten years old. The driver unloaded the little truck that looked like a miniature version of a real pickup, then pulled Sarah's fancy Mercedes up on the carrier and began to strap it down.

Jackson frowned. What the hell was going on?

Taking a last swig of coffee, he tossed the rest down the drain, grabbed his jacket off the coatrack beside the door and headed toward the cottage. Most of the snow had already melted, leaving the ground a muddy, soggy mess. His old work boots squished with every step. As he strode toward the cottage, he spotted Sarah standing on the porch, dressed in jeans and the same white sneakers she'd had on the last time he saw her. He wondered why she didn't have the good sense to buy herself a decent pair of boots.

"All set, Ms. Allen."

"Thank you, Mr. Roderick."

The driver waved, got back into his truck, turned the carrier around in the open space between the cottage and the barn, and headed back down the lane toward the road.

"Car trouble?" Jackson asked, wondering if she would explain or tell him it was none of his business.

"I sold my car. It wasn't any good for country living, anyway."

He walked over to the little Toyota pickup. The first thing he noticed was that all four tires were bare.

"I know I probably shouldn't say this, but you realize those tires have got to be replaced."

She frowned. "What do you mean?"

"I mean they aren't safe for you to drive on, let alone haul your little girl back and forth to town."

She started toward him down the steps, the white sneakers instantly sucking down in the icy, slushy mud. "Are you sure?"

"I'm sure." He walked around the pickup, saw that the leather seats were cracked and the carpets worn. "Did you have anyone look at this truck before you bought it?"

"I didn't know who to ask. I don't know anyone around here anymore. It looked like it would get good gas mileage and it has four-wheel drive."

"The damned thing's ten years old."

She stiffened. "It was all I could afford. Now if you will excuse me—"

"Whoa—wait a minute." She turned back to him. He tried not to notice how pretty she looked in the morning sun with her dark hair pulled into a long gleaming braid and her skin glowing as if it were lit from within.

"What do you mean, 'all you can afford'? Word around here was you married some wealthy guy in L.A. If he just passed away, you ought to be pretty well fixed for money."

"Well, I'm not. By the time the estate paid Andrew's debts, there wasn't much of anything left."

"Couldn't tell by that fancy fur coat you were wearing when I saw you on the road."

Her chin inched up. "That's sold, too, if it's any of your business." She turned and started walking and when he looked at her mud-covered sneakers, it occurred to him that she really might not have any money. He should have been elated by this little crumb of payback but he wasn't.

Christ.

No wonder she wanted to stay in the cottage. It was all she could afford. Which could be the reason she didn't seem particularly grief-stricken by her husband's death. She had probably married the guy for his money and then found out he didn't have any.

Sarah disappeared inside the little house. Against all his better instincts, he followed. He rapped on the door, and an instant later, she pulled it open.

"Was there something else you wanted?"

"I just thought I'd check, see if you're getting settled in all right."

"The rest of our things are supposed to arrive tomorrow."

"The rest?"

"There isn't all that much. I sold everything I could to get enough money to come out here." She sighed, looped a wisp of dark hair behind her ear. "I don't know why I'm telling you this. It's hardly your concern."

"Maybe not." But somehow it almost seemed as if it was. "How's Holly doing?"

"She loves it here."

"Mr. Raines!" She spotted him on the porch just then, bolted through the door and slid to a halt at his feet. "Mama said the next time I saw you I should ask you if it's all right if I get a puppy?"

He couldn't help a smile. His foreman, Jimmy Threebears, and his two boys had a couple of mutts. One more could hardly hurt. Still, it would just make things harder if he decided to send them packing.

Holly was looking up at him with big blue eyes so full of hope Jackson groaned inside. He loved kids.

There was no way he was going to say no to this sweet little girl.

"It's all right. Matter of fact, my foreman's dog just had a litter. They're border collies. You want to take a look? You might like to have one of the pups."

Holly whirled toward her mother, her long blond ponytail swinging out behind her. "Mommy, can I, please?"

Sarah smiled. She had pretty white teeth and full pink lips. Jackson remembered that smile and his jaw tightened. That same warm smile had been deceptive in the past.

Likely, it still was.

The UPS truck delivered the boxes with the rest of Sarah's clothes and personal items the following day. Olivia Jones, the housekeeper she had met the day after her arrival, came over with a hamburger-mac-and-cheese casserole that smelled so good her stomach growled.

"Looks like you got plenty of work ahead of you. I figured with this you wouldn't have to stop and cook dinner."

"Thank you, Mrs. Jones. It looks wonderful."

"It's just Livvy, same as when you used to come into the ice-cream shop."

Sarah remembered her from back in those days. Livvy had always been friendly and smiling, just as she was now.

Livvy set the casserole down on the kitchen table. "I figured macaroni might be something your little girl would like."

"Holly likes just about everything. Except avocados." Sarah laughed. "She calls them squishy green things."

Livvy chuckled. "I'll remember that."

For the rest of the day, Sarah unpacked and put things away while Holly played with the puppy Jackson had given her, a black-and-white border collie Holly named Rags.

Sarah had gone with them out to the barn so that Holly could choose which pup she wanted. They met Jackson's foreman, a big Sioux Indian named Jimmy Threebears. Jimmy had two boys, one ten and one twelve, but no wife.

According to Livvy, Annie Baylor Threebears, a waitress at the Wind Canyon Café, had left her husband and sons five years ago and never been heard from since. From what Sarah could tell, Jimmy had done a good job raising his boys.

Eventually, the long day came to an end and Sarah surveyed her work in the cottage, pleased with all she had done. Tomorrow would be her first day working at the newspaper. She had found a day-care facility not far from the office and Holly was excited at the prospect of making new friends. Sarah was excited to be starting her first real job as a reporter.

Oh, it wasn't anything big. Not much happened in a town the size of Wind Canyon, which was one of the reasons the job appealed to her.

She smiled as she broke down and stacked the last of the empty cardboard boxes. Writing stories about everyday occurrences, working to make them interesting and entertaining, was going to be fun. She had done something similar when she had written for the

Daily Bruin at UCLA—before she had dropped out in her senior year to marry Andrew.

An image of her husband in one of his rages popped into her mind and a shudder ran down her spine. God, what a fool she had been.

She shook her head, dislodging the memory. A few years after the marriage, she had started taking correspondence courses and eventually gotten her Bachelor's degree, which had helped in getting her the job in Wind Canyon. Andrew wouldn't let her take night classes or she would have finished sooner.

Sarah thought of the husband she had once believed she loved, the cruel, hateful man he had become, and resisted an urge to shiver. She walked over to the window and stood in the sunshine pouring through the glass, hoping to erase the chill.

Chapter 4

Sarah pulled her blue pickup over to the curb in front of the Busy Bee Day-Care Center. Holly waited on the porch, along with a couple of other kids. The little girl ran around to the passenger side and climbed into the truck, settled herself in her booster seat, and Sarah helped her fasten the seat belt. The pickup was sporting a new set of tires, thanks to the small amount of room she had left on her credit card, so she wasn't worried about getting safely home.

She turned the vehicle onto the street leading out of town and settled in for the drive back to the ranch. She looked over at her daughter, who peered at the thick growth of forest passing by outside the window.

"How was your first day, honey?" Sarah asked.

"I met a girl named Alice. Everyone calls her Allie. She showed me how to play a really cool card game called Go Fish."

Sarah smiled. "That's great, baby."

She thought of her own first day. She had been introduced to the owner of the paper, Smiley Reed, an older, pudgy, balding man with a penchant for cigars. And just like in the movies, everyone called him "chief."

The paper's only other reporter, Mike Stevens, was a couple of years younger than Sarah but had more experience. He was tall, sandy-haired and not bad-looking. Mike covered the headline news, weather and sports, while Sarah was assigned to personal interest stories, and pretty much anything newsworthy that she could come up with.

"To start with, just get out there and get acquainted with the town," Smiley had said, handing her a box of business cards he'd had printed especially for her. "Stop in the stores and meet the owners, see who's doing what. You'll be surprised what you might find out."

Sarah proudly held on to the cards, the first she'd ever had. She was fine with the idea. She'd had to come up with news for the college paper. This shouldn't be any more difficult.

She spent the afternoon milling around town, getting reacquainted. Wind Canyon looked just like a Wyoming town should, with a long main street that still had old covered boardwalks running along both sides. Bars, restaurants and boutiques lined the street, a lot more of them now that the quaint little Western town had been discovered by tourists.

Wind Canyon had grown quite a bit in the years Sarah had been gone and now there were shops and restaurants on the side streets, as well. She was sur-

prised to discover some of the people in town still remembered her.

"I sure was sorry about what happened to your
folks," Fred Wilkins said, owner of Wilkins' Mercantile. "They were real nice people."

"Thank you." Sarah fought a wave of sadness she
hadn't let surface in years, not since the awful news
of her parents' death had reached her when she was in
college. Her overwhelming grief and loneliness were
part of the reason she had married Andrew that year.

Sarah left the mercantile, leaving a card with Mr.
Wilkins, as well as Mrs. Potter at the antiques shop
and a number of other business owners, asking them to
call her if they had something of interest for the paper.
She smiled to think how well she had been received.

Sarah was still smiling when she arrived back at
Raintree Ranch and she and Holly drove up in front
of the cottage. Then she saw the front door standing
wide-open and her smile disappeared.

"Who's in our house, Mommy?"

"I don't know." She cracked open the car door and
climbed out. "You wait here, okay?"

She walked toward the house, wondering if the wind
or an animal might have pushed open the door. The
lock was old. Maybe it had just given way. As she
climbed up to the porch to inspect the lock, she caught
a glimpse of the living room through the front window.

"Oh, my God!"

She forced herself to walk inside, her legs beginning
to tremble. The entire cottage was a shambles, the sofa
cushions ripped open, the curtains torn down from the
windows, pots and pans tossed out of the cupboards,

broken dishes all over the floor. "Oh, my God," she repeated a second time.

Holly raced through the front door. "Mama! Someone tore up our house!" The little girl started crying and it was all Sarah could do not to join her. She lifted Holly into her arms and turned at the sound of a man's deep voice.

"What the hell...?"

"Jackson..." Of all the people she didn't want to see in that moment, Jackson Raines topped the list. She had promised there wouldn't be any trouble. This looked like very big trouble to her.

She set Holly back on her feet and the little girl clung to her waist. Sarah swallowed. "Someone... someone broke in."

"I can see that."

She covered her mouth with her hand to hold back a sob.

"You stay here," Jackson commanded. "I'll make sure they're not still around." He left her there and went through each room in the house, then returned to the living room.

"Whoever did it is long gone. You have any idea who it might be?"

Sarah shook her head. She looked at him and her eyes filled with tears. "Why would someone do this?"

Jackson's gaze held a trace of pity. It was overshadowed by anger. "I don't know, but I'm sure as hell going to find out." He surveyed the overturned sofa and chairs, then the destruction in the bedroom, which looked as bad as the rest of the house.

"What are we gonna do, Mama?" Holly stared up at her with tears in her big blue eyes.

Jackson strode toward the little girl, crouched down in front of her, and she went into his arms as if she had done it a thousand times. "Don't you worry, honey. We'll put this place back just the way it was." He looked over at Sarah, must have noticed the pallor of her face and the way she stood there trembling.

He came to his feet, but kept hold of Holly's hand. "That goes for you, too, Sarah. I'll get Livvy over here to help and between the three of us we'll have this place back in shape in no time."

She just nodded. Her throat was too tight to speak.

Jackson let go of Holly's hand and she ran back to Sarah.

"Nothing like this has ever happened on the ranch before," Jackson said. "We'll find out who did it and make sure it doesn't happen again."

Sarah made no reply. *Nothing like this has ever happened before.* The words sent a chill down her spine. Surely this had nothing to do with her, nothing to do with Andrew and the past she had run from in L.A.

Surely her problems hadn't followed her.

But as she looked at the destruction in the cottage, Sarah felt sure they had.

Jackson met Sheriff Weber in front of the cottage and they walked inside together. Livvy had taken Sarah and little Holly up to the main house and was distracting them with milk and cookies.

Weber, a tall, heavyset man with iron-gray hair, lifted his brown felt cowboy hat and scratched his head. "Worst case of vandalism I've seen round these parts in years. Any idea who might have done it?"

"No, but a woman and her little girl just moved

into the place. I imagine they aren't feeling real safe right now."

"Who's that?"

"Sarah Allen. Her family used to live here. Livvy tells me her folks died about ten years ago in a car accident. Husband died not long ago."

"I remember the accident that killed her folks. Some drunk crossed the centerline out on the highway coming into town. I'll talk to Sarah, tell her we're looking into this. Odds are it was a bunch of teenagers, maybe someone whose family is camped around here. I'll take a drive through the campgrounds, see what I can come up with."

"Thanks, Ben."

The sheriff went out and got his camera, took a string of photos documenting the damage. "Insurance gonna take care of this?"

"Only the building's covered."

"Figures." The sheriff walked back outside and the two of them went up to the main house so Ben could speak to Sarah.

As soon as Weber left, Jackson led the small group back to the cottage to begin cleaning up.

"Looks like you'll need a new sofa and chairs," he said to Sarah. "Some new curtains, too. Soon as you get time, we'll go into town and get whatever you need."

She gazed up at him in surprise. "You're going to replace everything?"

"You didn't think I would? What happened wasn't your fault."

Sarah glanced away. "Thank you."

When she looked back at him, there was something in her face… It had never occurred to him that Sarah's presence might have anything to do with the vandalism. Watching her now, he wondered.

Jackson made a mental note to call his brother, Devlin, have him do some digging. Dev owned a chain of security companies in the Southwest, including one in L.A. Mostly he managed them from his house in Scottsdale, close to the Phoenix branch. These days, his employees did most of the legwork, but Dev was still one of the best investigators in the business.

Jackson would ask Dev to sniff around, find out what he could about the young widow and her daughter.

Dev wasn't home. His brother was off somewhere with one of his lady friends, or so Devlin's Phoenix office manager said. Jackson wasn't surprised. A few years back, his youngest brother had suffered a bad breakup with the girl he planned to marry and since then, had become a dedicated bachelor.

"Can I take a message?" the manager asked.

"Tell him Jackson called. Tell him I need to talk to him." Jackson hung up the phone. He'd get a return call sooner or later, but he wasn't holding his breath. Dev liked to live big and he usually did just that.

Instead of waiting anxiously to hear from him, Jackson spent the morning in the basement, working out on the weights, punching the heavy bag, then spending some time on the speed bag. He liked the physical exercise that had come to be a habit, liked to keep in shape. When he finished, he showered and pulled on his jeans and headed down to his foreman Jimmy Threebears's house, part of the original ranch compound, three bedrooms with a wraparound, screened-in front porch.

The residence, which sat on a knoll across from the barn, had been remodeled a number of times, and Jackson had done a bit more modernizing of the old wooden structure when he bought the ranch four years ago. As he approached, he saw Jimmy's boys playing ball out in front.

"Where's your dad?" Jackson asked.

"He's up on the ridgeline, sir." Sam, the twelve-year-old, shoved a hand through his gleaming black shoulder-length hair. He was a good-looking kid—both of them were. They got good grades and were very good athletes. Jimmy had a right to be proud of them.

"Dad says those loggers are filling the stream up with mud again. He went up to take another look."

Jackson's jaw tightened. He had actually thought he'd had problems when he'd worked in Houston. After high school, he had used his boxing scholarship to earn a degree in geology then landed a job with the small, newly formed Wildcat Oil. He had taken part of his salary in stock—the smartest move he ever made.

When the company expanded, then went public, he made enough money to retire from the oil business and live in comfort, buy the old Simmons ranch and become a cattleman—which had been his lifelong dream.

One thing he'd learned—a rancher faced just as many problems as an oil company and made a whole lot less money.

And now the damned logging companies were making things worse. They were cutting down trees in the national forest that bordered the ranch and causing him all kinds of trouble.

He shook his head. He still couldn't believe the taxpayers paid to build roads so the bastards could cut down trees. They were taking out those big seven-hundred-year-old ponderosas as if they had a right. Only God had a right to those trees as far as Jackson was concerned. Somewhere along the way, the politicians had sure as hell gotten things screwed up.

He looked over at the older boy, who was nearly as tall as his dad but lean and lanky instead of muscular like Jimmy. Sam tossed the baseball into the air and caught it.

"I could use a little help," Jackson said. "You boys game?"

"Sure." Gibby grinned, a ten-year-old version of his older brother with slightly shorter black hair. "Just tell us what you need us to do."

Always ready for a little diversion, both boys followed him off toward the barn. Half an hour later, they had loaded the old sofa he remembered storing in the loft into the back of his truck, dusted it off real good, then the boys jumped up in the bed and he drove the load down to Sarah's cottage.

Sarah's. Jackson blew out a breath, amazed he already thought of the place that way and none too pleased about it.

"Found a couch you can use," he said when she opened the door. "Hope this'll do till we can buy you a new one."

"Anything we can sit on will do." She gave him one of her pretty white smiles and he felt the same kick in the stomach he used to feel in high school. He wished he could believe that smile was real.

With the boys' help, they situated the sofa in front of the fireplace. With the rest of the house cleaned up, the place was again in fairly livable condition. He made a mental note to have Livvy bring down a few of the extra dishes, enough to make do until he could buy some to replace the ones that were broken.

The boys took off, leaving him with Sarah.

"So when can you get away?" he found himself asking, wishing like hell he wasn't so eager to hear her answer.

"I'm working in town tomorrow, but I'll be done by three. Holly can stay at the day-care center while we go shopping if you want."

He nodded. "Great. I'll pick you up in front of the newspaper office."

She flashed him another warm smile and his groin tightened. He tried to tell himself he shouldn't be the least attracted to a money-hungry woman like Sarah but in his mind's eye he was untying that long, thick chestnut braid and running his fingers through it, unbuttoning her blouse and—

Jackson clamped down on the image. He needed to go a couple more rounds with the heavy bag, maybe let the speed bag hit him a few times in the head.

He had been fooled by Sarah Allen once. It wasn't going to happen again.

Sarah's cell phone rang. Sitting behind the desk Smiley had assigned her, she jumped, startled by the unexpected jangle. Ever since the break-in, her nerves had been on edge. Thank God nothing else had happened, which made her think she might be wrong, and it was, as the sheriff believed, just teenagers bent on making trouble.

The phone rang a second time before she could dig it out of her oversize leather purse. Hoping someone might be calling with a news story, she answered the phone without checking the caller ID and heard Martin Kozak's rusty smoker's voice on the line.

"I've been trying to reach you, Sarah. Don't you check your messages?"

Her hand shook. Vaguely she heard the bell ring above the door, but didn't look up to see who it was. "I've been busy, Marty. And my phone's been out of service." That was the truth. There were only certain places around the cottage where she could get cell reception. She reminded herself to get a landline, though she had few people to call.

"I need to talk to you, Sarah."

"I don't have anything to tell you, Marty. I don't have what you're looking for. I don't know anything about Andrew's business. We never discussed it."

"You moved out of the condo. Where are you, Sarah? Tell me where you are, and I'll meet you."

She swallowed. Her hand kept shaking. She tightened her fingers around the phone to make it stop. "Leave me alone, Marty." Sarah hung up the phone. She was breathing hard, her pulse racing. She closed her eyes, trying to bring herself under control, and when she looked up, Jackson Raines stood next to her desk.

"Who's Marty?" he asked. The look in his eyes said he had overheard her conversation. He expected an answer, and he wasn't going to settle for less.

"H-he was a business acquaintance of my husband's."

"What did he want?"

She moistened her lips, worked to make them form the words. "I don't know."

Jackson slid a hand beneath her elbow and urged her up out of her chair. "You're trembling. Come on, let's get out of here."

She didn't argue. Marty's call had shaken her. She had been so sure he would leave her alone once she left L.A. Now she wondered if Marty had been lying about not knowing where she lived and had followed her to Wyoming.

If he had sent his thugs to search the cottage for whatever it was he was looking for.

She waved to Mike as they walked out, letting him know she was leaving, and stepping outside, into the crisp mountain air. Sarah took a deep breath, felt a little steadier. Jackson just kept walking, hauling her around to the passenger side of his truck, opening the door and boosting her up into the seat. His hand accidentally brushed her thigh as he helped her get settled and a little tingle of awareness went through her.

She was wearing a lightweight apricot sweater and a pair of tan slacks—and it was a darned good thing. She imagined what that light touch might have felt like on bare skin and a rush of heat slid into her stomach.

Embarrassment sparked a little burst of hysterical laughter.

"What's so funny?"

She shook her head, then sobered at the sudden memory of Martin Kozak's call. "Not a damned thing."

One of his dark eyebrows arched up. He pinned her with the same look he had used in her office. "Why don't you tell me what's going on." It was an order, not a question.

Sarah sighed and leaned back against the black leather seat. "I suppose, since I'm living in your house, you have a right to know." And there was something about him that made her want to tell him. Maybe it was just that she had known him from before, or maybe it was that he seemed so strong and capable, a solid shoulder to lean on. Whatever it was, she just hoped that once he knew, he wouldn't toss her out in the street.

He drove the truck to a shady area off the road at the edge of town and turned off the engine, then shifted on the seat to face her.

"I overheard some of your conversation. Does the guy you were talking to have something to do with what happened at the cottage?"

She looked over to where he sat. His dark eyes were mostly hidden by his battered cowboy hat, but the hard line of his jaw and the indentation in his chin were clear. "I don't know. I don't think he even knows where I live."

"Then why were you so upset?"

She bit her lip, wondering how much she should tell him. "To put it bluntly, my husband—that is to say, my *late* husband—was a crook. I didn't know it when I married him and I was never involved in any of his shady business dealings, but I knew whatever he was up to wasn't good."

"Why didn't you leave him?"

"I tried more than once. He was…determined I would never get a divorce. He said he would do whatever it took to keep me from taking his daughter." An ugly memory surfaced of Andrew's fist connecting with her cheek and Sarah fought not to flinch. "I believed him."

She looked out the window, into the dense grove of dark, shadowy pines trees that climbed the sides of the hills. "I came here to start a new life. I just want to be left alone."

For several moments, Jackson said nothing. Maybe he was the one person she knew who understood what it was to want to start over. In high school, Jackson Raines had a wild reputation. He was in trouble off and on all through his early teenage years. Until he'd been recruited by the boxing team. After that, he had settled down, come up with a solid set of goals, and become the sort of boy she found attractive.

She hadn't dared let on. He had made an enemy of the varsity quarterback, Jeff Freedman, the most popular boy in school. Jeff had taunted him into a fistfight then taken a beating for his foolishness. Jackson had been completely ostracized, and unless Sarah wanted that same treatment, she was forced to ignore the attraction she felt for him.

But Sarah was a woman now and Jackson no longer a boy. It was far more difficult to ignore that attraction today than it had been back then.

"What's this guy's name?" Jackson's deep voice jolted her back to the present.

"Martin Kozak."

"You said you didn't have what he was looking for. So what is it he's looking for?"

She sighed. "Marty called me a number of times before we moved. He said Andrew had something he needed. A list of some kind, maybe a flash drive or a notebook. I told him I didn't know anything about it and I don't."

"So what makes you think Kozak's not responsible for ransacking the cottage?"

"On the phone Marty asked me where I lived. He

said if I would tell him, he would come and meet me. It seemed like he really didn't know. I said to just leave me alone."

Jackson watched her closely. "Why do you suppose he's come after this now? You said your husband passed away some months back."

"I don't understand that, either."

Jackson cast her another penetrating glance. "Do you think Kozak is a danger to you and Holly?"

She looked away. There was something about Marty Kozak that frightened her. She wasn't sure what it was. "He lives in L.A. I can't imagine he would come all the way up here, even if he knew where to find me. I'm just hoping the sheriff is right and it was just a bunch of kids."

Jackson studied her face, searching for the truth, she supposed. "All right. For now, that's the assumption we'll go on. In the meantime, let's forget about Kozak and go buy that sofa. We'll worry about the rest of it as it comes."

She looked at him and something squeezed inside her. "You're…you're going to help me?"

"If we're lucky, you won't need my help. This guy will stop looking for you and that will be the end of it."

"And if he doesn't?"

He shrugged a powerful set of shoulders that must have been a nightmare for his boxing opponents. "If he doesn't, we'll figure out where to go from there."

Her throat closed up. It had been so long since anyone had done anything at all to help her. One by one, Andrew had managed to destroy her personal friendships. Oh, she had tennis partners, mostly the women at the country club, and there were the wives of his business acquaintances. But none of them were real friends.

Her grandmother was still alive, but she was in her seventies and she had a heart condition. Sarah had been afraid that if she called her, she would inadvertently spill out her pain and it might aggravate her heart condition. With no friends or family she could talk to, she had no one to depend on but herself.

"I know what you must think of me," she said. "I know you haven't forgotten what I did to you in high school."

He flicked her a glance. "Maybe not. But we're not in high school anymore. And we're both too old to play games." He cranked up the engine, started to put the truck into gear, but she caught his arm.

"I'm sorry about what happened that day. I know it doesn't change anything, but it's true. I've regretted the way I behaved, the way I treated you, a thousand times."

Jackson said nothing, just shifted the truck into Drive and stepped on the gas. She didn't think he believed her. He probably thought that she was just being nice to him because he was successful now, obviously a man of some means, instead of a boy from the wrong side of the tracks.

Maybe he was right and what she'd done no longer mattered.

Oddly enough, it still mattered a great deal to Sarah.

Chapter 5

Jackson called himself ten kinds of fool. It was sheer insanity. Total stupidity. But every time he saw her, watched her doing some simple task, desire for Sarah Allen hit him like a fist to the solar plexus.

Something had shifted, changed the day she had told him about her husband's shady dealings and the man she was afraid of, Martin Kozak. Maybe it was the vulnerability he had seen in her face, maybe it was the way she had looked at him when he had offered to help her. Whatever it was, since that day, the attraction he had felt had grown into full-blown lust.

Jackson lifted his cowboy hat and settled it low on his forehead. He told himself it was just that he hadn't had a woman in a while. He wasn't like his brother, Dev. He wasn't into one-night stands. He dated, got to know a lady before he took her to bed. His relationships usually lasted until the heat was gone and the affair turned into friendship. The women knew from the start he didn't make promises and didn't want a woman who expected them.

Which didn't mean he was *completely* opposed to marriage. Hell, he always figured someday in the distant future he'd get married and have a couple of kids. Just not right away.

Still, he liked sex and he didn't have much trouble finding a willing bed partner, even in a town as small as Wind Canyon. It was just that lately, he'd been busy.

Or maybe he just hadn't met a woman who appealed to him.

As he strode toward where Jimmy Threebears worked with a couple of new saddle horses, he passed Sarah's cottage and caught a glimpse of her sweeping the porch. She bent over to use the dustpan, pulling her jeans tight over a very round, very nice ass, and pressure began to build in his groin.

It was insanity. Total stupidity.

He told himself he ought to give Maddie Gallagher a call. They had dated off and on. Maddie was a few years older, divorced, always up for a round of steamy sex. Maybe he should call her...but he didn't really want to.

He forced himself not to look back at the porch, carefully kept his attention on the big man working one of the geldings on a lead line in the pen. From the corner of his eye, he saw Jimmy's two boys tossing a ball to little Holly, whose black-and-white puppy sniffed and yapped at her feet. The boys had already grown protective of her.

Just as Jackson had grown protective of Sarah.

It was insanity. Total stupidity.

Sarah was probably playing him, just like she had in high school.

"Hey, boss!" Jimmy waved, dark-skinned and dark-eyed, his long black hair pulled into a ponytail fastened low on his neck. He handed the lead to one of the hands and walked out of the pen.

"You been up to the ridge today?" Jackson asked as Jimmy approached.

"Not today. But it sure didn't look good the last time I was there. There's slash clogging the water upriver, making it overflow the banks, and with the trees clear-cut on the north side of the hill that last storm washed a shitload of dirt into the stream. Those cows in the upper pasture are having a helluva time getting anything decent to drink."

"Let's move 'em down into Pine Meadow. The grass isn't quite as good, but at least the water will be clean."

"I'll get a couple of the hands and trailer some horses. Won't take long to move 'em."

"Keep an eye open while you're up there. I don't trust those loggers. The Barrett brothers are in for the quick buck and they don't care what they do to get it. If we aren't careful, they'll do something else we'll have to pay for."

Jimmy nodded, turned and started organizing the men. He was hardworking and efficient. Jackson couldn't run the place without him. On top of that, not counting Gabe and Dev, Jimmy was his closest friend.

Jackson left the men and returned to the house. As he walked into his study, he saw the message light blinking on the phone.

He pushed the button, heard his youngest brother's deep voice. "Hey, bro, what's up? Give me a call."

Jackson dialed Dev's home number and his brother picked up on the second ring.

"Thanks for calling me back," Jackson said. "Sorry to bother you, little brother, but I got what could turn into a problem and I was hoping you might be able to help."

"What's going on?"

"You remember a girl in your high school class named Sarah Allen?"

"Sarah Allen... Sarah Allen...dark hair, big blue, heartbreaker eyes and a luscious little body? The girl who had you tied in knots half your senior year? Nah, I don't recall."

"Very funny. The thing is, Sarah is back in Wind Canyon and I think she might be in some kind of trouble. I want you to find out everything you can about her and get back to me."

"What can you give me to work with?"

He dug out the application Livvy had taken from Sarah over the internet and read what little was on the printed page: her social security number; her residence address in Santa Monica, a former address on Sunset Drive, the make and model of her Mercedes, which had now been sold. Jackson told Dev about the break-in, and about the call from a guy named Martin Kozak, who wanted some kind of list that Sarah's husband supposedly had.

"I'm trying to tell myself the break-in had nothing to do with Sarah's past, but I don't believe in coincidence."

"Neither do I. What else can you tell me?"

"Sarah has a six-year-old daughter named Holly. Her husband's name was Andrew Hollister."

"*Late* husband, is it?"

He could almost see Dev's knowing grin. "Just do what you can, will you?"

"You got it, bro." Dev signed off and Jackson hung up the phone.

His brother was an ex-Ranger. Both his brothers had gone into the service after high school. Gabe had enlisted in the Marines, then a year later, Dev, the youngest and determined to prove himself, had joined the army and become a Ranger. Once he got out, he had used the specialized skills he had learned to start a security company, and eventually became one of the best investigators around.

Officially, he didn't take cases anymore, just ran his business. Unofficially, he still got involved whenever a case intrigued him—and he was always there if one of his brothers needed his help.

Jackson thought of the destruction in Sarah's cottage, of the ominous phone call she had received, and hoped his brother called back soon.

Three days later, Sarah stood at the window in the living room, watching Jackson at the barn. She liked the way he moved—his long, confident strides, the purpose that was clear in every step. She liked the narrow, masculine span of his hips in contrast to the width of his shoulders.

Something had changed between them the day she had told him about Marty. She still wasn't sure why she had done it—not that he had left her much choice.

Maybe it just felt good to talk to someone instead of being afraid to open her mouth.

She hadn't told him everything, of course. The years she had spent with Andrew were too ugly, too frightening—the end too terrible to recall. And she had no idea how much she could really trust him.

Still, she didn't leave the window, just stood there watching, smiling at the way he angled his hat over his eyes, how natural he looked in his worn jeans and boots, as if he'd been born to ranching—which she knew he hadn't.

In truth, he had lived in a ramshackle house at the edge of town. His mother had been a drunk and his father had left when Jackson was a boy. Thanks to boxing, he had been able to stop the downhill spiral that had been leading him into trouble and turn his life around.

He paused to talk to some of his ranch hands, saw them nod and head out to do whatever it was he asked. He was truly a man's man, but then he always had been. Maybe that was what she had liked about him even way back then.

"Are we going to work today, Mama?"

Sarah looked down to see Holly standing in front of her. "Yes, honey. I got a call from Mr. Wilkins at the mercantile. He reminded me about the big Memorial Day celebration coming up the end of the month. The paper needs an article written about it." She loved the fact she was a freelance reporter. It gave her a wonderful control of her time—as long as she got her work done.

"So you're gonna write it?"

"That's my job, honey. There's a picnic and a parade every year and the whole town turns out. Doesn't that sound like fun?"

Holly jumped up and down. "I love parades!"

Sarah smiled. "I know you do." And the community spirit in Wind Canyon was one of the things that had brought her back home to raise her daughter. "After I get finished in town, we'll drive over and see your great-grandma, just like I promised." Sarah had been anxious to visit her grandmother, a woman she hadn't seen in years.

Holly fell silent. She ran the toe of a small bare foot over the planked wooden floor. "Do you think she'll like me?"

Sarah reached out and caught her daughter's small hands. "Grandma Thompson is going to love you. I brought you to see her once when you were a baby, but you were too small to remember. She thought you were the prettiest baby girl she'd ever seen."

But Sarah had paid for that defiant visit dearly. When she'd gotten back to L.A., Andrew had been furious. During the terrible fight they'd had, he had blackened her eye and broken her arm.

Sarah took a deep breath and shoved the painful memory away. She smiled down at her daughter. "Go get your socks and sneakers, grab your jacket, and we'll get going."

Holly dashed off, and Sarah went to collect her sweater and purse. She glanced around the cottage. The new sofa and chair and the rest of the furnishings she and Jackson had purchased wouldn't be in for a few more weeks. She told herself the vandalism was never going to happen again. It was just out-of-control kids, nothing more.

But even if it weren't, she was home and she was going to stay. She had paid long enough for the foolish mistakes she had made.

And nothing—not even one of Andrew's crooked friends—was going to drive her away.

Jackson spotted Livvy's stout figure hurrying toward where he unloaded sacks of grain from the back of a flatbed truck.

"Jackson! Jackson, your brother's on the phone! He says it's important!"

Jackson waved, thought again that he should add a line out in the barn so he could take his calls. Then again, he didn't like talking on the phone. He'd talked from dawn to midnight when he had been in the oil business, which was the reason he hadn't put a phone out in the barn in the first place.

He started jogging toward the house, passed Livvy on the way and took the call in his study.

"Hey, Dev."

His brother's deep voice reached him over the line. "Are you sitting down?"

He sank down in the chair behind his desk. "That bad, is it?"

"Afraid so. You said Sarah's husband was Andrew Hollister?"

"That's right."

"Ever heard of Louis Hollister?"

"Seems to ring a bell, but I'm not sure why."

"Louis Hollister was a blue-collar guy from the San Fernando Valley who made it big in the heavy equipment business. He owned Blacktop Tires, owned some big manufacturing plants, a couple of mining operations, a demolition company—the list goes on and on. The guy dabbled in just about everything that dealt with machinery and usually made money. By the time he died, he was worth a nice round forty mil."

"Not exactly chump change."

"Not exactly. His estate went entirely to his son, Andrew—money, business interests, even his Spanish-style house on Sunset Drive."

"I guess Sarah found what she was looking for."

"No quite. For a while, Andrew lived high on Daddy's money. So high, in fact, he began to run out. He was a big-time gambler and he liked life in the fast lane. He married Sarah and they had a kid, but it didn't slow him down. Andrew kept right on spending."

"Sounds like a great guy."

"Yeah, well, according to my sources, he made enemies wherever he went. Four months ago, he was murdered, apparently by someone he pissed off. Probably one of his business cronies or someone he owed money."

"So the police never found the killer."

"I don't think they were highly motivated. No one thought much of Andrew. The Feds were looking at him for tax evasion, probably the only thing they could hang him on, but everyone knew he was into a lot of bad shit. I think the cops wanted to pin a medal on the guy who offed him."

Jackson mulled over the information, trying to imagine Sarah with a no-good like that. "I really appreciate it, Dev."

"There's one more thing."

He braced himself. "What is it?"

"Hollister was a wife-beater, Jackson. Sarah went

to the hospital on more than one occasion. It was fairly common knowledge that he used his wife as a punching bag whenever he felt the urge. Rumor mill says his wife was scared to death of him."

He said he would do whatever it took to keep me from taking his daughter. I believed him.

Jackson took a steadying breath. He couldn't believe how angry he was. His chest was squeezing as if he'd fought ten rounds, and one of his hands had unconsciously fisted.

He forced himself to relax. "What about the little girl?"

"Hollister worshipped her. No record of any hospital visits. I don't think he ever laid a hand on the kid, just took out his frustrations on Sarah."

"Thanks, Dev."

"Listen, I'm supposed to head down to Mexico with a lady friend for the next ten days. If you need me here, I'll cancel."

"So far I'm just trying to stay ahead of the game. Have fun in ole Meh-he-co."

Dev chuckled. "You've got my cell number…though I'm not sure there'll be any service."

"Not to worry. Watch out for bandits," he said.

"You, too," said Dev, and hung up the phone.

For long moments he just sat there, trying to wrap his mind around the fact that pretty little Sarah Allen had married some bastard who had hurt her so badly she'd wound up in the hospital. A gangster involved in gambling and shady business deals. If he'd had any doubts about the man or men who had tossed the cottage, he didn't anymore.

He needed to talk to Sarah. Unfortunately, he'd seen

her drive out this morning in her beat-up truck. He'd have to wait until she got home.

He told himself not to worry.

But he couldn't seem to make himself stop.

"She's a lovely child, Sarah." Her grandmother, Abigail Benton Thompson, watched fondly as Holly chased a butterfly across the covered porch in front of her small wood-frame house. "You've done a good job raising her."

"Thanks, Gran."

"Sometimes I wondered if I'd ever see the two of you again." She was silver-haired and broad-hipped, robust on the outside, though her heart was frail.

"I know. My calls were far too rare. The truth is, I had problems at home and I was afraid you'd be able to hear it in my voice. I didn't want to worry you."

"I worried anyway, darlin'. I'm your gran. You should have called. I might have been able to help."

Sarah managed a wobbly smile. There was nothing her grandmother could have done—nothing anyone could do. "It doesn't matter—not anymore. Andrew is gone. He's out of my life and I'm finally able to do what I want." Sarah kept other thoughts of him at bay, as she had learned to do, though sometimes they crept in anyway.

She leaned over and hugged the older woman. "I've missed you, Gran. It's going to be wonderful to be living so close again."

The town of Sheep River sat just the other side of the Wind Canyon County line. It was a good long drive, but manageable. And it was worth the time it took to get there to be with the only family, aside from a few distant cousins, Sarah had left.

"It's getting late," she said. "We'd better be getting home. I promise I'll be back next week."

"You'd better. Else I might have to pull that old Ford of your granddad's off the blocks in the garage and drive myself on over to your place."

Sarah laughed. Her grandfather had been dead since Sarah was seven years old, but Gran had insisted on keeping his car, the only new vehicle he could ever afford to buy. The tires were rotted off now, but Gran still went out to the barn just to look at it. She said it made her remember the good times.

Gran was still a romantic, even after all these years.

Sarah wasn't. Not anymore.

It was dark by the time she and Holly reached the cottage. Yesterday, she'd had a landline installed and the phone was ringing when she walked through the front door. She lifted the receiver.

"Sarah Allen?"

Her stomach knotted. Almost no one knew her brand-new number. "Yes…?"

"This is Deputy Carson of the Sheep River Sheriff's Department. I'm sorry to have to tell you, but your grandmother's had a heart attack. She's been taken to community hospital."

"Oh, my God!" Her knees turned to water and she sank down in the chair next to the phone. "I—I was just there. She seemed fine when I left."

"I'm afraid there was an incident. Two men broke into her house. They threatened her, told her they wanted whatever it was you gave her to keep for you."

"But I didn't give her anything! All I brought was a bouquet of flowers." *She always loved flowers.*

"I guess she told them that, but they didn't believe her. They tore up her house pretty bad, looking for whatever it was they were after. I gather your grandmother tried to stop them, but her heart began acting up. She called 911. She gave the medics your phone number when they got there."

Sarah swallowed, her lips trembling. "Is she...is she all right? Is she going to be okay?"

"I'm afraid I can't tell you. At the moment, she's in intensive care."

She beat down her fear and swallowed past the knot in her throat. "I'm on my way. I'll be there as fast as I can." Sarah hung up the phone, her hands shaking so badly she could barely get the receiver back into its cradle.

She whispered a silent prayer. *Please, God, don't let her die. We only just found each other again.*

When she turned, Holly stood there, holding on to Jackson's hand.

"I could tell it was something bad, so I went to get help," Holly said.

Sarah glanced up at Jackson, saw that his jaw was hard, his face lined with worry. She swallowed, tried to pull herself together when what she wanted to do was walk into his arms and just let him hold her.

She fixed her attention on Holly. "Grandma's had a heart attack, honey. Mama has to go to the hospital to make sure she's all right."

Holly started crying. "I don't want her to die like Daddy did. Please, Mama, I don't want Gran to die."

Sarah lifted the little girl into her arms. "She isn't

going to die. But she needs us right now. Can you be brave for her?"

Holly nodded, sniffed back tears.

Jackson's gaze locked with hers. "I'll drive you. I'll get my truck and be right back."

"You don't have to—" But he was already gone and she didn't think he would let her go without him even if she wanted to.

He had only been gone a moment when Livvy knocked on the door. "Your little one says you got a problem. Anything I can do to help?"

Sarah released a shaky breath. "My grandmother's had a heart attack. Jackson is driving us to the hospital over in Sheep River."

"If that's the case, you're liable to be there a while, all night maybe. Why don't you leave Holly with me?"

Sarah bit her lip. She hated the idea of her daughter sleeping in a corridor all night. She trusted Livvy. She remembered how good she had been to the kids who came into the ice-cream shop. The salt of the earth was Livvy.

"Are you sure?"

"Of course I'm sure. Don't be silly. There's a spare room off the kitchen. I stay there whenever it storms. I'll stay tonight and Holly can sleep in the other twin bed."

Relief swept through her, so strong it made her dizzy. She knelt in front of her daughter. "I want you to stay here with Livvy. Will you do that for me?"

"We'll bake some of those chocolate-chip cookies you like," Livvy promised. "What do you say?"

"What about Gran?"

"Gran's going to be all right," Sarah said, praying

it was true. The heart attack was all her fault. Her past had followed her, just as she had feared. If she caused her grandmother's death, she would never be able to live with herself.

She squeezed Holly's hand. "I'll call you as soon as I know for sure she's okay. Be a good girl and do what Livvy says."

"I could sure use the company," Livvy added. "You and me can worry together."

Sarah's heart squeezed. Somehow in returning to Wind Canyon, she had begun to make friends. She couldn't believe how good it felt.

Holly said nothing, just walked over and caught Livvy's thick-fingered hand.

"Thank you, Livvy," Sarah said. "You don't know how much I appreciate this."

"You just go on and take care of your family."

Sarah nodded, heard Jackson's big Ford pull up in front of the house.

"Holly's staying with Livvy," she told him as she walked to the truck.

Settling a hand at her waist, he walked her around and helped her climb into the passenger seat. In minutes they were rolling down the highway, headed back to Sheep River.

Neither of them talked until they passed through Wind Canyon and started farther east along the road.

Jackson tossed her a glance. "We need to talk, Sarah."

At his tone of voice, anxiety trembled through her. She wasn't sure if she was more worried about her grandmother—or what Jackson had to tell her.

Chapter 6

"It's a ways to Sheep River," Jackson said. "You're gonna sit there and worry until we get there. You might as well tell me what I need to know."

He could read the uncertainty in her face. Sarah sliced him a glance and nibbled her lip. "What exactly are you asking me?"

"You just got back from visiting her, right?"

"Yes."

"I want to know if what brought on your grandmother's heart attack has anything to do with what happened at the cottage?"

She kept her eyes straight ahead, staring at the yellow line in the middle of the darkened highway. "I went to see her today. After I left, two men broke into her house. They thought I had brought whatever it is they're looking for to my grandmother for safekeeping. She told them I hadn't brought anything, but they didn't believe her. They tore up her house, just the way they did the cottage."

Her lips trembled. "She tried to stop them. She has a heart condition. If something happens to her, it's my fault. Everything that's happened is my fault."

She started crying and pressed her fingers against her lips to hold back a sob. Jackson pulled the truck to the side of the road. Leaning over, he caught her face between his hands.

"This isn't your fault. You married some bastard who gave you nothing but trouble. That trouble followed you here. This is where it's going to end."

He let go of her and she straightened, seemed a little steadier. "Y-you know about Andrew?"

"Some of it." Jackson fought an urge to pull her into his arms, tell her everything would be okay. Instead, he put the pickup in gear and pulled back onto the road.

"When Kozak called," he continued, "I figured your past was somehow connected to the destruction in the cottage. My brother's in the security business. I called him, asked him to do some digging. He called me back this afternoon."

Sarah pulled a tissue out of her big leather purse and blew her nose. "How...how much did he tell you?"

"Enough to know that Andrew Hollister was a no-good SOB who treated you badly. I know he inherited a fortune from his father and spent it like there was no tomorrow—which for him, apparently, there wasn't."

"Then I guess... I guess you know he was murdered."

"Sounds to me like he got exactly what he deserved. Are you the one who found him?"

Sarah's hand went to her chest. He could tell she didn't want to remember.

She took a deep breath and slowly released it. "We... we were still living in the house on Sunset, but Andrew had put it up for sale. He'd bought a condo in Santa Monica and I had already moved in. I went back to the Sunset house to pick up some more of my things, but Andrew was there so I didn't stay long. After I left, I picked Holly up from her ballet class and drove on to the condo. The cleaning lady found him in the morning."

"You weren't worried when he didn't show up that night?"

"After the first few years we were married, Andrew rarely spent time at home. I didn't expect to see him that night."

"So the two of you were estranged?"

"If by *estranged* you mean we barely spoke to each other, had separate bedrooms and hadn't slept together in years—yes, we were estranged."

"Must have been a rough ten years."

Sarah gazed out the window as if she looked into the past. "He wasn't always that way. In the beginning, he treated me very well. He had a lot of money and he showered me with presents. He was handsome. To a twenty-two-year-old girl, he seemed like Prince Charming. I actually thought I was in love with him."

"Coming from a small town like Wind Canyon, I can understand how you might be impressed."

She sighed, raked a hand through her hair. "He started having money problems and as those problems grew, he turned violent. The slightest thing could set him off. I wanted to leave him but I was afraid. I'm only grateful he never hurt Holly. But I always worried that sooner or later he would."

Jackson made no reply. Every time he thought of what Sarah had suffered, he wanted to kill Andrew Hollister himself.

They finally reached the hospital, a three-story brick building big enough to service the rural community surrounding Sheep River. Jackson dropped Sarah off in front then drove into the lot to park the truck.

He found her outside the intensive care unit, talking to one of the doctors, a woman in her forties with salt-and-pepper hair.

"Do you think she's going to be okay, Dr. Ellis?" he heard Sarah ask.

"No heart attack is good, but we don't think she suffered any major damage. We'll be moving her into a private room in the morning."

Sarah's shoulders sagged in relief. "Thank God."

"You won't be able to see her tonight. Why don't you get some rest and come back in the morning?"

"I don't want to leave her."

Jackson introduced himself to Dr. Ellis. "I'll take care of Sarah," he added. "See she doesn't overdo. For now we'd like to stay."

"Suit yourself. I'll let you know if there's any change."

"Thank you, Dr. Ellis," Sarah said. The doctor walked away and Sarah looked up at Jackson. "You don't have to stay."

"Neither do you, but we will."

Her eyes misted, a soft clear blue, like the sky on a cloudless day. "Thank you." He felt sucker punched by the look in those eyes, the need and the trust. She was getting to him again.

Jackson told himself it would be different this time, but he was afraid it wouldn't.

Sarah called Holly at the ranch house and told her Gran was going to be all right. She urged Jackson to go home and said she would call him in the morning. Jackson solidly refused. He wasn't the kind of man to abandon a friend in her time of need.

Or at least that was the way he seemed.

But in the beginning, Andrew had seemed a different man than he actually was. Sarah wrapped her arms around herself against the chill in the empty corridor. Just the smells and the sounds dredged memories of her time in the emergency room, once with a broken arm, twice with broken ribs and lacerations, not to mention the concussion.

After a while, Andrew got better at hurting her without leaving traces. And over the years, she learned to stay out of the path of his anger.

It was his threats that kept her from leaving.

He had said he would kill her.

Sarah was certain he would.

She and Jackson sat in the hallway all night. In the morning, a tall blond nurse walked over to where they sat on a padded vinyl bench that didn't feel the least bit padded.

"We're moving Mrs. Thompson into a private room on the second floor. As soon as she's settled, you can go up and see her. Just don't stay too long."

"Thank you." Sarah waited with Jackson for another half hour before the nurse was ready for them to go upstairs.

"She's in Room 204. Like I said, don't stay long."

Sarah stretched to loosen her stiff, aching muscles. Sometime during the night, she had fallen asleep against Jackson's shoulder. She wondered if he'd gotten any sleep at all.

She flicked him a glance as they made their way along the second-floor corridor to her grandmother's room. His dark hair was mussed and a shadow of beard lined his jaw. He only looked more attractive.

"I'll wait for you out here," he said when they reached the room.

Sarah nodded. The door was open and Gran was awake when Sarah walked in. Her gray hair stood out all over her head and she looked tired, but some of the color had returned to her face. They talked for several minutes, Gran reassuring her, as the doctor had that morning, that she was going to be all right.

"I brought it on myself," the old woman said. "I knew those men were dangerous. I should have stayed out of their way, but they just made me so darned mad."

Under different conditions, Sarah might have smiled. "This wasn't your fault, Gran."

Watery blue eyes fixed on Sarah's face. "This has something to do with your husband, doesn't it?"

Gran had always been perceptive.

"I don't have a husband anymore, but yes, it has something to do with Andrew. Unfortunately, I don't know exactly what." Sarah squeezed her grandmother's hand. "Can you tell me what the men who broke in looked like?"

A sound of disgust came from Gran's throat. "One

was skinny and blond. He had a tattoo on his hand that said Mother. The other was Mexican...what do they call it now... Hispanic?"

"That's right, Gran."

"He was short, lots of muscles, wearing one of those tight black T-shirts with a skull on the front. Neither one of them seemed to care—" she dragged in a shaky breath "—that I'd seen their faces."

"Probably because they don't have a record." Jackson walked up beside the bed and Sarah introduced him as the friend who had brought her to the hospital. "They probably weren't concerned because they have no prints on file, no criminal record, that kind of thing."

"He brought you here?" The old woman's shrewd gaze surveyed the man at her bedside head to foot.

"Jackson owns the Raintree Ranch, Gran, where Holly and I are living."

She nodded with obvious approval. "A Western man. 'Bout time, girl."

Sarah flushed. She didn't dare look at Jackson. "Those men didn't find anything in your house. I don't think they'll bother you again. And while you're in here, I'm going to make sure your house is put back in order."

Gran patted her hand. "You're a good girl, Sarah. You didn't deserve a husband like that." The old woman's eyes began to droop and Sarah gently eased her hand away, letting her grandmother drift back to sleep.

She leaned over and kissed the old woman's forehead. "I'll be back tomorrow," she whispered and caught a last faint smile on her grandmother's wrinkled face.

Jackson walked her out into the hall. She shouldn't be thinking how sexy he looked in his low-slung jeans and scuffed boots, shouldn't be feeling this sweep of desire as he walked beside her—not with her grandmother lying in a hospital bed—but it was happening just the same.

How long had it been since a man had appealed to her the way this one did? In truth, not even Andrew in the days when she so foolishly thought she was in love with him.

"She sounded good," Sarah said, determined to distract herself. "I think she's going to be fine. I told her I'd come back tomorrow."

"So I guess that means we can go home."

She nodded. "I imagine we're both ready for a few hours in bed." Her cheeks flushed at her poor choice of words.

She flicked a glance at Jackson, hoping he hadn't noticed, and sucked in a breath at the flash of heat that burned in those dark brown eyes. For the first time she realized she wasn't the only one feeling the attraction.

After her nightmare marriage to Andrew, she wasn't ready for a serious relationship. She wasn't sure she ever would be. But she hadn't had sex in years. Maybe it was time she gave in to the growing need she felt for the man beside her.

His hand settled at her waist, guiding her out of the hospital, and that slight touch made her stomach contract. She could only imagine what it would feel like to kiss him, touch him, have him touch her.

She was a grown woman. For the first time in years, she was free to live her life as she pleased. And it was becoming increasingly clear, it would please her a very great deal to make love with Jackson Raines.

Jackson cast a glance at Sarah, who rode in the passenger seat as they drove out of the hospital parking lot. "There's something I need to do before we go home."

"What's that?"

"Take a look at your grandmother's house. We need to see if there's something there that might give us a clue who's behind this."

"I know where the spare key is—if the door's even locked. Gran figured living in a place like Sheep River, she didn't have to worry about locking her doors."

"Used to be that way. Unfortunately, times have changed." As he drove toward the old woman's house at the edge of town, Jackson glanced over at Sarah. He tried to concentrate on his driving and not think of the desire he felt for her that was growing all out of proportion. During the night just listening to her breathing as she slept against his shoulder made him hard. Her soft breasts had nestled against his arm, and desire clawed into his belly. He'd been hard off and on all night.

Damn.

He couldn't remember when a woman had gotten to him the way Sarah Allen did.

He amended that. As his brother had reminded him, the same woman had tied him in knots through most of his senior year. Though she had never known how strongly he wanted her, she had never been far from his thoughts.

She wasn't now.

Christ.

Boxing had taught him self-control and he prided

himself on being a master. Unfortunately, when Sarah was around, that control grew thin and strained. He flicked her another quick glance. He wanted to kiss her more than anything he could think of. He wanted to feel those soft breasts in his hands. He just flat out wanted her—to a degree that had rarely occurred in his orderly world.

Jackson didn't like it.

Not one damned bit.

They pulled up in front of Abigail Thompson's little wood-frame house and he turned off the engine. He rounded the truck and helped Sarah down, tried to ignore the brush of fine strands of chestnut hair that floated across his cheek.

His groin throbbed. When he looked at her again, she hadn't moved, just stood there staring up at him as if she felt the heat pulsing between them. He couldn't stop himself. He bent his head and kissed her.

Soft, full lips. Cinnamon from the breakfast roll he'd bought her in the hospital cafeteria that morning. She softened against him and his body went achingly hard. He started to pull away, end the kiss while a thread of sanity remained, but her sweet mouth opened in invitation and his tongue slid inside.

His arm went around her waist and he hauled her flush against him, deepened the kiss, lost himself in the taste of her, the feel of her slender body pressed the length of his. Her breasts were even fuller than he had imagined, softer, the tips like firm little berries. It was all he could do not to rip open her blouse and fill his palms, to bend his head and taste them.

It took a moment before he realized she was pressing her hands against his chest, trying to break free of his hold.

Instantly, he let her go.

"God, Sarah, I'm sorry. I didn't mean for that to happen. I can't believe it did." He ran a hand along his jaw, felt the roughness of his morning beard. "I know the kind of man you were married to, the things he did to you. I didn't mean to scare you. I don't exactly know what happened."

The tension left her shoulders and a faint smile rose on her lips. "You're a man. I've learned to distrust them. You scared me a little, but I think I mostly scared myself." She reached up and lightly touched the roughness along his jaw. "It's been a long time, Jackson."

His erection pulsed. He ached to kiss her again. Instead he stayed where he was. "You don't have to be afraid of me, Sarah. Not ever."

She studied him a moment, then turned away and started for the house. Jackson followed, not the least bit happy with his loss of control.

And aching for it to happen again.

The front door was locked when they got there, a small piece of yellow crime scene tape still attached to the porch. The tape was mostly gone now, but the sheriff had obviously been there. When Jackson got back to the ranch, he would call Ben Weber, tell him about the second break-in. Maybe the two law officers could piece something together.

They went into the house, saw that it looked pretty much the same as the cottage, the sofa cushions torn open, the chair upended, the lace curtains pulled down.

Sarah went over and examined them. "The curtains aren't torn. If I had a ladder, I could put them back up."

Jackson walked over, reached up and did it for her.

She gave him one of those soft smiles that turned him upside down. "Thank you."

The kitchen drawers had been pulled out, the contents strewn on the kitchen floor. Sarah bent and picked up the silverware, put it in the sink, and Jackson helped her. They worked for a while, Jackson searching while he helped Sarah straighten. As he walked out on the back porch, something dark and shiny caught his eye near the base of a flowerpot, the object partly covered by the blooms of a pink petunia. He picked up an empty matchbook, examined it in his palm.

"Look at this." He showed the blue-and-gold matchbook to Sarah. "It came from a place called The Blue Parrot." He turned it over, read the address. "It's in California, on Ventura Boulevard in Studio City. Ever heard of it?"

"No, but Marty Kozak is a smoker. Unfortunately he doesn't fit Gran's description of either of the men who were here."

"Maybe he hired them." He stuffed the matchbook into his pocket and finished inspecting the house, which wasn't torn up quite as badly as the cottage.

"I'm coming back to visit Gran tomorrow. I'll buy some throw covers for the sofa and chair. I don't think she'll mind. In fact, she'll probably be happy for the change. She's always been kind of adventurous."

"I'd be happy to buy—"

"This isn't your problem, Jackson. It's mine. It isn't your responsibility to replace Gran's furniture, and I can't afford to do it myself right now. But I'm pretty good with decorating. And the men didn't do that much damage. As I said, Gran will probably like the change."

He nodded. He was beginning to think he'd been wrong about Sarah. Or maybe she had just learned that money wasn't everything. Sometimes the price you paid for having it was just too high. It occurred to him that he could like this Sarah Allen.

And as he thought of the men who had put an old lady in the hospital, he was even more worried about her.

Chapter 7

Sarah drove to Sheep River for the next two days to visit her grandmother in the hospital and put the little wood-frame house back in order. She took Gran home the morning of the third day and smiled at the surprised, pleased expression she received for the work she had done.

"Looks real nice, honey," Gran said, assessing the dark blue flowered throws over the sofa and chair, the light and dark blue accent pillows. "Place has been needin' some sprucing up. I guess there's always something good comes from everything."

Sarah wasn't convinced about that, but she didn't say so. "Are you sure you'll be all right?"

"Dr. Ellis says I'm good as new. I've got a couple of check-ups along the way, but Doc says, long as I take it easy, I'll be fine."

Sarah hated to leave her there alone, but as Gran reminded her, she had been living by herself for the past twenty-five years. And the men had already been there, searched and found nothing.

Satisfied Gran would be all right, Sarah returned to the office to finish the articles she was writing about the Memorial Day celebration coming up the end of the week.

Using memories from her childhood in the first article, combined with old photos from the 1980s she found in the newspaper's archives, she hammered out a piece she felt pleased with. She printed the pages at the end of her shift and set them aside, and headed for her pickup, parked in the lot down the street.

She had just reached the corner when a man stepped up beside her, tall, mid-forties, with a long, pointed nose and very smooth dark skin. He was wearing an expensive dark brown sport coat and tan slacks and looked as out of place in Wind Canyon as he actually was.

She stiffened as she felt hard steel shoved into her ribs. "Keep walking," he said. "Make a sound and I won't hesitate to pull the trigger."

Her pulse kicked into high gear. The man looked foreign but his accent was purely American. She had no idea who he was, but she knew he must be somehow connected to Andrew. She had known Andrew's business dealings bordered on illegal, but she hadn't believed they would haunt her from the grave.

He urged her around the corner, into the parking lot. "What…what do you want?"

"I want the USB key your husband kept—the one he was using to blackmail his customers."

"Andrew was…blackmailing people?"

He prodded her with the gun. "I want the USB. I think you know where it is."

"I—I don't know anything. Do you work for Martin Kozak?"

He frowned, ignored the question. "Just tell me where to find the USB and you'll never see me again." She gasped as he shoved her hard against the rough brick wall.

"If…if I had it, I'd give it to you." She dragged in a shaky breath. "Andrew never trusted me with anything. He certainly didn't give me any blackmail list."

His hard look sharpened. "Then how did you know it was a list?" he said smugly, not really expecting an answer.

Sarah wet her lips, tried to push him away, but his body was as hard as the wall behind her and the forearm he pressed beneath her chin felt like an iron bar.

"I want that list. If you don't have it, you'd better figure out where it is." He shoved her again, slamming her head against the wall.

For years she had let Andrew bully her, let him hurt her. "Get off me!" She shoved the man with all her strength but he moved barely an inch.

A slow smile curved his narrow lips. "I'll be back. You say anything to the cops, you won't like what happens when I get here."

Turning away, he started walking and Sarah sagged against the wall. At least she'd fought back. She remembered the day she had been watching TV when an item came on about an online battered women's group. There were other women just like her, she had discovered, and the chat room they shared became her refuge.

And her strength.

She bit back a sob. She had no idea where Andrew might have kept a flash drive that apparently held information he used for blackmail, but she knew she had to find it.

The man had threatened her. He hadn't mentioned Holly, but there was no doubt Sarah wasn't the only one in danger.

She pushed away from the bricks and moved on shaking legs toward the pickup. From the corner of her eye, she spotted Jackson striding across the parking lot in her direction. Without thinking, she turned and ran toward him. When he saw her face, he hauled her straight into his arms.

"You're shaking all over. For God's sake, what's happened?"

Sarah clung to him. For a moment, she couldn't speak.

"Take your time," he said. "I've got you. I won't let anyone hurt you."

She lifted her head from his shoulder, saw by the hard set of his jaw he meant every word. "A man came…" She swallowed. "He…he had a gun. He said he wanted the list Andrew was using to blackmail his customers."

"Blackmail? That's what he said?"

"Yes."

"Was he one of the men your grandmother described?"

She shook her head. "He seemed more…sophisticated than the men who ransacked Gran's house." She glanced around the parking lot, but saw no sign of him. "I've got to find that flash drive, Jackson." She felt the sting of tears and blinked to keep from crying. "Somehow, I've got to find it."

Keeping an arm around her, he started walking her back toward her truck. "We'll talk to the sheriff, tell him what's going on, see what he can do."

She jolted to a halt in the middle of the parking lot. "No sheriff—not unless we absolutely have to. These men... Jackson, they're dangerous. And if they were associated with Andrew, they're powerful. I'm afraid of what they might do."

Jackson made no reply, but a muscle flexed along his jaw.

"Can you drive?" he asked when they reached her blue truck.

She nodded. "I'm just a little shaken. I'll be fine."

"We'll pick up Holly then I'll follow you back to the house."

She opened the door of the pickup. "What were you doing in town?"

"I had some grocery shopping to do. You usually finish around three. I thought I'd buy you a cup of coffee or a soda or something." His gaze shifted toward the brick building where the man had dragged her. "Too bad I didn't get here a little sooner."

Her stomach churned. If Jackson had tried to rescue her, the man might have shot him. A sweep of nausea rolled through her. She didn't want him getting hurt because of her.

What on earth was she going to do?

Sarah pretended everything was normal. She picked up Holly at the day-care center, then turned onto the highway leading back to the ranch. Jackson followed to make sure she got there safely.

"Everyone is going to the parade tomorrow," Holly said as they rolled toward home. For the past fifteen minutes, she had been chattering away, mostly about the upcoming weekend. "Allie says her brother's going to be on the Boy Scout float. She says her dad's going to take her while her mom helps with the picnic."

Holly prattled on, excited at the prospect of the big celebration. The thought of going made Sarah sick to her stomach.

What if the dark-skinned man were there? What if he threatened Holly?

"Mama, what time does the parade start?" Holly shifted in her seat. "Mama, did you hear me?"

Sarah forced herself to smile. "I'm sorry, honey, what did you say?"

"I asked what time does the parade start?"

She had to think. It seemed impossible to concentrate. "It starts at eleven."

"Is Jackson going with us?"

Jackson. Just the sound of his name sent her pulse up a notch. "I don't know." But secretly she hoped he would. She didn't think the man would bother her if Jackson were with them.

She pulled up in front of the cottage and as soon as she turned off the engine, Holly unfastened her seat belt and jumped down from the truck.

She ran straight back to the big Ford pickup pulling up behind them. "Jackson!" It seemed her daughter and her landlord were now on a first-name basis, as Holly also was with Livvy. "Are you going with us tomorrow?"

"Tomorrow?" Bending down, he scooped her up in his arms and settled her against his shoulder. "What's going on tomorrow?"

Watching them, Sarah felt a pang in her chest. Andrew had adored Holly, but he rarely had time for her. Jackson was just the opposite. No matter how busy he was, he always made time for Holly, or Jimmy's boys, Gibby and Sam.

"Tomorrow's the parade, silly. Everyone's going to be there—Mama said so."

He set Holly back on her feet, cocked an eyebrow at Sarah.

"I'm covering the celebration for the paper," she explained. "I have to go."

He looked more resigned than excited. "Looks like we're going then," he said to Holly.

"Yippee!" She jumped up and down, her ponytail bobbing. Jackson looked over at Sarah and smiled. He had the nicest smile, the straightest, whitest teeth. She tried not to think of the searing kiss they'd shared, but the image was crystal clear, and soft heat curled in her stomach.

She clamped down on the dangerous memory. "You don't mind going with us?"

"You think I'd let you go alone?"

She didn't answer but relief trickled through her. Though deep down, she had known he would insist on coming along.

"Why don't I see if Jimmy and the boys want to come with us? We'll go to the picnic, too, make a day of it."

Sarah smiled and nodded, figuring he probably wanted Jimmy there in case there was trouble. The first time she'd met Jackson's big brawny foreman, Sarah had sensed the bond between the two men.

From the corner of her eye, she caught a flash of color and turned to see Olivia bustling up to them in a pale pink sweater and jeans.

Livvy set her hands on her plump hips. "I heard what you said. Tomorrow's the big celebration. Everyone in town will be there and don't think for a minute you're leaving me home." She grinned. "I'll make us all some nice fried chicken and potato salad. We'll have a real old-fashioned family outing."

Something squeezed in Sarah's chest. If it weren't for the trouble that had followed her to Wind Canyon, she would be delighted at the prospect of a family outing—even if the family wasn't truly her own.

If it weren't for the trouble that had followed her...

Sarah's stomach churned.

Jackson left Sarah and Holly and headed for the house. Before he reached the back door he spotted his top hand, Wheeler Dillon, hurrying toward him.

Blond and gangly, Wheel was a cowboy in the truest sense of the word, a man who, at forty, had the suntanned, weathered features that came from spending most of his life out of doors.

"What's up, Wheel?"

"It's those damned loggers, Jackson. They had an accident up there along that new area they started working. Log pile broke loose, knocked down a big section of fence. The crew boss called, said some of our cattle got loose and were wandering around their equipment. I was just heading out with Shorty and Mac to round them up and move them down with the rest of the herd in Pine Meadow."

"Where's Jimmy?"

"He's out on the south range. Ought to be back any minute."

He spotted Jimmy's pickup just then, pulling up in front of the barn. Jimmy jumped down from the driver's seat and started walking toward them.

"What's going on?" he asked, and Wheel filled him in. "I'll go with you," Jimmy said.

"We can go up together," Jackson told him. "I've got a couple of phone calls I need to make, then we'll take the ATVs and ride on up. I want to take a look, see for myself what's going on up there."

Jimmy nodded, his long black ponytail blowing in the wind. "Sounds good."

Wheel took off with the men, a trailer and three horses, and Jackson went into the house to use the phone. If they were going to find that flash drive, they would have to go to L.A. He picked up the receiver to make arrangements with Mountain Air for a trip to California.

As soon as his calls were finished, he and Jimmy headed out on the four-wheelers, taking the road to the top of the mountain to assess the damage that had been done.

"They'll have to pay for that fence," Jimmy said as they pulled the four-wheelers to a stop in a spot that overlooked the upper pasture.

Jackson grunted. "You can be sure I'll send them a bill—but I won't hold my breath waiting for the check."

Bannock Logging was notorious for the destruction it caused. It was the kind of company that took its profits, then filed bankruptcy to avoid any claims for financial restitution or having to replant any trees.

Jackson figured the two brothers who owned the company were just the sort Andrew Hollister would have had dealings with, the sort he had been trying to blackmail. No wonder the guy had been murdered.

Wheel sauntered up beside them. "We'll need more fence line and posts than I thought."

"You and the boys get started with what you've got. Jimmy and I will go back down and get the rest of what you need."

"You got it, boss."

"The bastards," Jimmy muttered, surveying the ugly sea of stumps that dotted what had once been dense, old-growth forest.

They called it fire protection.

Well, they were right about that. You didn't have to worry about a forest fire if you cut down all the trees.

Jackson and Jimmy drove the dirt road back down the mountain, loaded a flatbed trailer with posts and barbless wire fence line. As they worked next to the barn, Jackson explained to Jimmy what was going on with Sarah, about her murdered late husband, and the danger she and her daughter might be facing.

"We're going to have to go to L.A., try to figure out what the hell is going on."

"If you have to go—then go. Things are pretty well under control around here, and Livvy and I can look after Holly. You just take care of Sarah."

Jackson clapped Jimmy on the back. "Thanks, Jim."

"Just call if you need anything."

"I will." But there was only one thing Jackson needed. His gaze strayed to the cottage and the dark-haired woman he could see through the living-room window.

Heat pooled low in Jackson's groin. Softly, he cursed.

Chapter 8

The parade was flashy, with lots of red, white and blue. The Cougars high school marching band in their red-and-gold uniforms played rousing John Philip Sousa tunes. There were a string of floats: Chamber of Commerce; the district recreation baseball team, the Wolverines; a war veterans VFW float sponsored by Fred Wilkins at the mercantile.

"There's Allie's brother, Rex!" Holly waved at the group of boys atop the Boy Scout float, jumping up and down as if she knew the boy, though she had never met him. Next came the sheriff's posse, riding palomino horses wearing silver-mounted saddles. Clowns on bicycles tossed out candy near the end.

Sarah scribbled notes. She had thought about bringing her pocket tape recorder, but it was noisy along the parade route and a regular old notepad worked just as well. Unfortunately it reminded her of the notes Andrew must have kept to blackmail the people with whom he did business.

She wondered what they had done that Andrew could hold over them, knew it must be illegal if someone wanted the information back so badly.

She had to find that flash drive.

Sarah closed her notepad and sighed. The last thing she wanted to do was go back to L.A. Too many bad memories, too much fear. Still, she needed to talk to Stan Greenberg, Andrew's attorney. Maybe he could tell her where to look for the list.

Then again, Andrew had died owing Stan money. There wasn't enough in the estate to pay him for all the hours he had billed. She wasn't sure how much help he would be willing to provide. Or if he knew anything at all about the blackmail list.

Or if he did, if he would admit it.

She tried to think what else she might do. The house on Sunset had finally sold—way below market value because of the death that had occurred there. The escrow had closed and what was left of the furniture that hadn't been sold had been moved into storage. Eventually that would go, too—more money into the probate coffers to pay the attorneys and a little more of Andrew's staggering debts.

The Santa Monica condo was up for sale but hadn't sold yet. She wondered if the apartment had suffered the same fate as the cottage and thought that it must have been the first place the men had searched.

It just indicated how bad the market was that the Realtor hadn't shown the place, discovered the vandalism and called her with the news.

"Look, Mommy, a fire engine!" It followed the last float, signaling the end of the parade.

"We'll drive over to the park," Jackson said, "and find a nice place to eat that chicken Livvy fried." He made another sweeping glance of the area. She noticed he had been doing that ever since they arrived in town.

"Let's head back to the cars," Jimmy said. "You boys look out for Holly."

Rags yapped and danced on the end of the leash Holly held. Sam and Gibby's little dog, Feather, one of two they owned, was also there for the festivities.

All kinds of activities were scheduled at Wind Canyon Park: a pie-eating contest, a three-legged sack race, a kayak race in the small lake in the middle of the park. The Memorial Day weekend weather was perfect—crisp, clear and sunny—just a few puffy clouds floating across the sky.

Still, Sarah was nervous. She hadn't seen any sign of the man who had accosted her, but there were a lot of people milling about. She told herself to relax, that she was with Jackson and Jimmy. She was safe and she should enjoy herself.

They were busily climbing into the pickups when she heard someone calling her name.

"Sarah? Sarah Allen, is that you?"

Turning, she spotted a freckle-faced redhead with a big wide grin. Sarah let out a shout of excitement. "Nancy! Nan Marcus! I can't believe it's really you!"

The two women hugged. "It's Nan Hargrove now," said her old friend. "You look fantastic!"

"So do you!" Nan was a few pounds heavier, but still curvy in all the right places.

"Actually, I'm divorced," Nan said, casting a sideways glance at Jimmy.

Sarah took the hint. "Do you know everyone? You probably know Livvy. This is Jackson Raines and his foreman, Jimmy Threebears. These are Jimmy's sons, Gibby and Sam."

"I know Livvy and Jackson. I've seen the boys and Jimmy around but we've never actually met."

"Nice to meet you," Jimmy said, and there was a tightness in his features Sarah didn't understand.

She smiled at Nan. "And this is my daughter, Holly."

Nan lowered herself to the little girl's level. "It's very nice to meet you, Holly. You're just as pretty as your mother."

Holly grinned. "Thank you."

Nan returned her attention to Sarah. "I never had any kids. I wanted them but Ron said we should wait, and then things…well, things just didn't work out."

"I'm sorry, Nan."

She shrugged. "It's all right. We never were very well suited. I just felt like it was time to get married and so I did. Not a good idea."

"Are you here by yourself?"

"I'm here with my mother. She's waiting for me in the car."

Sarah glanced at Jackson, caught his faint nod. "Why don't the two of you join us for lunch? Livvy made fried chicken and she always makes more than enough."

"I'm afraid my mother gets tired pretty easily. I was about to drive her home."

"Then come back and join us. Please, Nan. I'd love

a chance to catch up. It's been so long and it's so good to see you."

Nan's gaze strayed to Jimmy then back. "All right. I won't be long."

"We'll watch for you."

For the next few hours, Sarah was actually able to think of something besides the problems she was facing. Nan joined them and they ate fried chicken, potato salad and peach cobbler on a picnic table covered by a white cotton cloth in the shade of an old sycamore tree.

She and Nan shared old memories of their youth and lots of laughter. It was heaven.

Until a big-bosomed woman with long blond hair and even longer legs in tight jeans walked up to the table.

"Hi, y'all." She flashed a smile that was clearly meant for Jackson.

"Hi, Maddie," he replied and there was something in the look that passed between them that told Sarah he knew the woman well—very well. He introduced Maddie Gallagher to Sarah.

"It's nice to meet you," Sarah said.

"Same here."

Nan knew Maddie through her ex-husband's restaurant, The Cedar Inn, where Maddie worked as a part-time waitress.

"I guess you been busy," the woman said to Jackson, glancing from him to Sarah as if she were sizing up her competition.

"A little."

"Give me a call sometime. I'll fix you supper—just like I used to."

"I'll do that," Jackson said, but he didn't seem enthused.

As the woman walked away, Sarah couldn't help wondering if Jackson would make the call. It was clear Maddie Gallagher could give a man what he needed.

Sarah felt a stirring inside her, a combination of jealousy and heat as the thought occurred that if Jackson needed a woman, why not her?

The afternoon passed and all too soon it was time to head home. Sarah's nervousness returned as Jackson took her hand and led her away from the group.

"I wish I didn't have to bring this up, but we can't put it off much longer. Whoever these guys are, they aren't going to give up—not as long as they think you've got whatever it is they want...or know where to find it."

"I know." She looked up into that ruggedly handsome face, felt the same hot stirring she had felt before. She forced herself to concentrate. "I've got to go back to L.A. Since I don't have the flash drive, it must be there."

"We need to know who these people are. If we can't find the flash drive, we're going to have to deal with them some other way."

A chill slipped through her even though she stood in the sun. "Marty owns Kozak Construction," she said. "It's a pretty big company. He rented heavy equipment from one of Andrew's companies. Maybe he was using the stuff for something illegal."

"If so, we need to know what it was."

She nodded. "I'll talk to Andrew's attorney, see what I can get him to tell me."

Jackson dug the blue-and-gold matchbook out of his pocket. Sarah had forgotten all about it.

"This might be a lead. The Blue Parrot. We'll need to find out."

She plucked the matchbook out of his hand. "I'll make a point to go there, see what I—"

"*We,* Sarah. You're not going to L.A. alone—I'm going with you."

"But—"

"There's no point in arguing."

"But—"

He cocked a dark eyebrow and she closed her mouth a second time.

"Livvy can take care of Holly while we're away. Monday's a holiday. Can you be ready to leave first thing Tuesday morning?"

"I—I guess so."

He smiled. "Too bad my brother, Gabe, isn't up here. He flies a big twin Aerostar. But he's living in Texas these days. Be kind of out of the way for him."

She remembered Gabriel Raines, who had been a year ahead of her in high school. Like Jackson, Gabe had been a bad boy, always in trouble. When Jackson had begun to change, so had his two younger brothers. He had that kind of influence on people. From what she could tell, he still did.

"I've already called Mountain Air. Their planes are comfortable and well maintained. I use them whenever I have to fly."

"I can't afford—"

"I can."

Sarah glanced away. It was funny. Jackson was the sort of man who took charge, took care of things. At first she'd believed Andrew was that way. But Andrew mostly took care of himself, and he got what he wanted by force, not the lift of an eyebrow.

She shouldn't have liked being looked after. She should have craved the independence Andrew had stolen from her. But Jackson didn't make her feel cheated. He just did what he thought a man ought to do.

Sarah almost smiled.

Then she thought of the trip to L.A., of what they might find, of the demons she would have to confront, and any thought of smiling slipped away.

Chapter 9

They flew out at eight-thirty Tuesday morning in a twin-engine Cessna Jackson had chartered a number of times before. He hated the crowds and the security hassles at the airports and he could afford to fly private.

After a four-hour flight, plus a refueling stop, they arrived at the Santa Monica Airport, their destination, and a smaller, easier place to land than LAX. They grabbed their bags and made their way over to retrieve the rental car Jackson had reserved.

As Sarah watched him wheeling his carry-on bag across the asphalt, she found herself smiling. He looked almost as good in tan slacks and a short-sleeved shirt as he did in faded jeans and boots. He loaded their luggage into the trunk of a snappy red, four-door Infiniti and they climbed into the plush interior. Jackson checked the map he had printed off the internet and pulled the car out onto the road.

"Where are we going?" Sarah asked.

"I think we should check into the hotel first, get settled and get our bearings, then we can head out again."

She was only a little surprised when he drove the rental car up in front of Loews Santa Monica Beach, an expensive hotel that fronted the ocean.

"Can't beat Expedia," he said as he pushed through the doors leading into an impressive lobby lined with potted palms. "Living so far out of town, the internet is invaluable for travel."

Sarah had been to the hotel bar for drinks with Andrew and his friends. She caught hold of Jackson's arm, felt his very solid bicep harden at her touch, forced herself to ignore the little flutter in her stomach.

"Are you sure, Jackson? This place is expensive."

He smiled. "You know how much a gallon of gas costs in L.A.?"

"Depending on the economy, as much as four dollars."

"Until a couple of years ago, I owned a pile of oil stocks. They made me more money than I can spend. If my conscience hadn't started nagging me, I'd still own them. As it is, I'm now investing in Green."

"Green?"

"You know, wind machines and solar products developed to benefit the environment. So far, my stocks are doing great. I'm not Bill Gates, but I'm more than comfortable. I can do pretty much what I want."

He had reserved a two-bedroom suite with ocean views, a lovely room, she saw as they walked in. The bedroom doors were open. The minute he noticed the king-size bed, his gaze turned dark and smoky.

"Take your pick," he said, his eyes never leaving her face.

Sarah swallowed. She wanted to tell him that whatever room he chose was the one she wanted to sleep in. That she wanted him to make love to her and this was the perfect place.

She didn't. Just turned and walked into the nearest bedroom, leaving him the one with the ocean view. She picked up the phone and dialed the ranch house, spent a few minutes talking to Holly, telling her they had made it safely to L.A.

"Me and Livvy baked a cake, Mama. We're gonna invite Sam and Gibby and their dad over for supper."

"That sounds great, honey. I'm glad you're having fun."

"Sam says if it's okay with you, he could teach me to ride Midnight. She's a pony, Mom, and she's just my size. Can I?"

Uncertainty rolled through her. Sarah glanced over at Jackson, who had just walked into the doorway. "There's a pony named Midnight. Do you think it's safe for Holly—"

"Midnight's twenty years old. Both Jimmy's boys learned to ride on her. Holly couldn't be safer."

Sarah turned back to the phone. "You can ride her— as long as Livvy or Sam's dad is out there with you."

"Yippee!" The sound of clanging pots and pans came over the line. "I gotta go, Mom. Livvy's taking the cake out of the oven."

"Have a good time, sweetheart." The line went dead and Sarah hung up the phone, wishing she were there instead of in L.A.

"Everything okay?"

"Everything's fine. She's having a great time. I don't think she's missing me—especially not when she's got a pony to ride."

He chuckled. "She's living on a ranch. She needs to learn to ride."

"I suppose. I just… I worry about her."

"That's what mothers are supposed to do. Don't worry, she'll be fine." His expression changed and so did the subject. "Do you still have a key to your condo?"

She nodded. "I meant to leave it there when I left that last day, but I was so anxious to get on the road I forgot."

"We'll go there first."

"All right. I'd like to call Gran before we go, make sure she's doing okay."

Gran was fine. She told Sarah to enjoy the trip with her handsome cowboy.

"We're just friends," Sarah tried to convince her, but Gran just chuckled into the phone.

The rental car still sat in front of the hotel. Jackson waited until Sarah got in, closed her door, then went around to the driver's side and slid behind the wheel.

It didn't take long to reach the impressive Whispering Sands condominium development where Sarah had been living before her move to Wyoming. They parked in guest parking, then Sarah used her key to the private elevator, which they took to the seventh floor.

She steeled herself, expecting the worst, and handed Jackson the key to the door. When the door swung open, she saw that the apartment had been trashed as she had feared.

"Look familiar?" Jackson asked.

"Unfortunately, yes."

"I was pretty sure they'd hit here first."

"So was I." She surveyed the overturned cream-colored sofa and chairs in the living room, the cushions sliced open and the stuffing torn out. They had done a thorough job, she saw, even pulling up the carpet in the bottom of the closets. Still, the impact wasn't nearly as painful as it had been in the little cottage she thought of as home.

"When we get back to Wyoming, I'll call the real estate office," she said. "Tell them what's happened. They'll need to get the place cleaned up."

"You'd better call the police."

She stiffened, turned away from surveying the wreckage to face him. "I'm not calling the police, Jackson. I had more than my share of dealings with them after Andrew died. If I call, it'll start all over. I can't go through that again."

He said nothing for several long moments, just stood there studying her face. "All right, we'll play it your way. For now."

She knew he was worried about the danger she might be facing. But there was a danger in all of this that Jackson didn't understand. She turned away from him, walked into the master bedroom, surveyed the destruction in there.

Jackson walked up beside her. "Looks like they did a pretty thorough job."

"Very thorough."

"Any place they might have missed?"

"That's what I was trying to figure out." She gazed past the cream-colored bedspread to the black lacquer nightstands and matching armoire. The furniture had been thoroughly searched, the drawers and doors left standing open.

"There was a safe at the back of the closet," she said, heading in that direction, "but once my clothes were gone, it would be easy to spot." She walked inside, saw the door to the safe standing open.

"From the looks of things," Jackson said, "Andrew didn't leave the flash drive in the condo or your friends would have found it and they wouldn't be bothering you."

"As I said, Andrew didn't spend much time here."

"Where *did* he spend his time?"

She glanced away, barely able to look at him. "He traveled a lot. He spent a lot of time in Vegas. And then there was his mistress."

One of his dark eyebrows went up. "Sounds like Andrew was a very busy man."

"Thank God for that."

"Do you know her name?"

It was embarrassing to have a husband who openly flaunted his women, even if their marriage had been over for years. "The latest one you mean? I heard him call her Mitzy. I don't know her last name or where she lives. I didn't really care."

"We need to talk to her, Sarah. Maybe she has the flash drive—or at least some kind of information about it."

"If she had the flash drive and they threatened her, she probably would have given it to them." Sarah looked up at him, read the tension in his face, ignored the pity. "We need to talk to Stanley Greenberg. Stan was Andrew's attorney—his right-hand man. He would know where to find Mitzy."

Ditzy—Sarah had secretly called her. Though she had never seen the woman, she could describe her: perfect body, perfect face, pea-size brain. That was the kind of female Andrew always chose.

Too bad he'd made an exception in Sarah's case.

Too bad she hadn't figured it out before she'd married him.

"Let's go," Jackson said, catching her hand and pulling her out of the bedroom toward the front door. "Like I said, if the flash drive was here, they would have found it."

They left the apartment and Sarah gave Jackson directions to Stan Greenberg's office in Santa Monica. They drove into the underground parking lot, then took the elevator up to Stan's office.

Recognizing the attractive older woman seated behind the reception desk, Sarah summoned a smile. "Hello, Rosemary. Is Stan in? I need to talk to him."

The woman wheeled back her chair and stood up, smoothed the skirt of her apricot linen suit. "Mrs. Hollister—I thought you'd moved out of town."

"I have. I'm just here a few days on business. As I said, I need to speak to Stan." She continued to smile. "It shouldn't take very long."

"I'll see if he's in." Which meant, *I'll see if he'll talk to you.*

They waited only a moment before Rosemary returned. "He says you can go right in."

"Thank you."

Jackson followed her into Stan's office, elegantly decorated in dark wood and forest green.

"Sarah!" Stan rose and rounded his desk to greet her, kissing her on each cheek in the Hollywood style that always seemed so phony. "It's good to see you, Sarah." He was a balding man in his forties with the hint of a paunch beginning to show above the waistline of his navy-blue suit pants.

"You, too, Stan."

He turned a smile on Jackson, extended his hand. "I'm Stan Greenberg."

"Jackson Raines." The men completed the handshake.

"So how can I help you two?"

"A couple of things, Stan." Sarah went on to explain about the men who had pursued her to Wyoming, about the book or flash drive or whatever it was that they wanted.

"Andrew was blackmailing someone, Stan. We think it was Martin Kozak. Do you know anything about that?"

"Of course not. You know I would never do anything illegal."

Sarah refrained from rolling her eyes. "I'll need a copy of the probate documents. I need to find out what was going on."

"Are you sure you should be involving yourself in this, Sarah?"

"Involving myself is the last thing I want. I don't have any other choice."

"I see."

"I need a copy of the probate, Stan."

"That shouldn't be a problem. I'll ask Rosemary to mail you one. Just give her your address before you leave."

"I'll just wait here while she gets it."

It was clear he wasn't pleased. Still, he leaned over

and pressed the intercom button, instructed Rosemary to get the information Sarah had requested. Though she had signed a lengthy prenuptial agreement before she and Andrew were married, giving him sole rights to the companies he owned, she was his widow and a party to the probate proceedings.

She just hoped the information would help.

"The copies will be ready for you when you leave," Stan said.

"Thank you."

He walked behind his desk, sat down and opened the file in front of him.

"There's just one more thing," Sarah said.

He looked up. "Which is…?"

"I need to talk to Mitzy. Maybe she knows something that will help us."

His face colored slightly. "I didn't realize you knew."

"I've known for years, Stan. Before Mitzy, it was Gloria, and let's not forget Susie. The list goes on and on."

Stan flipped open the card file sitting on top of his desk and dug out the information. "Her name is Mitzy Bender. Unfortunately, she left town just after you did. I tried to call and check on her—as Andrew would have wanted—but I never reached her. She seems to have disappeared completely."

"I think I know why," Jackson said softly.

"Are you sure there's nothing you can tell us that might help us find the flash drive?"

Stan shook his head. "I wish I could. If anyone comes to me asking questions, I'll tell them you have no idea where to find whatever it is they're looking for."

"Thanks, Stan."

They left his private office. Sarah collected the probate paperwork from Rosemary and they carried it down to the garage. Sitting in the front seat of the Infiniti, she began to skim the documents, paying particular attention to the page listing the companies requesting payment of debt from the estate.

"God, there are dozens," she said, a sick feeling in her stomach.

Jackson leaned over to examine the list. "Looks like your late husband owed money to half the people in California."

"And most of the people in Nevada—though his gambling debts don't appear on the list."

She turned to the page showing his current assets. "Andrew's been selling off his father's businesses for years. Here's a list of the businesses he still owned when he died. Doesn't look like there's that many left."

"Read off the names, tell me what you know about each one."

"Not much, I'm afraid. Andrew wasn't very forthcoming when it came to his business dealings." But she looked down and began to read. "Blacktop Tires. That's a chain of retail tire stores located throughout the West."

"I've seen them."

"Speedway Manufacturing—a small company that makes specialty racing tires. It's kind of an offshoot of Blacktop."

"What else?"

"Axis Mining. As I recall, they closed down operations a couple of years ago. Andrew used to own a company that made ore crushing machines, but he sold that sometime back." She looked at another name on the list. "Hollister Equipment is a company that leases heavy machinery for big construction projects. I'm pretty sure that was Andrew's connection to Kozak. Kozak Construction builds roads, mostly. I'm not sure what else."

"That it?"

"There's one more listed—Southgate Demolition. They tear down buildings. That's all I know."

"It's a start."

"I guess. But what exactly are we looking for?"

"I'm not sure. If Kozak was doing something illegal, we need to figure out what it was."

"So how do we do that?"

He shook his head. "I wish my brother was back in the country. He's got lots of friends in low places, people who can dig up dirt when no one else can."

"When will he be home?"

"Not soon enough. We'll have to do the best we can while we're here."

"There's something that's been bothering me," she said. "I've been thinking about the man who accosted me in the parking lot… I'm not convinced he works for Kozak."

"Why is that?"

"I don't know exactly…just a couple of things he said."

"If he isn't Kozak's man, there may be more than one company Andrew was blackmailing."

"That's what I'm afraid of." Sarah sighed and leaned back in the deep red leather seat as Jackson stuck the key in the ignition.

"It's late and both of us are tired," he said. "We'll

get something to eat, get a good night's sleep, and start again in the morning."

Sarah glanced over at Jackson. His gaze locked with hers and her heartbeat quickened. It wasn't food he wanted, those hot brown eyes said. And it wasn't sleep.

As the engine roared to life, Sarah ignored the flood of heat that roared into her bloodstream.

Chapter 10

They decided on room service. As much as Jackson liked the idea of taking Sarah to one of the fine restaurants along the beach, he also liked the notion of sharing a meal with her alone.

He tried to tell himself not to think what might happen after they had finished eating and enjoyed a bottle of wine. He told himself not to imagine running his hands through all that glorious chestnut hair, capturing her face between his hands and kissing her until he'd had his fill. He tried not to think of undressing her, carrying her into the bedroom, easing her down on the king-size bed and making love to her.

She was exhausted, worried, and on top of that was the not-so-small matter that the last man she'd been with had abused her so badly she had wound up in the hospital.

Letting him make love to her was probably the last thing she wanted.

They ordered two filets, medium rare, and Jackson added a bottle of Stags' Leap, Napa Valley cabernet. The plates came piping hot with fully loaded baked potatoes, two big green salads, and there was strawberry shortcake for dessert.

The server had placed the food on the linen-draped table in front of the sliding glass doors to the balcony overlooking the ocean. Mostly Jackson just picked at the food on his plate, his mind on Sarah and how pretty she looked in the moonlight streaming in off the white sand beach and how much he wanted her.

He had no idea what Sarah was thinking. She made pleasant conversation and smiled often enough, but she didn't eat even as much as he did.

When the meal was finished, Jackson rounded the table and pulled out her chair.

"We've got a big day tomorrow." They planned to start with Hollister Equipment, investigate the connection to Marty Kozak, and make some calls, see what they might learn. "Why don't you go on to bed, try to get some sleep?"

Exactly what he knew he wouldn't be able to do—not with Sarah in a bed on the other side of the wall.

"I suppose we should." But she didn't move away from him, and the longer he stayed close to her, the harder it was going to be. He was so damned hard now he ached with every heartbeat.

"Good night," he said gruffly. Turning, he walked into his bedroom.

It took every ounce of his will.

Jackson closed the door and leaned against it. *Dam-*

mit to hell. But it wasn't fair to Sarah to press her. Not after what she'd been through.

With a sigh, he stripped off his shirt and tossed it over the end of the bed, took off his loafers and socks, then padded over to his suitcase and pulled out a paperback book. He tried not to listen for sounds in the room next door. It was going to be torture just knowing she was in there. Knowing he couldn't kiss her, touch her, couldn't pull off her nightgown and run his tongue over those soft, full breasts.

Jackson groaned.

Sarah paced the bedroom. She knew he wanted her. Or at least she thought he did. All through dinner, whenever he looked at her, the heat in his eyes made her giddy. Desire was there in every gesture, every glance. She'd been sure when they were finished with the meal, he would kiss her, do something that would lead to making love.

Instead, he had practically run from the room.

Sarah paced the bedroom. She remembered the kiss they had shared in front of Gran's house. True, she had been a little frightened. She had never been with a man whose passions ran so hot—and clearly his did. She had known it the moment he had touched her.

But mostly she had been afraid of herself—of her own fierce need, stronger than she ever could have guessed.

It was that kiss, she believed, that kept Jackson in his room, instead of in her bed. He was afraid he would frighten her, that he might lose control and hurt her in some way. He knew how cruel Andrew had been and he was going out of his way to protect her.

From himself.

Sarah glanced at the clock. Half an hour had passed and still desire pulsed through her. Her skin felt so sensitive the slight breeze coming in through the bedroom window seemed to scorch her flesh. Her nipples were as hard as diamonds and the place between her legs throbbed and burned.

All day she had thought of what it would be like to make love with Jackson. She had been so sure, so certain it would happen tonight.

She paused in front of the mirror, opened the silk robe she had put on in the hope he would come. At thirty-two, her body was still firm, her waist small and her hips nicely rounded. Her breasts were a little heavier since she'd had a child, but they were high and nicely shaped and as she looked at them in the mirror they seemed to swell with anticipation.

A noise sounded in the room next door.

Jackson was still awake. What would he do if she simply walked into his room? Would he send her away? Or would he take charge, as was his nature? Would he make love to her as she had dreamed he would do?

Her shoulders straightened. There was only one way to find out.

Refusing to allow the terrifying thought of how she would feel if he rejected her, she walked into the living room, crossed the carpet, and knocked on his bedroom door. She didn't wait for permission to enter, just turned the knob and walked in.

Jackson lay propped on a pillow, his rugged, handsome features immersed in the pages of a book. He spotted her, came up off the bed in the same tan slacks he'd had on earlier—and nothing else. Sarah sucked in a breath. He was tall and lean and all solid muscle—wide, muscled shoulders; slabs of muscle across his chest; an abdomen laddered with sinew. A light furring of dark hair spanned his chest and arrowed down into the waistband of his slacks. She had never seen a man with a more beautiful body.

"You must...must have kept up your boxing."

He stood there unmoving, his chest heaving in and out. "There's a gym in the basement at the house. I like to stay in shape."

She wet her lips. "Yes... I—I can see that."

He reached for the shirt lying across the foot of his bed, but Sarah held up a hand.

"Don't. You look perfect the way you are."

Dark brown eyes burned into her. "Sarah..."

"Do you know how badly I want to touch you? It's all I can do not to—"

"God, Sarah..." He didn't let her finish, just moved the short distance between them and hauled her into his arms.

His kiss was hot and fierce, a wild, burning, taking kiss that turned her inside out. He opened the front of her robe and one of his suntanned hands cupped a breast, began to mold and caress her.

"I've dreamed of this," he whispered, sliding the robe off her shoulders, lowering his head to take the fullness into his mouth. He tugged softly. His tongue curled around the hardened tip and it felt so good she swayed against him. She slid her fingers into his thick dark hair and arched her back to give him better access.

"Jackson..."

A shudder passed through him. His white teeth fastened on a nipple, raked gently, and hot sensation poured through her. Her legs gave out and Jackson caught her, lifted her into his arms and strode back to the bed.

"I've never wanted a woman as much as I want you," he said, settling her on the mattress and capturing her lips in another scorching kiss.

The words thrilled her, burned away any second thoughts she might have had. Held in thrall by his magnificent body, she watched him strip off his slacks and white cotton briefs. He was big and hard and her insides tightened at the thought of him entering her. Her mouth watered as if she wanted to eat him up.

"I want you, too," she said, and then he was kissing her again, joining her naked on the bed, taking her deeply with his tongue. Her own tongue swept in, tangled with his, and she heard him groan.

Jackson kissed the side of her neck, trailed hot kisses down over her breasts, and he suckled her there. Sarah began to writhe, to arch upward in a silent plea for more.

"I need you," she whispered, moving restlessly, urging him to take her.

"Soon, darlin'. First I want to taste you." She wasn't sure what he meant until she felt his tongue circling her navel, moving lower, felt the wetness of his kisses on the inside of her thighs.

"Jackson!" she cried out at the feel of his mouth on her sex, the slick heat of his tongue. Hot sensation flooded into her core, gripped her like a fist. The first climax hit like a tidal wave, shattering the last of her reserve, immersing her in a wave of pleasure that threatened to pull her under and never let go. She came a second time before he left her, moved above her, settled himself between her legs.

She tasted herself on the kiss that followed, and renewed desire swamped her, so powerful she barely noticed when he paused to slip on a condom. She was drenched and ready but, as big as he was, it took an effort to ease his way inside.

"It's all right, darlin'." He kissed the side of her neck. "We don't have to rush."

When he filled her completely at last, he paused and she realized he was fighting for control.

"Don't move," he whispered, bending to press a soft kiss on her lips. "Stay exactly where you are."

Sarah just smiled. She loved that she could do this, keep him on the very edge. She shifted, took him deeper still.

Jackson cursed softly, and then he began to move. She could feel the hot need burning through him as he pounded into her, took her with long deep, furious strokes that had her moaning and arching beneath him.

"Jackson!" she cried out as a fresh climax shook her, splintered her into a thousand pieces. An instant later, he followed her to release, his muscles tightening, a low growl coming from his throat.

Long seconds passed. He was still hard inside her when he rolled over, taking her with him, letting her lie across his chest.

He looped a strand of dark hair behind her ear. "You were amazing," he said, pressing a last soft kiss on her lips.

"So were you," she said. From somewhere deep inside her, Andrew's image flashed through her head—Andrew demanding she yield to him, Sarah giving in though whatever they had shared was long gone, enduring his touch but gaining no pleasure. Until he no longer came to her at all.

She shook her head, refusing to let him intrude—not now, not in a moment that belonged to her and Jackson.

"Are you all right?" he asked, his voice changing, roughening with concern. "I didn't scare you?"

A sweet warmth filled her that he should care. "You didn't scare me." In fact, she had never enjoyed lovemaking so much, never really known how good it could be.

She leaned down and kissed him, her hair falling forward, cocooning them in a world of their own. Jackson's erection stirred inside her, grew thicker, turned rock hard.

"I want you again," he said, "but I don't want to hurt you."

But the only one who had hurt her was Andrew and he would never hurt her again.

Sarah shifted, sat up astride him. She smiled as she lifted herself a little, then slid back down his hardened length. She moved that way again, felt the tension return to his body, felt his building desire. She had no idea what tomorrow might bring, whether the past would put an end to her future. Soon tomorrow would come, but tonight belonged to her.

Sarah meant to take this moment and hold it close to her heart.

As was his habit, Jackson awakened in the gray light of dawn. Beneath the covers he was hard. A beautiful woman lay beside him and he wanted her again.

He would not wake her. She needed her sleep, needed her strength to face the day ahead.

He sighed into the dim light slipping into the bedroom. The morning traffic was still sparse enough he could hear the waves rolling up on the beach. He looked over at Sarah, admired the way her glossy dark hair spread over the pillow, noticed the swell of a breast, barely covered by the white cotton sheet, and hardened even more.

Jackson softly cursed. Sliding out of the bed, he padded over to the closet, pulled out one of the terry cloth robes the hotel provided, and went into the living room to order coffee and breakfast rolls. He closed the door softly behind him, thinking of Sarah and the fantastic night they'd shared.

He couldn't stop wondering about her, how she had survived a man like Andrew, what made her the strong woman she seemed to be when she should have been defeated and weak.

He would find out, he vowed. There was something about Sarah Allen that made him want to know all of her secrets.

Then again, the more he knew, the more he might be drawn to her, the more easily he might fall prey to the charms that had captured him sixteen years ago.

He wasn't ready for that.

He would have to be careful.

But then *careful* was Jackson's middle name.

Sarah awoke with a start. For an instant, she didn't know where she was. Then she remembered—she had seduced Jackson Raines.

Embarrassment burned through her. There was no

denying it. She had gone brazenly into his room and practically demanded he have sex with her.

Not that he had minded.

Her embarrassment slowly faded. Jackson was an extremely virile man and an amazingly satisfying lover. It had been no hardship for him to make love to her.

And certainly no hardship for her.

They had made love three times last night, and it was one of the best nights of her life.

No, *the* best night, she corrected. Everything that had happened between them had been wonderful.

But wonderful had a way of disappearing, leaving heartbreak in its wake.

Sarah shivered. What she had shared with Jackson was special, but it couldn't last. There was too much pain in her past—and too many problems ahead.

She rose from the bed, grabbed her silk robe off the floor and slipped it on. She refused to lie to herself. She was free of Andrew but her life was still a mess. Danger lurked behind every corner. Beginning any sort of relationship wouldn't be fair to Jackson.

And it wouldn't be fair to her and Holly.

Sarah wasn't ready for any kind of commitment. Her one-night stand with Jackson—the first ever for Sarah—had perfectly filled her needs. Of course she wanted him again already—which could only be expected. Jackson was exactly the sort of lover every woman wanted: passionate, considerate and tireless. Sarah was thirty-two, at the height of her sexuality. It was only normal that she was attracted to such a virile male.

Still, she knew the terrible consequences of falling

under a man's spell—even one who, on the surface, appeared to be exactly the sort a woman would want. Sarah had learned the hard way how deceiving appearances could be.

One thing she knew for certain, the closer she allowed herself to get to Jackson, the more difficult it would be to end the affair.

No more hot, unbridled sex, she told herself. *No more fierce kisses and heated embraces, no more touching, aching, wanting.*

She had to stop now—before it was too late.

Jackson didn't notice Sarah standing in the bedroom doorway until she walked barefoot into the living room, wearing the same sexy, flowered silk robe she'd had on the night before. As she made her way toward the coffeepot, he went hard beneath his white terry robe.

She poured herself a cup of coffee but never once did she look at him, and right then, he knew he was in trouble. "You might as well say it. I kind of thought you would."

She added cream to her coffee, carefully stirred it in, then turned toward where he sat on the sofa. "All right, I'll say it. Last night was great—fantastic, in fact—but…"

"But it was a mistake."

She sighed, unnecessarily stirred her coffee a few more times, set the spoon back down on the tray. "It was my idea, so if it was a mistake, I'm the one who made it."

"That so? Maybe it wasn't a mistake. Maybe it was just great sex and we both enjoyed it."

She smiled at that, seemed a little relieved. "Yeah,

maybe it was. It's been years for me. I suppose I'm entitled."

That was exactly what he wanted to hear. Great sex, no strings. So why did hearing it make his insides draw into a knot?

"Actually, I've been wondering about last night…" he said.

"Wondering?"

"Yeah. Wondering why you weren't cowering in fear. I'm a man, after all, and a fairly demanding lover. After what your husband did—"

"Fairly demanding?"

"All right, I like sex. I like a partner who enjoys it, too."

"So you thought that after Andrew, I'd be afraid of you, afraid of your passion?"

He nodded. "I'm surprised you didn't run screaming from the room."

Sarah sighed, shoved back a lock of her heavy dark hair. "The truth is, for a long time, I was the coward you expected me to be. I was terrified of Andrew. I did whatever he told me to."

"Considering he beat you so badly he put you in the hospital, I can understand that."

"You know about that?"

"My brother's fairly thorough."

She walked toward him but sat down in the chair instead of taking a seat beside him on the sofa. "I was afraid to leave him. I was sure he'd wind up with custody of Holly—one way or another. And I was terrified that if he did and I wasn't there to take the brunt of his wrath, he would take it out on her."

"You thought he would kill you and then hurt your daughter."

"Yes." She glanced away, staring out the wide glass sliding doors as if she could see into the past. "Three years ago, I found a site on the internet, a support group for abused women—SBW. It stands for Support for Battered Women. I had my own laptop—something Andrew gave me so he could email me from wherever he happened to be, make sure I stayed close by."

"Kind of like Big Brother."

"Exactly. But it worked against him. Once I was in the chat group, little by little the women made me understand that I didn't have to let him break me, that I could find ways around him, ways to be my own person, even if I stayed."

"Do you still interact with the group?"

She nodded. "As soon as I get home, I'm logging in. Some of the women have become close friends. I've missed talking to them."

"I see." And he did. She had endured and become stronger, found ways to protect her daughter and herself. He couldn't help admiring her for it.

"So what about the flash drive?" she asked. "Where should we begin?"

He moved the paper lying open on the coffee table and she spotted the probate documents he had been reviewing. "I read through the paperwork this morning. I didn't see anything that rang a bell. Like we figured, Kozak's our primary lead. He wants the flash drive and he's willing to go to extreme lengths to get it."

"Which means there's something on it he doesn't want anyone to see." Sarah took a sip of her coffee. "Kozak is linked to Andrew through Hollister Equipment. Their main office is in West Covina. I'm sure they'll let me in—I'm Andrew's widow, after all. Let's go down there and dig around, see what we can find out."

"What about your husband's personal office?"

"The office was closed after Andrew died. It was only for show, anyway. Each of the companies he owned ran independently. Andrew liked to play, not work. He liked to keep things simple."

"Then we'll go out to West Covina, take a look at Hollister Equipment."

She nodded. "I'd better shower and get dressed." She rose from the chair, the flowered silk parting, showing a long length of her sexy legs. Jackson felt a jolt of heat that went straight to his groin.

He watched her refill her coffee cup then disappear inside the bedroom she had claimed but not slept in. He wondered where their relationship was headed— wondered if there would be any sort of relationship at all or just the memory of a heated night of sex.

Whatever happened, it was going to take patience on his part, patience and a will of steel. As he rose from the sofa, his erection hard as granite, it was all he could do not to walk through that bedroom door, join her in the shower, and make love to her until neither of them could move.

For the second time that morning, common sense prevailed, and he went in to shower and change.

Chapter 11

Sarah turned off the water and toweled herself dry. She blow-dried her hair and dressed in a beige skirt, turquoise silk blouse and sandals. When she returned to the living room, she found Jackson in a yellow short-sleeved shirt and dark chinos, drinking a cup of coffee.

God, he was handsome. She knew the iron-hard body beneath those clothes, knew the scent of him, the texture of his skin, the exact feel of the roughness along his jaw. Memories of last night did ridiculous things to her body.

"Ready?" he asked, setting the coffee cup down and striding toward her.

"I'm ready." She forced herself not to take a step backward as he approached. He was a powerful force and ignoring his sexual appeal wouldn't be easy.

They left the hotel and took the 10 Freeway out to

West Covina. Hollister Equipment was in a gray stucco building on a huge open lot where a variety of heavy equipment was stored. Sarah didn't know the name of each piece, but there were heavy earth movers and gigantic dump trucks with wheels the size of a small house, big yellow Caterpillar graders, steamrollers and dozens of miscellaneous trucks of every size.

"Big operation," Jackson said.

"I've only been here once. I'd forgotten it was so impressive."

"Let's go inside, take a look around the office." His hand settled at her waist and she ignored a little spark of awareness, waited while he opened the door, then walked inside.

There were two women working, each at a beige metal desk. One of them got up and walked over.

"What can I do for you?" She was short, late thirties, blond hair teased and pulled into a twist. She stuck a pencil into her hairdo and used it to scratch her head.

"I'm Sarah Hollister." At least she was for as long as it was necessary. "The probate on my late husband's estate is moving forward and I need to take a look at some of the company files."

The blonde flicked a glance at the other woman, older, with silver streaks in her short brown hair.

"It's all right," the older woman said. "Mr. Hollister is certainly not going to protest."

"Go ahead," the blonde said. "The records are all in the manager's office. It's right through there." She pointed toward a closed door. "Mr. Wallace is out on a job."

Good news, Sarah thought. At least she wouldn't have to concoct a story for him. Jackson followed her into the office and closed the door behind them.

"I wonder if they searched this place," he said. "If they did, they were careful not to leave any traces."

"It's one thing to tear up a cottage in Wyoming or vandalize an empty condo. Hollister is a big company that employs a number of people. They would have been worried about bringing in the police."

Sarah sat down at the desk and began to pull open the drawers while Jackson walked over to the file cabinets.

Finding nothing but the manager's personal items, she left the desk and joined him, saw him open the drawer marked J–M and begin to skim the records, searching for Martin Kozak's name.

"Here it is." He pulled out a manila file and they both read the information as he turned the pages.

"These look like mostly highway projects," Sarah said. "Kozak rented big pieces of machinery from Hollister to complete the jobs."

"Nothing here that looks suspicious."

"Let's take the file anyway," she suggested. "Just in case there's something in it we might need later on."

They made a cursory examination of the rest of the files, but saw nothing that might indicate a blackmail scheme. They left the office, the file under Jackson's arm. None of the women seemed to notice—or maybe they just didn't care.

"Where to now?" Sarah asked.

Seated behind the wheel of the Infiniti, Jackson opened the file. "Here's a project Kozak started last year. Leased a lot of equipment from Hollister. Looks like his company's still working on it."

Sarah leaned over and read the information. "They're

building an overpass on Highway 91. I'll show you how to get there."

Jackson cranked the engine and they drove out of the parking lot. With the congested L.A. traffic, they didn't reach the site until almost an hour later.

Work crews were everywhere, dust flying, engine noise so loud Sarah had to shout to be heard. Jackson pulled the car off onto a dirt road that led into the construction zone and turned off the engine, staying some distance away.

"I don't want them to come over and make us leave. I think if we stay back here, we'll be all right."

A gusty afternoon breeze whipped powdery dust into the air as each piece of Hollister machinery did its job. "What do you suppose Kozak could be doing that's illegal?"

They watched the equipment moving vast loads of dirt, flatbed trucks hauling long lengths of rebar to reinforce the concrete used to support the bridge. Huge chunks of earth were being scooped out then dumped into piles that provided the height necessary to cross the road below.

"I've read about companies using inferior grade products," Jackson said, "substandard concrete or rebar they bought for a song. Ultimately the structure failed and cost lives. Could be that kind of thing."

"I remember something like that happened in a hotel in Kansas City, though I think it might have been faulty design. Walkway gave way. Killed more than a hundred people."

"Or it could be faulty compaction. It's a lot cheaper to do a half-assed job than to spend the time necessary to compact the earth just right."

"Andrew might have stumbled across the truth. Or he might have paid someone to keep track of what was going on."

"The trick is to figure out what it was."

"And what to do with the information once we find out."

Jackson cast her a glance. "Use it to get Kozak off your back."

That sounded like a very good idea. She looked back at the massive building project. "If Kozak was doing anything that might affect the quality of the construction, wouldn't he have to deal with an inspector, someone in charge of checking to be sure the project was built to code?"

"Yeah—and that's damned good thinking. The only way Kozak could get away with substandard construction of any kind is if the highway inspector was on the take."

"How can we find out?"

"Let's go back to the hotel and make some calls, see if we can come up with a little more information." Jackson started the engine.

"Do you really think it could be that simple?"

"There's nothing simple about it. The only reason we're following this line of thinking is that we're pretty sure something crooked is going on."

Sarah fell silent, her mind spinning with possibilities. She had known Andrew was involved in shadowy activities. She had always worried that somehow his dealings might affect her and Holly.

She shuddered, afraid to consider the price she might yet have to pay.

* * *

The suite had been cleaned and fresh sheets put on the beds. No evidence remained of their heated love-making last night. Still, just a glimpse through Jackson's open bedroom door sent a ripple of heat into Sarah's stomach. She quickly glanced away, then flushed to find his dark eyes watching her.

He crossed the carpet to where she stood, came up behind her, set his hands around her waist and pressed his mouth against the back of her neck. "So you just want great sex, nothing more."

"No, I..."

"It's been years, you said. If that's so, one night isn't going to be enough." His warm breath fanned her nape. He slid her hair aside and kissed her just below her ear, bit down lightly on the lobe.

She moistened her trembling lips, felt his fingers working the buttons at the front of her blouse, pulling it open, sliding inside the lacy cups of her demi-bra. He grazed the tips of her breasts as he pressed more kisses along her throat, kissed the shoulder he bared, unhooked the front of her bra and filled his hands with her breasts.

Sarah's knees went weak. "Jackson..."

"You want this, don't you? Just as much as I do?"

She swallowed, told herself to pull away, to ignore the hot little tremors that came with each tug of his skillful fingers on her nipples.

His teeth grazed her shoulder. "Tell me you want me. Say it out loud."

She whimpered.

"Say it."

She could feel his erection pressing against her bottom, remembered how good it felt to have him inside her. "I...want you."

She started to turn but he held her in place, leaned around and kissed her on the mouth. She sucked in a breath at the feel of her skirt sliding over her hips, exposing her bottom and the white lace thong that matched her bra. At least the expensive underwear, one of the few remnants of Andrew's money, was being put to good use.

"Very pretty," he said, running a hand over the rounded globes, bending down to press soft nibbling kisses against her skin. "The panties, too."

He slid the thong aside, found her softness and began to stroke her. Sarah squirmed, arched into his hand. She was trembling all over, any thought of resisting a memory. She was wet. Dear God, the man could make her wet. She heard the buzz of his zipper, felt the thickness of his heavy erection. Her palms flattened on the wall as he tipped her forward, parted her legs and filled her.

Sarah gasped at the rush of pleasure, at the heat and need pouring through her.

Jackson was a fiercely demanding lover, she had learned, but as he eased himself out and filled her again, as his fingers found her cleft and stroked her to the very edge of climax, she understood that here was a man who demanded but also gave, a man who could satisfy her as no man ever had.

A man even more dangerous than Andrew.

A hot climax shook her and sweet pleasure rolled through her, filling every cell in her body. Sarah cried out Jackson's name as he surged deeply, pounded into her and brought her to fulfillment again. Then his hard body tightened, he drove into her one last time and reached a powerful release.

For long seconds they just stood there, Sarah's eyes closed, her insides still tingling, a soft smile on her lips. Jackson eased himself out of her body and disposed of his condom while she worked to straighten her clothes.

Her smile remained in place, but as she continued to spiral down and the pleasure began to fade, warning bells went off in her head and the old fear returned. Jackson was a man with the power to reach her as no man ever had—and therein lay the danger.

Silently she vowed to find the courage she would need to resist him.

Jackson sat in the living room, poring over the equipment leases and notes in the Kozak file, then he went over the probate papers again. Sarah had showered and at his insistence lay down for an afternoon nap.

She'd had little sleep last night, thanks to him. And though she had made it clear she wanted to put some distance between them, he had beaten down her defenses and taken her again.

It hadn't been difficult. All day, sparks of sexual tension had crackled between them, sparks ready to burst into a roaring blaze. Sarah was a far more sensual woman than she realized. She had been without a man for years, and it was clear the two of them were good together, that they could satisfy each other's needs.

Jackson frowned. He wanted Sarah Allen. He couldn't seem to get his fill. And yet he wasn't sure, beyond sex, what he expected of her—or what she expected of him. He wasn't sure how deeply he should get involved.

He remembered the old Sarah, driven by a fierce desire for money and social position. Maybe that hadn't changed and the attraction she felt for him came from the money and influence he now commanded.

A line from a country song popped into his head—"How do you like me now?" Now that he was wealthy and successful. Now that he was no longer just a boy from the wrong side of the tracks.

His gut was saying it wasn't so, but he didn't know her well enough to be completely sure.

And even if he decided a relationship with Sarah was what he wanted, he wasn't sure how much involvement she would allow. After ten years with an abusive husband, she might not be ready to jump back in.

He only knew he didn't want to hurt her. Whatever her thoughts and motives, Sarah and her daughter had been hurt more than enough already.

It was half an hour later when she walked into the living room in one of the hotel's fluffy white terry robes, her hair damp from the shower and curling softly around her face, looking so damned sexy he wanted to tumble her again.

"You want a Coke or something from the minibar?" he asked, careful to keep his thoughts to himself.

"Diet Coke, if there is one. That would be great."

He filled a glass with the ice he'd retrieved from the machine down the hall, walked over to the minibar and took out a Diet Coke, poured it into the glass.

Sarah was on the phone as he approached, seated on the sofa with her legs curled up beneath her, the receiver pressed against her ear. She held up the message pad and he read the words she'd written, *highway dept*.

"Yes, well, my name is Carrie Johnson," she said, making up the words as she went along. "I'm a secretary with Kozak Construction—the company that's building the overpass on Highway 91? I was wondering…hoping…you could help me."

She reached up and took the frosty glass from his hand, took a quick sip and continued her conversation.

"You see, today is only my second day on the job and I'm embarrassed to say I've managed to lose the information my boss gave me with the highway inspector's name written on it. Do you think you could look it up for me? I really hate to ask my boss for it again." She sipped her Coke. "Sure, I'll be happy to wait."

A moment later, she set the glass down and picked up the pad, plucked up the pen beside it and began to scratch out a name. Vernon Rimmer.

"He's not new, is he? He's been doing this a while?" She gave him a nod. "You're a lifesaver, Dottie. Thank you very much." She hung up the phone and looked up at him with a grin. "Here's our man."

"I didn't realize I had myself a first-class detective."

She laughed. "It's a start. Unfortunately, we need to find out if Mr. Rimmer is legitimate, and I haven't the foggiest notion how to do that."

"I'll call my brother, see if he's back from Mexico." Jackson sat down in the chair instead of sitting next to her on the sofa as he wanted to do. He had pressed her enough for now. In boxing he'd learned to bide his time, to read his opponent, then wait till the moment was right before striking. He had a lot left to learn about Sarah Allen.

Jackson picked up the receiver and called Arizona. Dev wasn't at his Scottsdale home, or in his Phoenix office, but he had been calling for messages and he was expected back soon. Jackson left word both places.

"It's getting on toward evening. We need to stop by the Blue Parrot. Afterward we'll get some supper."

"All right. I'll go get dressed. And I need to call Holly, make sure she's all right."

Jackson had already showered and changed into fresh clothes. He emptied the other half of her Coke into a glass and drank it while he waited. A few minutes later, Sarah returned to the living room wearing a slinky little black cocktail dress that made the blood in his veins rush south.

"You look gorgeous," he said. "Ought to make the boys at the Blue Parrot sit up and take notice."

She smiled, looked pleased. He was always surprised at how little it seemed to take to please her.

"Thank you."

"I'll have the valet bring the car around." He called the front desk, grabbed his light-colored sport coat off the back of a chair but didn't put it on, and they left the suite.

The car was waiting when they reached the front door. He drove out into traffic, took the 405 Freeway to the Ventura Boulevard off-ramp, then cruised the busy street until they spotted the Blue Parrot, a few miles down the road.

The place didn't look fancy, just a white stucco, flat-roofed building with a motel facing the parking lot in the rear. A blue-collar joint of the sort that might appeal to Andrew Hollister's blue-collar clientele, guys like Kozak in the construction business.

"You ready for this?" Jackson asked as he turned off the engine.

Sarah released a slow breath. "As much as I'm ever going to be. Let's go."

Chapter 12

The Blue Parrot. A plastic palm tree stood at the end of a long bar lined with red vinyl bar stools. Neon beer signs on the wall, Formica tables and multicolored plastic chairs that looked as if they came straight out of the fifties. Jackson could see into a back room that had a shuffleboard and two pool tables. The place should have been smoke-filled, undoubtedly was until the city passed an ordinance against smoking indoors.

"Nice place," he said sarcastically. "I don't imagine it's the sort your husband might have frequented."

"Andrew liked the finer things in life, but he was forced to mingle with his customers on occasion. He might have come here at one time or another."

Jackson's hand went to Sarah's waist, urging her toward the bar, and she slid up on one of the stools. She tugged on the skirt of her sexy black cocktail dress, pulling it down to cover as much as she could of her shapely legs. As short as the dress was, the gesture was pretty much futile. Enjoying the view, Jackson bit back a smile.

"What'll you have?" The bartender, a blond guy slightly past his prime in a tight black T-shirt, leaned on the top of the bar. He had blue eyes and they ran over Sarah, taking in the soft swells of her cleavage exposed in the V of the dress. Jackson ignored an unexpected shot of jealousy.

"I'll have a glass of white wine," Sarah said.

"I'll have a beer," Jackson added. "Make it a Bud."

It was a beer-and-whiskey kind of place, a little shoddy, but the sparse crowd didn't look rough, just slightly worn out. Jackson sat down on the bar stool next to Sarah and casually surveyed the room, noting the aging features of the women and the disinterested expressions of the men, none of whom fit the description of the ones they were looking for.

Halfway through his beer, he returned his attention to the bartender. Earlier, he'd noticed the guy's thick biceps but figured him for a weight lifter. Then he spotted the broken nose and roughened ears.

"You look like a fighter. You box some?"

He made a slight nod of his head. "Boxed a little after high school. For a while I was the Great White Hope around here. Didn't last long." He looked Jackson over, taking in the muscles in his arms, the scar along his jaw and the one bisecting his eyebrow. "You, too?"

He nodded. "Made the Olympic team. Did pretty good till some Russian kicked my ass."

The bartender hooted a laugh. "There's a gym just down the street. We get a lot of muscle-jocks in here.

A few decent fighters. You want another beer? This one's on me."

Jackson shook his head. "Rather have a little information."

"Yeah?"

"I'm looking for a couple of guys—one's blond, skinny, has a tattoo on his hand that says Mother. The other one's Hispanic. Short and stout. Might be a fighter. Maybe he's one of those who come in here from the gym."

"Sounds like Billy Hinman and Jose Delgado. They hang together a lot. Billy's okay, a little slow on the uptake. Delgado thinks he's a tough guy. Competes in the local boxing competitions. I guess he's been doing okay."

Jackson pulled the napkin from beneath his beer, wrote down his cell number, slid it and a fifty-dollar bill across the bar. "You see either one of those guys in the next day or two, give me a call."

The bartender picked up the fifty. "I see Delgado right now... He's just walking in the back door." He tipped his head toward the rear entrance leading in from the parking lot. Jose Delgado strode in as if he owned the place.

"Stay here," Jackson said to Sarah, sliding off the bar stool.

"Are you sure you should—"

"I won't be long." He was sure, all right. The bastard owed him for the mess he'd made of the cottage. Jackson strode the length of the bar, across the empty dance floor toward the back door. He stopped dead in front of the fighter.

"You Delgado?"

"Who wants to know?"

"I do. I believe you owe me some money."

"I don't even know you, man. Why would I owe you money?" With his dark complexion, black eyes and straight black hair slicked back from a square-jawed face, he was good-looking—or at least Jackson figured the women would think so.

"Maybe because you and your buddy broke into my property in Wyoming and tore the hell out of just about everything."

Jose scoffed, but the truth was there in his eyes. "I don't know what you're talking about, man."

"Maybe not. Tell you what…you give me the name of the guy who paid you to do it and we'll forget the whole thing."

"Get lost, man." He tried to walk past, but Jackson moved in front of him, used a shoulder to shove him against the wall.

"I want the name."

Delgado grinned, a look of pure anticipation twisting the contours of his face. His hand fisted, shot out with the speed and power of a cannonball, a punch that could send a man to his knees. Jackson blocked the blow, drilled him with two sharp jabs and a punch that had Delgado's head slamming hard against the wall.

The amazement on his face turned to fury. He growled low in his throat and charged. Jackson turned at the last instant, hit him with a blow that came up from the floor, and Delgado went down like a sack of oats.

Seconds passed, not quite the count of ten, Jackson figured. Delgado staggered to his feet. He shook his head and wiped the blood off his lips with the back of his hand. "You're gonna pay for that, man."

Jackson just smiled. The kid was strong as a bull, but he'd had no real training. And he let his temper get in the way of his boxing. He threw a fierce punch at Jackson straight from the shoulder. Jackson jerked sideways, missing the blow, jabbed him two more times, then went in for the kill. Two hard punches, one to the head, one to the midsection, another blow to the head and the kid went down.

Delgado wasn't unconscious but he was smart enough not to get up. Jackson rolled him onto his back and planted a knee in the middle of his chest. "The name."

He spit out a mouthful of blood. "Screw you."

Jackson drew back his fist. "You sure that's the way you want it?"

Delgado swore a dirty word. "Kozak," he said through swollen lips.

"You went to Wyoming looking for a flash drive Andrew Hollister had."

"Yeah." Delgado tried to sit up but Jackson's knee forced him back down.

"The lady doesn't have it," Jackson said. "She doesn't know anything about it."

Jackson put pressure on his knee and Delgado groaned. "Mostly it was…a message," the kid said. "Kozak wants her…to find it."

Jackson came to his feet, letting Delgado go. "All right, now I'm the one sending a message. You tell Kozak if he doesn't want more trouble than he can handle, he'd better leave Sarah Hollister alone."

* * *

No one called the police. It was over too quickly and the patrons were probably used to an occasional show of bad temper. The bartender just grinned, one boxer to another, as Sarah and Jackson walked out of the Blue Parrot.

Sarah's legs were shaking. She felt Jackson's hand at her waist all the way to the parking lot. There was something about his natural sense of protectiveness she found comforting. She told herself she didn't approve of Jackson's brutal treatment of Jose Delgado, that she'd dealt with enough violence to last a lifetime.

But somehow this was different. Jackson was trying to protect her, not hurt her.

"You okay?" he asked as he waited for her to get settled in the passenger seat and snap her seat belt in place.

"I'm all right."

"At least we know for sure it was Kozak." He shut the car door, walked around to the driver's side and climbed in.

She studied his profile as he pulled the seat belt across his muscular chest. "I remember your fight with the Russian," she said, referring to the comment he had made to the bartender. "He didn't beat you by much."

He shrugged the powerful shoulders she had just seen in action. "I lost. That was all that mattered."

"I think it mattered that you competed and gave it your best."

His dark eyes ran over her, sending a sliver of heat into her stomach. "So you watched the Games?"

"Everyone in Wind Canyon watched. They were proud of you. So was I." Jackson seemed surprised. "I had a crush on you, Jackson. I was just afraid to let anyone know. I was afraid they would treat me the way they treated you."

He scoffed. "You had ambitions that didn't include a poor boy like me."

She glanced away, knowing it was true. "I wanted out. I admit it. I was tired of being a small-town girl. I wanted to see what life was like outside Wyoming. I wanted to travel, to visit places like Paris and Rome. Believe me, I paid for it."

Jackson made no reply, just started the engine and drove out of the parking lot. "We've got dinner reservations at a place called The Dove. It's supposed to be very good."

"I've never been there, and to tell you the truth, I'm glad. I have some pretty awful memories of dinners with Andrew."

For the first time, he smiled. "Then let's make a good memory tonight."

Sarah's heartbeat quickened. She already had too many memories of Jackson, memories of a hot, steamy night in bed with him, of outrageous sex, memories that urged her to let him make love to her again.

Not tonight, she told herself. Tonight she would say no and she would mean it.

In the meantime, she would enjoy a delicious meal in the company of a handsome man. She deserved that much, she told herself.

Tomorrow she would think of Marty Kozak and what she needed to do to make sure she and Holly were safe.

A warm, early-June sun beat down on the asphalt surrounding the Serv-U Storage facility off Sunset

Boulevard west of the 405 Freeway. After Andrew's death, when his father's big Spanish-style house had been sold and finally closed escrow, the Realtor had arranged an estate sale for the furniture that remained in the house, donated miscellaneous items, then put what was left into storage.

The items in the unit weren't something Marty Kozak was likely to know about and even Sarah had no idea exactly what was in there, since none of it held the least sentimental value to her. In fact, the only memories she had of living in the house on Sunset were bitter and painful.

Including the fact that the house was the scene of the murder.

Sarah shivered though the breeze fanning the palm trees around the perimeter was warm. She had worked hard to deal with the memories of what had happened that last night in the house—the terrible fight she'd had with Andrew she had never revealed to the police.

The awful, nauseating fear.

She closed her eyes, refusing to let the unwanted memories return.

"You all right?" Jackson asked.

"I'm fine." And for the most part, she was. The images of that terrible night came mostly in nightmares, and after her move to Wyoming, they occurred less and less.

Jackson examined the padlock. "You've got the combination, right?"

She nodded. "The Realtor gave it to me before I left. I figured we'd need it once we got to California so I brought it along."

Jackson examined the lock, worked the tumblers, removed the device, then slid up the heavy rolling door.

Sarah stared at the dusty stacks of boxes and miscellaneous bits and pieces of furniture, most of which were broken or damaged, and felt a sweep of nausea. Perspiration broke out on her forehead.

Jackson caught her arm. "You look like you're going to faint. Maybe you'd better wait in the car."

She shook her head. "I'll be all right in a minute. I just… I wasn't quite prepared." She wasn't prepared to see a lamp Andrew had once thrown at her in a fit of temper, the expensive silk shade ripped and bent beyond repair. Or the chair he had been sitting in behind his desk that last night.

She took a deep breath and slowly released it, clamped down on the old fear she refused to let grab hold of her again.

"Not much to show for a lifetime," she said, surveying the miscellaneous items in the storage room, a carton of books meant as a donation for the library, a stack of pillows from one of the beds, the cases now yellowed and stained.

"Your life is just beginning," Jackson said.

Sarah took a deep breath, praying he was right. "After the estate sale, Andrew's clothes and personal effects were given to the Salvation Army."

"If the flash drive was in any of that, it's history."

"He kept his business life completely separate, so likely it wasn't." She moved silently into the debris that had once been part of her life. "We need to go through these boxes, see what's inside."

Jackson walked past her into the storage locker, his lean body brushing against her as he moved. She told herself she wasn't disappointed that last night he had brought her back to the hotel after supper and played the perfect gentleman. She wasn't the least disappointed that he had kissed her on the forehead and told her to get some rest.

Sarah ignored a twinge of irritation at the memory. All evening, she had been constructing her defenses, preparing for the battle she would wage when they returned to the suite and Jackson began making love to her. Her biggest enemy was her own desire for him, but she was ready to say no and mean it.

Instead, Jackson had respected her wishes and ruined her plans.

· She flicked him a glance. The man was just full of surprises.

She watched him open one dusty box after another, setting anything aside he thought she might need to go through.

"These look interesting," he said about a series of boxes he found in the corner. "Looks like they may have come out of his home office."

They had, she discovered as she started on the first of three, digging out an old fax machine Andrew had never used, paper trays, a phone with the receiver missing, a broken pencil sharpener, Scotch tape dispenser, stapler and other miscellaneous objects.

But there was no notebook or flash drive, or anything that might have concealed something like that.

Sarah dug through several more boxes, while Jackson did the same. The dust in the storage room made her eyes water and she sneezed but kept on working.

"There's more office stuff in this one," Jackson said, pulling over another dusty cardboard box. Sarah wiped her hands on her jeans, knelt and began digging again. As she lifted out a leather desk pad, she recognized the coffee cup warmer that had sat on Andrew's desk. This year's Week At A Glance calendar was among the items. She set it aside to look at later, lifted out a tray that held pencils and pens. One of the pens caught her eye. It looked different from the others, shiny black-and-gold, and she remembered seeing it in Andrew's pocket.

"What is it?" Jackson asked as she picked it up to examine it more closely.

"Andrew's pen. He carried it a lot."

"Let me see it." Jackson took it out of her hand and pulled off the top. He smiled. "Well, look what we have in here."

"Oh, my God!"

"It's a pen drive. Works like a flash drive. Information's easy to carry this way. Whether it's got the right information remains to be seen."

But she couldn't help being excited, and she could tell he was, too.

"We're about finished in here," he said. "Let's go back to the hotel and see what we've got." He made a last survey of the storage unit. "See anything we might have missed?"

She took a good long look. She was anxious to get back to Wyoming, back to Holly. She didn't want to have to return for something they had overlooked.

"We've gone through all the boxes. The rest is mostly broken furniture the Realtor couldn't sell."

"All right, then, let's go."

Sarah took the hand Jackson held out to her. It felt warm and strong and not the least bit threatening.

When they reached the car, Jackson handed her the pen drive. It held the blackmail list they were looking for—she was sure of it! She would bargain with Marty Kozak and be free of the past at last.

Sarah stuffed the black-and-gold pen deep into the pocket of her dusty jeans. Sending up a silent plea, she prayed the drive held the information she needed and she could get on with her life.

Chapter 13

Sitting behind one of the computers in the hotel business center, Sarah opened the list of files in the pen drive. "There's only three of them."

"Good, let's take a look."

Her heart was pounding. This had to be it. It had to be!

The first was labeled Calendar. Sarah opened the file to find Andrew's schedule for the month of January, the last month of his life.

"I don't see anything exciting, just his usual meetings, golf and lunches."

Jackson was kind enough not to point out the weekends Andrew had marked off to Mitzy. Sarah ignored them, as well. She closed the file and opened the next.

Disappointment struck her. "The second file has notes from a meeting with the management of Southgate Demolition. Looks like the company had a contract to demolish a building in Northridge. It was scheduled to be pulled down the end of the month."

"January."

"That's right."

"What's in the third file?"

She was afraid to open it. If the list wasn't in there, they were right back where they'd started. Sarah watched the screen, her heart thumping almost painfully. She frowned. The file opened, but she had no idea what it meant. "What is it?"

"Looks like an address."

"Yes, I see that. 1542 Rocky Mountain Road, #14A, Palm Springs. But what's that other number?"

"Twenty-eight, thirty-two, eleven. Sounds like the combination to a lock."

"Like the storage room. That was thirty-six, eighteen, three." She gazed up at him, her spirits gradually sinking. "This isn't the blackmail list we were looking for. That means it isn't the right drive."

"No, but it's not a dead end, either."

She sighed. "So we're going to Palm Springs?"

"Looks like it."

Sarah just wanted to go home. She was missing Holly and the quiet of her charming little Wyoming cottage. And as much as she enjoyed being with Jackson, the desire that simmered between them, the constant yearning, left her on edge.

"Better to go now than make another trip."

He was right. Thank God she had turned in enough articles to keep Smiley happy at the newspaper. She sighed again as she printed out the information—everything on the drive, just in case, and picked up the printed pages. "When do we leave?"

"We can make it before dark if we start now."

And the traffic in the early afternoon would be better than in the morning. "I guess I'd better go up and pack."

Returning the pen drive to her pocket, determined to hide her disappointment, Sarah started for the elevator leading up to their suite.

It was a long drive to Palm Springs from Santa Monica, but they were getting out of town just after noon so the traffic wasn't as bad as it would be later in the day. Sarah sat back in the seat, trying not to think of the pen drive and Andrew, trying not to think that somehow he was trying to destroy her even from the grave.

Determined to distract herself, she made the mistake of looking over at Jackson. His dark gaze cut sideways, touching hers for a moment, and heat tugged low in her belly. Lord, the man could make her think of sex without saying a word.

Flustered and unwilling to let him see, Sarah dug her cell phone out of her purse. She had yet to change to a company with better service in the mountains, but this one still worked fine down here.

The first call went to the Realtor who was handling the sale of the Santa Monica condo.

"Mrs. Hollister!" Jane Perkins said. "I'm so glad you called!"

"It's Allen, now," she corrected. "Sarah Allen."

"Oh. Well, as I said, I'm extremely glad you called. You see, the thing is, yesterday I tried to show your condo to a really good buyer, a Japanese businessman who wanted something in that exact location. I was sure he would make an offer, since your place was so nice and the price is so low, but, you see, the thing is, when I opened the door—well, you just wouldn't believe it."

Oh, yes, I would, Sarah thought, relieved that now she would not be connected in any way with the break-in. The police wouldn't even have to know she was there.

"So I guess the showing didn't go all that well."

"Well, that's just it. You see, the thing is—the entire place was a shambles!" Jane went on to describe the vandalism in the condo, how the whole unit had been trashed, and Sarah pretended to be shocked.

"I've phoned the insurance company," Jane continued, "and of course, the police—but the thing is..."

Sarah mostly tuned out the rest. When the woman was finished, Sarah told her to contact Stan Greenberg, the probate attorney, in regard to whatever needed to be done. She hung up the phone and let her head fall back against the headrest.

"Seems like the lady had plenty to say."

Sarah sighed. "Her name is Jane Perkins. She's a friend of Stan's. I'm beginning to think she is more than a friend, otherwise, why in the world would Stan have listed the property with someone like that?"

Jackson chuckled. "You're getting cynical in your old age, Ms. Allen."

She blew out a breath. "I guess I am." She didn't tell him that being married to Andrew had irreparably destroyed whatever naive notions she'd once had about life.

"Why don't you give Holly a call," Jackson suggested. "See how she's getting along?"

She had called Wyoming that morning before they left for the storage room, but she called again now. Livvy answered then put Holly on the line.

"Mom!"

"Hi, honey, how are you doing?"

"I'm okay, but I miss you. When are you coming home?"

"Soon, baby. Maybe tomorrow." She looked over at Jackson for confirmation and saw him nodding. He was probably as eager to get back as she was. He had a ranch to run, after all, and if the address in Palm Springs turned out to be a dead end, there was nothing more they could do in L.A.

Holly chatted pleasantly, telling her about Sam and Gibby and about the pony riding lessons, about seeing her very first eagle in the sky above the pasture, making Sarah smile.

"And Livvy taught me how to make brownies."

"Good, you can make some for me when I get back."

"Do you really think you'll be coming home tomorrow?"

Sarah felt a tug at her heart. She and Holly were so very close. The little girl had never really had a father. Andrew was just a shadowy part of her life, someone who was almost never there. It was the reason Holly rarely mentioned him, the reason Andrew's death hadn't hit her as hard as it might have.

"I hope so, baby. I'll call you as soon as I know for sure." Sarah hung up the phone feeling more homesick than she had before.

Jackson cast her a glance. "How's she doing?"

"She loves the boys and Livvy."

"But she misses her mother."

Sarah nodded.

"What about her dad, Sarah? How's she dealing with that? I've never heard her talk about him."

Sarah sighed, the question mirroring her earlier thoughts. "Andrew was never around. He talked about Holly as if he really cared about her, but he rarely saw her. He came home late and left early. He never had time for a child."

"We'll go home tomorrow no matter what we find. We can come back if we need to."

Relief swept through her. They were going home. She could be with her daughter, and she could get back to work. She had told her boss that she needed a few days to take care of some loose ends in L.A. Now she could get back to her job as a reporter, back to her charming little cottage and the new life she had been trying to build.

She flicked a glance at Jackson, caught the lean, hard jaw, the slight indentation in his chin. His eyes were a rich dark chocolate brown, his lashes black and thicker than she had noticed before. The hands he wrapped around the steering wheel had long, sun-browned fingers, skillful fingers that had stroked her to climax more than once.

She felt that same, sensuous tug in her belly, closed her eyes and willed herself not to remember what it was like to make love with him.

What would happen once they returned to Wyoming? Could she live in such close proximity to such an attractive man and not succumb to her desire for him?

She wasn't sure what else she felt for him. She liked

him. She was grateful for his willingness to help her, valued the kindness he had shown her. Perhaps they could come to an arrangement, enjoy a friendship that included occasional sex, but went no further.

"You're awfully quiet," he said, breaking into her thoughts.

She shifted in the seat, hoped he didn't notice the flush that crept into her cheeks. "I was... I was just thinking about Marty Kozak," she lied. At the moment, the man was the farthest thing from her mind.

"Delgado will deliver my message. There's a good chance Kozak will accept the fact you don't have the list and leave you alone."

Sarah said nothing. She hoped Jackson was right, but she knew Marty Kozak.

And her cynical nature just wouldn't let her believe it.

"There it is." A small condo development in the rugged, arid mountains outside Palm Springs, a chic, expensive town in the California desert. Tile-roofed, tan and dark brown stucco, thirty-five units built around a big, kidney-shaped swimming pool. They parked the car and went in search of unit 14A, making their way along wandering pathways landscaped with rocks and cactus in a desert motif.

"There it is." Unit 14A sat on the ground floor; 14B was a second-story unit above.

"So what do you think we should do?" Sarah asked in quiet tones, her nerves kicking up.

"Let's try knocking." Jackson took her hand and started for the door. "Maybe someone's home."

It seemed obvious, but there was no way to know

what Andrew might have been doing with the condo or who might be inside. They walked the cement path, climbing an occasional wide step, then up the stairs to the covered front porch. Jackson rang the doorbell, but neither of them actually expected anyone to come to the door.

No one did.

"Let's go round back," Jackson suggested, "see if we can find a way in without being seen."

There was a walkway between each four-unit complex. They passed the single-car garage marked 14A, went round to the back and saw a door that went into the garage from the rear. Jackson tried the door but it was locked. They continued to a glass sliding door that led out onto a small patio. Jackson walked over, lifted and jerked, and an instant later, the glass door was slightly off its track and moving backward, creating an opening big enough for them to slip through.

She flicked him a glance. "A man with hidden talents."

His mouth edged up. "A trick I learned in my misguided youth."

The condo looked surprisingly clean—too clean. No dust on the countertops or the small kitchen table, and there were freshly washed dishes in the sink.

"Anybody home?" Jackson called out.

A movement in the doorway alerted them. "Don't move or I'll shoot!" A flashy blonde pointed a gun straight at Jackson. Though the woman held it arms out in front of her, her hands were shaking and it was clear she had no idea how to properly use the weapon. Which made her even more dangerous.

"Take it easy," Jackson soothed. "We didn't think anyone was home."

She was wearing very short white shorts and a black-and-white halter top—and she looked really good in them. She was perfectly tanned, had long blond hair, and she was extremely pretty.

A light went on in Sarah's head. "You must be Mitzy," she said, certain she was right. All of Andrew's women looked pretty much the same. Sarah was amazed he had ever been attracted to *her*. But then, apparently her late husband was one of those men who wanted a lady in the living room and a whore in the bedroom—literally.

Sarah forced herself to smile. "I'm Andrew's wife, Sarah."

The gun wavered. "You're...you're Sarah?"

"Put the gun down, Mitzy," Jackson said with firm command. "We didn't come here to hurt you."

She tipped her head toward Jackson, but didn't lower the weapon. "Who's he?"

"His name is Jackson Raines. He's a friend. We came here to find a flash drive Andrew had." She caught the fear that flashed in Mitzy's blue eyes. "I think maybe Marty Kozak thought you had it. Is that the reason you're hiding out here?"

Mitzy cautiously lowered the pistol, and Jackson reached out and took it gently from her hand.

"I—I told him I didn't have the flash drive but he didn't believe me. I was afraid of what he might do. I had a key to the condo so I came here." So this was Andrew's little love nest, a place he came with his mistress-of-the-moment. "Andrew said no one knew about the place. He said he paid cash for it a long time ago."

Andrew actually owned something he hadn't mortgaged to the hilt? *Amazing.*

"You won't say anything, will you? You won't tell Mr. Kozak I'm here?"

"We won't say anything," Sarah promised.

Jackson held out a slip of paper with the numbers twenty-eighty, thirty-two, eleven printed on it. "We just need to figure out what this means. It's probably the combination to a lock of some kind. Is there a safe or a storage room around here?"

"There's a safe in the back of Andrew's closet. I don't think he used it much. At least I never saw him. I found it when I was hanging up some of my clothes."

Some clothes turned out to be a boatload, two closets full—expensive designer dresses, slacks, shoes and purses that Andrew must have bought her.

Sarah couldn't help wondering what price, beyond the use of her incredible body, Mitzy had paid for them. One thing Sarah knew—if Andrew hadn't beat her for some imagined transgression, sooner or later he would have.

She fought to control the shudder that filtered through her body.

"Here it is." Mitzy shoved aside some of the clothes on the rod. "Behind my suit."

A lovely white Chanel. Of course, in the beginning, Andrew had bought Sarah clothes with those same expensive labels. In the past few years, she hadn't wanted them, hadn't wanted anything that came from him.

"All right, let's give it a try." Jackson moved past Mitzy. So far, he hadn't seemed to notice her gorgeous face and amazing body. Or maybe he was just more subtle than most men.

He turned the dial slowly, carefully working the tumblers into place. He must have missed a number on the first try because it didn't open. He started over, went round again, back and then forward, and *click*. The combination fell into place. Jackson turned the handle and the small safe slowly opened.

Sarah leaned forward to peer inside. "It's empty," she said, not sure if she was disappointed or relieved.

Then Jackson reached into the shadows and pulled out three narrow colored envelopes. The words *Varig Airlines* were printed on the front.

"Looks like he was planning a trip."

Sarah felt a rush of nausea. "H-he talked about it. He threatened to move us all to Rio. I told him I wouldn't go—that I wouldn't let him take Holly. We fought about it."

She looked away. They'd fought, all right. A scene that had ended with Sarah's nose bloodied and her lip split. Like most of their arguments, they happened late in the evening—downstairs in his study where he demanded her presence—long after Holly had been put to bed upstairs.

"Looks like he expected you to give in, sooner or later."

She swallowed. They had argued about it again that last night.

"I'm going," Andrew had said. *"You want to stay here, fine with me, but I'm leaving the country and I'm taking Holly with me."*

She closed her eyes to block out the rest of the ugly scene. She refused to let her mind stray past the moment when he had risen from behind his desk and started toward her, when she had felt the awful, sickening fear.

Jackson's arm went around her, steadying her. "You okay?"

"Yes, I... I just wish we'd found the USB."

But they hadn't, and there was no telling what Kozak might do.

"Do you think he'll give up?" Mitzy asked.

"I hope so," Sarah said.

"Sooner or later, he'll quit looking," Jackson said. "And we're still working on a couple of things that might help. Odds are he'll eventually figure the flash drive is lost and therefore no longer a threat."

Sarah made no reply. They were still trying to find out why Andrew had been blackmailing Kozak. If they could find the answer, they would have a bargaining chip to use against him.

She thought of Kozak and Andrew and her mind returned to the airline tickets Jackson held in his hand. She couldn't help wondering what would have happened when she had finally convinced Andrew she wasn't going with him. Would he have forced Holly to go, changed her ticket into Mitzy's name and taken his mistress to Rio instead?

Or would he have simply taken Holly and made Sarah disappear?

Chapter 14

They were almost home. Sarah's anticipation built as Jackson's Ford pickup rolled toward the ranch. The minute the truck pulled up in front of the sprawling two-story ranch house, Holly rushed out to great them.

"Mama! Mom!"

Her daughter was growing up. She was *Mom* now. Holly hadn't called Sarah *Mommy* since a few weeks after their arrival in Wyoming.

"Hi, baby." Sarah lifted her up and propped her against her hip. "Good heavens, I think you must have grown a bunch since I left town."

Holly giggled. "Just like Rags. He gets bigger every day." She turned. "You should see him, Jackson—I think he's gonna be really big."

"Well, maybe not too big," Jackson said, running a hand over the top of her small blond head. "Maybe just right."

Holly grinned up at him. "I'm glad you're back."

"Me, too," he said.

Sarah returned Holly to her feet and the little girl took hold of Sarah's hand. "Come on, Mom. I wanna show you Midnight. She is so cool."

"I need to take my stuff inside, then we can go down to the barn and you can show me."

"I'll take your luggage inside," Jackson offered. "You can unpack when you're finished."

He was always so thoughtful. She wished it didn't make her so nervous. She wished *he* didn't make her so nervous. Then again, maybe *nervous* wasn't the right word. She flicked him a glance, caught the heat in his dark eyes he was usually so careful to hide, and her stomach contracted. He was back in his jeans and boots and looking so damned sexy her thoughts strayed to the bedroom and she blushed.

She turned her attention to her daughter, a thread of worry filtering through her. They were home, back in Wyoming, but nothing had changed. Marty Kozak still posed a threat to her and Holly.

And Sarah still wanted Jackson Raines.

"Welcome home." Livvy's robust figure stood in the kitchen when Jackson walked into the house towing his black, wheeled, carry-on bag behind him.

"It's good to be back."

"Did you get things straightened out for Sarah?"

"We're still working on it."

Livvy moved toward the sink, spatula in hand. "Your brother, Dev, called this morning. He's back in Scottsdale. I told him you'd call him when you got in."

He nodded, started toward his study, stopped and looked back. "Thanks for taking care of Holly."

Livvy smiled, stretching her double chins. "She wasn't a bit of trouble. That little girl is a treasure. She can stay with me anytime." Livvy had wanted kids when she married, he knew, but somehow it just never happened. Jackson thought Olivia Jones was also a treasure, and he was damned glad to have her there on the ranch.

"She's going to be a real heartbreaker," he said. *Just like her mother,* popped into his head. He forced the old uncertainties away and continued along the hall, went into his office, and over to his big oak desk. Picking up the telephone, he dialed his brother's home number.

"Ey, *muchacho*—how was Mexico?"

"Hot." Dev chuckled. "In more ways than one."

"Yeah, well, I hope your mind's back on business because I'm going to need a favor."

"Seems like I've heard that one before."

"True—and it probably won't be the last time."

Dev's smile reached into the phone. "This still about Sarah Allen?"

"We just got back from L.A. Went to look for the missing flash drive."

"I guess you didn't find it."

"Not yet."

"Why don't you bring me up to speed on this thing?"

So he did, telling his brother about the break-in at Sarah's grandmother's house before they'd left Wyoming that had put the old woman in the hospital, about the threats Sarah had received from the dark-skinned man in town, his run-in with Jose Delgado and that Delgado had a partner named Billy Hinman.

"Looks like Andrew Hollister was blackmailing Martin Kozak," he said. "We're trying to find out why."

"You're looking for leverage."

"That's about it."

"In a situation like this, leverage can be a very good thing."

"Kozak is big-time in heavy construction, builds highways and bridges, that kind of thing. Currently he's working on an overpass on Highway 91, leased the equipment from one of Hollister's companies. Could be he's cutting corners, using substandard material or something. The inspector on the project is a guy named Vernon Rimmer. I need to know if Rimmer's on the take. Any chance you can find that out?"

"Maybe. Sounds like you two have been doing your homework."

"Unfortunately, we've pretty much reached a dead end—unless you can help."

"Let me see what I can do. I'll get back to you as soon as I know something."

"Thanks, bro."

"No problem." Dev rang off, and Jackson felt a sense of relief. His brother was good. *Very good.* If they could find out what Kozak was doing, they could ensure he left Sarah and Holly alone.

Jackson checked his messages, returned a couple of calls, then left the study and went out to find Jimmy Threebears. The spring branding was done, so it wasn't as busy as it had been a few weeks back, but they were moving cattle to graze different pastures and there were always fences to mend, along with just keeping track of the animals' general welfare.

He found Jimmy out in the barn, stacking some of

last year's hay to make room for this summer's crop. They had weed sprayed last year and fertilized this spring so the grass was growing tall and thick, and rich in nutrients.

"Hey, boss!" Jimmy strode toward him, his long legs eating up the ground between them. "How'd it go in L.A.?"

"Not as well as I'd hoped. Dev's looking into a couple of things for me. We'll see what he comes up with. Everything okay here?"

"We could use a little rain. Weather's been pretty warm for this early in the year. Ground gets too dry, we're gonna have a problem with fires."

Jackson nodded. In the past few years, what had rarely been a problem had become a very big one. Drought and forest fires were a huge concern. And having a logging operation creating sparks with their heavy machinery could make the situation even worse.

"I guess we'd better pray for rain."

Jimmy grinned. "I'll talk to Dennis Redhorse, see what he can do."

Redhorse was the local tribal medicine man, or at least his grandfather had been. Dennis was doing his best to follow in the old man's footsteps. Unfortunately, in these modern times, a lot of the old ways were lost as they passed from one generation to the next.

Jackson just smiled. "You do that."

He looked over Jimmy's shoulder to a door leading out to the corral. Sarah sat on the fence while Sam led the little black pony, Midnight, around the ring— Holly riding in the pony saddle. A few feet away, Gibby added an occasional instruction.

"She's been doing real good," Jimmy said. "Sam's done a great job of teaching her."

Jackson watched the way Holly held the reins just like Sam told her, not too tight and not too loose, and felt the pull of a smile. She was the sweetest little girl, exactly the sort he'd want if he ever had a kid.

His gaze drifted to Sarah. The sun was gleaming on her heavy chestnut hair, highlighting fine strands of red and making her skin glow. She smiled as she watched her daughter on the pony. The soft, full lips he remembered so well curved up at the corners, and inside his jeans he went hard.

Damn. He reminded himself to stay away from her, as he had done last night and the night before that. He wanted to give her some breathing room, some time to consider what might lie ahead for them.

He wanted some time to consider those things himself.

But time wasn't going to change the hot desire he felt whenever he looked at her. Or whenever she looked at him—the way she was now.

The air seemed to heat and thicken between them. Sexual awareness crackled like invisible lightning around them. He knew she felt it, knew she fought it, just as he did, but it only made the wanting worse.

She jerked her gaze away, off toward the lane leading from the main road into the ranch. Jackson turned to see a plain brown sedan driving up the lane, pulling to a stop in front of the cottage. Two men in dark suits got out and started toward the front porch.

"I guess I better go see what they want," Sarah said, but she didn't look happy about it.

"I'll go with you."

Sarah seemed relieved. "Thanks." When they reached the cottage, she paused at the bottom of the wooden steps and looked at the men on the porch. "May I help you?"

"FBI. We need to speak to you, Mrs. Hollister—in private."

Her cheeks paled. "Could I please see your credentials?"

The men pulled out their IDs and flipped them open and Sarah climbed the steps to examine them. Jackson joined her.

"Can we go inside?" one of the agents asked, older than the other, maybe forty-five, his blond hair sparse.

"What is this in regard to?"

"As you know, your late husband was being investigated for tax evasion. We need to ask you some questions."

Sarah's head jerked up. "I—I don't know anything about an investigation. I had no idea."

Dev had mentioned it. Jackson knew the Feds had been after Hollister, but clearly Sarah didn't know.

He could see she was fighting for composure. "I'm Jackson Raines," he said to give her the time she needed. "I own Raintree Ranch."

"I'm Special Agent Lee Brooker," the blond man said. "This is Special Agent Matt Davis." Davis was tall, African American, the shoulders of his dark brown sport coat snug over a solidly muscled frame.

"Mr. Raines is a friend," Sarah said as the men shook hands. "He'll be coming inside with me. We can speak in the kitchen."

Sarah led them into the house and they all sat down at the old oak table in front of the kitchen window. She didn't offer them refreshment, just went straight to the point. "You've come quite a distance to see me. What is it you need to know?"

Jackson didn't miss the slight tremor in her voice.

Brooker began the conversation. "As I said, your husband was under investigation for tax evasion. Since you signed on the return, so are you."

"But that...that isn't possible. I didn't know anything about Andrew's business. I don't even know how much he paid in taxes."

"Not enough," Matt Davis drawled, a slight Texas twang in his voice. "We figure, even if no criminal charges are filed against you, with interest and penalties, you'll owe somewhere around five million dollars."

Sarah's shoulders drooped. Her complexion had faded to the color of sand. "Andrew left me virtually penniless. I couldn't possibly pay that kind of money."

"Which you gentlemen undoubtedly know," Jackson put in. "So why are you really here?"

Brooker flicked him a look of respect, then returned his attention to Sarah. "We think your husband was blackmailing someone, maybe several someones. Whoever it was is involved in illegal activities on a very large scale. We want to know who it is and what they were doing."

Sarah swallowed. "As I said, I don't know anything about...about Andrew's business dealings. I'm afraid I can't help you."

"Word is your husband kept a record," Brooker continued, "probably copied onto a USB key. It's got the names of the people he dealt with and a record of their illegal endeavors. He was trying to sell that information back to them."

"Extorting them for money," Jackson said, which they already knew.

"That's right."

"What does that have to do with me?" Sarah asked.

"From the information we've uncovered, we believe the people he was blackmailing are trying to find the USB. We think they'll contact you—if they haven't already. They won't feel safe until the information is returned to them."

"Andrew's been dead for months. Why would they wait until now to go after the flash drive?"

"Probably waiting for things to cool down," Davis drawled. "Hollister was murdered. There was a police investigation. By now, enough time has passed for them to crawl out from whatever rock they were under."

"Well, I don't have it," Sarah said, "and I have no idea where to find it."

Brooker's voice softened. "We need to know who these men are, Mrs. Hollister. We want to know what they were doing and we want proof. In other words— we need the information on that USB."

"And in return," Jackson added, "you'll see that Sarah is cleared of any responsibility for Andrew Hollister's tax problems."

Brooker smiled. "That's about it."

Sarah looked sick. "I'm not a detective. I'm a mother trying to raise a child. I have no idea how to go about this kind of thing."

Brooker looked directly at Jackson. "Maybe not, but I have a feeling your friend here may be able to help you."

Sarah flicked a glance at Jackson. "But I don't know what to do. I haven't the slightest—"

"To start with," Brooker interrupted, "keep us informed. Let us know when someone contacts you. And try to figure out where your husband hid that information."

Sarah made no reply. She had wisely made no mention of their trip to L.A. or that Martin Kozak had already been pressing her for the flash drive.

"Sarah needs time to think this through," Jackson said, "see how she might be able to help you." They needed time, all right. Time to figure out what the hell to do.

The men rose from their chairs around the table. "You've got three days, Mrs. Hollister. We'll expect to hear from you by then."

"It's Allen," she belatedly corrected. "My name is Sarah Allen."

The men ignored her. "If you hear from someone or need our help in any way, call this number." Brooker handed her a white business card. "Be sure the line is secure. We wouldn't want Andrew's *friends* to know what you're up to. In fact, there's a very good chance that list of his is the reason he wound up dead."

Jackson walked the men to the door, then returned to the kitchen. Sarah stood pale and shaken next to the sink.

"What...what am I going to do?" Her eyes slowly filled with tears. "I don't know how to catch a criminal."

She didn't resist when Jackson eased her gently into his arms, just rested her head on his shoulder. "You're going to do exactly what we were doing already. To begin with, we're going to find out why Andrew was blackmailing Marty Kozak. We just need the leverage we were after a little bit more."

"Is this ever going to end, Jackson?"

His chest tightened at the fear he heard in her voice. "We'll make it end, Sarah. I promise you, we'll find a way."

In that moment he realized he would do anything to keep Sarah safe.

And that was the moment he knew he was in trouble.

Chapter 15

June in the mountains, wildflowers blooming in fields so green it made your eyes hurt, while blinding-white snow still crowned the tops of the surrounding peaks. In the early mornings, the pasture was alive with deer.

It was tempting to stay home and simply absorb the beauty of a late Wyoming spring, watch the tiny striped chipmunks frolic on the porch.

Instead, Sarah went to work. After her visit from the FBI, Jackson convinced her that until they heard something from his brother, or Marty Kozak contacted her again, there was nothing more they could do.

"We just have to wait," he had said. "Dev will call as soon as he knows anything. Three days from now, you'll call the Feds and tell them you're willing to co-operate. That'll buy us a little more time."

"Maybe I should just tell them it's Kozak. That Marty's the guy Andrew was blackmailing."

"We still don't know why, and there may be others. You tell them about Kozak, they'll want more. We need to hold them off for as long as we can."

"All right, we wait, but in the meantime, we need to live our lives. That means I go to work and you go run your ranch."

He frowned. "If you go into town, you might be putting yourself in danger."

"I don't think Kozak is going to hurt me—not as long as he thinks there's a chance I'll get him that information."

"Maybe. But I still don't like—"

"I need this job, Jackson. I've got a daughter to support. Besides, I enjoy what I'm doing. I've always wanted to be a writer. Someday I'd like to write a book, but for now being a reporter is enough. I'm doing what I love and I'm not going to let anyone—including Andrew's crooked *friends*—screw things up."

Jackson walked to the door, lifted his battered straw hat off the rack beside it and settled it low on his forehead. He turned to face her. "All right, if you're that determined, I guess I can't stop you. But let's get you a cell phone that works so at least we can stay in touch."

"Good idea. And I want to get internet service."

He grinned. "I paid to have a line brought in from the road. It was worth it."

And so Sarah signed up with Qwest for internet and cell service. That Monday morning, she dropped Holly off at day care and went to work.

"Welcome back, stranger." That from Mike Stevens, the tall, sandy-haired reporter who worked with her at the paper. Except for the creak of the old wooden floors as she walked to her desk, the place was quiet.

"It's good to be back." She glanced around, saw that she and Mike were the only ones in the office.

"Smiley's out of town," Mike explained. "Myra isn't due in until this afternoon."

Myra Cunningham, the part-time receptionist, bookkeeper and head of the advertising section, was an older, no-nonsense, curly-haired blonde with a ready smile and an easy disposition. She and Smiley were an item, which everyone knew, though they tried to pretend it was a secret.

Sarah plunked her oversize bag down on top of her desk. "So what's been going on in town? Anything exciting?"

"Well, we had some big news day before yesterday. Bob Springer's teenage boy, Teddy, stole his old man's car and went for a joyride with his girlfriend. Bob thought the car had really been stolen so he called the sheriff. Kid was picked up and taken to jail. Bob was so mad he left the boy there overnight."

"Might be an interesting family angle for a follow-up article."

"Yeah, if you can get the Springers to talk to you. I think it shook 'em up pretty good—their perfect, never-do-anything-wrong son arrested for stealing a car."

"Well, it was the family car, not someone else's."

"Bob and Susan didn't see it that way. Ted isn't old enough to drive. He could have killed someone."

"Or been killed himself. I'll talk to them, see if it leads anywhere."

Mike nodded. "Umm…by the way… I've been wondering…any chance you might let me take you out to supper sometime? Food at the Sheepherder's Inn isn't too bad. Tonight they've got prime rib."

Sarah nervously moistened her lips. The Inn was the only steakhouse around, a ten-minute drive down the road to Sheep River. It wasn't the invitation that bothered her. It was that the invitation forced her to consider her relationship with Jackson. She wondered what he would say if she accepted a date with a good-looking younger man.

"So what do you think?" Mike pressed. His tenacity was the reason he made a good reporter. She just didn't want it used on her.

"I appreciate the thought, Mike. I really do. But things are kind of up in the air right now, and I'm just not ready for that kind of thing."

"That kind of thing? Dinner, you mean? You have to eat, you know."

"Yes, but—"

"Yes, but not unless the guy asking you happens to be Jackson Raines."

Heat rushed into her cheeks. She hadn't realized her feelings were so transparent. She had no idea exactly what his feelings for her were or what hers were for him, but the truth was, he was the man she wanted to be with and if she started dating other men, he would likely start dating other women—a thought that didn't sit well.

Of course he might do that anyway. He was a man, wasn't he? Still…

"As I said, I appreciate the invitation…"

"No problem. Maybe lunch sometime—just to go over some story ideas."

She smiled. "Maybe. I could sure use the help."

Mike wandered back to his desk and Sarah went to work. She read each edition of the paper she had missed while she was away, searching for something that might develop into a human-interest story.

She found it on page three of yesterday's paper—among the foreclosure notices.

She recognized the name of the property and the borrower who had defaulted on the loan. She and Cody Ballard had gone to high school together. Cody was the son of an old-time ranching family. Apparently his father had died and Cody had inherited the Three Forks Ranch, which, like a lot of other property, seemed to have fallen on hard times.

With all the foreclosures going on in the country, there was a great deal of interest in the subject. She might be able to do a story on what happened when a lender called a loan and include information on the unfortunate lending practices that had cost a number of people their homes. She wondered if that was the kind of thing that had happened with the Three Forks Ranch.

She drove out the following morning, hoping for an interview with Cody and his wife, Marilyn. Cody was working in the hay field with their two sons, Mark and Patrick, but Marilyn was more than eager to talk.

"We had a couple bad years in a row," she said. A slender woman at least five years younger than Sarah, with long brown hair pulled back in a ponytail, the calluses on her hands said that she was a rancher's wife.

"We saw this ad on TV," she continued, "how you could consolidate your debts, you know, with an equity loan? We thought three years was plenty of time to get things straightened out. Now the loan is due and our credit's not good enough to get another one. We just don't know what we're going to do." Tears rushed into her eyes and she glanced away.

Sarah handed her a Kleenex, which she used to blot her cheeks and blow her nose.

"It's too soon to give up," Sarah said, her heart going out to the young couple. "Maybe something will come along, some way to get an extension or something."

It was so easy to get sucked into a loan that could wind up ruining you. Years ago, Andrew had gotten involved with a loan shark to pay off some of his gambling debts. He had managed to extricate himself before the leg-breaking started, though Sarah had no idea how he had done it.

Maybe he had used one of his blackmail schemes to raise the money.

"There's so much of this kind of thing happening," she said. "Let me look into it, see if there are any resources for you to use."

Sarah wound up the interview, and they walked together to the door. Marilyn reached out and took hold of her hand. "Thank you, Sarah. Even if things don't work out, I appreciate your trying to help."

Sarah left feeling terrible for the Ballard family but good about a story that would give her a chance to make people aware of the dangers involved when you went into a mortgage without completely understanding the consequences. She would also talk to Jackson, see if he knew any way the Ballards might be able to hang on to the family ranch.

Returning to the office, she worked on the article the rest of the afternoon, digging up information on mortgage companies and the problems in the subprime market. As soon as she finished, she grabbed her briefcase and was just leaving the office when the phone rang. She recognized the voice though it didn't hold the least trace of an accent—the dark-skinned, foreign-looking man who had accosted her in the parking lot.

"How was your trip?" he asked amiably, his pleasant words in contrast with the underlying tension in his voice.

"How did you—"

"We know you went to Los Angeles with your cowboy, Sarah."

"You—you followed us?"

"We didn't need to. We want that flash drive. We need you to get it for us and we have every confidence you will."

She swallowed, took a slow breath, determined not to let him intimidate her. "Then you'll be happy to know you're right. I'm doing everything in my power to find it. When I do, you'll be the first to know."

"I believe you, Sarah. You're trying. The problem is we need you to try a little harder."

"Who are you working for? Kozak?"

"Just get me that flash drive." The line went dead. For a few more seconds, Sarah held the phone against her ear. On a shuddering breath, she closed the phone and dropped it into her purse.

She told herself she wasn't frightened. She was getting used to being accosted, to people threatening her. After Andrew, she could handle it, she told herself. After Andrew, she could handle anything.

But she had Holly to think of.

She was going to speak to Jackson, see how he would feel about letting her hire Livvy to take care of Holly whenever she went to the office.

She trusted Livvy completely and Holly would be safe at the ranch. As she left the building and walked to where her car was parked in the lot, she found herself glancing over her shoulder, looking to see if someone was watching.

She wasn't as frightened this time, she told herself again.

But something warned her that might just be a mistake.

Sarah didn't tell Jackson about the phone call. She knew he would try to talk her out of going to work, and though she could do some of her work from the house, her job demanded she come into town. And so she spoke to Livvy—who refused to take money for watching Holly, until Sarah refused to leave her unless she did.

A deal was struck.

Holly stayed safe at the ranch and Sarah went to work.

The rest of the week was uneventful. On Friday, Sarah's article about the Three Forks Ranch foreclosure came out in the newspaper and several people called to congratulate her on writing a story of such importance to the community.

Jackson was one of them. "I didn't know about the foreclosure till I saw your article in the paper. I'll call Cody, find out the amount of the loan. If Cody will sell me that triangular piece that abuts my property for a fair price, I'll see he gets a new loan on the rest of the property—at a reasonable rate, due in a reasonable period of time."

Sarah's heart warmed. "I was going to talk to you about it this weekend. I was hoping you might come up with some way to help."

"I'll call Ballard. See if we can work something out."

Sarah smiled into the phone. "I'm sure he'll be interested. I think he'd do just about anything to save his family's ranch."

Sarah rang off, thinking of Jackson and how different he seemed from Andrew, whose thoughts revolved mostly around himself.

Saturday came. Since she mostly set her own hours, she rarely worked weekends. Sarah stood at the window of the cottage watching her daughter race down the steps and off toward the corral, Rags trailing along in her wake. Holly loved it here in Wyoming. She was blossoming in the warm sun and clear mountain air. Sarah smiled, thinking what a good decision she had made in leaving the city.

If only she could find a way to solve the multitude of problems Andrew had left her.

Giving in to a sigh, she turned away from the window, meaning to finish her housecleaning, but stopped as she spotted a compact silver car driving toward the cottage. For an instant her nerves kicked in, then the car pulled to a halt, the engine went still, and Nan Hargrove climbed out of the car, long red hair flashing in the brilliant morning sun.

Nan pulled a potted plant out of the backseat and walked toward the front porch steps as Sarah hurried to open the door.

"Nan! Come in!"

"Welcome home." Nan handed her the plant, a lovely blooming lilac. "It's a little late in coming, but as they say, better late than never. I figured you could find a place to plant it."

Sarah carried the lilac inside, set it on the coffee

table, turned and gave Nan a hug. "It's wonderful. And it smells so good. You didn't have to buy it, but I love it."

"I hoped you would."

"I've been meaning to call you. Things have just been so hectic time slipped away."

"That's okay. You're just getting settled. Eventually things will calm down." She glanced around the living room, at the mismatched sofa and chairs that replaced the ones destroyed by Kozak's goons.

"Jackson ordered some new furniture. It's due in any day."

"That's nice, but the place is already starting to look like home. I like the hooked rug and the old kerosene lamps."

"Jackson found them in the top of the barn."

"You were always good at decorating. I remember your bedroom when we were kids. The whole place was done in pink and white. You had a pink-and-white-striped dust ruffle and a matching pink comforter on the bed. You even painted pink flowers on the old antique mirror above your dresser. I loved that room. It was so *girlie*."

Sarah laughed. "It was, wasn't it?" She ignored a bittersweet pang at the memory of the happy days when her parents were still alive.

Nan walked over to the window, looked out to where Jackson and Jimmy Threebears were working. They had the hood up on one of the older ranch pickups, which apparently had broken down.

"How are things going with Jackson?" Nan asked.

Something warm unfurled inside her at the mention

of his name. Oh, boy, was she in trouble. "Jackson's a very nice man. He's been a good friend."

Nan's dark red eyebrows went up. "*A very nice man?* Girl, have you lost your mind? This is Jackson Raines we're talking about. Mr. Tall-Dark-and-Handsome? He's one of the sexiest men on the planet. Tell me you just think of him as a friend."

She flushed and glanced away. "All right, so maybe it's a little more than friendship." *Like spending hours in bed with him and wishing they could make love again.* "But I don't think either one of us knows where it's going." She noticed Nan hadn't turned away from the window, but seemed to be watching Jimmy, not Jackson.

"What about you? Any new men in your life?"

Nan turned and Sarah caught a flash of sadness in her eyes. "I went out with Jimmy Threebears. It was pretty much a disaster."

"A disaster? Really? Why?"

Nan blew out a breath. "Because—like half the men in Wind Canyon—Jim thinks I'm a slut."

"But that's crazy. Why on earth would he think that?"

Nan walked over and sank down on the sofa. "For a while after Ron and I got divorced, I kind of was." She smoothed a wrinkle in one of the sofa cushions. "I hung out at the Canyon Club—you know, that place out on the Sheep River highway?"

"I remember it."

"When I'd get lonely, I'd go out there. Sometimes I'd pick up a guy. I saw Jim there a couple of times. The night we went out, he pressed me for sex. When I said no, he said I put out for every other guy, why not him?"

"Lord, Nan, what did you do?"

"I slapped his face and made him take me home." She looked up and tears sprang into her eyes. "I wanted to tell him I'm not like that anymore—not for years. That I never really was that way. I didn't, of course."

"Oh, Nan."

"I've wanted to go out with him forever. I really wanted him to like me."

Sarah sat down beside her, leaned over and gave her a hug. "People make mistakes. Nobody's perfect—not even Jimmy Threebears. Jimmy doesn't deserve you. You keep that in mind."

Nan smiled wanly. "I didn't mean to get into that. I almost didn't drive out because I was afraid I'd see him."

"Forget him. Come on in the kitchen and I'll make us a nice cup of tea."

And so she did, and they sat together drinking Earl Grey and enjoying the pretty view outside the kitchen window, watching a fat gray squirrel foraging food from beneath a pine tree.

But long after Nan left, Sarah thought of Jimmy Threebears and the way he had treated her friend. She never would have expected Jimmy to behave so disrespectfully to a woman.

Which only went to prove how careful a woman had to be.

Chapter 16

Jackson was flat-out tired. Tired of waiting for his brother to call, tired of worrying about Sarah and little Holly. Tired of waiting for Sarah to give in to her desire and invite him back into her bed.

He couldn't do much about his brother, or the problems with Marty Kozak. But he could do something about Sarah.

Saddling Galahad, a big sorrel quarter horse gelding he favored, and a paint mare named Daisy he trusted for Sarah, he led the animals toward the cottage. Holly and her puppy were playing with Sam and Giddy and their dogs out in front of the barn so he knew Sarah was home alone. Before he left the house, he'd asked Livvy to keep an eye on the little girl so Sarah wouldn't worry.

Arriving at the cottage, Jackson tied the horses

to the railing in front of the flower bed, climbed the wooden steps and knocked on her door. Another quick knock and Sarah pulled it open.

"Jackson. Hi."

His gaze ran over her feminine features, pretty blue eyes and luscious curves, and the blood began to settle in his groin. Since it was far too soon for that kind of thinking, he clamped down on the heat burning through him and smiled.

"You're wearing jeans. Great, you won't have to change." He grabbed her hand. "It's too nice a day to stay in the house. Come on, we're going for a ride."

"Wait a minute—"

"Holly's with Sam and Gibby, and Livvy's keeping an eye on them."

She continued to resist, pulling against his hand, then she spotted the little paint mare. "That isn't fair. She's too pretty to resist."

"That was my plan."

"I haven't ridden in ages." But he could feel her eagerness as he led her toward the horse. "Not since I left Wyoming. I don't know if I remember how."

"It'll come back to you. It's the same as riding a bicycle—once you know how, you never forget."

She cast him a not-so-certain glance. "I hope you're right."

He led her over to the paint—brown and white, small, well-shaped head and nice markings. "Sarah, meet Daisy. She's got a good rein and she's very sweet tempered."

Sarah scratched Daisy between the ears. "Aren't you a sweet girl?" The mare nickered softly and leaned into her hand.

"See, she likes you already."

And from the adoration on Sarah's face, the feeling was mutual. Jackson swung her up in the saddle, took a moment to check the stirrup length, saw that he'd guessed about right. She was wearing the same white sneakers she usually wore and he made a mental note to take her into the mercantile and buy her a pair of boots.

Sarah settled deeper in the saddle and took hold of the reins, placing them correctly in her left hand. She rode Daisy in a small circle, just to get the feel of the horse, and it was clear she hadn't forgotten much of anything. It was hard to live in a small, rural town in Wyoming and not know how to ride.

"Where are we going?"

"Up to the top of the ridge. I need to check on those loggers, make sure they aren't causing any trouble." And it was a beautiful ride up an easy, meandering trail. Livvy had packed a picnic lunch, and there were nice places along the way where they could stop to eat.

"Ready?"

"As I'm ever going to be."

The kids had disappeared inside the barn. Jackson led Sarah out a dirt road that followed the creek, then they branched off up the trail.

The path started up steeply.

"Jackson?" There was a hint of nervousness in Sarah's voice.

"It's only a little way to the top of the rise, then it's a gentle climb the rest of the trip. Just give Daisy her head and hang on."

Sarah handled the climb like an expert and pulled the little mare to a halt behind Galahad under a canopy of trees. She looked at him and grinned. "I forgot how much fun this is."

He smiled back at her, thinking how pretty she looked in the dappled sunlight filtering down through the branches. A rush of wanting hit him that had nothing to do with sex, then the familiar throb of desire settled deep in his loins.

The woman was in his blood, had been since he was a boy. It was a worrisome thought; one, for the moment, he chose to ignore.

The trail continued, passing grand vistas of greengrass valley below and craggy mountains in the distance where a hawk soared over the treetops. The path wound into deep, old-growth forests, and the scent of cedar and pine filled the air. Saddle leather creaked beneath him and a thick mat of needles muffled the clop of the horses' hooves.

An hour into the ride, Jackson pulled Galahad to a halt in a quiet little meadow next to a bubbling stream.

"Livvy packed us a picnic lunch." Swinging down from the saddle, he slung a rope around Galahad's neck, pulled off the bridle and tied the horse up to graze. He dragged a blanket out of his saddlebag and whipped it open on the grass then walked back to where Sarah sat on Daisy.

She was staring at the rocky, snowcapped peaks as if she had never really seen them. "Oh, Jackson, this is wonderful! Thank you so much for bringing me."

"My pleasure." He refused to let the thought linger, just slipped a rope around the little mare's neck, took off Daisy's bridle and tied her to the nearest tree. Reaching up, he lifted Sarah off the saddle, holding her so close she slid down his body as he set her on her feet.

He was hard and he let her know it. Her eyes found his and he felt the thrum of her pulse speeding into a faster gear. He kept his hands at her waist, though he wanted to move them higher, wanted to cup those sweet breasts he remembered so well.

"Livvy made us sandwiches." His voice came out gruff since his mind was not on food.

Sarah reached up and touched his face. He could read the uncertainty, knew the instant she made her decision. "Let's eat later." Twining her arms around his neck, she went up on her toes and kissed him. Her soft curves melted against him and Jackson groaned.

Damn, he wanted her.

His tongue found its way into her mouth, and she sucked on it, tangled her own tongue with his and pressed herself more fully against him. Desire slammed through him like a heavyweight punch, set off a roaring in his ears and a pounding in his blood.

Sweet Jesus. His hands found her breasts, just the way he had imagined. He palmed them, cupped them over the crisp white blouse she wore with her jeans. He told himself to go slow, but when Sarah deepened the kiss, when it turned hot and fierce, any thought of a slow, easy loving evaporated like water on a heated stone. Jackson drove his hands into her heavy hair and tilted her head back to lay claim to what was his.

Sarah couldn't think. She could barely breathe. Jackson kissed her wildly, a deep, slick kiss that fired the fever burning through her blood. She wanted this, wanted him. There was no use denying it. Jerking the snaps open on the front of his Western shirt, she ran her palms over his magnificent chest, felt the slabs of muscle tighten, felt the roughness of his curly, dark chest hair, felt his erection leap against the zipper of his jeans.

She leaned toward him, pressed her lips against a flat copper nipple, and the last of his control seemed to snap.

"I want you," he said, cupping her face between his hands. "God, I want you so damned much." Dragging her mouth back to his, he plunged his tongue inside. He walked her backward till they reached the blanket, then lowered her to the ground and came down on top of her.

Long, deep kisses followed. Wet, openmouthed kisses as he unfastened her bra then clamped his lips over a rigid nipple. He sucked until he had her moaning, stopped only long enough to tug off her sneakers, unzip her jeans and drag them down her legs. He pulled them off and his hot gaze devoured her, snagged on the little blue thong panties that barely covered the dark brown curls above her sex.

Sarah reached for him, her hands trembling as she unzipped his jeans, urging him to take them off. "I want to see you. I want to touch you, Jackson."

He clenched his jaw as if he were in pain. He was naked in an instant—boots, jeans and shirt all gone. Slabs of muscle tightened across his chest as he moved, spreading her legs, positioning himself above her.

He didn't wait, and Sarah didn't want him to, just parted her softness and found the entrance to her passage, began to ease his powerful erection inside. She was wet and slick and as the penetration deepened, the pleasure was so intense she started to come.

Sarah bit back a cry as ripples of sweetness washed

over her and her body tightened around his hardened length.

Jackson hissed in a breath. "God, lady…"

She could see he was fighting for control, his breath coming fast, every muscle tense. His movements quickened, his hips pumping, driving him hard inside her. Pleasure swamped her, pulled deep in her stomach. He felt so good, so totally amazing. She closed her eyes and bit her lip, dug her fingers into his powerful shoulders and held on through a second searing climax.

"Damn…" he ground out, and finally let himself go. His skin was slick with sweat, his biceps bunching as he spent himself inside her. The muscles across his chest teased her nipples. She loved the weight of him above her, loved every inch of his rock-solid body.

She'd had sex before, but never like this, and she loved it.

I can handle this, she told herself. Sex with an incredible lover. All she had to do was keep things on an even keel—keep herself from falling in love with him.

The words stirred a trickle of unease inside her. She wasn't ready for that kind of involvement. Maybe she never would be.

I can handle it, she told herself again. She wanted this time with Jackson. After what she had suffered with Andrew, she deserved this special time with this very special man.

"All right?" he asked, slowly lifting himself from above her, lying down on the blanket beside her and easing her into his arms. Cool mountain air rushed over her bare skin, raising a fine spray of goose bumps. Sarah loved it.

"I'm fine. Wonderful, in fact."

He leaned over her, kissed her softly on the lips. "So am I." He smiled. "Hungry? Because if we don't get dressed pretty soon, I won't give a damn about that chicken."

Sarah laughed. "I'm starving." She hadn't eaten all day. Even so, when Jackson leaned over to kiss her one last time, she slid her arms around his neck and deepened the kiss. Sparks ignited. They made love slowly this time, learning each other's body, giving each other pleasure.

After they finished, they lay there in the sunshine, Sarah on the edge of slumber till the breeze began to chill her bare skin. She leaned over for a last quick kiss, then left him there on the blanket.

While Sarah washed in the little stream and pulled on her clothes, Jackson dressed and went to retrieve their picnic lunch. As she returned to the blanket, an image stirred of him naked, all dark skin and lean bands of muscle.

She hid a small, inward smile. She hadn't realized what a brazen hussy she was until she met Jackson. Or maybe that was just the way a normal woman reacted to a man who attracted her as strongly as he did. She had so little experience with men she didn't really know.

They ate the sandwiches and drank iced tea. When they had finished, he tugged her to her feet. "I'd rather stay here and make love to you again, but it looks like it's getting ready to rain. Storms blow up fast around here. I'd rather not be stuck on the mountain."

"We're going back?"

A few drops began to fall, dappling the ground around them. "I think we'd better," he said.

"What about the loggers? I thought you wanted to check on them."

"There's a road that goes to the top. I'll take one of the ATVs and go up in the morning." Jackson hauled her into his arms and very thoroughly kissed her. "I'm glad you enjoyed the ride."

She blushed, and he laughed.

"That one, too. Come on, we'd better get going." He had readied the horses. He boosted her into the saddle, then collected his reins and swung up on Galahad. Adjusting his battered straw hat to shade his eyes, he led the way out of the meadow and they started back down the trail.

It was raining steadily by the time they reached the ranch and Sarah's gaze went in search of her daughter.

"I need to find Holly."

"I'm sure Livvy brought her into the house. Let's get you in where it's dry and I'll send her home."

Sarah hesitated. She wasn't used to anyone looking after her daughter but herself.

"Come on," he gently coaxed, riding past the barn and reining up in front of the cottage. "It's getting wetter by the minute."

With a last glance back toward the ranch house, Sarah jumped down and Jackson swung down beside her.

"Sorry about the rain."

She smiled up at him. "It was worth it." She handed him Daisy's reins, went up and kissed him full on the lips. "Thanks for the lunch."

"As I said, my pleasure." The edge of his mouth curved up and the devil twinkled in those flashing dark eyes. Sarah ignored the little flutter in her stomach and the urge to invite him inside.

"Tell Holly to come straight home."

He nodded, pulled his hat farther down against the rain that was falling even more heavily, turned and led the horses toward the barn.

"Mom, I'm home!" It hadn't been ten minutes, but still Sarah was relieved to hear the sound of her daughter's voice. Everything was fine. Holly was home and safe.

"I'm in here, honey—in the bedroom." She had finally gotten her laptop up and running and was now able to get her email.

The friends she had made in SBW, the online support group for battered women, all stayed closely in touch. One woman in particular. Patty Gorski, the founder of the small collection of women, was as tough as nails and as solid as a rock. Sarah sorted through her emails, looking for a message from Patty as Holly dashed into the bedroom.

"Hey, Mom!"

"Hi, honey." Sarah smiled down at her. "Sounds like it's stopped raining." She listened but no longer heard the soft patter on the roof.

"It's mostly stopped. Jackson says he wished it would rain all week."

Sarah shoved aside a memory of their incredible lovemaking in the meadow, knowing the danger of that line of thinking. "Your clothes are damp. You better go put on something dry."

"Jackson says the next time you two go riding, I can

come with you. He says I can ride with him on Galahad—that's his horse."

"If you keep up your lessons on Midnight, someday
you'll be able to ride by yourself."

Holly chattered on about her morning with Sam
and Gibby—Rags had to stay outside because he was
too muddy to come in the house—then dashed off to
change and watch TV.

Sarah went back to her email. Among assorted
spam, she found several anxious messages from Patty,
who was worried about her. Patty wanted to be sure
she had made it to Wyoming safely and that everything
was working out all right.

Sorry to take so long getting back to you, Sarah
replied. Just got my email up and running. Hope you
weren't too worried. Andrew left me with some problems, but we're coping. Holly and I both love it here.
Maybe someday you can come for a visit.

Sarah didn't say more. Though she and Patty had
never met, in the ways that mattered the woman was
the best friend she'd ever had. Patty Gorski lived in
Chicago, the only daughter in a poor Polish family
of six. She'd gotten pregnant her junior year in high
school, had an abortion, then a year later married the
guy who had fathered the baby.

For years, she had lived as a battered wife, unable
to build up the nerve to leave, but with the help of a
support group, she had finally found the courage to
break free.

If it weren't for Patty...

Sarah shook off the thought, refusing to imagine

what might have happened if she hadn't become friends with such a strong, caring woman.

Sarah returned the emails in her inbox, then decided to work on the synopsis of a book she had been dabbling with for more than a year. *Trials of Passage* was the working title, a novel about a young woman from a small town trying to raise a child and make her way in a troubled world. It was loosely based on her own life, but not entirely.

There were things she would never write about, things that were too frightening or too painful—and the book *was* a novel, after all.

If she ever got the project off the ground.

"The rain's all the way stopped," Holly called out from the living room. "I'm going back out to play."

"Try to stay out of the mud!" Sarah called back to her. She glanced out the window. The ground was so dry the rain had soaked right in, but if there was a puddle, Holly was sure to find it.

The front door slammed as Holly ran out, and Sarah thought of the changes in her daughter since their move to Wyoming. Here the little girl was outside most of the time instead of inside watching TV. With the harsh winters, hot summers, bugs and wild animals, it wasn't an easy place to live, but for Sarah and Holly, the trade-off was worth it.

Sarah opened the file marked *Passage*. She hadn't worked on the novel since before Andrew died. It was something he knew she was doing, patronized her about, but didn't take seriously. Since she had been at it for what seemed ages, maybe in this instance he was right.

She was going over the opening chapter—which

was as far as she had ever gotten—when she heard a faint knock at the door. Rising from the chair behind the small oak desk in her bedroom, she walked into the living room and, through the window, saw Jimmy Threebears standing on the porch.

"Hello, Jimmy."

He held his damp felt cowboy hat in his hands. "Hello, Sarah… I was…ah, wondering if you might have a minute to talk."

He was a tall man, and imposing, with all that long black hair, black eyes and dark, smoothly carved features. She opened the door, curious as to why he was there. "Come on in."

Jimmy pulled off his muddy boots and left them by the door, the way most people did in Wyoming. They walked into the living room and sat down on the sofa and chair in front of the rock fireplace.

"I saw you had a visitor yesterday." Jimmy turned the hat in his hands.

"Nan Hargrove. Yes, she was here."

"Did she…ah…tell you we went out?"

"She mentioned it. I don't know what you want me to say, Jimmy. Nan is a friend. She told me what happened, and to be honest, I was surprised you would treat her that way."

Jimmy glanced off toward the window. "That's the reason I'm here."

"I'm listening."

Jimmy released a slow breath. "I don't know exactly what happened that night. I'd been wanting to ask Nan out for a real long time. I knew Ron, her ex-husband, before the divorce. After they split up, I tried to work up the nerve to ask Nan for a date, but then I started seeing her down at the Canyon Club."

"She told me about that. It was a bad time for her, Jimmy. Her marriage had failed. Ron was gone and she was lonely."

He turned the hat in his hands. "The truth is, those times I saw her at the Club… I wanted to be one of the guys she went home with. I was jealous she picked one of them and not me."

"Nan's not really that kind of woman. She never was, and the way I understand it, that was several years ago."

He nodded. "I know. Like I said, I don't know what happened. I guess my feelings kind of spilled over. I took my past jealousy out on Nan."

"And you expect me to do…what?"

He ran a calloused finger around his sweat-stained hatband. "Talk to her, I guess. See if you can convince her to give me another chance."

"I don't know if she will, Jimmy. From what Nan told me, she wanted to go out with you, too. The way you acted, those things you said… You hurt her, Jimmy. I don't know if she'll take the risk."

He looked her straight in the face. "I know about your husband—the way he treated you. I've never abused a woman and I never will."

When Sarah made no reply, Jimmy shoved to his feet and started toward the door.

He turned back when he got there. "Tell her I'm sorry. Will you at least do that?"

Her heart pinched. Even after Andrew, she was a sucker for an old-fashioned romance. "I'll tell her," she said softly.

Jimmy nodded, pulled open the door, picked up his boots and stepped out on the rain-soaked porch to pull them back on. He closed the door behind him, and Sarah sighed.

Everyone made mistakes. Some were smaller than others. Maybe Nan and Jimmy could get past this one. She would tell Nan what he had said and leave the decision up to her.

Chapter 17

Jackson sat in front of the old wood-burning stove in his study. Most of the house had been remodeled, but this room remained much as it had been when the ranch was built in the 1920s. He propped his boots up on the coffee table Jimmy had made for him one Christmas out of deer antlers. The antlers formed the legs beneath a thick slab of varnished tree trunk.

Jackson had a fire burning in the stove tonight. Though the days were growing warmer, up here in the mountains the nights were still cold—perfect weather, Jackson thought. If only the rain had lasted more than a couple of hours, the summer might be all right.

Thinking of the storm that had passed through the mountains so quickly brought memories of a grassy meadow and the beautiful woman he had made love to. The rain hadn't lasted long enough and neither had the lovemaking.

Jackson sighed, wishing Sarah were there with him, that he could pull her down on the thick bear rug in front of the iron stove, strip off her clothes, and—

The ringing of the doorbell put a stop to the train of his thoughts. It was past eight o'clock. Livvy had gone home and it was nearly dark outside. Walking out of the office, he made his way to the front door, flipped on the porch light, and opened the door.

His youngest sibling, Devlin, stood there grinning. "Hey, big brother, got an extra room for the night?"

Gabriel stood behind him. "Make that two."

"I'll be damned." Jackson shook hands with each of his brothers, pulling them into a quick bear hug, then stepping out of the way so the men could carry their duffel bags inside the house. "What in blazes brings the pair of you way up here?"

"I was in Phoenix on business," Gabe said, tossing his duffel at the bottom of the stairs. "Dev said you were having a little trouble. He had some information he figured he would rather deliver in person, so I offered to give him a ride."

"Pretty far out of the way for a side trip."

Gabe shrugged a set of linebacker shoulders. All of them were about the same height, Jackson being tallest, but Gabe had the most muscular build—which had proved useful since he actually *was* a linebacker on the high school varsity football team. After that, four years in the Marines, just a grunt, he'd always said, but the service had given him the confidence he'd needed to start a successful career in real estate and construction.

Jackson fixed his attention on Devlin, the pretty boy of the family, though with their startling blue eyes, both his brothers managed to charm more than their fair share of women. "So I guess you've got news."

"Big news, *hermano.* The kind that could get your lady off the hook with Martin Kozak and his bad boys."

Jackson liked the sound of that. "Why don't you two go upstairs and get yourselves settled in a couple of the spare bedrooms. I'll make us some coffee and meet you in the study."

"I take it Sarah's still living in the cottage," Dev said. He grinned. "I thought by now you'd have her moved in here."

Jackson felt an unexpected pang at the notion. "Mostly, we're just friends," he said, ignoring a memory of making love to her in the meadow.

Gabe slapped him on the back. "Yeah, right—mostly."

"She's going to want to hear this," Dev said.

"It's late and she's got her daughter to think of. We'll go over all of it again in the morning." Besides, he wanted to hear the news first, find a way to soften the blow if one was coming.

The men pounded up the staircase, and Jackson went into the kitchen and began to make coffee. He was damned glad to see his brothers, the best friends he had in the world. Only the fact they thought it was necessary to fly all the way up to deliver the information in person made him uneasy.

Dev and Gabe arrived in the study, poured themselves a mug of coffee from the pot keeping warm on the stove, then sat down on the brown leather sofa and chairs around the fire. Jackson opened the heavy iron door, tossed in a couple of logs, closed the door and joined them.

"All right, what have you found out?"

Dev didn't hesitate. "Kozak's running two or three different scams all at once. On some jobs, he's using fewer supports than the project calls for, spacing the rebar a little farther apart than is legal. In projects the size of the ones he builds, it saves him millions."

"What about the inspector?"

"I'll get to him in a minute." Dev took a sip of his coffee. "Kozak's also got an interesting deal going with the labor he's hiring. The state requires the contractor to pay the prevailing wage. Kozak's bringing in Mexican illegals by the truckload, willing to work for substandard wages. I figure he's cooking the books so the state doesn't know. There may be more—I just haven't run across it yet."

"How's Kozak getting away with all this?"

"That's where his old buddy, Vernon Rimmer, comes in."

"Who's Rimmer?" Gabe asked, clearly aware of most of what Dev had been working on. Gabe owned a construction company in Dallas. Lately, he'd been doing redevelopment projects.

"Rimmer's a state highway inspector," Dev answered. "It took a little doing to find them, since they were buried pretty deep, but Rimmer's got several offshore bank accounts in the Caymans. He's on Kozak's payroll and getting paid off big-time."

"So even after paying Rimmer," Jackson said, "Kozak is still ahead of the game."

"Way ahead," Dev agreed. "And this has been going on for years. My guess is, Andrew Hollister found out about it sometime back. Maybe he had an informant. Clearly he kept a record of what was going on."

"So what happened to make him decide it was time to cash in?" Gabe asked.

"The IRS, I'm betting," Jackson said. "Hollister must have figured he could either get enough blackmail money from Kozak to pay his back taxes, or make a deal with the Feds not to prosecute in exchange for the information on the flash drive."

Jackson explained about the two federal agents showing up at Sarah's door, threatening her with prosecution if she didn't help them find out who her husband was blackmailing.

"Not good," said Gabe, rubbing a hand over his square jaw.

"Maybe that's how the Feds knew Hollister had the kind of information they would want," Dev said. "He was in touch with them before he got whacked."

It made sense.

"Maybe Kozak whacked him," Gabe suggested.

"Or hired someone to do it," Dev added.

Jackson took a slug of his coffee. "The guy had enough enemies it could have been just about anyone."

"So what's the next step?" Gabe asked.

Jackson sat back in his chair. "Good question. Since the FBI is now in the game, the whole thing's a lot more complicated. In the morning we'll fill Sarah in, then put our heads together and see what we can come up with."

Dev nodded. "Sounds good to me." He yawned, rubbed the shadow of black along his jaw. "I was out pretty late last night—not that I'm complaining."

"Missy or Babs?" Gabe asked.

"Maria." He shook his hand as if he had burned it. "That lady is hot!"

Jackson inwardly sighed. Since Devlin's breakup with longtime girlfriend Amy Matlock two years ago, he was a confirmed bachelor. He went through women like a scythe through wheat. Jackson wondered whether it was really helping his brother forget the woman he had loved or if he was fooling himself.

"It's been a long day," Jackson said, rising from his deep leather chair. "I want you both to know I appreciate your help in this."

"Not a problem, bro." Dev shoved to his feet.

"I needed a vacation anyway," said Gabe, which was probably true though he would be hard-pressed to actually take one. He rose from the sofa to join his brothers. "Good night, y'all," he drawled with the slight Texas accent he had slowly been acquiring since his move to Dallas ten years ago.

"I've got a little more to do down here," Jackson said. "I'll see you both in the morning."

The men left the study and Jackson sat down in front of the stove, watching the low-burning flames through the open iron door. Propping his boots on the coffee table, he leaned back on the sofa.

Dev had found the information they needed. Now the question was, what to do with it? The things Kozak was doing weren't just illegal, they were dangerous. If one of those overpasses collapsed because of shoddy construction…

He didn't even want to go there.

Making any sort of deal with Kozak was no longer an option. The trick was to figure out how to get the Feds off Sarah's back, stop Kozak—and keep all of them in one piece.

* * *

Sarah sat in the living room of the cottage the following morning. Across from her sat three of the best-looking men she had ever seen. Jackson, the rugged Raines brother, sat next to Gabe, who was the brawniest of the trio. Both had the same dark brown hair, though Gabe's shone with traces of red in the light coming in through the window. His square jaw led to a strong chin with the same cleft all three Raines brothers had inherited.

Dev was leaner than the other two, but with his shirtsleeves rolled up, she could see muscular forearms, hinting at a solid body that matched those of his brothers. He had nearly black hair, incredible eyes the same brilliant blue as Gabe's and thick black lashes that a cover model would kill for.

"So that's about it," Jackson said, summing up the information Devlin had discovered, drawing her mind back to the information he had been delivering, information she would rather not have known, the kind of illegal activities that made her stomach burn. "Now we need to decide our next move."

Sarah sighed. "Well, we can't let Marty Kozak continue to build bridges that might fall down. I think we should call the FBI, set up a meeting with agents Brooker and Davis."

"I think we're all in agreement on that," Dev said.

"I'll get hold of my attorney," Jackson added. "We need someone there who knows the ropes when we talk to those guys, someone we can count on to see you get a fair deal."

Her stomach tightened. "I can't afford to hire—"

"I can," Jackson said as he had before.

Sarah came to her feet. "I can't take money from you, Jackson. I don't want to be in your debt and that's exactly where that would put me."

Gabe was staring at her with a trace of pity. "You think he'll want something in return, don't you?"

"My brother's trying to help you, Sarah," Devlin said gently. "You won't be the first person he's done that for—Gabe and I can both personally vouch for that. You won't be the last."

"And he isn't going to require any kind of repayment," Gabe finished.

She stood there feeling humiliated and embarrassed. Jackson had never asked her for anything. He had been a friend from the start, one she needed very badly. He wasn't like Andrew or any other man she had ever known.

"I'm sorry." She sank back down in her chair. "I'm not used to people helping me." She looked at Jackson and blinked to hold back tears. "Thank you," she added.

Jackson looked away from her, hiding the emotions she had read in his face—concern, relief that she had agreed, and something more she couldn't name.

"Where were we?" he said, clearly wishing to turn the conversation back to their plans.

"Thomas Carson, your attorney," Gabe reminded him. "You were going to set up a meeting with the Feds and ask Carson to be there."

"Right."

"Not in Wind Canyon," Dev warned. "We don't want Kozak or his goons getting wind of this."

"Carson's office is in Cheyenne. We'll ask for a meeting there tomorrow."

"That'll work," Dev said. "They'll be eager to know what you've got."

"I'll fly you down," offered Gabe.

Sarah took a deep breath, trying to pull her thoughts together, feeling a surge of gratitude for the help the brothers were giving her.

She looked over at Jackson, who had turned to speak to Gabe, and found herself studying his profile: the straight nose and hard jaw; the dark hair, a little too long, that brushed the collar of his Western shirt. A sweep of desire stirred deep in her stomach—which was ridiculous, considering they weren't alone and they were discussing a deadly serious situation.

Sarah returned her thinking to the problem at hand, listened as the men worked out the details. She would have to take time off work—again. But she didn't really have set hours and she could always work at home a few nights to make up the time. She was surprised when they asked her opinion and actually seemed to listen to what she had to say, including her in the planning as Andrew never would have done.

"All we need to do now is to set up that meeting," Dev said.

"I'll take care of it," said Jackson, rising from his place on the sofa, and Sarah had no doubt that he would.

As soon as the men left the cottage, Sarah grabbed her briefcase and headed into town. Holly was staying with Livvy. Earlier, the little girl had met Dev and

Gabe, who both had an easy way with children and really seemed taken with the little girl.

Holly had been instantly charmed by Jackson's two handsome brothers, and disappointed she had to leave while the adults had their meeting. She did so only with the promise that the men would come down to the corral and watch her ride Midnight, which they all agreed to do.

Sarah smiled as she sat at the desk in her office reviewing the article she was currently writing. She had gotten an appointment with Susan Springer to discuss her son Teddy's arrest for joyriding in his parents' car, promising to keep Teddy's name out of the article. She explained that she wanted to write about the problems parents had today communicating with their teenage children and how important it was to keep those lines of communication open.

Susan seemed to like the idea, telling Sarah over the phone that she regretted not having talked to Teddy more about his responsibilities, as well as drugs, alcohol and sex, and that she and Bob were making much more of an effort to listen to what their son had to say.

Her interview was scheduled for two o'clock. There was still plenty of time, so Sarah called her grandmother, which she did as often as she could, wishing she could drive over to Sheep River to see her. With things the way they were, it wasn't going to happen right away.

"How are you, Gran?" Sarah asked.

"I'm doing just fine, sweetheart. Feels real good to be back home. Everything okay with you and Holly? You haven't had any more trouble like before?"

Things were far from okay, but she didn't say that to

Gran. "I'm trying to get the whole thing straightened out." And maybe tomorrow, after her trip to Cheyenne, the situation would look better.

She and Gran chatted for a while, then Sarah hung up the phone on her desk, picked up her big leather purse, and started for the door, waving to Myra Cunningham as she passed the front counter.

"See ya later," Myra called out, shoving a pencil into the frizzy gray-blond curls she had pulled back into a bun.

Sarah stepped out on the boardwalk and took a couple of paces before she spotted Nan Hargrove walking toward her.

"Sarah!"

"Nan! I've been meaning to call you." *Would have if it weren't for the trouble that seems to follow me wherever I go.*

"I know it's a little late for lunch, but have you eaten yet? I thought maybe you could get away for a sandwich or something."

"I wish I had time. I have an appointment with Susan Springer to discuss an article I'm writing."

"Well, maybe next time." She started to turn away, but Sarah caught her arm.

"Listen, Nan, Jimmy Threebears came to see me. He wanted to talk about what happened the night he took you out. He asked me to speak to you about it."

Nan's fiery red eyebrows went up. "Jim asked you to talk to me?"

Sarah tugged her a little way down the boardwalk, where no one could hear. "Jimmy said he screwed up that night. He said he was jealous of the men you'd dated. He said he had been wanting to take you out for years. He said to tell you he was sorry."

"If he was sorry, why didn't he call and tell me?"

"I don't know. I guess he didn't think you'd forgive him."

Nan faintly smiled. "I might. If I thought he really meant it." She tossed her long red hair back over one shoulder. "Tell him to call me. Tell him I'll listen to what he has to say."

Sarah smiled. "I'll tell him the first chance I get."

Nan reached over and hugged her. "Thanks, Sarah. You're a good friend."

And for the first time Sarah realized that Nan was also a dear friend. The number of them had been growing since her arrival in Wind Canyon, something she hadn't really expected when she had decided to move back.

"I'll talk to you later," Sarah said with a smile as she started walking toward the parking lot.

Her smile slowly faded. She hoped Nan wouldn't rush into a relationship with Jimmy. He had hurt her once. There was no telling what kind of man he really was. He said he had never abused a woman, but verbal abuse could be just as hurtful. Still...

Sarah shook her head as she climbed into her blue truck. It wasn't fair to assume every man was like Andrew. Surely she should know that by now.

But deep down inside she knew that for her, trusting a man completely would never be an easy thing to do.

Chapter 18

Cheyenne, the state capital, was an interesting small Wyoming city. Interesting because, like Wind Canyon, the town was so completely and utterly Western. It's 1860s beginnings were apparent in the old brick buildings, the charming Victorian houses, the Wild West statues of buffalo and gunfighters that were scattered all over town—and the people themselves, men and women comfortable in worn jeans, cowboy hats and boots.

Summer visitors roamed the streets along with locals, and more would be arriving for the annual Cheyenne Frontier Days Rodeo next month. Sarah had never been to the event and she vowed to bring Holly sometime—after she got her life back in order.

Gabe's plane had landed safely. Sarah gazed out the windows of the white Buick sedan Jackson had rented at the airport and now drove toward the domed capitol building where the meeting was scheduled. As a kid, she had visited Cheyenne a couple of times with her parents, but she barely remembered.

Now that she was older, the Western atmosphere captivated her completely. It would be fun to visit the museums or check out the old steam trains that once ran on the Transcontinental Railway tracks heading through town.

Not today.

Today all she wanted to do was to finish her meeting with the FBI and get the hell out of Dodge—or in this case, Cheyenne.

Jackson walked next to Sarah along the corridor leading to the small conference room down the hall in the capitol building, an historic brick structure completed in the early 1890s.

His brothers weren't coming to the meeting. Whatever means Dev had used to gain access to Vernon Rimmer's offshore accounts was undoubtedly illegal. Dev didn't want his name connected to the case in any way. Gabe just didn't like Feds.

Jackson spotted Thomas Carson, his attorney, a tall, imposing man with dark brown hair streaked with silver though he wasn't much past forty. Jackson had filled him in on the particulars of the situation during a lengthy phone call yesterday, and earlier this morning, he and Sarah had gone to Carson's office for a discussion of the case. Jackson had no doubt Carson would be prepared.

Sarah stopped when they reached him. In the brief time she and the lawyer had spent together, she seemed to have come to trust him. "Thank you for being here, Mr. Carson."

Carson gave her a reassuring smile. "I thought we agreed you'd call me Thomas." Sarah returned his smile. "You look like you're holding up. If we're lucky, this won't take too long."

She seemed to relax a little.

"I just have a couple more questions before we go in," the attorney said.

Sarah nodded. "All right."

Thomas asked her to confirm a few more bits and pieces of information. Sarah asked him a couple of questions, then Jackson asked a few. Satisfied that they were all on the same page, Carson tipped his head toward the door.

"I think we're ready." He turned to Sarah. "Once we're inside, let me do as much of the talking as possible. Don't volunteer any information. Answer only what's asked, and look to me for a nod before you do even that."

"Okay," Sarah agreed.

"Ready?" Jackson asked her.

She took a deep breath. "I guess."

She was nervous. That much was clear, and yet when she walked into the room and caught sight of special agents Brooker and Davis seated next to an FBI-higher-up—the guy with the power to make the deal—Jackson caught only the subtle squaring of her shoulders.

The men rose as she approached. "Mrs. Hollister, thank you for coming. I believe you know special agents Brooker and Davis. My name is Richard Kemp."

Six feet tall, medium build, dark blond hair, power tie and a decent navy-blue, pin-striped suit.

Sarah gazed at him steadily. She was wearing a simple white cotton suit with white embroidery on the lapels, not too expensive but classy, the perfect choice for an occasion like this.

"Legally, my name is Sarah Allen. This is Jackson Raines and my attorney, Thomas Carson."

Carson was no longer the big-time Chicago lawyer he had once been, but he still had a big reputation. Business was his specialty, which meant he had worked with a number of clients in tax-related matters. And this wasn't the first time criminal charges were involved.

All of them sat down around a long mahogany table. Carson slid a manila file across the table and Richard Kemp opened it. He took his time, carefully examining the contents, then looked over at Sarah's attorney.

"According to this letter, your client wishes to trade the name of the man she believes her late husband was blackmailing, along with information about his criminal activities and proof that will lead to the man's arrest. In exchange, she wants complete exoneration from any charges resulting from the ongoing investigation of Andrew Hollister's tax records."

"As well as any other illegal matters in which he might have been involved," Carson added. "She was, after all, an unknowing participant in her husband's affairs."

Kemp flicked Sarah a glance. "We would have to know the name of the person or persons involved, the nature of the criminal activity and what you're offering as proof before we could agree. In other words we need to determine the value of what we are buying before we can make any sort of a deal."

Carson's look fixed on Kemp. "But assuming you're satisfied with what we've brought to the table—information your agents strongly indicated you needed—the government will agree."

"As I said, we'll need to hear what you have, but if the information is all you claim—and your client only culpable as an unknowing spouse, we'll accept your terms."

Jackson looked at Sarah. He could read the anxiety—and her hope that all of this would come to an end. Jackson wanted that same outcome. He cared about Sarah Allen. He wanted to explore a relationship with her and her daughter, see if there might be a future for them.

It was an idea that had started that day in the meadow. Watching her, seeing the joy on her face as she absorbed the beauty of the mountains, the way she seemed to respond to the land and to him had stirred something deep inside him. There was something about Sarah that drew him as no woman ever had, and since that day the feeling had been growing. He wanted to see where it led.

Still, there were obstacles to overcome. Three of them sat at the table across from her.

For the next half hour, Sarah sat rigidly at the table listening to Thomas Carson discuss Martin Kozak's illegal activities. Carson told the FBI about the bribes a state inspector had been taking to ignore Kozak's shoddy construction practices and offered to give them the inspector's name and the account numbers that contained the bribery money he had received.

"Let me get this straight," Richard Kemp said. "Your client has somehow been able to obtain the numbers of the offshore accounts that contain the money this inspector was being paid?"

"That is correct."

"I presume this information was contained on the flash drive Andrew Hollister was using in his blackmail attempt."

"Ms. Allen knows nothing about the alleged flash drive and never has."

Kemp leaned over and said something to the blond agent, Brooker. He looked back at Carson. "If that's the case, we'll need to know how she obtained the information."

"I'm afraid that isn't possible," Carson said.

Kemp turned to Sarah. "Mrs. Hollister?"

She refused to reply to the name.

"Excuse me, I meant, Ms. Allen."

"I won't divulge my sources. That was never required when your agents came to see me demanding information."

"As I said, in order to agree to your terms, we'll need—"

"We'll give you the inspector," Jackson interrupted, "and his account information. You pressure him enough and he's going to roll over on Kozak. And you can simply follow the money. In the course of your investigation, there is every chance you'll run across other illegal activities Kozak is involved in. You'll have more than enough to prosecute."

"My client won't even need to testify," Carson added, "which means you won't need to worry about offering her protection."

The men glanced back and forth, mentally going through their options. Even their years of training couldn't mask their excitement. It was clear they were interested in Marty Kozak, maybe had already suspected his criminal activities.

"So do we have a deal?" Carson quietly demanded.

The men spoke briefly one last time.

"We have a deal," Kemp said.

"Good," said Carson with the faintest of smiles. "In reliance upon your promise here and in exchange for the information I am about to hand over, I'll expect a memo to that effect sent to my office this afternoon."

Kemp gave a curt nod and Sarah breathed a sigh of relief. Martin Kozak would be dealt with. She would be free to get on with her life. She watched as Thomas Carson slid across the table a sheet of paper with Vernon Rimmer's name on it, along with a list of his bank account numbers in the Cayman Offshore Corporation. The knowledge of Rimmer's participation and the threat of a long jail term, Jackson had told her, would be enough to gain his cooperation and probably the return of the money.

Everyone stood up from the table.

"Thank you for your assistance, Mrs.…Ms. Allen."

Sarah didn't bother to smile. "Good afternoon, gentlemen." Turning, she walked out of the conference room. She had nothing more to say to the FBI.

And she hoped to God they never had anything more to say to her.

* * *

"I think we should celebrate." Jackson reached out and caught hold of Sarah's hand, gave it a gentle squeeze. "I told my brothers I'd call as soon as we had a decision." He pulled his cell phone out of the inside pocket of his navy blue sport coat. "I know a great little restaurant we can all go to for lunch." He grinned. "I'm buying."

"I wish I could join you," Carson said, "but I had to rearrange my schedule to make time for this morning's meetings. I promise I'll make it the next time you're in town—and I'll be the one to buy."

Sarah looked up at the attorney and smiled. "Thank you, Thomas. You can't know how much this means."

"You understand, this isn't completely over—not yet. It'll take a while for the government to move on this."

"Not too long, I don't think," Jackson said. "They won't want anything to happen to their case."

"I'd say a couple of weeks. But until they have Kozak in custody and he realizes the FBI already knows about his illegal activities, you'll need to be careful, Sarah."

"I will. And thank you again." She took Carson's hand, leaned over and kissed his cheek.

Ignoring a twinge of jealousy at the smile Carson gave her, Jackson settled an arm around her waist and led her toward the white Buick parked in the lot. He dialed his brothers.

"We made the deal. We're out of the woods—mostly. I'm buying lunch at Buffalo Bill's."

"Great news!" said Dev. "We'll be there."

Jackson closed the cell and slid it into his coat

pocket. "Everything's going to be okay," he said as he walked Sarah to the car.

She looked up at him. "That's what I keep telling myself."

But there was something in her face that said she wasn't completely convinced.

Two weeks passed. Sarah had seen no sign of Kozak or his thugs. She had received a single phone call from Richard Kemp, telling her an arrest had been made. That same day, Jackson got a call from his brother in Scottsdale. According to people in his L.A. office, Kozak's arrest had made the front page of the *Times*.

"Dev says it's all over the news out there." Jackson stood in the living room of the cottage, making the room feel smaller than it actually was. He had arrived with the news just moments ago. "I don't think you'll be hearing from your old buddy Kozak again." He smiled. "He's too busy trying to stay out of jail."

Sarah felt a sweep of relief so strong her legs went a little weak. Kozak had been dealt with. At last her life was her own.

Hearing a noise outside, Jackson walked over to the window to see the delivery truck pull up with the furniture Sarah had chosen to replace the pieces Kozak's goons had destroyed—a comfortable overstuffed sofa and chair in a dark green color, along with accent throw pillows.

"Looks like your furniture is finally here."

Excitement filled her. The cottage already felt like home, but it would be nice to have something she had picked out herself. Jackson helped the men carry the furniture inside, but she knew he wouldn't stay long.

She told herself she was glad he was giving her time to get her life back in order, that he hadn't pressed her to have sex with him.

She was glad, she told herself, but as she watched him helping the men carry the old furniture out and setting the new sofa and chair in place in front of the fireplace, she noticed the way his lean muscles bunched beneath his shirt and felt a soft tug low in her belly. An hour later, when she spotted him working in front of the barn, it was all she could do not to go to him, drag him into the straw in one of the stalls, unzip his jeans and do delicious things to his magnificent body.

At the end of the day, when she saw him ride off on his beautiful horse, she wanted to follow him into the woods and demand he make love to her as he had that day in the meadow.

It was ridiculous. Embarrassing, even. She was afraid to look at him, afraid he could read the lustful thoughts she was trying so hard to hide.

Jackson didn't bother hiding his. The hot looks he gave her, the deep rusty tone of his voice when he spoke to her, told her how much he wanted her in his bed.

At least she had fulfilled her promise to Nan and spoken to Jimmy Threebears, relaying Nan's message to him.

"She said you should call her, Jimmy. She says she'll listen to what you have to say."

He just nodded, his expression solemn. "Thank you," was all he said.

Then Gran called, wanting to know how Sarah would feel about letting Holly spend a few days with her in Sheep River.

"I'm not getting any younger, you know," Gran said. "And the two of us…well, we've never really had a chance to get to know each other."

Sarah adjusted the phone against her ear, the idea gaining momentum as it rolled around in her head. The threat from Kozak was past and she could certainly use a little time to herself. Raising a daughter was a full-time job. Except for the few hours she spent in town writing articles for the newspaper, she rarely had time alone.

And she could go to Jackson, accept his blatant if unspoken invitation. Sarah ignored a little tremor of heat and concentrated on her phone call.

"Are you sure you're feeling well enough, Gran? A child can be a heckuva lot of work."

"I'm not so old I don't remember what it's like to raise a child. And I feel just fine. So what do you say?"

Sarah smiled into the phone. "I know she'd love to come for a visit. I'll bring her over in the morning."

And she had been right. When she mentioned the idea to Holly, it was clear her daughter wanted very badly to go.

"Can I, Mom? Please?" Holly jumped up and down, her blond ponytail bobbing. "I never had a real grandma before."

"She's actually your great-grandmother—my mother's mother."

"Cool! I promise I won't be any trouble."

"I'm sure you'll be a good girl and do exactly what your gran tells you."

"I will, I promise."

They packed that night. Early the next morning as Holly finished dressing, Sarah summoned her courage and stepped out into the warm July morning. Jackson stood in front of the barn talking to Jimmy. The moment he saw her walking toward him, he turned and started her way. His worn jeans clung to those long sinewy legs and gently cupped the impressive bulge of his sex. The sleeves of his shirt were rolled up and she could see the powerful muscles in his forearms.

A little sliver of desire snaked through her, giving her the courage she needed to do what she had come for.

"Good morning," he said as he reached her, shoving his hat back on his head.

"Yes, it is." She smiled up at him. "It's beautiful." She flicked a glance toward the house. "I'm driving Holly over to my grandmother's place this morning. She's going to stay for a couple of days. I was wondering…hoping you might come over for dinner tonight. I mean… I owe you at least that much."

She couldn't miss the hunger that burned in those dark eyes. "I'd love to come. What time?"

"I know you start work early. How about six o'clock?"

"Perfect," he said, his eyes still on her face.

"All right, then." For a couple of seconds neither of them moved. Sarah felt a blush creeping into her cheeks, turned and started walking briskly back to the cottage. Already her heart was pounding and all he had done was agree to her supper invitation.

The man could make her body feel hot just by looking at her.

She should have been worried. And she would be—later. For the next few days, she was simply going to enjoy being a woman. An image of Andrew flashed into her head, but Sarah firmly pushed it away. Andrew was dead. Her life was her own now.

Chapter 19

After a drive through the glorious Wyoming countryside, Sarah left Holly at her grandmother's house.

"If you need anything," she said to the slightly bent, silver-haired woman, "just call me. You've got my numbers."

"Stop worrying," Gran said. "Holly and I will be just fine. Besides, you deserve a little time to yourself."

Which she truly believed, but of course, now that it was time to actually leave Holly behind, she worried.

Still, her decision was made, and she wanted to give the two people she loved most in the world this special time together.

On the way back to town, she stopped at the market to pick up the groceries she would need for tonight's supper, along with a bottle of Chianti to go with the Parmesan chicken she planned to serve. As she climbed back into the truck, a jolt of excitement went through her. She was seeing Jackson tonight! They would make love and it would be wonderful!

From the store, she drove to her office, which was empty with Mike out on a story and Myra taking her afternoon break.

Sitting behind her desk, Sarah grinned as she opened the word file on her computer and reread the humorous article she had been working on—the mostly true story of Homer the Rebellious Squirrel, the bane of the Wind Canyon Fire Department.

Homer had been stashing pinecones in the tailpipe of a big RV near his tree. When the owner started the engine, the cones caught on fire. The exhaust spit flaming pinecones into the dry grass and set small fires all over the area.

Fortunately, the fire trucks arrived in time to put out the burning grass and keep the fire from spreading. No harm was done and Homer escaped to the safety of his tree.

Sarah leaned back, smiling, pleased with the finished article. She printed it and put it on Smiley's desk, then glanced up at the sound of the bell ringing above the door. A man walked in and her chest squeezed so hard no air could get into her lungs. For a minute she thought she might faint. The only sound she could hear was the ringing in her ears.

She knew the man with the straight brown hair, bad complexion, and nose that spread out as if it might have been broken. Still, if it weren't for his hard-as-nails, I-hate-the-world attitude, Detective Ed Mercer might have been in a strange way attractive.

Today he was dressed in khaki pants and a yellow

Izod shirt. Usually he wore cheap suits and faux leather loafers. After Andrew's murder, Detective Mercer of the Los Angeles Police Department had given her nothing but trouble.

He sauntered past the counter wearing the same smug expression he had worn the last time she had seen him, walked over to her desk and propped his hip against the edge.

"Hello, Sarah."

Her mouth went paper dry. She swallowed, managed to make her voice work. "Detective Mercer. You're... you're a long way from home. What are you doing in Wind Canyon?"

She had never liked Mercer and suspected the feeling was mutual. During the murder investigation, one of the other detectives had told her Mercer was recently divorced and on a hate-all-women jag that seemed to have no end.

"I came here to talk to you. I think we have some unfinished business."

She glanced around, heard Myra on her way back from lunch coming in through the back door and quickly stood up from her desk. "We can talk in the conference room." Which was about the size of a large broom closet but was a place they wouldn't be overheard.

He followed her down the hall, walked in behind her and firmly closed the door.

Summoning every ounce of her composure, Sarah turned to face him. "What can I do for you, Detective?"

"I think you know why I'm here. I told you when you left L.A. you hadn't seen the last of me."

He'd said he wouldn't be done with her until the details of the case had been tied up. She had tried not to worry about what that meant.

"So you're here because of Andrew?"

"That's right."

"I thought the investigation was over."

"It won't be over until we find the person who murdered your husband."

"But I thought…" She swallowed, clamped down on an urge to run out of the room and just keep going. "Lieutenant Delaney said he was sure it was someone Andrew was in business with or someone he owed money."

She didn't mention Kozak. She didn't know how much the police knew about her husband's blackmail schemes, and she didn't want to be connected in any way to Martin Kozak's arrest.

"Come on, Sarah. We both know the truth. Why don't you make it easy on all of us and admit you were the one who shot him."

Her stomach contracted so sharply she thought she was going to be sick. No longer sure her legs would hold her up, she sat down in one of the chairs around the small Formica-topped table in the middle of the room.

"What…what are you talking about?" But Mercer had made a similar accusation before.

"The spouse is always the most likely suspect," he had said. *"In your case, Sarah, you had more motive than most."*

He might have officially accused her, but his boss, Lieutenant Tom Delaney, had been sure Mercer was looking in the wrong direction.

"Hollister had a dozen enemies. His shady business

dealings alone were enough to get him killed—to say nothing of the big boys he owed money to in Vegas. In Hollister's case, his wife would have had to stand in line to get a shot at him."

Mercer's voice drew her out of the past. "Let's take a look at the facts," he said as he pulled out a chair, spun it around and straddled it backward. "You were there the night he was murdered. You said that when you left he was still alive, that someone came in and shot him after you were gone, but who's to say you didn't shoot him and *then* leave?"

Sarah said nothing. Her insides were shaking. She had been so sure the police were satisfied the murder had nothing to do with her.

"Then there's your motive," he went on. "You found out Andrew had a girlfriend and was buying her expensive gifts. You knew he was seeing Mitzy Bender and you didn't like it."

She stared at him in amazement. "You think I was jealous of Andrew?"

He studied her face, saw the revulsion she didn't bother to hide. "So maybe the girl wasn't the reason. Maybe it was the money."

"What money? Andrew left me buried in debt."

"True enough. And that's what our investigation discovered. But since you left, I dug up a little tidbit we missed."

She frowned. "I told you—there wasn't any money."

"No, there wasn't. But at the time, you didn't know that. Hollister had a big fat life insurance policy—two million, to be exact—and you were the beneficiary. You didn't find out he hadn't paid the premiums until he was already dead. By then it was too late."

Beneath the table, her legs shook. "You're wrong."

"Am I?"

"If…if you really believed I was the one who killed him, why did you wait until now?"

"I always figured you were the one who did it. I tried to tell myself I was wrong, but the more I thought about it, the more it made sense. And the idea of you getting away with murder…well, that just doesn't set well with me."

Sarah said nothing.

"And then just the other day, I ran across this other little loose end…"

She swallowed, hoped her face wasn't as pale as it felt. "What…what loose end?"

"Your daughter's ballet class. It wasn't over till eight o'clock that night. I guess somehow that information got overlooked. You were there to pick her up when the class finished, just like you said. But where were you between six—when you said you left the house—and eight, when you picked her up?"

"Holly's ballet class is in Westwood. I had to drive there. I—I got stuck in traffic. I told the police that at the time."

"Yes, you did. So the fact is you don't really have an alibi for the time of the shooting, which the coroner figures was somewhere between six and eight."

If she could have made her voice work, she might have said something. As it was, she didn't dare.

"There's only one thing missing," he said.

She worked up a shot of courage. "What's that, Detective?"

"The gun. I still haven't figured out how you got

hold of a thirty-eight caliber revolver, or how you got rid of it."

"I don't own a gun. I never have."

"But you know how to shoot one, don't you, Sarah? A Wyoming girl? Raised out here in the Wild, Wild West?"

Sarah made no reply. She knew how to shoot. Her dad had taught her. They'd had fun target practicing and she had become a very good shot.

Mercer got up from his chair. "Don't worry, though. In time, I'll figure it out. Once I do, you can bet you'll be seeing me again."

Sarah felt sick to her stomach. "I didn't shoot my husband."

Mercer just smiled. "I guess we'll just have to wait and see." He turned and started for the door. "In the meantime, I'm here on vacation. I've never been to Yellowstone Park. Think I'll drive on up and take a look."

Sarah didn't stand up as Mercer opened the door and stepped out into the hallway. Her legs were shaking too badly. She wasn't sure how long she stayed in the room, but she didn't make an effort to move out of her chair until Mike Stevens knocked, then opened the door.

"Sarah. I thought you'd gone home."

She summoned a little fortitude and forced herself to her feet. "I was just on my way out."

"Are you all right? You look a little pale."

She managed a shaky nod. "I'm fine." Moving past him out the door, she made her way along the hallway to her desk, picked up her purse and started to leave.

"Will you be in tomorrow?" Mike asked.

She nodded. "I—I think so. I'll see you then." Hurriedly she pulled open the door. All she could think of was reaching the safety of her home, the safety of Raintree Ranch.

She stepped out onto the boardwalk and a wave of nausea hit her. She wasn't safe at the ranch. She wasn't safe anywhere.

From the moment a bullet had pierced Andrew's heart, she had never been truly safe.

Jackson knocked on the door to Sarah's cottage at exactly 6:00 p.m. As he stood there waiting, a bottle of good red Napa Valley wine in his hand, he rubbed the toes of his boots on the back of each leg to bring up the shine and straightened the collar of his white Western shirt.

He was really looking forward to the evening, looking forward to a supper Sarah cooked especially for him, looking forward to making love to her for most of the night.

His mouth edged up. He wasn't a fool. Sarah might keep him at arm's length but she wanted him. He could see it in those clear blue eyes whenever she looked at him.

And, by damn, he wanted her.

The door swung open and Sarah's eyes widened. "Jackson! Oh, my God, is it six o'clock already? I sat down for a couple of minutes. I guess I must have fallen asleep. I—I meant to call you. Something's come up and—"

He walked into the house, over to the round oak dining table, and set down the bottle of wine. He turned to face her. "What's going on, Sarah?"

She swallowed, glanced away. "Nothing. I just… I fell asleep and I didn't get supper ready, that's all."

"Fine. I'll do the cooking." He turned and started into the kitchen. Sarah caught up with him and grabbed hold of his arm. She looked as though she wanted to say something but didn't quite know how.

"You...you can cook?"

"I didn't always have a housekeeper. In Houston, I had to take care of myself. And I like good food."

He opened the refrigerator door and looked inside, spotted the package of chicken breasts she had apparently meant to cook, took it out and set it on the counter.

"I just... I guess I'm not used to Holly being gone. It would be better if we made supper another night."

He opened the package. "I'm hungry. You promised to feed me. Since I sent Livvy home early and we both have to eat, we might as well eat together." He prepped the chicken then started digging around, pulling out pots and pans. He knew the little kitchen, since he had furnished the place himself.

"You're staying—is that it?"

He looked at her. "Yup."

"You're not leaving me any choice?"

"Nope."

She blew out a breath and some of the tension in her shoulders seemed to ease. "Well, okay, then." Stepping up beside him, she opened the fridge and took out a head of lettuce, along with tomatoes and the rest of the fixings for a salad. "I thought Parmesan chicken breasts and a salad with balsamic vinaigrette and blue cheese crumbles."

He smiled. "Perfect." The lady was definitely gun-shy. After her no-good husband, she still had a deep distrust of men, and yet he sensed a need in her. He thought that secretly she was glad he was staying.

Not nearly as glad as he was.

Sarah held up a bottle of Chianti. "I bought this at the market. Shall I open it?"

"I brought a bottle, too. I guess we won't run out."

Sarah retrieved the bottle he had brought and set it on the counter, then opened the Chianti and poured each of them a glass. They made supper together, working jointly at the task surprisingly well. He talked about his trip up to the top of the mountain that morning to check on the loggers, and she told him about the article she had written about the squirrel. Both of them laughed at that.

Jackson ignored the little cloud that seemed to settle over her when she finished. Something was wrong but he wasn't about to press her. At least not yet.

The aroma of tomato sauce, oregano, garlic and vinegar filled the kitchen. Sarah tossed the salad and set the table, and they filled their plates and carried them into the dining area at the end of the living room.

"The place is really shaping up," he said, glancing around as he took a sip of wine. "You've got a knack for decorating, Sarah."

She smiled, seemed pleased. She pointed toward the old steamer trunk she had placed beneath the window. "I found it up in the attic. It's wonderful, isn't it? I didn't think you'd mind."

"I like to see things put to use."

She sipped her wine. "I bought that oak bookshelf down at Potter's Antiques. I gave most of my books to the library before I left L.A., but I love to read so it won't take long to fill up."

Jackson watched her, noticed that she looked a little less pale than she had when she'd first pulled open the door. They finished the meal and ate spumoni ice cream for dessert. By the time they had cleared the table, Sarah seemed completely relaxed.

"I'm glad you stayed," she said as they stood at the kitchen counter.

"So am I." He leaned toward her. He only meant to kiss her cheek, but she looked so good standing there with her dark hair loose and tomato sauce on her blouse, he couldn't resist. It was only supposed to be a thank-you-for-supper kiss, but weeks had passed and the minute his mouth touched hers, sparks seemed to leap between them.

"Jackson…" Sarah leaned into him and her arms went around his neck. Jackson pulled her hard against him, deepened the kiss, slid his tongue inside her mouth.

She tasted so damned good, a little like the ice cream they had been eating. He wanted to eat her up that same way. He shoved his hands into her dark hair, pulled her mouth up to his for another burning kiss.

Sarah kissed him back, pressing her full breasts into his chest, making his erection stiffen and throb against the fly of his jeans.

"God, Sarah, do you have any idea how much I want this?" He pressed himself against her, let her feel how hard he was, heard her moan. Jackson kissed her long and deep, felt her fingers move down to cup his sex, caress him through the heavy denim fabric.

"Jesus, lady…" He backed her up until her shoulders hit the door leading into the bedroom, unbuttoned the front of her blouse and filled his hands with her breasts.

They were full and heavy, her skin soft as silk, but her nipples were stone-hard, and so was he.

He had meant to suggest a walk down by the river. He could barely walk now and he was getting harder by the minute. He cupped her face and kissed her again, long, wet and slow. Sarah squirmed against him, reached back and turned the knob on the bedroom door.

They stumbled into the room. Jackson caught her up in his arms and carried her over to the bed. He stripped away her blouse and bra, dragged off her sneakers, jeans and skimpy thong panties, then stood there for a moment admiring her. Her sweet woman's body called to him, the soft curves and lovely breasts, the thatch of dark curls that marked her sex. Her light perfume mingled with the scent of her arousal, and his mouth watered. He wanted to taste her, pleasure her the way he had the first time they made love.

He shed his boots and the rest of his clothes and joined her on the bed, came up over her and kissed her long and deep, kissed her until he had her squirming beneath him. He suckled those luscious breasts, grazed the tips with his teeth, took the fullness into his mouth.

She was ready and so was he, and yet he waited, moved between her legs and lifted her knees up onto his shoulders.

Sarah squirmed. "Jackson, please... I—I want to feel you inside me."

"Soon, darlin'." And then he set to work, using his hands and his mouth, tasting her, stroking her, making her come two times before he sheathed himself and entered her.

Her eyes slowly opened and catlike, she smiled. He could read the renewed desire in the way her head fell back as he began to move, her hips arching upward, taking him deeper, making him groan. She was one helluva woman—but then he'd figured that out sometime back.

Her body quivered. Her sex pulsed around him, sending a fierce shot of pleasure roaring through him. He tried to hold on, give her as much as he could, but when she cried his name and her body convulsed around him, it drove him over the edge.

His muscles strained and tightened, jerked with the deep, intense pleasure of a mind-blowing climax. *Sweet God Almighty.*

Sarah clung to his neck and he rested his head against her shoulder as the heat spiraled down and the world slowly spun back to normal. Jackson kissed her one last time and settled himself beside her on the bed.

You're mine, he thought. *Even if you still don't know it.*

Chapter 20

Sarah slept deeply. The house was quiet, just the night sounds outside the window, the crickets and the coyotes. Jackson lay beside her. Some part of her knew he was there, felt the joy of it, the rightness. And yet, even in sleep, she knew it could not last.

As she slept, her mind shifted, slipped back in time. She saw Ed Mercer standing in front of her desk at the office.

Why don't you make it easy on all of us and admit you were the one who shot him. We both know you did it.

She tossed and turned on the mattress, her legs tangling in the sheets. Perspiration soaked the dark hair at her temples. Her thoughts shifted.

Suddenly, she was back in the house on Sunset, standing in the doorway leading into Andrew's study.

She'd been upstairs packing the last of her things to take to the condo in Santa Monica when he had arrived. He had called out to her, demanded she come downstairs.

"Sarah! Get down here! I want to talk to you!"

She could hear the anger in his voice, the fury.

He wasn't drunk. He didn't have to be.

As she stood in the open study doorway, she saw him rise from behind his desk.

"What...what is it you want, Andrew?"

"Do you think I'm a fool, Sarah?"

He was a no-good, rotten bastard, a true sonofabitch, but he was no fool. "Why would I think that?"

"Maybe because you didn't think I'd read your email, find out what you were planning to do."

He was bluffing. She had been extremely careful, deleted everything, all her messages to Patty Gorski and the other women in the support group. And she had always chosen her words with special care, sent nothing in a message that would give her away.

"I don't know what you're talking about."

He just smiled. It was the kind of smile she hated. The kind that made her stomach knot with fear, the kind that made her want to throw up.

"I told you we were going to Rio. The three of us. Did you actually think you were going to take Holly and run away?" His smile grew feral and the knot in her stomach tightened. "I went directly to the server. I saw what you wrote to those women."

She swallowed past the lump blocking her throat. "It was just conversation." She had never been specific, only hinted to Patty. But Patty had understood.

"I think it was more."

She straightened, determined not to let him know how terrified she was. "Holly and I aren't going with you, Andrew. You can leave if you want, but we're staying here."

His mouth thinned to a slash across his face. "You really believe you can defy me? You don't remember what happened the last time you tried?"

She remembered. He had beaten her so badly she'd ended up in the hospital. She'd had three broken ribs and thirty stitches in her arm. She hadn't reported him to the police, had, in fact, told the doctors he'd never touched her. She was afraid he'd take Holly and leave and she would never see her daughter again.

He stepped away from his chair, rounded the corner of his desk. Fury etched lines into his face. Anticipation glittered in his eyes. He liked this, liked to hurt her.

"Andrew, please don't do this." She forced herself not to back away, to hold her ground and face him. It was now or never. "Stay away from me, Andrew. Don't!"

She was shouting his name and crying when a big hand wrapped tightly around her shoulder and shook her awake.

"Easy, Sarah," a deep voice said, his hold turning gentle. "It's all right, darlin'. You're only dreaming. Everything's okay."

She opened her eyes to see Jackson leaning over her, his face filled with concern. Sarah burst into tears.

Jackson eased her into his arms and held on tight. "I'm right here, honey. I've got you. No one's going to hurt you. You're safe with me."

There was a gruffness in his voice that told her how upset he was, how worried. Sarah clung to him, fighting the memories, trying to shove them back into the past, as it had taken her months to learn to do.

She hadn't had the nightmare since her arrival in Wyoming. Not until Detective Ed Mercer had shown up in her office.

He wanted to arrest her, put her in prison. He believed she was guilty of murder and he was determined to prove it. She was afraid to tell Jackson. She couldn't involve him in more of her troubles and even if she were selfish enough to do it, there was nothing Jackson could do.

Nothing anyone could do.

"Are you all right?" he asked, pressing his lips against the top of her head.

She nodded, dragged back her perspiration-damp hair. "I'm all right."

"You were dreaming about Andrew."

She swallowed. She remembered. She'd had the dream a dozen times. "It was the night he was killed. The last time I saw him."

"You want to tell me about it?"

It was the last thing she wanted. "I'd rather not talk about it."

Jackson didn't press her. "All right." Lying back down on the bed, he eased her down beside him, nestled her in the circle of his arms. "Think you can go back to sleep?"

Tears burned her eyes. She wouldn't sleep anymore tonight. After the dream, she never did. Not unless... She turned to Jackson, ran her fingers along his hard jaw, felt the stubble of his night's growth of beard.

"Make love to me, Jackson."

He studied her face, saw the need there. He came up over her, cupped her face in his hands and kissed her. She could feel him go hard, grow thick and pulsing against her. His kiss was enough to arouse her, the feel of his muscular body pressing her down in the mattress. He started gently, but she didn't want gentle. She wanted hard and fast, she wanted to climax and she wanted to forget.

Jackson seemed to understand. He pulled her beneath him and filled her, surged into her in a single deep thrust. Long, heavy strokes shook her. Deep, penetrating strokes made her come, then come again.

Jackson gentled his movements, kissed her softly and took her with such tenderness her eyes filled with tears.

"Jackson…" she whispered, wishing he had been the man she had married, the man who was Holly's father, the man she would share her life with.

It wasn't going to happen.

Andrew had seen to that.

For the next few days, Jackson spent his nights with Sarah at the cottage. He had pushed her to let him stay and Sarah was glad. She didn't dream while he was there. They made love and she slept and they made love again and it was heaven.

Then it was time to pick Holly up at Gran's, time for her brief respite to end.

"It doesn't have to be over," Jackson said as they lay in bed that night. "I can come to you after Holly goes to sleep and leave before she wakes up."

It was tempting. So incredibly tempting. But the

risk was too great. Mercer was still on the prowl and sooner or later Jackson was bound to find out.

What would he think when the detective accused her of murder? What man would want a woman the police accused of killing her husband?

And there was the not-so-small matter of her heart. She was falling for Jackson Raines. She couldn't afford to let that happen. She trusted him more than any man she had ever known. Trusted him the way she had trusted her father. It wasn't enough.

Too much had happened. Too many years of abuse and misery. She couldn't take that kind of risk again.

Instead, tomorrow morning she would pick Holly up at Gran's and return to work. She had decided to let her daughter go back to the Busy Bee Day-Care Center so the little girl could play with her friends and make new ones. She prayed Ed Mercer would not return, that he would go back to L.A. and give up his search.

Surely he would, sooner or later.

Or he would convince the police he had enough evidence to charge her with Andrew's murder.

Sarah shivered.

Late in the afternoon of the next day, while Holly was outside playing with Rags and the boys, Sarah sat at the laptop computer in her bedroom. As soon as the machine geared up, she clicked on her email, watched it download, then deleted the junk mail that escaped her spam filter. There were a couple of actual messages, one of them from Patty.

Sarah smiled. Patty could be funny, and she was today, telling a story about her recent tooth surgery. According to Patty, the surgery had left a gaping hole that was meant to be filled by a porcelain tooth. While she was waiting for the false tooth to be finished, she had a minor accident, slipped and fell in her basement and hit her head on a wooden sign she was making for the shelter. Her eye turned black and blue. That, along with the missing tooth, had the women at the shelter certain that some man had beat her. They were all up in arms over it.

Sarah grinned as she read the email. She always loved hearing from Patty. She kept her reply light, but Patty was hard to fool, and apparently she was sitting at her computer when she got Sarah's email.

The reply came back:

What's the matter, kiddo? You can tell your big sister.

Why not? She knew she could trust Patty Gorski. Sarah typed in, Okay—here it is. Detective Mercer came to Wind Canyon. He is sure I killed Andrew and he is trying to prove it. He says he won't give up until he does.

Patty wrote back, Tell him to bugger off. He doesn't have anything or he would have arrested you a long time ago.

Sarah felt the pull of a smile. Patty was different from any woman she had ever met. She was intelligent. She was street-smart and she was courageous. And she had been there for Sarah when no one else gave a damn what happened to her and Holly.

Thanks, Patty. Take care of those teeth! Love you, Sarah and Holly.

She blew out a shaky breath, feeling better after talking to her friend. Whatever happened, she knew she could count on Patty.

She thought of Jackson, how protective he was, the way he had held her after her nightmare. She trusted him. She cared for him.

And she was afraid.

The Fourth of July arrived. In a small town like Wind Canyon, Independence Day was a really big deal. Sarah covered the fireworks display and picnic, which she attended with Jackson, Holly and Livvy. Jimmy invited Nan to join him and his boys, and all of them sat together to watch the colorful fireworks show.

Sarah knew Nan and Jimmy were seeing each other. She just hoped her friend took the time to really get to know the man before jumping into a relationship.

It was late by the time the fireworks were over, all the hot dogs and sodas consumed, and the folding chairs and blankets packed up for the trip back home. Jackson dropped Livvy off at her house just down the road from the ranch, then drove his big white Ford along the lane and parked in front of the cottage. Sound asleep in the backseat, Holly awakened as he began unloading the leftover picnic items they had taken with them to the park.

All of them climbed out of the truck and Jackson reached into the backseat for a bag of leftovers.

"I was wondering…" he said as he handed her the bag and reached for another. "I thought maybe this weekend we might all ride up in the hills and spend the night. I think Holly would really enjoy it."

Any residual sleepiness Holly was feeling instantly

faded. "Can we, Mom? Can we? Can I ride in front of you, Jackson, can I?"

He looked over at Sarah. "So what do you say?"

She should have been angry that he hadn't asked her first, considering there was no way now she could possibly say no, but instead she just thought how nice it was that he was willing to take all of them up into the beautiful mountains.

"I don't see why not," she said, and he smiled so wide her heart squeezed hard inside her.

Holly squealed and flung herself into Jackson's arms. He lifted her up on his back, locking her legs around his waist, piggyback style. "We'll ride up Saturday morning, make camp and spend the night. Maybe do some fishing up at the lake."

"Fishing! I get to go fishing!"

Sarah couldn't help laughing. "All right, you two, that's enough." Jackson set the little girl back on her feet. "Holly, it's time to go in. It's way past your bedtime."

As Sarah said the word *bed,* she made the mistake of looking at Jackson, saw his eyes go hot. Her breath caught. Just a hint of invitation and he would come in through the back door and join her in bed. Her body went liquid and warm. She wanted that so much.

Too much.

She turned to Holly, took her hand and led her up on the porch. "Good night, Jackson. Thanks for taking us tonight. It was really fun."

He just nodded, pulled his hat brim down over his eyes. "I'll see you tomorrow."

But tomorrow she would be working in town and it

would be a long day. She had her story to write on the fireworks display and some shopping to do.

Ignoring a hollow feeling of regret, she opened the door and led her daughter into the house.

Jackson tossed a couple of small logs into the old iron stove in his study. Leaving the door open so he could watch the flames, he sat down on the comfortable leather sofa. All evening, his mind had been on Sarah. From the moment he had first seen her that night in the snowstorm, he'd had a feeling his life was going to change.

He sat there now, contemplating that change and his growing feelings for Sarah. And what, exactly, he should do about them. He was deep in thought when the phone rang. Jackson came up off the sofa, walked over to his desk and picked it up.

"Hey, bro…" Dev's voice came over the line. "You got a minute? I'm not interrupting anything, am I?"

"I wish…" grumbled Jackson. "What's up?"

"To tell you the truth, I'm not sure. After I put the word out to my bloodhounds for information on Hollister, I never bothered to call them off. I figured, what the hell? You never know what might turn up."

"I take it something did."

"Maybe. I'm not sure. One of my people sent word… he says Andrew Hollister was getting big cash payments from a company called Ace Trucking. It's owned by a guy named Vincent Spalino."

"You think he was blackmailing Spalino?"

"I can't say for sure, but I don't think that was it. The payments had been coming in for years. Looks more like some kind of business arrangement, something they kept off the books."

"You know anything about the company?"

"Not much. I know their connection to Hollister was through Southgate Demolition, one of Hollister's companies. Apparently Ace Trucking did a lot of work for them."

"Could be kickbacks to Hollister through Southgate for getting them the work."

"Could be. I was just thinking that if Hollister was planning a trip to Rio, maybe he was stashing some of the cash he got from Spalino to set himself up when he got there."

"He'd need cash, all right. I figured that was why he made the flash drive—to get as much money as he could before he left the country."

"Or maybe that's one of the reasons Kozak was pressing Sarah so hard. Maybe he knew about the money. Maybe he was hoping the flash drive would help him find it."

"Anything's possible, I guess."

"I just thought you might want to know."

"Thanks, Dev. I appreciate it. If anything else turns up, give me a call."

"You got it."

Jackson hung up the phone. Hopefully, Sarah was out of danger, but it didn't hurt to stay informed.

He sat back down on the sofa, wondering if he should tell her about the phone call, then decided against it. She had been through enough. Hopefully, it wouldn't matter.

The fire crackled and popped against the sides of the old iron stove. Knowing warm summer nights were at hand, he enjoyed these final chilly evenings with the heat soaking into his bones.

Jackson sighed, his thoughts returning to Sarah, wishing he would be spending the night in her bed, instead of sleeping alone.

Chapter 21

July in Wyoming was breathtaking; dark green pines soaring up the hillsides; the deciduous trees fully leafed out; the sky a clear, crystalline blue. A pair of eagles nested at the top of the ridge, occasionally sailing out over the mountains in search of food. Though last night had been cool, the weatherman predicted a rise in the temperature. Summer was on its way.

Sarah sat at her desk, her workday nearly over. Once she had finished her grocery shopping, she could pick up Holly and enjoy the beautiful scenery on the ride back to the ranch.

She finished her article on the Fourth of July fireworks, mentioning what a good job the Wind Canyon Fire Department had done, what a fantastic show it was and how the city's firemen had kept everyone safe.

There had only been one incident. A little after midnight, a teenage boy had accidentally set off a string of firecrackers that set the dry grass in the field behind his house on fire. The fire trucks had arrived in time to bring the flames under control and keep it from spreading into the nearby forest.

Sarah reread the article and printed it, then packed up her briefcase, said goodbye to Myra and Mike and left the office. She smiled as she made her way along the boardwalk, enjoying the lovely weather and the cloudless blue sky. At the corner, she stepped off the wooden walk into the street and an odd sense of unease struck her. The hairs on the back of her neck stood up, warning her something was wrong.

"Just keep walking," said the dark-skinned, foreign-looking man who had accosted her before.

Sarah jolted to a halt, but he grabbed her arm and dragged her forward, around the corner into the parking lot. He slammed her up against the building, the way he had before.

"You were a very naughty girl, Sarah." He was dressed in expensive tan slacks, a short-sleeved blue oxford shirt and a pair of Italian loafers that had to run at least six hundred bucks.

"I don't... I don't know what you're talking about." Her legs were shaking, her heart hammering away. She told herself she wasn't in any real danger. He wasn't going to do anything to her in a public parking lot.

"We know you went to the Feds. We know you had something to do with Martin Kozak's arrest."

"You're crazy."

"You met with them in Cheyenne."

The bottom dropped out of her stomach. It was clear

the man had been watching her or knew someone in the FBI. "Are you one of Kozak's men?"

"This has nothing to do with Kozak."

That was some consolation, she guessed, though she had never figured Marty as the type for revenge. He was a businessman first, last and always. Money was his god—which was the reason he and Andrew had gotten along so famously.

She straightened, forced some courage into her spine. "I didn't go to the Feds. They came to me. They were investigating Andrew's tax records. They threatened to charge me with tax evasion if I didn't help them."

"Did you give them the flash drive? Make a deal to exchange it for dropping the charges?"

"I don't know anything about any flash drive. I told you that before."

His eyes drilled into her, black and fathomless. A chill swept down her spine. "Come on. We're going for a little ride."

He jerked her forward toward a row of cars across the lot, but she dug in her heels and tried to twist away from him. "I'll scream," she warned, then felt the heavy metal barrel of his pistol shoved into her ribs.

"Keep walking."

"What do you want?"

"We want you to understand what will happen to you if you open your mouth about your husband's business dealings again."

She moved a couple of feet toward the car, a nondescript white Ford sedan, probably a rental, her eyes darting right and left as she searched for an avenue of escape. She wasn't getting into a car with him. If he was going to shoot her, he'd have to do it right there in the parking lot.

Then she spotted Jackson. He was across the street, walking toward her office, more than a block away. Why his gaze happened to swing toward her she would never know, but the moment he spotted the foreign-looking man walking beside her, he started running.

The man spotted Jackson, as well. "Keep your mouth shut, Sarah. Think of your daughter." Hurrying off toward his car, he got in and started the engine.

She was shaking by the time Jackson reached her, and the sedan was merging into the traffic in the street, then disappearing around a corner.

"Did you get the plate number?" Jackson asked, not breathing nearly as hard as she would have been if she had run that far.

She swallowed and nodded. "Wyoming plates—23 619 N O."

"Twenty-three is the number for Sublette County. That's right here."

"I-it looked like a rental car, basic, no frills. It didn't seem to match the expensive clothes he was wearing."

Jackson glanced around, lifted his cowboy hat and repositioned it. "He's long gone by now. My truck is four blocks away or I'd take a run at finding him." He pulled her into his arms. "You okay?"

Sarah hung on to him, her tremors subsiding, thinking how good he felt and how glad she was he had come along when he did. "I'm okay."

"Tell me what happened."

Reluctantly, she moved away from him, regretting the loss of his warmth. She explained the encounter, telling him about the gun and repeating the subtle threats.

"He knew we'd met with the FBI in Cheyenne. He said he wanted me to understand what would happen if I talked about my husband's business dealings again."

Jackson rubbed his jaw. "Either someone's been keeping tabs on you or he's got an in with the FBI."

"That's what I figured." She looked up at him, felt a sudden jolt of fear. "Oh, my God—Holly!"

His glance shot down the street. He jerked out his cell phone and handed it over. "Call them. You know the number. Make sure she's okay and tell them to keep her inside until we get there."

She dialed the number with an unsteady hand.

"The day-care people won't let her leave with anyone but you, and I doubt he's willing to make a scene, but we don't want to take any chances."

One of the women at the center answered. Holly was playing Go Fish with some of the other kids. "I'll be there in just a few minutes," Sarah said, relieved. She looked up at Jackson. "She's okay."

"I figured she would be. It's you he's worried about. He thinks you know more than you do, and he wants to make sure you keep quiet. Still…" He urged her toward his truck, which was parked down the street. "We'll pick her up, then take that plate number over to the sheriff, see what he can find out."

Sarah stopped walking. "No way, Jackson. I'm not about to go against these people. I've got to think of Holly. I'm the only parent she's got. My daughter needs me."

"We don't know how far these guys are willing to

go. Your life could be in danger no matter what you do. Have you thought of that?"

Her eyes slid closed. She swayed a little and felt his arm go around her, drawing her against his side. "I don't know how much more of this I can take." She pressed her face into his shoulder, her eyes welling with tears. "I just don't know."

"We'll get through this, darlin', I promise." He turned her into his arms and held her, smoothed back loose strands of her hair. Finally easing away, he took hold of her hand. "Come on, let's get Holly and go home."

"What about my truck?"

"Leave it here. I'll drive you into town in the morning and you can pick it up."

She didn't argue. The adrenaline rush was beginning to fade and suddenly she was exhausted. When she had awakened that morning, Detective Mercer had been her biggest problem.

Now she was right back where she'd started, trying to figure out what in God's name Andrew had done that threatened her from beyond the grave.

They drove to the day-care center and picked up Holly, fastened her securely in the backseat then headed out of town. Jackson waited until he pulled up in front of the cottage and turned off the engine before reaching beneath the seat and dragging a plastic bag out from underneath.

"I bought you each a present."

Holly sat up straighter, her eyes bright with excitement. "You bought me a present?"

"That's right." He reached into the bag, pulled out

a cardboard box and handed it Holly. The other box was larger and he handed that one to Sarah. "I hope they fit."

Sarah took off the lid, saw a pair of soft brown leather cowboy boots nestled inside.

"Boots, Mama!" Tissue paper rustled as Holly pulled her pair out of the box, flashy red ones with great big eagles spread-winged on the front. "They're beautiful!"

Sarah ran a hand over the soft brown leather, checked inside for the size. "How did you know I wore a seven and a half?"

"I looked at the shoes in your closet. I checked Holly's, too. Of course, until you try them on, you still won't know if they fit."

So they went inside and tried them. Holly's fit perfectly and Sarah's fit nicely, too.

"Thank you, Jackson."

"We're going riding, aren't we? You can't ride without a decent pair of boots."

With the boots still on her feet, Holly ran over and hugged him. "Thank you, Jackson. I love them."

"You're welcome. Just be sure to wear them around a little so you get them broken in."

"I will," Holly promised, dashing back outside to show them to Gibby and Sam. Rags rushed up beside her and started barking. Holly gave his head a quick pat and kept running.

"Until I get things straightened out," Sarah said, "I think Holly should stay here on the ranch with Livvy again."

"So do I. I'll talk to Jimmy, fill him in on what happened in town. He can talk to the hands, ask them to keep an eye peeled for strangers. They're good men. They won't let anyone on the place who doesn't belong."

Sarah nodded, her mind still spinning with worry over the man in town.

"Tomorrow I'll take you in to pick up your truck and bring it home."

"I'm going to work, Jackson. I can't hide out here like a frightened rabbit."

"The guy had a gun, Sarah. I think you should stay close to the house."

She only shook her head. "There's no way to know how long this might go on. I've got a job. I intend to keep it."

Jackson blew out a breath. "I was afraid that's what you'd say. I'll tell you what. I'll take you into town in the morning. You usually only work four or five hours, right?"

"Usually."

"Good, then I'll follow you home when you get off. While you're at work, I'm going to have that old truck of yours gone over, make sure it's in A1 condition. We don't want to chance it breaking down somewhere on the road."

She didn't like it. She treasured her independence. But for now, she knew he was right. "Okay, but after tomorrow, I'll be all right on my own."

"We'll see," was all he said.

She looked up at him as they stood at the living-room window watching Holly outside playing with the boys. Jackson was always so strong and caring. And yet she didn't want to have to depend on him. She needed to be able to take care of herself and her daughter.

Sarah's lips trembled, the situation suddenly more than she could cope with. "What am I going to do, Jackson? I can't live this way, always looking over my shoulder, never knowing if Holly will be safe."

"We're going to do exactly what we did before. We're going to find out who this guy is and who he works for. We'll figure out what it is he thinks you know and find a way to end this."

Sarah swallowed. The man who had accosted her wasn't involved with Kozak Construction. He was harder, the people he worked for clearly more dangerous. He carried a gun and though she didn't think his intention was to shoot her, she was sure he wouldn't hesitate to do it.

She looked over at Jackson, saw the determination in the set of his jaw and tried to find the courage to do whatever it was she had to do.

Jackson made arrangements to leave for California on Monday. He didn't tell Sarah. He didn't intend for her to go.

After the incident in town, he had called in a favor and gotten an old friend at the motor vehicles department to run the plate number off the Ford. It belonged to Duff Oldman, one of the locals.

Since Duff was sixty-five years old, mostly into gardening and definitely not the criminal type, Jackson figured the guy had traded the rental plate for Duff's, used it while he was in town, then put it back on Duff's car before he left the area.

No help there.

He might be able to track down the rental car at

one of the airports, but the guy had undoubtedly used a false ID.

Jackson had to go back to L.A., see where Devlin's information might lead.

In the meantime, it was the weekend and there wasn't much he could do. As promised, he would take Sarah and Holly camping. One thing he knew—once Sarah was up in the high mountains away from her troubles and fears—it would be nearly impossible for her to worry. He knew because it was what he'd done when he was a boy and his mother got drunk, or when he had to spend his hard-earned, after-school-job money to buy his family food.

What he still did sometimes when the troubled world just got too heavy to handle.

For the next two days, up in the high valleys where the air was crystal clear and the scent of pine needles and campfire smoke rode on the breeze, Sarah could forget for a while and just enjoy herself.

Or at least he hoped so.

Where this lady was concerned, nothing was ever certain.

He got up early Saturday morning, long before the sun had popped over the hill, and began to get ready for the trip—brushing the horses down; collecting the tent, sleeping bags, cooking utensils, fire grate and the rest of the overnight gear they would need.

Once he had it all together, he set the pack saddle in place on one of the mules he'd had Wheel Dillon bring in from the lower pasture, put the panniers in place and carefully distributed the weight of the gear.

They could have gone without the mule, old Salty, taken less stuff and made do, but the trip would be more fun, more like the old days when the mountain men packed into the high country to hunt and trap, and he was sure the girls would enjoy it.

Jimmy showed up about the time he was ready to saddle the horses, Galahad for himself and Daisy for Sarah. Until she was a little older, Holly would ride with him.

He found himself liking the thought of the little girl getting old enough to have a horse of her own, then shook his head, not certain he was ready to think along those lines just yet.

"Need some help?" Jimmy walked up as he set the second saddle in place and adjusted it on Daisy's back.

"Just some company. Aside from that, I'm pretty well ready."

"Should be good weather for it," Jimmy said. "No rain in the forecast."

"I damned well wished there was. I'd be willing to put up with the wet if it helped get rid of this dry."

"I know what you mean."

Jackson tightened the cinch on Daisy's saddle, looked over at Jimmy and wondered what it was he seemed to want to say.

"You and Nan have a good time on the Fourth?" he asked, just to see if that might lead his friend in the right direction.

"Yeah, we did. We had a real good time. The boys sure like her."

He tugged on the latigo, checking to see if the cinch was tight. "What about you? You like her, too?"

"More than I should, I guess."

"Why is that? Nan seems like a nice enough gal."

"We haven't...well, you know, but I sure like having her around. I've even been thinking it might be the kind of thing that could wind up permanent."

One of Jackson's eyebrows went up. Jimmy had never talked this way about a woman. "That sounds good."

"Could be. The only problem is…"

"The only problem is…?" he prompted.

"I don't know if I can trust her."

Jackson thought back several years to the time Jimmy had mentioned his interest in dating Nan Hargrove. "You mean because of the guys she took home from the Canyon Club."

He nodded.

"She was single, Jim. She had a right to do what she wanted."

"I know. It's just…"

"It's just that Annie chased everything in pants and you don't want to go through that again."

Jimmy looked away. His ex-wife had been a real peach. Everyone in town knew she was wilder than a jackrabbit, but Jimmy had fallen for her anyway. Fallen for her hard. When he'd found out she was making the rounds with half the guys in Wind Canyon, it'd torn him apart.

The luckiest day of Jimmy's life had been the day Annie Baylor Threebears packed her bags and disappeared, never to be seen again. She'd signed the divorce papers, and Jimmy was free, but he'd never really gotten over Annie. Until now, it seemed.

"Give it some time, Jim. There's no rush."

Jimmy shot him a glance that traveled past him, off toward the cottage. "Back at ya, buddy. Sarah's a beautiful woman, but she's trouble. It seems to follow her around like a bad smell."

It was true. Too damned true. And yet he was in for the duration. In until whatever was going on was over.

He didn't have to think twice to know he wasn't going to be another man who had let Sarah Allen down.

Sarah hurried to catch up with Holly, who ran excitedly out of the house off toward the barn. Jackson stood waiting next to the horses, the big red gelding, Galahad, and the pretty little paint mare, Daisy. A pack mule stood at the hitching rail, his long ears twitching at the sound of Holly's small footsteps approaching.

Sarah made a last mental check of the stuff in the duffel bag she carried. Jackets, an extra pair of jeans for each of them, extra socks and sneakers in case their boots got wet. Along with a few miscellaneous personal items, she was ready—and far more excited than she had imagined she would be.

Jackson came forward before she reached him and took the canvas duffel from her hands. "This it?"

She nodded.

"Jackets in here? That high up in the hills, it still gets cold at night."

"It's all there. Once I got started, it all sort of came back. I used to go camping with my dad." She still avoided the bittersweet memory of those times. Her mother had been a true homemaker, Sarah a bit of a tomboy who loved spending time out of doors. "We really had fun."

"We're going to have fun this time." He loaded the duffel on top of the pack rack and tied it snugly in place.

"What's his name?" Holly asked, stroking the mule's soft nose.

"Salty. He can be cantankerous once in a while, but mostly, he's a good ole boy." He stroked the mule's long neck. "Aren't you, son?"

The mule brayed as if he understood, and all of them laughed.

"You ready?" he asked Holly.

"You bet!"

Jackson chuckled as he lifted her up on the front of his saddle then swung up behind her. "You okay? Got enough room?"

The little girl grinned and nodded.

Jackson took the mule's lead rope, looped it loosely around the saddle horn, and they started off up the trail.

Holly waved goodbye to Jimmy, Sam and Gib, who came to watch them ride out, then settled in for the three-hour ride up the trail into the mountains.

"We'll camp next to the lake," Jackson said. "I've brought a couple of poles so we can fish. We get lucky, we'll have fried fish for supper."

Sarah smiled as she watched him settle himself in the saddle, Holly's back resting against his chest. She was only a little nervous watching Galahad carry Jackson and Holly up the steep section of the trail leading off the road, relaxed as they reached the top and settled into a steady pace.

Jackson rode with the same ease he did just about everything, his shoulders wide and straight, his long legs comfortable in the saddle, boots shoved into the stirrups, hat pulled low over his forehead.

Sarah felt a little pinch in her chest just watching him, thinking how good he looked, how tempting. It was the kind of pinch that wasn't good. The kind that said where this man was concerned, she could be in serious trouble.

Sitting on his horse, looking like every woman's fantasy, Jackson turned and surveyed her with a long, heated glance that ran up her jean-clad legs, settled on her breasts and told her exactly the kind of ride he would rather be making.

Sarah sucked in a breath as a shot of lust hit her so fiercely the muscles in her thighs went taut. Her jeans chafed an intimate spot between her legs and every time Daisy took a step, she felt a jolt of sexual heat.

Good Lord, three hours was going to be a lifetime! And once they got to the lake, it would only get worse. She would have to watch Jackson setting up camp, those hard muscles flexing and tightening, making her stomach twist with longing. With Holly along, there was no way they could make love, no way to find relief.

Sarah watched Jackson riding steadily up the trail, not quite sure she liked this new, sexual side of herself.

Then she smiled. It felt good to desire a man. Good to be desired. Leaning back in the saddle, she relaxed for the first time in days. She had come on this trip to enjoy herself. Whatever happened, whatever the future held in store for her, that was exactly what she intended to do.

Unfortunately in life, nothing ever went the way it was supposed to. They were just approaching the lake when Sarah heard the whine of a chain saw.

"Sonofa—" Jackson broke off in deference to Holly, snatched off his hat and resettled it on his head.

"Loggers?" Sarah pulled Daisy to a stop beside Galahad and Salty in a wide spot on the trail.

The chain saw bit in and whined, and Salty's long ears went up. He began to back away, pulling on his halter, trying to tug the lead rope out of Jackson's hand.

"Easy, son." Leading the mule a few feet away, he swung down from the saddle and tied the animal to a tree.

"They aren't supposed to be working in this section," he said as he led the sorrel back to where Sarah sat on Daisy. "This lake is surrounded by national forest, but these days that doesn't mean the trees are protected."

He lifted Holly out of the saddle and set her on the ground, and Sarah swung down off Daisy. They had stopped a number of times along the route, but still her legs were a little sore.

"You okay?"

She smiled. "I'm fine." A little saddle soreness wasn't much of a price to pay for a trip through such spectacular scenery.

Jackson reached into his saddlebags and dug out a map, spread it open on top of a rock and studied it for several moments. "I thought so." He rolled the map up. "I need to check this out. I won't be gone long." Stepping into the stirrup, he swung aboard the gelding, whirled the horse and headed up the trail.

Chapter 22

"Where's Jackson going, Mama?"

The chain saw had stopped. Jackson must have reached the logging camp. The men couldn't be working that far away.

"I'm not sure, honey. Why don't we leave Daisy here with Salty, walk up the trail a ways and see?" She led the mare over and tied her to graze, then took Holly's hand and started up the trail.

She didn't like the idea of Jackson going head-to-head with a bunch of loggers by himself. If she and Holly were there—a woman and a child—maybe it would ease the situation.

She walked up the trail holding on to Holly's hand and the minute she rounded the bend, she saw them. A group of men clustered around a bunch of heavy equipment: bulldozer, flatbed trailer, some kind of crane for loading the logs onto the truck, other miscellaneous machinery. The words *Bannock Bros. Logging* were stenciled on the sides of the equipment.

"Take a look at the map," Jackson was saying to what appeared to be the foreman, a big burly, barrel-chested, red-bearded man. "Pine Lake is right there." Jackson pointed down the hill. "Black Bear Summit is off to the right, and you can see Badger Pass on your left." He drew a finger along a line on the map. "You were supposed to stop about a half mile back, at the top of Buffalo Ridge."

"So what's it to you? You act like those trees are your own personal property."

"Well, they sure as hell don't belong to you. This is public land, DeSalvo. Your company managed to horn-swoggle its way into a logging contract on far too big a chunk of it, but you're clearly over the boundaries that were set."

"So what? You think anyone gives a shit?"

"Wind it up, Red," Jackson warned, "and haul your crew out of here. You don't, I'm going to call the Forest Service and turn you in. I doubt the Bannock brothers will appreciate the big fat fine you cost them."

DeSalvo took a threatening step forward.

"Come on," Jackson taunted. "Throw a punch. I'd love an excuse to whip your sorry ass."

Sarah's stomach tightened. There were five of them and it was clear all of them were spoiling for a fight.

"Stay here," she whispered to Holly, then pasted on a smile, raised a hand, waved and started toward the men.

"Jackson! Jackson, there you are! I've been looking all over." She wasn't afraid the men would hurt her.

They were just working men trying to do their jobs. Jackson represented a threat to their way of life and it was clearly him they wanted to stomp into the dirt.

"Take Holly and go back to the lake," Jackson warned, his gaze still fixed on the foreman he'd called Red DeSalvo.

Sarah just kept walking. She paused when she reached the circle of men. "Jackson, we need your help. We can't figure out how to pitch the tent."

He sliced her a look that could have crumbled stone, then turned back to the foreman. "Pack it up or I call the authorities. Get back to the area you're supposed to be working in."

DeSalvo looked from Jackson to Sarah, flicked a glance to where Holly stood at the edge of the clearing, then turned to his men. "Move it, boys. Let's get back up the hill."

Sarah breathed a sigh of relief. She might have smiled if she hadn't looked, just then, into Jackson's furious face.

"Let's go," he said between clenched teeth. Grabbing her arm, he whirled her around and urged her toward the trail. She knew that look, recognized the barely leashed fury in his expression.

She stumbled and nearly fell. On legs that barely held her up, she made her way along the trail, forced herself to keep walking until they rounded the bend. Her vision blurred and she realized her eyes had filled with tears. Why hadn't she seen it sooner? What had she been thinking to trust him the way she did?

She stumbled again and this time Jackson caught her. She cringed and tried to pull away, but he didn't let go. He must have seen the tears in her eyes for the color drained from his face.

"Sarah...my God." He stopped there in the middle of the trail and pulled her into his arms. "Honey, it's all right. Everything's okay." He held her, felt her trembling and tightened his hold around her. "Just because I get mad, doesn't mean I'd hurt you. I'd never hurt you or Holly. Never." He eased away enough to look at her. "Surely you know that by now."

The tears in her eyes rolled down her cheeks. She did know. Somewhere deep inside her, she knew he was nothing like Andrew. And she was no longer the submissive, frightened young woman she had been before. Still...just for a moment...

"Mama, are you okay?"

Jackson knelt in front of Holly. "Sometimes your mama's just too brave for her own good." He came up beside Sarah. "You weren't afraid of five big loggers, but you were afraid of me?"

She caught his incredulous expression and her lips slightly curved. Now that she thought about it, it did seem ridiculous. "I just... I didn't want them to hurt you."

Jackson laughed, loud and long. Then he pulled her back into his arms. "You're something, Sarah Allen. You truly are." And then he kissed her, right there on the trail in front of Holly.

"It's getting late," he said gruffly as he drew away. "We'd better get started making camp." Swinging Holly up on his shoulders, leading Galahad, he headed down the trail, walking next to Sarah. When they reached the clearing, he left the trail and walked out into the meadow next to the lake.

"I think this will do," he said, picking a spot close to the pines at the edge of the water. While Holly ran off to gather kindling for a fire—with instructions to stay in sight—Jackson turned to Sarah.

"I'm not going to promise you I'll never get angry. You pull a stunt like that again—put yourself and your daughter in danger for any reason—I'm liable to get good and mad. I might yell. I might blow off a little steam, but I'd never hit you. I'd never do anything to hurt you. You need to believe that, Sarah, if whatever is happening between us is ever going to have a chance to work."

The words swirled around her, filled her with yearning. *If whatever is happening between us is ever going to have a chance to work.*

There was something in his eyes, something fierce and compelling, and an honesty that drew her as nothing had before. Sarah held his dark gaze for several long moments, then turned away, a new, different kind of fear settling deep inside her.

Fear of losing her independence, fear of the problems that still threatened her future.

And the fearful knowledge that she had fallen in love with Jackson Raines.

The trip was a grand success. Jackson taught Holly how to fish. They fried one of the fat lake trout they caught and ate it for supper, with camp potatoes and homemade Dutch-oven biscuits and some of Livvy's raspberry jam.

In the morning he fixed flapjacks and bacon and they sat in the warm sun around an early-morning campfire and ate until they were too stuffed to move.

"I can't believe how good this all tastes," Sarah said, apparently impressed with his cooking. "I used to help my dad cook over an open fire. I bet I could do it again with a little practice."

"I bet you could, too," he said, thinking there wasn't much Sarah Allen couldn't do if she put her mind to it. He would never forget the way she had come to rescue him from the loggers. Or how badly it had hurt to see the fear in her pretty blue eyes when she had looked at him on the trail.

She had nothing to fear from him and never would, and he thought that maybe, little by little, she was coming to realize that.

They were tired by the time they packed up the camp that morning and left the meadow and started back down the trail. Holly fell asleep against Jackson's chest as Galahad plodded along, and seeing the trust in her sweet little face made something tighten inside him.

Though he often worked with kids during the summer, mostly with the youth boxing team, he had never realized what he was missing in not having a family of his own.

The thought intrigued him more than it should have and he forced the notion away. He wasn't ready for that kind of thinking. At least not yet.

The small band was exhausted by the time, late in the afternoon, they arrived back at the ranch. Jackson walked the girls to their cottage, then he and Jimmy unpacked the mule, unsaddled, fed and put the livestock away.

"Everything go all right?" Jimmy asked as they turned the horses and Salty out into the pasture.

Jackson glanced back up the mountain. "Aside from a little run-in with Red DeSalvo and some of his loggers. They were half a mile or so over the boundary line." His jaw flexed. "They decided to move back to where they were supposed to be."

Jimmy chuckled. "Lucky for them."

Jackson just grunted.

"I'd better go fix supper," Jimmy said. "The boys'll be getting hungry."

Jackson could see Jimmy's two black-haired sons standing out in front of the house tossing a baseball back and forth. "I guess they aren't going to summer school this year." He had noticed they were there every day, which they hadn't been last year.

"They got nearly straight A's. I figured they deserved a little time to enjoy themselves. Sam's going to start working with Wheel and a few of the hands. Gib's going to do some chores for me and Wheel. I think it'll be good for them."

"So do I." That was how Jackson had learned to love ranching, working on a ranch in the summers. He grabbed his saddlebags off the fence, turned and headed up to the house, thinking of Jimmy and Nan, wondering where the relationship was headed, trying not to think of his own uncertain relationship with Sarah.

"There's supper on the stove," Livvy said as he walked into the warm, steamy kitchen, and he was damned glad.

"Thanks."

"I made enough for the girls. I thought I'd take it over. They're bound to be tired after the trip."

"I'm sure Sarah will appreciate that. Both of them were pretty beat by the time we got home."

"Did they have a good time?"

"You'll have to ask them, but yeah, I think they did. We all did."

Livvy gave him a warm, motherly smile and went to work, serving him up a plate, then putting the rest of the roast, carrots and potatoes, and the remainder of a loaf of crusty French bread on a tray, covering the food with foil, and heading out the door.

As soon as Jackson finished eating, he started upstairs to pack for his trip to L.A. He needed to act on the information Devlin had given him on Ace Trucking, the company that had been paying big chunks of cash to Andrew Hollister. It was likely that someone at Ace was behind the assaults on Sarah. He was going to California to find out exactly what was going on.

Once he reached his bedroom, Jackson set to work. He retrieved his shaving kit and put it in the carry-on he had opened and set on his bed. He packed a couple of pairs of slacks, a clean pair of jeans and a couple of short-sleeved shirts, then added underwear and socks. He turned at the sound of a light knock on his door.

Livvy stood in the opening. "Sarah's downstairs. She says she needs to talk to you."

"Actually, I'm right here." Sarah peered at him over Livvy's plump shoulder, then frowned. "Where are you going?"

He hadn't planned to tell her. He was going to call once he got there. Didn't look like she was giving him any choice.

"Out to your old stompin' grounds. Dev called a couple of nights ago. He had information on a company called Ace Trucking. They were paying Andrew big money under the table. Ace does work for Southgate Demolition." One of Hollister's own companies. "I want to find out what they were paying Andrew for."

"And you were going to tell me about this—when?"

He shrugged his shoulders. "I didn't want you to worry."

Sarah's chin firmed as she stepped out from behind Livvy. "This is my problem, Jackson. You're not going out there unless you take me with you." She turned to his housekeeper. "Will you watch Holly while we're gone?"

"You know I will."

"There's no reason for you to go," Jackson said as Livvy slipped quietly away. "We have no idea if this has anything to do with the man who threatened you in town."

"But it might. And even if it doesn't, maybe we can find out who the guy is and why he's after me."

Jackson sighed. Half of him wanted to insist Sarah stay here on the ranch where she would be safe. The other half was already seeing her in a plush hotel room, curled up in his bed. Damn, sleeping next to her in that little three-man tent was one of the hardest things he'd ever done. He was hard again now, just thinking about it.

He definitely wanted her to go.

And he knew damn well he shouldn't let her.

"You don't have a choice, Jackson. If you don't take me along, I'll fly out there myself. I may not have a lot of money, but I've got some, enough I can afford to get there. I'll march right into Ace Trucking, tell them who I am and demand to know what's going on."

She was bluffing.

Or maybe not.

"All right, dammit, you can go."

"Fine."

He raked a hand through his hair, shoving it back from his forehead. "I'll talk to Jimmy, let him know we'll be gone a couple of days."

"What time are we leaving?"

"Plane's set to leave at 7:00 a.m."

"Then I'd better go pack." She turned and started for the door.

"So why did you want to see me?" he called after her.

Sarah turned back. "I just wanted to thank you for the wonderful trip." She smiled. "I'll see you in the morning." And then she was gone.

Sarah did her homework that night. Sitting at her desk after Holly went to bed, she opened the bottom drawer and pulled out a file that held the pages she had printed off the pen drive they had found in the storage room. One of the pages, she recalled, held notes from a meeting with the managers of Southgate Demolition. She carefully went over the notes, looking for any mention of Ace Trucking.

She found it at the bottom of the page. Ace was working on a couple of Southgate's demolition jobs, but the information was five months old, before Andrew had died, the projects probably completed by now.

Reaching over, she flipped on her laptop. When Google popped up, she typed in *Southgate Demolition*. There were several articles in various newspapers in the L.A. area, as well as the Southgate Demolition home page.

She skimmed their website, which showed color photos of buildings being torn down, then clicked on the link that read *management*. The company was currently being run by a man named Theodore Schuler. Since she had never heard the name, she figured he had probably been appointed by the probate court.

Going back to the Google list of entries, she clicked on a recent article in the *L.A. Times* naming Southgate as the company hired to demolish a six-story building in East L.A. Sarah mentally placed the location, thinking it might border a fairly rough section of town. But then much of L.A. was being revitalized. Space in a city that was growing so fast was always at a premium. Jackson's brother, Gabe, had said he was doing a lot of that kind of work in Dallas.

She jotted down the address of the project, searched a little longer but found nothing that seemed particularly useful.

Next she typed in *Ace Trucking* on Google.

The Ace home page was informative. The company was owned and operated by a man named Vincent Spalino. Though Andrew had mentioned him, Sarah had never met him. There was a photo of Spalino on the page, an older man with beefy jowls, hard black eyes and thick, iron-gray hair. He looked more like a dock worker than a businessman, which didn't seem to fit with the exotic-looking, expensively dressed man who had threatened her here in Wind Canyon.

Then again, if the man who had accosted her was some sort of hired gun, how he dressed wouldn't matter to Spalino.

She yawned, satisfied she had learned all she could for now, turned off the computer and went to bed. They were flying out at seven and she wanted to have Holly settled with Livvy before she left the ranch.

The morning went as planned. Livvy had Holly nestled on the sofa watching cartoons in the ranch house living room by the time Sarah left. The road was clear on the way to the airport and the weather was good. The chartered, twin-engine plane departed right on schedule.

Sitting next to Jackson in one of the cream leather seats, she took a sip of hot coffee then handed him the information she had collected.

"This is the stuff we printed off the pen drive we found in the storage room and I also printed some items off the internet."

Jackson took the file. "Great minds, I guess. I went on the net last night, myself."

"Find anything?"

"I took a look at Southgate Demolition's web page and ran across the location of a couple of their current projects. I read about them in an article in *Heavy Equipment* magazine."

"I know they're tearing down a building on Brooklyn Avenue. That's East L.A. It was mentioned in a *Times* article on city revitalization."

"They're demoing a grammar school in Monrovia, too."

"You think they'll be using Ace Trucking?"

"We're going to find out." His foam cup crackled as he took a sip of coffee. "I also made a call to my brother. I asked him if he could arrange for us to talk to his informant, the guy who told him about Ace's cash payments to your late husband."

She ignored a sudden chill. She hated any reference to Andrew as her husband. "And?"

"And he said he'd see if he could make it happen. I expect to hear from him sometime today."

Sarah leaned back in her seat. It was the logical first step. Find out what else Devlin's informant might be able to tell them—if he was willing to talk.

"You think this man will meet us?"

Jackson shrugged. "Money talks," was all he said.

Sarah opened her mouth to tell him she couldn't afford to pay the sort of money it would take, but he held up his hand and simply shook his head.

Sarah sighed. There was no point in arguing. She reminded herself what his brothers had said. Jackson was helping her. Just as he had helped people in the past and would again in the future.

She bit her lip and closed her eyes, let the drone of the engines lull her. She relaxed and grew sleepy. She was just drifting off when erotic images of Jackson began to appear in her mind. She squirmed in her seat, softly whispered his name. She wasn't sure what else she said, something provocative, it was clear, for when she opened her eyes her blouse was unbuttoned, Jackson's dark head bent to the task of suckling her breast.

"Always happy to oblige a lady," he said softly, then returned to the job at hand.

Sensation swamped her. Sarah laced her fingers in his hair to pull him closer, urging him to continue. His teeth grazed her nipple, then she felt the sweet sensation of his mouth opening to take the fullness.

Sarah moaned. Her heavy-lidded gaze slid toward

the cockpit door but it was firmly closed. She glanced down to see that her slacks were unzipped as his tanned hand moved over her belly, slipped beneath the band of her thong panties into the tangle of dark hair between her legs. She was wet in an instant, plump and ready for him to take her.

"Jackson…" She was trembling all over, more than eager, but there was a pilot sitting behind the cockpit door and no possible way they could make love.

"As soon as we get to the hotel," he promised, claiming her lips in a slow, ravishing kiss. "In the meantime, I'll give you something to last until we get there."

Sarah arched upward as his long dark fingers slid inside her, stroking deeply, expertly. In moments, she was hovering on the verge of climax. A glance toward the cockpit door assured her it remained tightly closed, and she gave herself over to the exquisite sensations.

"Come for me," Jackson softly urged, and the deep, sexy cadence of his voice sent her over the edge. His hard kiss swallowed a cry of passion, and he held her as she trembled, then began to spiral down.

Her tremors slowly eased, replaced by a glow of satisfaction. A last soft kiss and he let her go, settled himself back in his seat.

Sarah looked down at her open blouse and unzipped slacks and hurriedly rearranged her clothes. Embarrassment pinkened her cheeks as Jackson leaned back in his seat, a smug male smile tilting the corners of his lips.

She couldn't believe it. She had let the man pleasure her in the seat of an airplane!

She glanced toward him from beneath her lashes.

"You don't have to be embarrassed," he said, clearly reading her thoughts. "I liked it, too."

"But you didn't get to—"

"No, but I enjoyed touching you just the same."

She glanced away. He was such a virile man. He liked sex and he made no secret of it.

Sarah rose from her seat and made her way to the tiny bathroom in the rear of the plane to freshen herself. As she closed the minuscule door, she gazed into the small oval mirror on the wall. Her dark hair was mussed and a soft flush colored her cheeks. She looked, well, satisfied.

The plane hit an air pocket just then, tossing her against the wall in the narrow, confining space. She had never liked flying. She glanced back at her reflection in the mirror, saw the glow in her face, felt the sweet tingling that hadn't completely left her.

Then again, there were definitely some advantages to flying with Jackson Raines.

Chapter 23

Jackson's cell phone rang as he slid behind the wheel of his rental car. They had flown into the Burbank Airport, which was close to Ace Trucking in the San Fernando Valley and not far from Southgate Demolition in Glendale. The day was California-warm, eighty-five degrees and sunny. But the weatherman had predicted light showers that night.

Jackson looked at his phone, recognized the caller ID. "Hey, bro."

"You on the ground?" Dev asked.

"Yeah, we just landed in Burbank."

"That'll work. My guy's name is Jorge Rodriguez. He's willing to meet you—for a price."

"Not a problem. When and where?"

"Tonight. Nine o'clock. A place called the Arizona Café. It's on Valley Boulevard in Alhambra." Dev gave him directions off the eastbound 10 Freeway. "He'll be wearing an L.A. Dodgers ball cap."

"How much do you know about him?"

"Jorge worked for Hollister up until he died. Did pretty much whatever the guy wanted him to. Nothing wet, I don't think. Just errands that required tight lips and muscle when it was needed, that kind of thing. He was out of a job after Hollister got snuffed. Does a little work for a guy I know. According to him, Jorge's got a family. He needs the money. He'll tell you as much as he knows."

"Thanks, Dev."

"It may not be all that much, but you were coming out anyway, so it's definitely worth a try. I'll expect to hear from you when it's over. Take care, big brother."

Jackson leaned back in the car seat. All three brothers were protective of each other. As kids, with a mother who was mostly drunk, there was no one but the three of them, nobody else who gave a damn whether they lived or died. The feeling had stuck. Dev would be worried until he got Jackson's call.

"So what did he say?" Sarah asked from the passenger side of the rental car, a midsize, nondescript Chevy that wouldn't attract attention.

Jackson turned the key in the ignition and the engine roared to life. "I'm meeting with his informant tonight at nine."

"*We,* Jackson. *We're* meeting him tonight."

He flicked her a glance, caught the stubborn tilt of her chin. *I'm going,* it said. *One way or another.*

He sighed, raked a hand through his hair. He put the car into gear and pulled out of the lot. "You can be a real pain in the ass sometimes, you know?"

Sarah grinned more broadly than he had ever seen her. "I'll take that as a compliment."

Jackson grumbled a word he didn't want her to hear. "Fine, but you do exactly what I tell you, okay?"

She nodded, pleased with herself for getting her way. "Okay."

He thought he understood. She was coming into her own, growing stronger every day, now that she was out from under her husband's brutal, domineering control.

"So where's the meeting?"

"Alhambra. I guess that's a town. You know it?"

She nodded. "It's south and east of here. We're staying in Burbank, right?"

"Afraid so. Nothing fancy, this time, just a little hotel I found on the internet that looked easy to get in and out of and seemed to have decent rooms."

The hotel, the Gramercy, was a little over four miles from the airport, a three-story, U-shaped building that looked clean and well cared for and had parking on all three sides. He had reserved a two-bedroom suite, small but adequate, though he hoped they would only need one of the bedrooms.

They checked in and were shown upstairs into room 318. Sarah rolled her carry-on through the door into the second bedroom.

"You sure you don't want to stay with me?" His hopes rose at the indecision he read on her face.

"I like my privacy. You don't really mind, do you?"

"Of course I mind. I want you in my bed, Sarah. I want to make love to you. I want you there when I wake up in the morning. But I know you need time and I'm willing to give it to you."

Sarah moistened her lips, making them glisten, and his blood began to heat.

"Thank you," she said softly.

He forced his thoughts in a safer direction. "We've got a little time before tonight's meeting. Let's take a drive past that demolition site I came across on the internet—the one Southgate is working on in Monrovia. I looked it up and I don't think it's that far away."

"All right. Traffic shouldn't be too bad this time of day. Maybe we'll run across something useful."

They finished unpacking, then went back downstairs to the car. Fortunately, even after plowing through traffic and checking into the hotel, it was still early afternoon, not yet the rush hour, so the drive didn't take too long.

The bad news was, when they got to the demo site, it wasn't Ace but another trucking company that was busily hauling away the big chunks of cement, bent and rusted rebar, broken windows, mountains of Sheetrock and lumber, and just plain piles of trash resulting from the destruction of a cluster of buildings.

"They aren't using Ace," Sarah said, disappointed. "I wonder why."

"Maybe their bid was too high. Southgate's tearing down a school. The contract would probably be awarded by the state."

They watched the men working, the bulldozers piling up debris, skiploaders scooping it up and dropping it into dump trucks.

"Andrew owned a lot of equipment," Sarah said. "Why do you suppose Southgate needs to hire a trucking company? Why doesn't Southgate just haul the stuff away?"

"Andrew owned equipment, but not all of it was the right kind. From what we've seen, Southgate Demolition uses on-site machinery—bulldozers, pavers, skiploaders, that kind of thing. Andrew was never in the transport business."

Sarah studied the activity on the site. "Still, he owned some trucks. Maybe Ace does some kind of specialized work for Southgate. Something that requires slightly different kinds of trucks."

"Good thought. Maybe tonight good ol' Jorge will be able to tell us." And if not, maybe they would at least pick up something useful. Jackson looked at his wristwatch. The afternoon was slipping away. The traffic would be worse going back. They hadn't had anything to eat since morning, and the long plane ride was always tiring.

"Why don't we head back to the hotel? You can call and check on Holly, then we'll get something to eat and maybe catch a nap. We'll regroup and be ready for Jorge."

Sarah nodded, yawned behind her hand. "Now that you mention it, I could use a little sleep." She looked up at him and a sexy smile curved her lips. "Besides, I owe you for that little present you gave me on the plane. I wonder…am I officially a member of the mile-high club?"

A rush of blood went straight to his groin. "Only an associate member, but I'll be glad to remedy that on the flight back home."

Sarah laughed, but her cheeks turned red. The lady was definitely an enigma, embarrassed one minute, bold the next. She wanted a room of her own, but she wanted to have sex with him. She had a lot to figure out about herself, he guessed.

"You don't owe me for that," he said, getting back to the subject at hand, "but I'd like nothing more than to take you to bed." Leaning across the console, he kissed her long and deep.

Sarah kissed him back and he figured they had just sealed the deal.

Sarah watched the big green freeway signs for the exit off the 10 that Devlin had said to take into Alhambra. The sun was almost down, the last faint remnants of light fading along the horizon. The heat of the day was easing, as well, the temperature cooled by a layer of clouds moving over the city. A light rain had begun to fall, just enough to dampen the arid land along the highway.

Earlier, after making love, a nap in Jackson's bed, and hamburgers and French fries from the hotel's limited room service menu, they set off for tonight's meeting, leaving early enough to get there even if they ran into trouble on the road.

Another freeway sign loomed ahead of them out of the darkness. "There it is." Sarah pointed. Jackson spotted the turnoff, signaled and eased the car toward the off-ramp. A few minutes later, they were heading down Valley Boulevard in search of the Arizona Café.

It was a coffee shop, Sarah saw as they pulled into the parking lot and Jackson turned off the engine. She had no idea why it was named for another state, except maybe for the dirt and tumbleweeds around the edge of the lot, making it look like it sat in the middle of the desert.

"We wait out here until it's time to go in," Jackson said. "I doubt Jorge would want us drawing any more attention than necessary."

They waited fifteen minutes, till exactly 9:00 p.m., then got out of the car, crossed the rough pavement, and pushed through the glass doors into the small café. A mix of whites, Hispanics, African-Americans and Asians sat in booths and at the long Formica-topped counter. A good spot to meet, Sarah thought, a place where, dressed in jeans and a T-shirt, her hair pulled back in a ponytail, with Jackson in jeans and a short-sleeved shirt, they would blend in fairly well with the rest of the customers in the café.

Jackson said Jorge Rodriguez would be wearing a Dodger's baseball cap and Sarah scanned the counter in search of him. He wasn't there, or in any of the pink vinyl booths along the wall.

"He's in the back, the last booth," Jackson said softly.

Sarah spotted him, average height, muscular build, plain white T-shirt snug across his chest. Jackson's fingers entwined with hers and he led her forward.

Jorge Rodriguez pulled his cap a little lower over his straight black hair as they slid into the booth on the seat across from him. He was drinking a cup of coffee, a dark-skinned, round-faced man with black eyes and an earring in his ear.

"Why'd you bring her?" he asked Jackson sullenly. "You should have come alone."

"She's Hollister's widow. She's the one who's on the hook for his mistakes."

A waitress appeared, stringy blond hair but a friendly smile. They ordered coffee, waited till she set the heavy white china mugs down in front of them and returned to her duties.

"Tell us what you know." Jackson shoved a folded newspaper across the table. Jorge peeked inside, saw four crisp hundred-dollar bills, closed it quickly and dragged it to his side of the booth.

"Ace made a cash payment once every month. I picked up the payments directly from Spalino and delivered the envelope to Hollister personally."

"What was the money for?"

"I don't know. I overheard them talking once... something to do with getting rid of waste."

Sarah exchanged a look with Jackson, neither of them had a clue what that meant. Still, the information might prove useful.

"What else?" Jackson slid another hundred out on the table.

"They talked about putting it somewhere safe. They didn't say where."

"Anything else?"

"That's all I got."

Jackson dropped a five-dollar bill on the table to pay for the coffee. With a nod at Jorge, he urged Sarah up from the booth, and they walked toward the door. Clues. Like pieces of a puzzle. Separately they meant nothing, but putting them altogether might just give them the answers they so desperately needed.

Outside in the parking lot, the light rain had already stopped, leaving a pattern of scattered drops in the dirt.

"It wasn't much, was it?" Sarah said.

"Might be more than you think. We're only getting started. Let's see what tomorrow brings."

Sarah just nodded. Her mind was spinning. So much

was happening. So many things seemed out of her control. She thought of the dark-skinned man in Wind Canyon who had threatened her in the parking lot. She thought of Detective Mercer, and a shudder moved down her spine.

If it weren't for Jackson...

A lump swelled in her throat. He was helping her now. But what would he do when he found out it wasn't just another of Andrew's crooked business partners who threatened her?

What would he do when he found out the police were after her, too?

Sarah slept poorly, even though she and Jackson had made love and he had convinced her to spend the night in his bed. Unconsciously, she snuggled closer, absorbing his warmth, his hard-muscled body enfolding her protectively even in his sleep.

Still, it wasn't enough to stop the nightmare from returning, slipping into her subconscious as it had done dozens of times before.

She was upstairs packing, getting ready to leave the house for good, when she heard Andrew's voice downstairs.

"Sarah! Sarah, come down here! I want to see you in my study!"

She could hear the anger in his voice, the fury. Fear cut through her, settled sickeningly in her stomach. Her glance strayed to the bed and uncertainty swamped her. She bit her lip, trying to decide, then stiffened her spine and moved forward. Her legs trembled as she crossed the bedroom, walked to the side of her bed and pulled the pistol out from under the mattress.

The pistol Patty Gorski had sent her.

"Use it if you have to," the brief note had said. "Don't let him hurt you again."

There were no serial numbers on the weapon. Patty was smart about those kinds of things. She'd sent it UPS, boxed like clothes ordered over the internet.

Sarah's hand shook as she stuck the gun in her purse, looped the strap over her shoulder. It took every ounce of her will to walk to the door, open it and make the trip downstairs. But the gun was there, lending her courage. She wouldn't pull it out unless she had to, but she wouldn't take another brutal beating.

She stood in the open study door, saw him rise from behind his desk.

"What...what do you want, Andrew?"

"Do you think I'm a fool, Sarah?"

Once she had thought he was handsome. Now his face looked pure evil. "Why would I think that?"

"Maybe because you didn't think I'd read your emails, find out what you were planning to do."

"I don't... I don't know what you're talking about." He couldn't know. She'd been so careful.

He just smiled. It was the kind of smile that made her stomach squeeze in fear, the kind that made her insides roll with nausea.

"I told you we were going to Rio. Did you actually think you were going to take Holly and run away?" His smile looked feral and her stomach rolled again. "I went directly to the server. I saw what you wrote to that woman."

She swallowed past the lump in her throat. "It was

only conversation." She had never been specific, only hinted to Patty. But Patty knew what Sarah had suffered, understood as no one else ever could.

Sarah straightened, determined not to let him know how frightened she was. "Holly and I aren't going with you. You can leave if you want, but we're staying here."

His mouth thinned to a slash across his face. "You really believe you can defy me? You don't remember what happened the last time?"

She remembered. He had beaten her so badly she'd wound up in the hospital. She swallowed, tried to block the memory.

He stepped away from his chair, rounded the corner of his desk. Fury etched lines into his face. Anticipation glittered in his eyes. He liked this, liked to hurt her.

"Andrew, please don't do this." She forced herself not to back away, to hold her ground and face him. When he just kept coming, she drew the pistol from her purse.

Her hand shook. "Stay away from me, Andrew. I'm warning you." A noise reached her. Was someone else in the house? "I—I won't let you hurt me again."

His cruel laughter rang in her ears. The hellish sound sent a jolt of adrenaline into her blood and awakened her from the nightmare. A shot?

Or maybe it was Jackson, whose face loomed above her as he reached out and caught her shoulders.

"Sarah? Sarah, are you all right?"

She swallowed past the bile that rose in her throat. Tears welled in her eyes, began to run down her cheeks. She was shaking so badly Jackson drew her into his arms.

"Take it easy, darlin'. It was only a dream."

Sarah clung to him, hung on as hard as she could.

"Easy," he soothed. "You're all right now."

She took a deep breath, exhaled slowly, fought to regain her composure. "I'll be okay. Just…just give me a minute."

"Take all the time you need." He stroked her hair, held her snugly against his chest. "It was him again," he said. "Andrew. You called out his name."

Her eyes slid closed. "Sometimes…" She swallowed. "Sometimes I remember the things he did and I get scared all over again. I wish I could forget, but at night…sometimes I can't."

She felt his lips against the top of her head. "It's all right, honey. Sometimes the past is hard to forget."

He talked as if he knew and she remembered his troubled childhood—the father who abandoned them, the mother who drank herself to death. Maybe he was like Patty. Maybe he understood.

They lay back on the mattress, and he curled her against his side, wrapped her in his arms as he pulled up the covers. She thought she wouldn't fall asleep, but his warmth and strength surrounded her, and she did.

The dream did not return. Jackson's presence banished it. But it would come again, she knew.

And if Mercer got his way, the nightmare she would face would be real.

Chapter 24

Jackson was in the shower when Sarah awakened. She heard the stream of water go off in the bathroom and a few minutes later, he opened the door. A rush of steam swept into the room, hiding him for a moment from view.

"I thought I'd let you sleep," he said. "After last night, I figured you could use a little extra time in bed."

A fluffy white towel rode low on his hips, exposing a flat abdomen ridged with muscle, a broad chest and powerful biceps. She allowed her gaze to run over him and wished he had awakened her with his lovemaking instead of letting her sleep.

"Keep looking at me that way and I'll take you up on what you're thinking. I'll have you again before we leave."

She laughed, wishing she could let him. "It's too late for that. We have too much to do."

He grumbled, and then he smiled. He had the most breathtaking smile. "There's always later." He walked over to the bed and pressed a soft kiss on her lips. "You'd better get going. We're driving all the way to East L.A."

She grabbed her silk robe, rolled out of bed and headed for the shower in the other bedroom. Twenty minutes later, she walked back through the door into the living room for some of the coffee and rolls he'd had room service bring up.

She sipped the rich black brew and nibbled the sweet pastry as she talked to Holly, laughing at the story of Rags chasing a big raccoon that turned and chased him back inside the house.

She smiled as she hung up the phone. "I miss her already."

"Maybe we'll have better luck today and we can go home."

Sarah hoped so. Last night Jackson had called Devlin after their meeting with Jorge Rodriguez. Dev had asked him to phone again if they found out anything more.

Sarah grabbed her purse, anxious to get started and see what they might discover. "Ready?"

Jackson nodded, walked over and opened the door.

As they drove out of the parking lot, she studied him, thinking of the call he'd made to Devlin. "You're very close to your brothers, aren't you?"

He shrugged, but it was clear it was an important subject. "We're all we've got," he said, as if that explained everything.

Sarah settled back against the seat. "You're lucky to have them. I always wanted a sister, but Mom had to have a hysterectomy so my parents never had more children. I have a friend in Chicago who's the closest I've got to a sister. It's crazy, since we've never even met."

"How did that happen?"

"She was one of the women in the battered women's group I told you about. She was the founder, the one who got the program started. We really seemed to connect." She told him a little about Patty, how funny she could be and how strong. How she hoped someday to meet her.

"I used to call her from a pay phone whenever I got the chance. She was my rock, the reason I could get out of bed in the morning." Sarah didn't say more, didn't even tell him Patty's last name. "She's the best friend I've ever had."

Jackson cast her a sympathetic glance as he took the 60 Freeway and continued along the road. Eventually, they found their way onto Brooklyn Avenue, the location of Southgate's project.

"You got the address?" he asked.

"Right here." She pulled out a slip of paper, read him the street numbers, and both of them started searching. The location wasn't hard to find. The demolition site was marked by a wide blue sign—Future Home of Freemark Plaza—a large office complex that would be a big asset to the neighborhood.

Just like the day before, one of Southgate's Demolition teams was hard at work. But this time, an Ace company truck sat next to the six-story building being torn down.

And the difference was instantly apparent.

"Oh, my God, they're hauling asbestos," Sarah said.

"'Something to do with waste,' Jorge said. The men must have been talking about asbestos."

Warning signs were everywhere, including on the trucks. Men completely enclosed in white protective suits, gloves, booties, and wearing sophisticated particle masks, worked in the interior of the six-story building which had been opened up on one side.

"The backs of the trucks are fully enclosed," Sarah said.

"Everything's enclosed, including the men."

The asbestos being removed was first sprayed down with water, she saw, then dropped through flexible tubing directly into the back of the trucks, or carried in tightly sealed plastic bags.

"Southgate does the demolition," Jackson said, "but they need special vehicles to haul the waste away."

They watched for more than an hour, but saw nothing but a group of men hard at work. One of the Ace trucks was finally filled and ready to leave. It had been tightly sealed to ensure none of the toxic particles escaped into the air.

"I don't know much about asbestos," Sarah said. "I know it causes cancer and lung disease."

But tonight they could find out more on the subject. Jackson had brought his laptop and the hotel provided wireless internet service.

They watched one of the trucks prepare to leave. The driver, wearing one of the white protective suits, climbed behind the wheel and drove the vehicle out through the chain-link fence surrounding the construction site.

"Come on. Let's see what happens next." Jackson started the Chevy, waited for the truck to pass, waited a few more minutes, then pulled in with the traffic headed in the same direction.

"Where do you suppose they dump that stuff?"

"Someplace that specifically handles toxic waste. I imagine the closest location is a pretty good distance away."

It wasn't as far as they thought, a disposal site located in the City of Commerce. The driver pulled up to a guarded gate, signed something on a clipboard and drove on into the facility. Jackson waited till the truck pulled back out, then followed its return to the construction site for another load.

"I hate to say this, but everything looked perfectly legitimate to me."

From their parking spot near the site, Sarah watched the Ace truck being filled with more of the wet asbestos. "It's daylight. Nobody does anything illegal in the daytime. I think we should do this like they do on TV—go down to Ace Trucking after dark and stake the place out."

"Stake the place out?" Jackson chuckled at the term. "You really think—"

"So far Jorge's information has gotten us nowhere. Have you got a better idea?"

He rubbed his jaw. "Not at the moment. All right, we'll give it a try. It'll be a damned long night, but I suppose it's worth a go."

They waited till eleven o'clock before leaving the hotel. Jackson helped Sarah into the car then drove toward the San Fernando Valley. The Ace Trucking compound was easy to spot. Rows of trucks sitting on an asphalt lot surrounded by a tall chain-link fence. A one-story building, flat-roofed and unimpressive, sat on one side of the compound. Inside, everything was dark.

"They look like they're locked up for the night," Jackson said, surveying the empty lot lit only by a few tall mercury lights.

"Maybe," Sarah said stubbornly. "Or maybe that's just what they want people to think."

Jackson didn't laugh. Sarah was smart. And considering the connection between Ace and Andrew Hollister—the cash payments and Jorge's comments—she just might be right.

The hours slowly passed. "You want some coffee?" he asked. They had stopped and bought a thermos at a Kmart they passed, drove through a McDonald's and had it filled with hot coffee.

"Sounds good."

Jackson poured some of the dark liquid into the plastic lid and they shared it. They were parked well out of sight, in a spot behind a patch of oleanders growing next to an empty metal building.

They sipped coffee, watched and waited. It was a warm night, only a quarter moon, making it easier for them to remain hidden.

At one o'clock, Sarah gave up a weary sigh. "I guess I was wrong. We might as well go back to the hotel."

Jackson surveyed the darkness, searching right and left one last time. The hair rose at the back of his neck. "Somebody's out there."

Sarah straightened in her seat. "Near one of the asbestos trucks?"

"No, just a regular truck and trailer. The guy just opened the door of the cab. Now he's climbing inside."

For a moment the dome light went on. "Yes, I see him. Another man just got in with him."

Jackson watched as the driver started the engine and slowly pulled the vehicle toward the gate. It opened automatically, then closed behind him. The truck continued slowly down the street, its headlights turned off. They didn't go on until the vehicle was nearly a block away.

Jackson waited until the truck turned the corner, then started the car and followed, careful to stay out of sight.

"I don't believe this," Sarah said.

"It might be nothing. Maybe just a job out of town that requires an early start."

"Or it might be what we've been looking for. Trucks don't usually drive around with their headlights turned off."

It was a little odd, he thought as the truck found its way onto the freeway. Jackson followed at a distance, taking the same on-ramp then an off-ramp several miles down the road, traveling the same streets, following a few cars behind. The truck turned into another fenced compound. The sign on the gate read, Hexel Pharmaceuticals.

The truck and trailer disappeared inside the compound, then drove through a huge roll-up door that led into an opening in one of the two-story buildings.

"Why would they need to come here in the middle of the night?" Sarah asked.

"Good question."

Fifteen minutes later the truck reappeared. When the driver drove beneath one of the lights in the yard,

Jackson saw that both men were wearing hazard suits, but this time the material wasn't white, it was black.

"White stands out too much," he said.

"Which means they don't want to be seen."

They waited till the truck disappeared down the street then pulled into the traffic and followed. The vehicle made its way onto the 15 Freeway, northbound.

"This is getting very interesting," Jackson said. "Not much out here. They may not be planning to stop anytime soon."

"Looks like we may be having breakfast in Las Vegas."

Jackson chuckled, thinking it could be true.

But a couple of hours into the drive, some miles east of the small desert town of Barstow in the middle of nowhere, the truck turned onto a frontage road. To maintain his distance, Jackson pulled onto the edge of the freeway just before their car reached the off-ramp and watched the truck until it turned onto a dirt road leading farther into the desert.

Sarah swiveled in the seat to face him. "You aren't going to stop now?"

He released a slow breath, wishing he could, but knowing how important this could be. "We saw where he turned. We'll wait another couple of minutes and go after them."

They waited, Sarah on the edge of her seat until Jackson took the off-ramp, then pulled onto the frontage road. When he reached the dirt road, he turned off the headlights.

"I hope we didn't lose them," Sarah said.

But there was no one around for miles out here. The

truck was running with only its parking lights on, but Jackson could easily make it out in the distance.

"It's turning again," Sarah said anxiously.

"I see that." He followed, keeping as far back as he could. The truck pulled to a stop. The dome light went on as one of the men got out.

Jackson was a quarter of a mile away when he pulled the car over to the side of the road and turned off the engine. Reaching up, he popped the plastic cover on the dome light and removed the bulb. "You stay here. I'm going to take a closer look."

"No way. I'm going with you."

"Sarah—"

She opened the door before he could argue and started walking along the road. Both of them were dressed in black and wearing comfortable shoes. Jackson swore softly and hurried to catch up with her.

"If you're determined to go, let's get off the road so we won't be spotted."

Sarah followed his lead, staying low, weaving in and out of the sagebrush and cactus that dotted the flat desert landscape.

"What about snakes?" she whispered as they hurried along.

"Just hope we don't step on any." Up ahead, the truck was parked at the base of a barren mountain where the road came to an end. Now as they watched, the vehicle started up again, drove inside a fenced compound, then into a hole in the side of the hill.

"It looks like a mine," Sarah said softly.

Jackson nodded. "There are probably a lot of them out here."

The area was surrounded by fencing, but a lot of it

was falling down. Near the gate leading into the yard, a sign hung at an angle. Dry Springs Mine. Another sign read, Axis Mining Company.

"Oh, my God."

"Yeah." Both of them recognized the names. The bankrupt mining company had been listed as one of Hollister's assets.

"I'm trying to remember…" Sarah said. "Andrew mentioned it a couple of times. As far as I recall, it was never productive, just an old, played-out gold mine Andrew's father bought on a whim." She looked back at the entrance where the truck had disappeared. "They must be dumping something from the pharmaceutical company in there."

"Biowaste would be my guess."

She started forward and Jackson caught her arm, stopping her. "We're pushing our luck, Sarah. We need to call the authorities."

For once she didn't argue. Whatever was going on, it appeared to be highly illegal. They needed to talk to Richard Kemp, tell the FBI what they had seen and let them find out exactly what was going on.

"Come on. Let's get out of here." Catching hold of her hand, he turned and took a step, came to an abrupt halt as he stared into the barrel of a gun.

"Too late for that," said a man's deep voice. The black hazard suit was gone. He was tall, lean and wiry, thin-faced, with hair as black as the night. Jackson might have gone for the weapon if the man hadn't swung it toward Sarah, pressed it up against the side of her head.

She made a little whimpering sound, but didn't move.

"Where's your car?" the man asked.

"Just down the road," Jackson answered.

"Let's go."

They walked along the dirt road, both of them moving in front of the man with the pistol, a big Glock 9 mm, it looked like.

He shoved Jackson toward the driver's side. "Get in and drive." He tipped his head toward Sarah. "You get up front with him."

She did as she was told while the man with the gun got into the backseat and aimed the weapon at the back of her head.

"Where are we going?" Jackson asked.

"Back to the yard. Mr. Spalino wants a word with you."

So they'd been in touch with the boss. Apparently cell phones worked even out here. Jackson started the Chevy, turned it around in the road, and headed back to L.A. He drove carefully. With Sarah the target, he couldn't afford to take chances.

It seemed to take forever to reach the trucking company back in the San Fernando Valley. The lights were on in the office when they drove through the gate, which stood open as if in welcome.

"Pull up in front."

Jackson did as directed, waited till the man climbed out of the car and yanked Sarah out, then climbed out himself. Another guy stood on the porch in front of the door, stocky, with a heavy thatch of iron-gray hair and a bulldog face.

Vincent Spalino.

"It's a little early for visitors—even around here." Spalino tipped his head toward the man with the gun. "Bring 'em inside, Floyd."

Jackson rested a hand on Sarah's shoulder, hoping to reassure her. If Spalino wanted them dead, there was no better time or place than out there at the mine.

They walked into Spalino's office, Spartan, with a metal desk and chairs, a brown vinyl sofa that looked as if it occasionally served as a bed, and a few family photos on the wall. The door closed behind them. The tall guy, Floyd, didn't come in.

Spalino walked behind his desk but remained standing. "Take a seat."

Jackson sat down next to Sarah in cushioned metal chairs on the opposite side of the desk.

"All right," Spalino said, "who the hell are you and what the hell do you want?"

Sarah cast Jackson a glance that told him she was the one who needed to speak. "I'm Sarah Hollister— Andrew's wife. This is a friend, Jackson Raines. We came to find out why you've been making threats against me and my daughter."

"So, you're Hollister's widow."

"That's right."

Spalino sat down in his black leather chair. "Well, I've got news for you, lady. Your husband had more enemies than fingers and toes. If someone's been threatening you, it ain't me."

"The way I hear it," Jackson put in, "Andrew Hollister was blackmailing you. You figured Sarah knew you were dumping pharmaceuticals out at the mine and you wanted to make sure she kept her mouth shut."

He grunted. "First off, me and Hollister were business partners. That's all. He didn't ask for anything more than we agreed on. Hexel paid me to dump the stuff, and I paid Hollister for the use of his property. He was happy to get the money."

Jackson mulled that over. Hollister had been blackmailing Kozak, but not Spalino. "If it isn't you, it must be the pharmaceutical company."

Spalino shrugged his bulky shoulders. "Could be. The company's got real deep pockets. Hollister might have figured he could squeeze a little more out of 'em."

"Would they come after Sarah?"

"They might. It's a small company with big plans. The guys who run it haven't been around that long. They still don't know the ropes."

Meaning they were wild cards, just the sort to cause trouble.

"The dumping has to stop," Sarah said.

Spalino leaned back in his chair. "We ain't paying your husband no more. I told those guys at Hexel that sooner or later it would have to end. With Hollister dead, the mine's in probate. Better to seal it up now, before somebody starts sniffing around."

"What do you mean, *seal it up?*" Sarah asked.

He eyed her with speculation, as if weighing how much he could say. "You got the cash, right? The money your husband got paid? He was thinking of leavin' the country. I figured he was putting away a little nest egg. When he died, you got the cash so we're in this together, right?"

Sarah opened her mouth.

"She's got the money," Jackson answered for her. "We're all in this together."

Spalino nodded. "The stuff's stored in fifty-gallon drums. The drums are stashed in one of the auxiliary mine shafts. A few sticks of dynamite to close the entrance to the shaft and the barrels are safely disposed of, all nice and tidy."

Jackson looked at Sarah. Now wasn't the time to argue. She made a faint nod of her head, clearly getting the message.

"What about Hexel Pharmaceuticals?" Jackson asked. "How do we get them to leave Sarah alone?"

"I'll talk to them, explain the deal." He turned to Sarah. "If they're the ones who been hassling you, they won't give you any more trouble."

Jackson caught Sarah's faint wash of relief.

"That...that sounds fair."

"Hey, we all came out winners, didn't we? Hexel will have to figure something out, but you know, that's their problem."

He rose from behind his chair. "Too bad about your husband. Him and me—we always got along real good."

Sarah made no reply. It was difficult to manage a nod.

"Your car's out front," Spalino said.

"Thanks." Jackson rose and so did Sarah. He set his hand at her waist and guided her toward the door.

"One more thing."

Both of them stopped and turned.

"You open your mouth to the wrong people—you won't be getting threats. You'll be dead."

Chapter 25

"I want to go home." Sarah turned as Jackson closed the door to their suite behind them. It was seven-thirty in the morning and they were just getting back to the hotel.

"All right. I'll call the airport, make arrangements to leave. We'll be back in Wyoming before dark."

Sarah paced over to the window and looked down into the courtyard. She watched a young valet pull a car up in front of the lobby, then wait for the driver to climb inside.

She turned back to Jackson. "This all seems so surreal."

"I know what you mean."

"I don't feel right about leaving that stuff in the mine. We don't even know what it is."

"Some kind of waste from whatever it is Hexel doesn't want anyone to know they're doing."

"I feel like I should do something, but—" She shook her head. "But I've got Holly to think of." She returned to staring out the window, watched the valet through a sudden film of tears. "How could I have married a man like that? How could I not have seen what he was like from the beginning?"

Jackson walked up behind her. Slipping his arms around her waist, he drew her back against his chest. "You were young. He was good at what he did and that included conning you."

She turned around and leaned into him, slid her arms around his neck. "I wish it had been you."

He moved a strand of dark hair off her cheek with his finger. "There's time, Sarah. You're young yet and so am I. Things can still work out."

She looked up at him and the tears in her eyes rolled down her cheeks. She stepped out of his embrace, felt a chill at the loss of his warmth. "I won't marry again, Jackson. Not ever. You might as well know that. If you're looking for a wife, you need to look somewhere else."

Jackson's gaze remained on her face. "I wasn't looking for a wife when you came along, Sarah. I'm not looking now. But unlike you, if the right person happens to come into my life—if I fall in love—I won't throw away the chance for happiness."

Sarah felt a sharp pinch in her heart. *If I fall in love*...

She was in love with Jackson. She didn't think he knew and she would never tell him. How could she? How could she drag a good man like Jackson into the kind of sordid life she had been living? The kind that seemed to follow her wherever she went?

"I need to pack," she said, turning away from him and heading for her bedroom.

"I'll arrange our flight home."

Sarah paused at the door and looked back at him, saw him reach for the phone. He was so handsome her heart squeezed. She had never met anyone like him. She never would again.

She was in love with him and she didn't deserve him.

She stepped into the bedroom, closed the door and leaned against it. If Spalino kept his bargain, she and Holly would be safe.

There was no reason to continue her impossible relationship with Jackson.

There was only one thing to do.

As soon as she got back to Wyoming, she was moving off Raintree Ranch.

The plane returned them safely home. Jackson drove his pickup, which he'd left at the Wind Canyon airport, back down the road to the ranch. Sarah sat in silence beside him.

"You're supposed to be feeling better," he finally said. "I've got a hunch Vincent Spalino is a man of his word, and I'm pretty sure Hexel Pharmaceuticals is behind the threats against you. Spalino will talk to them and hopefully, your problems will disappear."

She looked up at him with troubled blue eyes. "I hope you're right. I still don't like the idea of just looking the other way while Hexel dumps its garbage into the mine or somewhere else. They don't want to go to a legitimate toxic dump site because they don't want anyone to know what they're doing. God only knows what that is—or what the consequences might be."

Jackson slowed to let a deer cross the road. A small spotted fawn followed its mother. "I'll talk to Dev. Maybe we can come up with a way to handle the problem without involving you."

She nodded, sighed and settled back in the seat. She fell silent again as he turned down the private road leading into the ranch. A car sat in front of the main house, he saw as they drove up, a plain brown Ford Taurus with bald tires that needed replacing.

Jimmy stood in front of the driver's-side door talking to the man, who had straight brown hair cut short, a bad complexion, and wore wrinkled khaki slacks. Sarah made a funny sound in her throat as Jackson pulled the pickup to a stop in front of the ranch house next to the car.

Jackson turned. "You know who that is?"

She glanced away. He could see she was upset.

"Who is he, Sarah?"

She trembled. "He's...he's a policeman from Los Angeles...a detective named Mercer."

Jackson opened the door of the pickup, rounded the vehicle and helped Sarah climb down. Mercer turned away from Jimmy and started walking toward them.

"Welcome back," the man said to Jackson with a smile that looked anything but sincere. "I'm Detective Ed Mercer, homicide division, LAPD. I'd like a word with you, Mr. Raines."

"Why did you come back here?" Sarah interjected. "Why can't you leave me alone?"

"I'm just on vacation," Mercer said, "heading home

after two weeks off. I told you that when I came to see you before."

Jackson looked at Sarah hard. She hadn't mentioned the detective's visit. He couldn't help wondering why.

"If you'll excuse us, Sarah," Mercer said, "I'd like to talk to your friend alone."

Jackson could see she wanted to join them, but Mercer wasn't giving her a choice.

"Holly's probably with Livvy," Jackson said. "I'll send her home."

Sarah just nodded, watching as he and Mercer walked inside the ranch house. Holly spotted him and came running in from the kitchen, bubbling with excitement.

"Jackson!" She ran to him and he lifted her into his arms.

"You keep growing," he teased, "and pretty soon you'll be too heavy for me to lift."

She giggled at that. "I'm glad you and Mama are home."

He gave her a kiss on the cheek and set her back down on her feet. "Your mama's waiting for you in the cottage."

Holly flashed a grin, then took off running, heading back into the kitchen, slamming out the screen door and racing for home.

Jackson turned to the detective. "Why don't we go into my study? We can speak privately there." He headed that way and Mercer fell in behind him. Once the door was closed, he moved toward his desk instead of the sofa, forcing Mercer to take a seat in one of the brown leather chairs on the opposite side.

"So what can I do for you, Detective?"

Mercer surveyed the study, his gaze taking in the leather-bound books on the shelves and the old pot-bellied stove. Though Jackson didn't even know the man, there was something about him that rubbed him the wrong way.

Mercer leaned back in his chair. "Like I said, I was just passing through. I thought I'd stop by, see if there was something you might be able to tell me about Andrew Hollister's murder."

Jackson eyed him carefully. "How could I tell you anything? I wasn't there when it happened. I didn't even know the guy."

"No, but you know the woman who shot him."

Jackson's whole body tightened. He held on to his temper, but only by a thread. "As far as I know, Sarah Allen isn't even a suspect in her husband's murder."

"Oh, she's a suspect, all right. She was there that night. It isn't clear exactly what time she left the house but she could have been there at the time the murder was committed. She had motive. It was common knowledge the woman hated her husband. Hollister had a girlfriend and Sarah found out. Oh, and there was the life insurance policy."

"What are you talking about? Sarah got almost nothing from Hollister's estate."

"True enough. Turned out the policy was expired. But then, Sarah didn't know it at the time. She didn't find that out until later."

"That's all you have? She might have been there around the time he was killed and she didn't like him?"

"Motive and opportunity, my friend. And the spouse is always the number one suspect. In this case, it all adds up."

"And how, exactly, did she kill him? Point her finger at him and pull the trigger? Sarah doesn't own a gun."

"We haven't found the murder weapon yet, but sooner or later, something's going to turn up that proves she was the one who shot him."

Jackson came out of his chair. "This conversation is over. Unless you're here with an arrest warrant, Detective, it's time for you to leave."

Mercer stood up, too. "Like I said, I was on vacation. Two weeks this year. I just figured I'd drop by, see if you might have something you wanted to tell me."

"Yeah, well, I don't. And since this is private property, I'd suggest you get moving. I'm sure they could use your services back in L.A."

Mercer smiled the same unfriendly smile he'd flashed before. "I'll keep in touch. You never know... you might have a change of heart."

Jackson made no comment, just stood fuming as Mercer walked out of the study.

Change of heart? One thing he knew for sure. Where his heart was concerned, it was already too late for a change.

Sarah opened the door to let Holly and Rags out to play. She froze at the sight of Jackson standing on the porch, his fist raised to knock, as angry as she had ever seen him.

Two thoughts occurred: First, she wasn't actually afraid of him—not in a physical sense. She had finally realized Jackson would never hurt her. Second, he had come to talk about Andrew. He had spoken to Mercer. He knew the detective believed she was a murderer.

Holly and Rags rushed past him out the door, the

little black-and-white dog yipping as the pair ran off to play. Sarah just stood there.

"We need to talk," Jackson said, his jaw hard as steel.

Sarah managed a nod. "Come in." She stepped back out of the way, letting him walk past her into the living room. He didn't sit down and neither did she.

"He was here before, wasn't he?"

It wasn't exactly what she expected him to say. She had expected accusations. "He was here."

"Why didn't you tell me?"

"Because I've brought you more than enough trouble already."

"That isn't good enough. What are you leaving out?"

She swallowed past the lump that rose in her throat. "I couldn't bear to see the way you would look at me once you knew the police believed I was a murderer."

Jackson released a breath. "You still haven't figured it out, have you? You still aren't sure you can trust me. I'm your friend, Sarah. Whatever you tell me, I'm not going to look at you any differently. All I've ever wanted to do is help you. I can't do that if you don't tell me what's going on."

When she didn't move, Jackson reached out, drew her into his arms, and she didn't resist. It was hard to believe he was taking her side again and yet clearly he was.

"I'll talk to Dev," he said. "Ask him to find out who this guy is and what's going on with the murder investigation."

A trickle of fear slid through her and her shoulders stiffened. "Please, Jackson." She eased out of his embrace. "I'd rather you didn't. I don't want any more trouble. Lieutenant Delaney was the detective in charge of the investigation—he's Mercer's boss. The lieutenant thinks someone Andrew owed money to killed him. I don't think the police are trying that hard to find out. I keep hoping…praying that in time things will settle down and this will all go away."

Jackson made no comment. Clearly he wanted to do more than ignore the matter. His jaw flexed, but he didn't argue. For now it seemed he was willing to concede to her wishes.

"Next time you tell me if someone shows up and gives you any trouble."

Sarah opened her mouth, then closed it again and simply nodded. Jackson stalked across the living room toward the door. He was still angry but not because of Mercer's accusations. He was mad at her for not asking him for help.

She watched him walk out the door and close it solidly behind him, her heart squeezing hard in her chest. He was the best man she'd ever known and she was totally in love with him.

Still, she couldn't let things continue as they were, couldn't afford to get in any deeper.

How would she ever find the courage to leave?

It was dark outside, a warm summer wind blowing through the trees, making a soft whistling sound. As Jackson walked into his study, the phone started ringing. He headed to his desk and picked it up.

"Hey, brother."

"Gabe! Been a while since I've heard from you. What's going on?"

"Just thought I'd call and see how things went in

California. I spoke to Dev a couple of times, so I know a little of what's been happening to Sarah."

Jackson raked a hand through his hair. "Things have been pretty much upside down, I can tell you." He explained to Gabe about the stakeout and the waste being dumped in the mine, that it looked as if Hexel Pharmaceuticals had been behind the recent threats to Sarah, and that he hoped Vincent Spalino would help get things worked out.

"I was just getting ready to call Dev and fill him in," Jackson said. "I meant to call earlier, but somehow time slipped away." *Somehow. Like spending the afternoon talking to a homicide detective about Sarah's possible involvement in her husband's murder.*

He didn't believe for a moment that Sarah had murdered the guy. It just wasn't something she would do. What he needed was information on Ed Mercer and he hoped Dev could help him get it.

"You're into some serious stuff, bro. If anyone can help, it's Dev. Call him tonight, Jackson. Don't screw around with this."

"I'll call him right now." Jackson hung up the phone, thinking he was lucky to have two brothers he could count on no matter how tough things got.

He phoned Dev at his Scottsdale home. After the third ring, the phone went to voice mail. "This is Dev. I'm hard at work or doing something fun. Leave your number and I'll call you."

"It's Jackson. Ring me when you get the chance."

An hour later, Dev returned the call. He sounded sleepy—or satisfied. Jackson had a feeling it was the latter. Which was an irritating reminder that he could have had Sarah this morning before he left the

Gramercy Hotel, that he wanted her fiercely right now.
The feeling put a grouchy note in his voice.

"I called an hour ago. I hope you were enjoying
yourself."

Dev chuckled, then yawned. "The lady had to go
to work early or I'd still be enjoying myself. I gather
you're back in Wyoming. How did your trip go?"

Jackson exhaled deeply. "You'd better make yourself comfortable. This is going to take a while." Even
over the phone, Jackson could feel his brother tense.

"Tell me," he said.

For the next half hour, Jackson relayed the events of
last night, starting with the stakeout at Ace, following
the truck to Hollister's abandoned mine, the trip back
at gunpoint and the conversation with Vincent Spalino.

Dev whistled into the phone. "Now you know why
I'm mostly retired."

"You aren't retired—which is the reason I'm calling. I need you to see if you can find out what Hexel's dumping and why. If it's nothing that will do any
harm, we'll leave things the way they are. Unfortunately, considering the pressure they've been putting
on Sarah, I'm thinking whatever it is, it's probably not
going to be good."

"I'll see what I can do. That it?"

"There's one more thing...a detective named Ed
Mercer. He's LAPD. Showed up at the house this afternoon. It's his second visit. He's convinced Sarah
killed her husband and he's determined to prove it. It
seems personal, Dev. I want to know why Mercer's
made Sarah his personal target."

"I'll get started first thing in the morning." He

yawned again. "Meantime, I think I'll get some sleep. I'm damned well worn out."

Jackson grumbled a curse and hung up the phone.

He sighed into the quiet of the study. He had bought himself a handful of trouble when he'd let Sarah stay in the cottage. But right now, all he could think of was climbing back into her bed.

Sarah left the real estate office on Friday afternoon, a rental flyer clutched in her hand. She had gone to the office after work, spoken to a Realtor, and the woman had shown her a small house for rent at the edge of town that she could afford. It wasn't as nice as the cottage on Raintree Ranch, but every day she spent with Jackson, the harder it was going to be to leave him.

And there was Holly to think of. Her daughter was beginning to think of Jackson as the father she'd never had. Sarah couldn't let that happen. Not when it all might come to a crashing end.

She had to move. Mercer had left her no choice. In truth she should leave Wyoming entirely. Maybe in time, she would.

But she loved her job and she loved this town. She was beginning to make friends and so was Holly. Her grandmother was here and they were becoming a family again. She would stay for as long as she could. She was making her way along the boardwalk toward the parking lot when she heard someone calling her name.

"Sarah! Sarah, wait!" Nan Hargrove waved. Strands of red hair brushed her flushed cheeks as she hurried across the street.

"Nan, it's good to see you." The two women hugged.

"You, too." Nan settled in beside her, the two of

them strolling together along the walk. "I hear you've been traveling. Jimmy said you and Jackson went out to California. I hope you had fun."

Fun? Sarah inwardly shuddered at the memory of the man who'd held a gun against her head. "It wasn't exactly fun. It's a long story, Nan. Problems left by my late husband. I just can't seem to escape him, even now that he's dead."

Nan shifted her Wilkins' Mercantile bag from one hand to the other. "I guess in some ways, I was lucky. Ron and I are friends. Well, not exactly friends, but we get along. We don't try to hurt each other the way some divorced couples do."

They walked past a small shop called Mountain High, a new winter clothing store that was just getting ready to open. The town was growing, but slowly. Which suited Sarah just fine.

"So how are things going with you and Jimmy?" she asked.

Nan smiled dreamily. "I'm crazy about him, Sarah. And I think he really likes me." She stared down at her feet. "We, uh, spent the night together last weekend." She looked up and grinned. "It was fantastic. But then I always figured it would be."

Sarah couldn't help thinking of Jackson. He made her feel womanly and sexy. She had never really understood desire until she met him. And even as she had made the arrangements to move away from the ranch into the house in town, she'd wanted him. She wanted him now.

"What about you and Jackson? You guys moved in together yet?"

Sarah paused on the boardwalk. "I'm moving into

town, Nan. My husband's been dead less than six months. I'm not ready to get serious with a man."

Nan's red eyebrows arched up. "You told me you and your husband had been estranged for years. It's not like you had any kind of real marriage."

"I know."

Nan's shrewd gaze searched her face. "To tell you the truth, I thought…well, I thought you two were in love. I mean, the way you looked at him…and the way he looked at you." She rolled her eyes. "You could start a fire with a look like that."

Sarah smiled, but it was tinged with regret. "What I feel for Jackson doesn't matter. I'm just not ready, that's all."

Nan gently caught her arm. "Hey. I'm your friend, no matter what happens between you and Jackson, okay?"

Her chest squeezed. She treasured what few friends she had. She was grateful to have Nan as one of them. "Thank you. You can't imagine how much that means."

Nan leaned over and hugged her. "Maybe you just need a little more time."

"Maybe." But Sarah didn't think so. Not with a murder investigation hanging over her head.

Not with a bloodhound like Mercer digging and digging, determined to put her in jail.

Chapter 26

It rained through the night, a light, soothing patter against the roof. On Saturday morning, Sarah fixed breakfast for Holly then began to sort through her belongings, what little she had left after her move from California. She had been bringing home cardboard boxes, enough to make the move into town.

Her luggage sat open on the bed, some of her clothes neatly folded inside. She carted a couple of the boxes into the living room. It was warm this July morning, a little damp from the mist that still hung in the air.

In concession to what would likely be a hot summer day, she had left her feet bare and dressed in a sleeveless white blouse and a pair of cutoff jeans. She was trying to decide whether to start in the living room or go back to the bedroom when a familiar knock sounded at the door.

She peeked out the window to see Jackson standing on the porch, handsome as sin in his jeans, hat and boots. A memory surfaced of the last time they had made love, and a jolt of heat slid low into her stomach. She took a deep breath and opened the door, wishing the coming confrontation could be postponed for a couple more days.

Beneath the brim of his hat, his dark eyes ran over her face. "Good morning," he said.

She smiled back as he took off the hat and held it in his hand. "Good morning."

He looked past her into the living room, saw the string of open boxes and his eyebrows drew together. "What's going on?"

She thought how much she was going to miss him. How much she loved him, how hard it would be to explain.

"I'm leaving the ranch, Jackson. Holly and I are moving into town."

His frown deepened. "What are you talking about?"

"I—I'll be closer to my work, and Holly... Holly will be closer to school when it starts. She'll have a better chance to make friends—we both will."

Jackson looked at her as if she had punched him in the stomach. He looked past her to the boxes, looked into her face again. He didn't say a word, just stepped into the living room and closed the door firmly behind him. Sailing his hat onto the table, he moved toward her, slid a hand into her hair and dragged her mouth up to his for a long, scorching kiss.

Her insides melted. Oh, God, the man could kiss. His tongue found its way into her mouth and heat and need broke loose inside her. He tasted male and sexy.

His clothes carried the scent of leather and hay. Jackson deepened the kiss. Sarah felt the hardness of his erection pressing against the fly of his jeans, gripped his shoulders and just hung on.

She was way past stopping him. Instead, her tongue slid over his and everything inside her went liquid and warm.

Sarah heard him groan. Drawing her even more firmly against him, he deepened the kiss, and desire rose fierce and hot. He backed her into the bedroom, kicked the door closed with the heel of his boot, but didn't stop moving till her shoulders came up against the wall. The curtains were closed. He must have seen Holly outside playing.

"Jackson…"

"Maybe this will convince you to stay." He cupped her face in his hands and kissed her again then unbuttoned the front of her blouse and filled his hands with her breasts. His tongue ringed her nipple, turned the end diamond-hard.

Her knees started shaking as he sucked in the fullness, laved and tasted, grazed her nipple with his teeth. Capturing her lips, he kissed her as he worked the zipper on her cutoff jeans, shoved them down over her hips, along with her white thong panties. They slithered down her legs and pooled on the floor and he lifted her out of them.

Sarah whimpered as he unfastened his belt buckle, unzipped his fly and freed himself, wrapped her hand around his powerful erection.

"This is how much I want you."

He was big and hard and pulsing. "Dear God…" He

felt hot in her hand and when her fingers tightened, he hardened even more.

Jackson parted her legs and began to stroke her. One of his big hands caressed her breast, and pleasure tugged low in her belly. How could she have forgotten how good he was at this and how much she loved it?

Lifting her, propping her back against the wall, he wrapped her legs around his waist and filled her with a single deep thrust.

Sarah softly moaned.

"We're good together, Sarah—you know how good. How can you think about leaving?"

Beneath his shirt, the muscles in his shoulders moved and tightened. Bands of muscle bunched in his chest. Sarah grabbed the front of his shirt and popped the snaps, pressed her lips against his hot, sun-darkened skin, and Jackson hissed in a breath.

Cupping her bottom in his hands, he began to move, driving himself deep inside her. Pleasure merged with the love she felt for him, heightening the sweet sensations. Her head tipped forward onto his shoulder and goose bumps feathered across her skin.

"You don't want to go, Sarah." He nipped the side of her neck and thrust deeply again. "You know you don't."

It was true. Leaving was the last thing she wanted.

Jackson drove into her, eased out and drove into her again, and a deep, sucking orgasm hit her. Moaning, she buried her face against his shoulder, but Jackson didn't stop until she came again. Then a low, growling came from his throat and he followed her to release.

Long seconds passed. Limp and sated, she held on to him as he lowered her to her feet. He zipped his jeans and fastened his buckle, bent his head and very softly kissed her.

He handed Sarah her discarded garments. "I don't want you to go."

Sarah turned away from him and began to put on her clothes, needing a moment to compose herself.

Once she was dressed, she forced herself to turn and face him. "I have to go, Jackson. It's something I just have to do."

"Even if you want to leave, you can't—at least not right now."

"Why not?"

"Vincent Spalino is dead."

"What?"

"That's what I came to tell you. Dev called this morning. Apparently one of the people in his L.A. office saw it on the news. Spalino's secretary found him this morning sitting at his desk, dead of a heart attack."

A shiver went through her. She read the worry on his face. "It wasn't a heart attack, was it?"

"Dev doesn't think so. Neither do I."

"Hexel makes pharmaceuticals. They would know what to do to kill someone and make it look like a natural death." She raised her gaze to his face. "Oh, God, Jackson, what am I going to do?"

He moved toward her, eased her into his arms. "After our trip to the mine, I'm also on Hexel's radar, which means the question is the same as it always has been—what are *we* going to do?"

Sarah moved away from him, trying to think things through, trying to stay calm and failing. She saw him through a film of tears. "This is all my fault. I never should have come here."

"But you did, and I'm glad, and somehow we'll get through this."

"How?"

"I don't know yet."

She raked back her hair and glanced over at the empty cardboard boxes. "I should leave. Maybe if I did, they'd forget you're involved."

He chuckled but it wasn't with mirth. "Those guys at Hexel aren't going to forget. We have to find a way to stop them."

"Maybe it's time to call the police."

"Maybe. In that regard, it might interest you to know the reason Ed Mercer has it out for you is because you were Hollister's wife. Apparently, he got divorced about eight months ago. His wife took him to the cleaners. She got custody of his two kids and he got minimum visitation. He can't get to her, but he figures to make you and every other woman pay for what she did to him."

"Mercer may have had troubles in his marriage, but he couldn't begin to understand what it was like living with a man like Andrew. He couldn't begin to know the fear—not only for myself but for Holly."

"The good news is most of the cops think he's gone off the deep end. He hasn't got any real evidence and apparently they aren't giving much credence to his theory." He reached out and stroked her cheek. "For now, let's not worry about Mercer. Let's just figure out what to do about those guys at Hexel."

"Before they kill us, you mean. Just like Vincent Spalino."

Chapter 27

Sarah awakened to the low roll of thunder outside the cottage. It had rained again last night, for which everyone was grateful. She glanced at the glowing red numbers of the clock on the nightstand and shot up from the bed.

It was almost nine-thirty. She hadn't been able to sleep last night so she'd taken a couple of Tylenol PM. They had worked so well she had overslept. She was surprised Holly hadn't come in to wake her hours ago. Maybe she had overslept, too.

Grabbing her fleece robe off the foot of the bed, Sarah hurriedly drew it on and walked to the bedroom door. As she stepped into the living room, the house seemed oddly quiet and a little tremor of unease went through her.

"Holly?" She opened the door to her daughter's

bedroom, saw the rumpled bed, the colorful quilt that Livvy had made decorated with tiny fawns and bear cubs, but no sign of her little girl.

Certain Holly must be outside playing, she started to close the door then happened to glance at the window. She frowned as she walked toward it. Holly liked to sleep with the window partly open so she could feel the cool night air, but the window was completely closed.

She leaned in closer toward the glass panes and looked down to the ground. Big, deep footprints were stamped into the mud. Terror filled Sarah's stomach. Whirling around, the air stalled in her lungs as she caught sight of the square of paper lying on Holly's pillow. Her hand shook as she picked it up.

If you want to see your daughter alive, bring Jackson Raines and come to the old mining shack near Alpine Meadow. Take the Bear Flat Road. You've got till noon. No police or she's dead.

Biting back a cry of sheer panic, Sarah turned and ran from the room, the paper gripped in her hand. Tears threatened as she raced out of the house. Asleep on the porch, Rags's head popped up. He jumped up and barked and started running along beside her.

Through the open barn door, Sarah spotted Jackson working.

"Jackson!" She tripped and nearly fell. Tears burned her eyes. Fear made it hard to breathe. "Jackson!"

He ran toward her, caught her hard against his chest. "What is it? What's happened?"

"It…it's Holly." Her voice broke. "They've taken her." The tears in her eyes spilled onto her cheeks.

Her hand shook as she handed him the note. Jackson scanned the words and his jaw went granite-hard.

"We'll get her back, Sarah, I promise you."

"Oh, God, Jackson—"

"It's all right. Everything's going to be okay."

"Do you know this place? Can you get there?"

Jackson caught her arm. "I know you want to go with me, but—"

She jerked away from him. "I'm going. She's my daughter. Don't you dare try to stop me."

Jackson seemed to read her determination. "All right, go get dressed. I'll get my gear and meet you at the truck."

Jackson looked up to see Jimmy Threebears walking toward him. "What's going on? I heard you talking. What's happened to Holly?"

"It's a long story, Jim." He glanced back at Sarah and saw her dash into the cottage. "Same problem as before, different players. And these guys mean business." He handed Jimmy the note, which he read as the two of them strode toward the ranch house.

"What are you going to do?"

"They've got Holly. We've got to do whatever they say."

"These are city folks, right? How did they know that shack was even up there?"

"Must have paid someone who lives around here for information." Everyone in the area knew about the old abandoned cabin at the top of the mountain. In the winter, the local cross-country ski group took snowmobiles up there and used it as a warming hut. The rest of the year, few people bothered with it since it was difficult to reach.

"You need to call the sheriff," Jimmy said as they pushed through the back door into the kitchen. Livvy was off on Sundays so the room was cold and quiet. "You can't do this alone."

Jackson continued through the house into his study. He went directly over to the gun cabinet, unlocked it and opened the etched glass doors. Pulling out the .308 Winchester rifle he used for hunting, he set it on top of the desk, his mind running over his options—which were few and far between.

"All right, here's what we'll do," he finally said to Jimmy. "The road up to the cabin is bad in the best of weather. After two nights of rain, it's going to be a real sonofabitch. It'll take us a couple of hours to get there, even with four-wheel drive. Give me half an hour to get Holly out of there, then call Ben Weber. Tell him to get a chopper up there. He should be able to land in the meadow."

Jimmy reached past him into the gun case. He pulled out the Colt .44 revolver Jackson carried whenever he was in the mountains and laid it next to the rifle, silently telling him one was not enough.

"I've got a better idea," Jim said. "You drive the road. Make sure you get up there at exactly noon. In the meantime, Wheel and I will trailer a couple of horses and head for the trailhead. We'll ride in the back way. It's a shorter route. Should take about the same amount of time. With luck, we'll be there to cover you when you get there."

Jackson lifted his battered straw hat and tugged it into place on his forehead. "I'm not sure what we'll be facing up there, Jim. You've got your sons to think of."

"I wouldn't be much of a father if I taught them to abandon a friend when he needs my help."

Something tightened in Jackson's throat. He could always count on Jimmy. "What about Wheel? This isn't his problem."

"They took that little girl right off the ranch. Holly's been taken and that makes it his problem. Besides, I know Wheel, and I know we can count on him."

"All right, we'll play it your way. Tell Sam what's going on and have him call the sheriff at exactly twelve-fifteen. That doesn't give us much room for error, but if something goes wrong, maybe Ben can get there in time to pick up the pieces."

Jimmy nodded. He shoved both guns across the top of the desk. "I've got my own rifle and Wheel's got his." He grinned. "See you at the top of the mountain, Wyatt." And then he was gone.

Thinking of the days when they were kids playing cowboys and Indians—Wyatt Earp and Cochise—Jackson collected the rifle and pistol and headed for the door, stopping only long enough to grab his jacket off the coatrack.

Sarah was waiting next to the truck, dressed in jeans and a shirt, carrying her jacket, a blanket and a canvas satchel.

"Clothes for Holly in case she needs them," she said as she climbed in, and the lump returned to his throat.

His hand tightened around the stock of the rifle. He was tired of playing games with these people. They were in his territory now, not some shadowy street in L.A. And today—one way or another—he was going to end it.

Jerking open the driver's-side door, he shoved his

pistol under the seat and rested his rifle on the seat behind him. Once Sarah was buckled in, he cranked the engine, put the truck into gear and headed for the road leading up to Alpine Meadow.

Devlin Raines pulled his rental car up in front of the ranch house and turned off the engine. His brother was usually outside working, but at the moment, no one seemed to be around. Then he spotted Jimmy Three-bears and the tall, lanky cowboy, Wheel Dillon, loading a couple of saddle horses into the back of a trailer.

"Hey, Jimmy!" he called as he climbed out of the car and started walking toward them.

"Dev!" Features grim, the big Sioux strode in his direction. "Am I glad to see you."

Something was wrong. Dev could hear it in Jimmy's voice. It was the reason he had flown all the way to Wyoming. After what had happened to Vincent Spalino, he'd had a bad feeling his brother was in trouble.

"What's going on? Where's Jackson?"

"Headed for that old mine shack near Alpine Meadow. Someone took Holly. They've demanded Jackson and Sarah come up to the cabin. Wheel and I are riding in the back way."

Dev clenched his jaw. "I was afraid something like this might happen. I'll need a horse."

Jimmy nodded. "We're on a tight schedule. I'll fill you in once we're on the road."

"Let me get my boots and gear and we're out of here." He ran upstairs, slid open the closet door, and grabbed the boots and jacket he kept at the ranch for whenever he came to visit. On the way back down, he went into the study, got one of Jackson's hunting rifles, then stopped at the car to retrieve the Browning 9 mm in his shoulder holster and a pair of high-powered binoculars.

Another vehicle was pulling up just as he shut the car door. Even with the shit that was about to rain down on all of them, he couldn't stop a grin.

"Hey, Gabe! Good to see you, brother." He and Gabe had talked last night. Neither of them had mentioned making a trip to Wyoming in case Jackson needed help, but Gabe had clearly been worried. Dev wasn't surprised to see his brother there.

"We got trouble," Dev continued. "Go get one of Jackson's rifles." He glanced down to be sure his brother was wearing his usual pair of boots. "I'll saddle you a horse."

"I brought my own firepower," Gabe said, obviously ready for whatever trouble he might find. He opened the trunk of his rental car and dragged out a jacket with something heavy in the pocket, reached back in and pulled out his big 7 mm Weatherby rifle.

The brothers strode toward the stable. Having spotted the second car, Jimmy was just tightening the cinch on a second horse. Battered hat pulled low, Wheel Dillon mumbled a greeting, then took both animals' reins and led them toward the back of the trailer. Obediently, the bay and sorrel geldings climbed in with the first saddled pair.

"Just like old times," Jimmy said, referring to their younger days when one of them always seemed to be in trouble. "I'll bring you both up to speed on the way."

Dev just nodded.

Gabe's jaw looked hard. "Let's go."

* * *

Holly huddled on an ugly brown blanket in the corner. Beneath another itchy blanket, she wore only her cotton nightgown, the one with the big-eyed owls on it. Two men sat at an old wooden table across the room playing cards. One had a scraggly blond beard and she thought she might have seen him once in town. The other man was skinny as a snake and looked just as mean.

The third man was the scariest of all, though she couldn't quite say why. Just that his nose was too long and his eyes were a shiny black. His lips were thin, too, and when he smiled at her, it made her shiver.

"I want to go home," she said, not for the first time. It took courage because they had warned her not to say it again.

"I told you to keep quiet," the man with the blond beard said, casting her a look that made her pull the blanket tighter around her.

Last night, he was the one who'd come into her bedroom. She had only seen him for a minute before he pressed something over her nose and mouth that made her go back to sleep. This morning, she woke up in the cabin with her head hurting and her mom nowhere around.

"Your mother is coming to get you," the dark-skinned man said. His hair was as black as his eyes, which always seemed to be looking at her. One of the men had called him Turk so she guessed that was his name.

"When is she coming?" Holly wasn't even sure her mom knew where she was. If she did, though, Holly knew her mom and Jackson would come for her.

The man named Turk looked at his watch. "An hour, maybe less. The road's bad. It might take a while, but your mother will be here."

"With Jackson?"

His thin lips curved. "He'll be with her." He was sure of that, she could see, and hope rose inside her. Still, she couldn't figure out why the men had brought her here. Why they had come into her room in the middle of the night and carried her out of her house.

"You two better get outside with Beckman," Turk said. "Make sure he's still covering the road. They could show up anytime now."

Holly watched the man with the scraggly beard walk out the door with the skinny man. There sure were a lot of them and they all had guns.

Fear slid through her and she shivered beneath the scratchy wool blanket. She told herself not to cry and whenever she did, she didn't let them see.

She tried not to think what the men meant to do when her mom and Jackson came to get her. Whatever it was, she was afraid it wasn't good.

The pickup crawled along the narrow, rutted, muddy road. Thanks to the rain, it was nearly impassable in places. Mostly the truck was axle-deep in sludge, making the tires spin and the vehicle slide sickeningly on the curves.

At first, Sarah had been afraid they wouldn't be able to make it to the cabin, but Jackson knew this country and how to drive a road like this and the four-wheel truck just kept going.

"I shouldn't have taken those pills last night," she said as the vehicle rolled along in a spot that was a little less rutted. "If I hadn't been sleeping so soundly I would have heard them. I could have stopped them." Her eyes burned. She glanced out the window and hung on to her emotions, refusing to cry again. She had to be strong for Holly.

"You only took a mild sleep aid and even if you'd heard them come into the house, chances are you couldn't have stopped them. They probably would have taken you both. But they want me, too. This way, they make sure that happens."

"Why do they want us to come way out here?"

"To control the situation. As far as they know, we're the only real threat to them. They want to get rid of us before we can tell the police about the mine. And they want to take care of the matter as neatly as possible."

She clamped down on a stab of fear. "You would have gone to the police already, wouldn't you? If it weren't for my troubles with Mercer."

Jackson made no reply.

If she had known this would happen, she would have called Richard Kemp at the FBI as soon as they had talked to Vincent Spalino. But they hadn't imagined that Spalino might get killed.

"What we should have done isn't important," Jackson said. "Right now we need to focus on how we're going to get Holly and get the hell out of there."

Sarah suppressed a shudder. "What's our plan?"

"Unfortunately, until we know what we're facing, we'll have to play it by ear."

Sarah said nothing more and neither did Jackson. Both of them just watched the road, hoped and silently prayed that by some miracle—and Jimmy's and Wheel's help—somehow they would succeed.

* * *

If there was one thing Dev was good at it was digging up information. He knew people all over the country, kept in touch with old army buddies and had developed a sophisticated network of informants that had been invaluable over the years. He paid well for information and kept his mouth shut about where it came from.

Which was the reason he knew the name of the guy who was running this operation.

Or at least believed he did.

From the description Jackson had given him and the talk he'd stirred up, his name was Rene Abaz, a hired gun currently employed by Barry Helman and Frank Eldridge, the owners of Hexel Pharmaceuticals. Rene's family had been in this country since the thirties, regular upstanding citizens. His father was first-generation Turkish-American, his mother mostly French, and Rene didn't even speak his family's native language. Still, everyone called him the Turk.

Abaz was smart and he was ruthless, and he was being well paid to cover up whatever it was Hexel was doing. And since money seemed to be no object, he had all the help he needed.

Dev swore softly as the sorrel's steady pace ate up the trail. His instincts had been warning him, but he hadn't known about Abaz until last night and he hadn't figured on how quickly the man would move.

Saddle leather creaked beneath him. He hadn't ridden in nearly two years. Under different circumstances, he would have been enjoying himself, enjoying the ride and the scenery. At the moment, he barely noticed the dark green pines and jagged peaks. He was too busy scanning the rocky slopes in search of movement, anything that might be a sign of trouble.

They were less than half an hour from the summit, had pushed hard to make up for the extra time it had taken them to get on the road.

A squirrel chirped loudly, signaling their passage along the route. The gelding's ears went up and the horse's nostrils flared. Dev's hand went to the butt of the pistol in his shoulder holster. He straightened in the saddle, felt the comforting weight of Jackson's rifle slung across his back.

Several seconds passed, time enough for another scan of the mountains. No problem, just Mother Nature's warning system. He had learned to pay attention to it when he'd been with the Rangers.

Riding ahead of him, he saw that Gabe had also gone on alert. Seeing nothing out of the ordinary, both of them relaxed. He was glad to have his brother along. They were both ex-military, able to communicate in a language that didn't require spoken words. He didn't know much about Jimmy's friend, Wheel Dillon, but Jimmy was as solid as a stand of timber. If Jimmy trusted Wheel, then Dev figured he could trust him, too.

He checked his watch. Almost noon. They were right on schedule. Another quarter mile and they'd leave the horses, go the rest of the way on foot.

It wouldn't be long until they knew what they were up against. Dev felt the familiar adrenaline rush and prepared to do battle in a different kind of war.

Chapter 28

Jackson rounded the last bend. A tall, bone-thin man with an assault rifle stood on a dirt mound at the side of the road where it flattened out in front of the cabin.

"Pull up there and turn off the engine," the man instructed, pointing to a spot out in the open.

Jackson looked over at Sarah. Her face was paper-white, but her chin was set with determination. He wished he could have left her back at the ranch but there was no way. Sarah loved her daughter more than her own life. She was going after her child come hell or high water. Better to have her with him than doing something foolish on her own.

His mind strayed to the Colt revolver on the floor of the truck beneath his feet and the rifle on the seat behind him. There was no way he could take either weapon with him. He'd have to go in unarmed except for the knife he'd strapped to his calf, and they'd likely find that when they searched him.

He hoped Jimmy and Wheel had made it to the top of the trail and gotten into position. If they had, he and Sarah might have a chance.

"Both of you! Raise your hands and get out of the truck!"

Jackson looked over at Sarah. He reached out and clasped her hand, gave it a reassuring squeeze. It was a helluva time to realize how much he loved her.

He prayed he would get the chance to tell her before it was too late.

Dev crouched next to Jimmy. "Dammit, the truck just pulled up in front of the cabin. I was hoping for another five minutes."

"Gabe's in position. I saw him drop behind that rock to the left of the clearing. Wheel's moving to the right."

"You okay here?" Dev asked.

Jimmy set his rifle in a notch between two rocks and peered into the scope. "I'm just fine."

Dev used his binoculars to scan the area below. "There's a man about ten o'clock, sixty yards out. Another a little left of your three."

Jimmy used the scope to locate the threat. "I got 'em."

Dev started moving as the pickup doors opened and Jackson and Sarah slowly climbed down from inside, their hands raised into the air. Jimmy, Wheel and Gabe were all in position and so far none of them had been spotted.

Then a rifle shot roared, echoing into the hills. Rock chips flew, and Dev caught a glimpse of Wheel slam-

ming backward, his cowboy hat spinning into the air
as he hit the ground and lay unmoving.

Son of a bitch.

The crackle of a walkie-talkie split the quiet, letting the bad guys know Jackson and Sarah were not
alone. It was bad news for all of them, but at least it
gave Dev the shooter's position. He started moving in
that direction, keeping low as he darted between the
sharp-edged rocks.

In the clearing below, all hell had broken loose. A
burst of rapid gunfire followed Sarah as she ran to the
back of the pickup. Jackson ducked behind the door of
the truck, reached beneath the seat and retrieved his
revolver, dodging and weaving past a series of bullets
that struck the ground as he ran to the rear of the Ford.
Crouching next to Sarah, he aimed his big Colt .44 and
took out the guy firing the assault rifle, who ran for
cover off the mound.

Dev moved silently, making each step count as
he came up behind the first shooter. Locking an arm
around his neck, he twisted, dropping the man to the
ground before he knew what hit him.

It wasn't something he liked doing, but at least he
hadn't forgotten how.

He crouched and used his binoculars to check on
Wheel, saw that Gabe knelt beside him, working to
stop the flow of blood from what appeared to be a
shoulder wound. Dev headed toward the cabin in search
of Holly while Gabe moved Wheel under cover and
ducked back out of sight.

Dev had nearly reached the cabin when he glanced
toward the rear of the truck and saw that both Sarah
and Jackson were gone.

He spotted Sarah behind the thick trunk of a downed pine tree and Jackson running along the bottom of a shallow gully that bordered the road. Jackson disappeared out of sight and Dev started moving, silently praying that his brother and his lady would be all right.

Sarah's heart raced. A shot tore into the trunk of the fallen tree in front of her and she ducked out of sight. Her breath froze as she spotted Jackson to her left, moving toward a man with a thin blond beard armed with what looked like a machine gun, scanning the area with the muzzle, searching for a target.

Sarah trembled as she watched Jackson creep closer, coming up behind the man and wrapping an arm vise-like around his neck. Jackson pressed his pistol against the side of the blond man's head and ordered him to drop his weapon, which fell to the ground with a noisy clatter. Then Jackson slammed his revolver down hard on the blond man's head and he collapsed into the dirt.

Sarah's heart pounded as her terrified gaze swung to the cabin. Holly had to be inside. She wondered how many more men were in there with her daughter. The shadowy outline of a figure appeared for an instant behind the window, but dropped quickly out of sight.

Jackson was heading for the cabin door. He jerked to a halt and dropped down into the rocks as the door swung wide and the tall, dark-skinned man Sarah recognized from the parking lot stepped into the opening, holding Holly up in front of him like a shield.

Sarah's stomach knotted with fear for her little girl. She stifled a terrified sob and forced herself to remain where she was instead of rushing into the clearing to beg the man not to hurt her daughter.

* * *

"Put down your weapons! Do it or the child is dead!"

Gripping his Colt in both hands, the barrel leveled at the man who held Holly, Jackson stepped out into the open. Holly's abductor held her flush against him, one arm locked around her waist, his pistol pressed against the side of her head.

"Do it, or I kill her!"

Jimmy stood up but continued to hold on to his rifle. Wheel staggered to his feet, his rifle steadied against his hip. Blood soaked his shirt and dripped onto his jeans.

"Where are you, Sarah?" the black-haired man called out as if they were old friends. Jackson recognized him as the guy who had accosted her in the parking lot.

"If you want your daughter to live, you'll come forward. Now!"

Sarah came out from behind the fallen log, her jeans and shirt covered with mud and dead leaves. Her face looked even paler than it had before, and her legs were shaking as she hurried to Jackson's side.

"Now…like I said, drop your weapons. Tell your men to throw down their guns, Raines. Do it or the little girl dies."

"Do it, Jackson," Sarah begged. The terror in her voice cut into him like a blade. But if they gave up their weapons, all of them would die, including Sarah and Holly.

Jackson glanced around the clearing, stalling for time. The rest of the gunmen were all injured or dead. He knew there was at least one more man out there on his side of the fight, someone who had ridden in with

Jimmy and taken out at least one of the gunmen. In the rocks to his right, a man rose up, a rifle resting against his shoulder. Jackson recognized his brother, Dev, and a fresh shot of adrenaline poured through him.

"You shoot the girl, Turk, you're a dead man," Dev said. The barrel of his rifle pointed at the gunman's head and it never wavered. "Holly's your only way out of this alive."

Sarah made a little whimpering sound.

Following Dev's lead, Jimmy and Wheel held their positions. So did Jackson, though the fear in the little girl's eyes and the terror in Sarah's face made it the hardest thing he had ever done.

"Give it up, Turk," Dev shouted. "You don't, this isn't going to end well for you."

"I've got the girl. You'd better remember that." And then he started running, holding Holly up in front of him to keep the men from firing, moving in such a way none of them could get a clear shot without risking the little girl's life.

All of them started moving, following the pair as they raced across the clearing and disappeared behind a row of pines that stood between the cabin and Alpine Meadow.

"Holly!" Sarah cried out, stumbling as she ran after the man with her child.

Jackson raced ahead of her, moving fast, narrowing the distance between him and Holly's captor. That was when he heard it—the *whop whop whop* of a chopper. It was preparing to lift off, not landing, so it couldn't be Sheriff Weber. The chopper had brought the kidnappers up to the cabin and as soon as the man named Turk reached it, he would be gone.

Jackson ran faster, his heart pounding in rhythm with his running feet, desperate to stop the man from boarding the chopper with Holly. The blades were spinning when Jackson burst through the row of pines into the clearing, the dark-skinned man racing for the door of the helicopter.

As the chopper began to lift off, Turk dropped the child and reached for the door. A shot roared from somewhere in the rocky terrain to the right and a bullet slammed into Turk's chest. Blood gushed through the hole in his shirt as he went down, his pistol landing in the grass a few feet away.

Jackson just kept running, keeping his head low beneath the whirling blades. He grabbed Holly and cradled her protectively against his chest, then turned and raced away from the chopper. Dev and Jimmy ran forward, their rifles aimed at the glass bubble where the pilot worked the controls.

Jimmy fired a single shot through the glass just missing the pilot, who put his hands up. The helicopter began to sink back down into the deep green grass. The engine turned off, and the rotor blades began to slow.

Sarah raced toward her daughter. "Holly! Holly!"

"Mama!"

As soon as they were a safe distance from the blades, Jackson set the little girl on her feet and she rushed into her mother's open arms. Both of them started crying. Relief hit him so hard his eyes began to burn. Jackson watched the two people he had come to love so much, alive and clinging to each other, and a lump swelled in his throat.

He turned away and when he did, he saw Gabe walking toward him, his rifle slung over one wide shoulder. Relief was etched into his face. Dev was right behind him.

Both his brothers had come to help. Jackson clenched his jaw against the fresh rush of emotion that seeped into his chest.

"How'd you know?" he said to Gabe, clapping a hand on his brother's shoulder.

"We didn't. Dev and I talked last night. He had a hunch trouble was about to come down. I figured a little trip to Wyoming wouldn't hurt. I guess he thought the same thing."

For the first time since that morning, Jackson smiled. "You two always did have a good sense of timing."

They walked over to where the pilot stood next to the chopper, covered by the rifle Wheel held in his hand, Gabe's makeshift bandage wrapped around his injured shoulder. A few feet away Jimmy knelt next to Turk, who lay bleeding and unconscious. Dev found some rope in the chopper, and he and Jimmy tied up the rest of the gunmen. Kneeling next to Turk, Gabe tore open the man's bloody shirt to check the wound in his chest.

"I didn't kill him," Gabe said to Jackson. "I figured the way things were going you might need him."

Gabe was a crack shot. If he'd wanted the man dead, he would be. But his brother was right. There was still the matter of Hexel Pharmaceuticals and whatever they were dumping in the Dry Springs Mine.

The company still posed a threat that needed to be dealt with. Jackson hoped the FBI would be able to solve the problem.

Dev left them there and went to check out the cabin. His blue eyes looked hard when he returned.

"Bastards wired the place. From the way it looks, they meant for the three of you to be in there when it blew."

"You disarmed it?"

He nodded. "It's safe now."

Jackson looked at his two brothers, and gratitude for the family he had been given filled his chest. His gaze went to Sarah and little Holly, who still hung on to each other in the meadow. They were part of his family, too.

He loved them both and he wanted them with him. He just hoped he could make Sarah see.

Chapter 29

Jackson believed it was over. He would never know how much Sarah wished that were true.

Though the day was warm, she sat in front of the empty hearth in her living room, feeling cold clear to her bones. Out in front of the barn, Holly laughed as she played with Rags and Sam's dog, Feather, safe once more at the ranch, accepting in the way children seemed able to do that her life was already returning to normal.

Sarah was no longer sure what normal really was.

She leaned back in the antique rocker she had retrieved from the attic just a few days before all of this started, felt the comforting back-and-forth motion.

As Jackson had hoped, Sheriff Weber and his deputies had arrived in the meadow by helicopter soon after the shooting had ended. He had taken the gunmen into custody—three wounded, one dead—and arrested the pilot. The man with the stringy blond beard had turned out to be a local, a hand who'd been fired off the Whittaker Ranch for stealing and now lived in Sheep River. He had only wanted money, he said.

Weber's pilot had flown Sarah and Holly back down the mountain along with Wheel, who'd been taken directly to the hospital. Later that afternoon, the sheriff had come to the ranch to take her and Holly's statements. He had said not to worry, that he would take care of everything.

If only that were true.

Sarah leaned back in the rocker. She was exhausted. She hadn't slept in the past three nights, not since that awful day in the meadow. Whenever she closed her eyes, all she could hear were the sound of bullets. All she could see was blood: the man on the mound with a bloody arm; the blond man moaning, pressing a hand over his bleeding head; the black-haired man, the Turk, lying in the grass, a spreading stream of crimson pumping out of his chest.

Sitting in front of the empty hearth, she thought of those men, and a memory of Andrew arose, as it had a hundred times before.

Andrew lying on the floor of the study, scarlet soaking the front of his jacket over the perfect hole in his heart.

She squeezed her eyes shut, trying to block the memory, but it wouldn't go away.

"Do you think I'm a fool, Sarah?"
"Why...why would I think that?"

He just smiled, the kind of smile that made her insides roll with nausea.

"I told you we were going to Rio. Did you actually think you were going to take Holly and run away?"

She straightened, determined not to let him know how frightened she really was. "Holly and I aren't going with you. You can leave if you want, but we're staying here."

His mouth thinned to a slash across his face. "You really believe you can defy me? You don't remember what happened the last time?"

She remembered. He had beaten her so badly she'd wound up in the hospital. The fear inside her swelled, nearly overwhelmed her.

Andrew stepped away from his chair, rounded the corner of his desk. Anticipation glittered in his eyes. He liked this, liked to hurt her.

"Andrew, please don't do this." She forced herself not to back away, to hold her ground and face him. When he just kept coming, she drew the pistol from her purse.

Her hand shook. "Stay away from me, Andrew. I'm warning you." A noise reached her. Was someone in the house? She glanced around, but there was no one there. "I won't...won't let you hurt me again."

He laughed, the sound almost demonic. Even the gun wasn't enough to frighten him.

"You dare to threaten me? I'm going to kill you for this, Sarah. I'm going to make you disappear and then I'm taking Holly with me to Rio." He took another step closer.

"I'll shoot you. I swear it."

His lips curled. "You don't have the guts."

She tried to blot out the rest, but it was fixed in her mind and it wouldn't go away—Andrew rushing forward, his features distorted in fury. She remembered closing her eyes for an instant, but she didn't remember pulling the trigger. Not the exact moment, just the roar of the bullet, and the feel of the pistol bucking in her hand.

Andrew's eyes bulged in disbelief. He took one more step, swayed and fell backward, landing on his back on the floor of the study. Fear froze her where she stood. Fear and denial.

This can't be happening! *Her gaze swung toward the phone on his desk.*

Call 911. Call 911.

But when she looked at Andrew, she saw that his chest wasn't moving. His eyes were staring straight up at the ceiling and she knew for certain he was dead.

Dear God, what have I done!

For several long seconds, she just stood there, listening for the wail of sirens, the gun a deadweight in her hand.

But no police cars came. No one walked through the front door. The house sat at the end of a long, private drive, and no one had heard the gunshot.

Holly's sweet face rose in her mind. If she called the police they would take her away from her daughter. Even if she could prove it was self-defense, she'd be arrested. They would put Holly in foster care. There would have to be a trial. It could take weeks, months. She didn't have money for an expensive lawyer. She might even be sent to prison.

Hysteria threatened. She thought of Holly and forced herself to stay calm.

Opening her purse, she dropped the gun back inside, her hand shaking almost uncontrollably. On legs that felt rubbery and numb, she turned and walked out of the study. She retrieved the bag she had packed, the last of her things left in the Sunset house, and headed for the car.

Stay calm, *a little voice ordered.*

Andrew had any number of enemies, people with a reason to want him dead. Just keep going. Pick up Holly and drive to the condo. Pretend nothing has happened. You can do it. You have to. Holly needs a mother. Without you, she has no one.

Sitting there now in the rocker in her cottage, Sarah brushed a tear from her cheek, fighting to bury the memories, staring into the empty hearth as if it were her empty soul.

She had tried so hard. But trouble had followed her even here. She had to leave. She couldn't face Jackson, couldn't continue the lie a moment more.

She couldn't bear to think of what he would say, of the way he would look at her if he knew she had killed her husband. The reason wouldn't matter. No man would want a woman who had done a thing like that.

And there was the future to consider, the awful certainty that in the end, Detective Mercer would come for her.

Sarah rose from the chair, feeling sick inside. She was in love with Jackson. The desperate, forever kind of love. She knew that now, had known it the moment he had run through a hail of gunfire to save her daughter. Known it by the moisture in his eyes when he realized she and Holly were safe.

He had risked his life for her and her daughter.

Sarah loved him, and now she was going to repay him for the kindness he had shown her.

She was going to leave him. She was going to give him back his life.

It would be the hardest thing she'd ever done.

Sarah didn't know how long she stood there staring into the empty hearth. At a knock on her door, she glanced up. Wearily, she crossed the living room, wondering who was there. Pausing at the window, she saw Jackson standing on the porch, looking masculine and virile without even trying. She summoned her courage and opened the door.

"I've brought news," he said as she stepped back to let him into the living room. He took off his work-stained cowboy hat and held it in one of his calloused hands. He always seemed so big, larger than life. There would never be another man like him.

"Would...would you like something to drink? Some iced tea, or something?"

He smiled. "It's hot out there. Iced tea sounds great."

For the past few days, he had left her mostly alone, just stopping by to check on her and Holly, but careful to give them plenty of space, time to adjust to all that had happened.

"I'll be right back." She went into the kitchen, filled two glasses with ice and poured in the sun tea she had made by setting a jar filled with tea and water out on the porch. Jackson rested his hat on the back of the sofa as she handed him one of the frosty glasses, and both of them sat down.

"You said you brought news. I hope it's good for a change."

He took a long drink of his tea, the muscles in his throat moving up and down. He set the glass down on a coaster on the coffee table in front of him. "It's kind of good news/bad news."

She braced herself. It seemed lately, everything had been that way. "Give me the good news first."

"Richard Kemp called. They've arrested Barry Helman and Frank Eldridge, the guys who owned Hexel. According to Kemp, Rene Abaz turned state's evidence, and Helman and Eldridge were charged with conspiracy to kidnap and attempted murder, and that's just for starters."

"What about the mine?"

"That's the bad news. Turns out the Dry Springs Mine didn't live up to its name."

"The springs weren't dry?"

"Not completely. There's a little town south of the mine north of Interstate 40. It's called Mineral Wells. Apparently, people there have been getting sick. The EPA tested the water and found out they had arsenic poisoning."

"Oh, my God—and it came from the mine?"

He nodded. "From an old underground spring that ran into the town's main water supply."

"Are you saying those barrels Hexel was storing were filled with arsenic?"

"Not exactly, but arsenic was in the waste that was in the barrels. Now that this is all out in the open, some of the scientists working for the lab have come forward. They say they were working on a variation of a product called arsenic trioxide. It's a powerful drug used to treat leukemia. Hexel was secretly trying to expand the applications. Helman and Eldridge believed they could make some changes to the drug and come up with a cure for cancer."

"Couldn't they do that kind of research legally?"

"I guess their greed got in the way. Their lab wasn't approved for the use of arsenic and they didn't want to spend the time or money it would require to qualify for whatever permits were needed. They figured once they found the cure, none of it would matter."

"And Helman and Eldridge would wind up filthy rich."

"That's about it. Kemp says they'll be charged with conspiring to conceal health risks and knowing endangerment, among at least a dozen other violations. Strict liability applies in cases like this, so Hexel will be on the hook for everything that's happened in Mineral Wells. The company is out of business for good."

Sarah glanced away, guilt rising in her chest. "I wonder how much Andrew knew about this."

"Whatever he knew or didn't know had nothing to do with you. You're an innocent bystander in all of this."

She tried to convince herself, but it all came back to the question of how could she ever have married a man like that? How could she have lived with him for all of those years?

"I'd better get going," Jackson said, finishing the last of his tea and setting the glass back down on the coaster. He came up off the sofa and Sarah stood up, too. Neither of them moved. All she could think about was how much it was going to hurt to give him up.

"There's something I need to tell you," she forced herself to say.

One of his dark eyebrows lifted. "What is it?"

"I'm moving, Jackson. I've rented a place at the edge of town, just south of the road to Sheep River. I told you I was going to leave before all of this happened."

"Sarah..."

"I want to be closer to work. Smiley's been great or I would have already lost my job. Holly will be closer to school and I can see my grandmother more often. It'll be better for all of us."

"Not all of us, Sarah," he said softly. He reached out and rested a hand against her cheek. "It won't be better for me." His dark gaze locked with hers and she felt the pull of it deep inside her. She wanted to touch him, erase the pain in his face. "I love you, Sarah. I want you and Holly to stay here on the ranch. I want you to mar—"

"Don't say it!" She jerked away, backed up a couple of paces. Jackson wanted to marry her! It was exactly what she wanted and absolutely could not have. Dear God, she couldn't bear it.

"I—I'm not ready for a serious relationship. I don't think I ever will be."

"Sarah, listen to me..."

"My mind is made up, Jackson. I'm leaving." She looked at him and couldn't hold back tears. "Please let me go. Let me go and get on with your life."

Those strong, suntanned hands settled gently on her shoulders. "Tell me you don't love me and I'll walk away. I won't ever bother you again."

She bit back a sob. How could she do it? How could she lie about something that meant so very much? It took every ounce of her will, every ounce of courage she possessed.

"I don't love you, Jackson. I wish I did, but I don't."

For long moments, Jackson said nothing. Then he turned away from her, picked his hat up off the back of the sofa and headed for the door.

He stepped out onto the porch. "Whenever you're ready, I'll send a couple of the hands over to help you move the boxes." Very softly, he closed the door, the faint click as loud as a gunshot in the silence of her heart.

Sarah pressed a hand over her mouth to hold back a sob of pain. She loved him so very much.

She told herself she had done the right thing.

Chapter 30

Sarah had been living in her new place in town for almost two weeks. The house was more modern than the cottage, with a newer kitchen and bath. But it didn't feel homey like the little cottage on the ranch, and it wasn't surrounded by a clear bubbling stream, beautiful vistas and towering pine trees.

The furniture inside was modern, too, and Spartan. She hadn't even brought the few antiques she had purchased for the cottage. There was no fireplace here, just a heater in the wall, and no old, worn, wooden floors. The antiques seemed to belong up there, not here.

She kept telling herself she could fix the place up a little, make it more comfortable, but so far she never seemed to find the time.

Holly didn't like the house, either. At first she had cried and begged Sarah not to move away from the ranch, but she was a sweet, loving child, and sensing her mother's unhappiness, she had resigned herself and let the matter rest.

Holly missed Jackson, though. Whenever his name came up, a wistful look crept over the little girl's face. She thought of him as the father she had never really known, and Sarah blamed herself for that, too.

That Sarah missed him didn't surprise her. She ached for the sound of his voice, the thud of his heavy boots on the wide plank floors as he walked into the cottage. She missed the warmth in his eyes whenever he looked at her, missed his lovemaking.

She swallowed past the lump in her throat. Most of the time, she was able to keep thoughts of him away. Once in a while, like today, the loneliness crept in and memories of Jackson returned, along with the terrible pain of losing him.

Sarah shook her head, forcing his beloved image away. She checked her watch, saw that it was nearly three o'clock and went in search of her car keys. Holly had spent the day with Gran, but it was time to drive out to Sheep River and pick her up.

The phone rang just as she found her key chain and picked it up off the table. Sarah walked into the kitchen and lifted the receiver.

"Ah, Sarah…there you are. How are you enjoying your new home?"

Her stomach instantly knotted. She knew that voice, recognized the hint of derision. She swallowed, forced a note of calm into her tone. "Detective Mercer…good afternoon. What can I do for you?"

"Actually, I'm just calling with a little bit of news. I

thought you might be interested to know we found the murder weapon…the gun that killed your husband."

Nausea hit her with such force she doubled over, wrapped her arms around her waist and fought not to be sick. Drawing in a breath, she clung to her composure by a thread. "You…you found the gun?"

"That's right. Guess where it was?"

"Wh-where?"

"A couple of divers were doing some work under the Santa Monica pier. Imagine their surprise when they turned up a .38 caliber pistol, lying under the sand at the base of one of the pilings. I guess all sorts of things get tossed off the pier, but this was certainly one of the more interesting items they found."

Sarah said nothing. She was afraid of what her voice would sound like if she tried to speak.

"Rather an interesting coincidence wouldn't you say—being as you live just a few blocks away. When did you toss it there, Sarah? Right after you shot your husband through the heart?"

She fought for control, prayed her voice would not tremble. "Any…anyone could have thrown it there. Unless you can prove it was me—"

"Oh, I will—sooner or later. Count on it, Sarah."

The line went dead, and for several seconds, Sarah just stood there, holding the phone in her hand. She was shaking all over, her stomach rolling, threatening to erupt.

She set the phone back in its cradle, walked over and sank down in a kitchen chair. For the past two weeks, every time she'd thought of Jackson, the notion had arisen that maybe she had made a mistake. Maybe she

should call him, tell him she loved him. Tell him she
wanted to marry him more than anything in the world.

But deep down, she knew she couldn't keep lying
to him. That in not telling him the truth about Andrew, she was betraying his trust in the worst possible manner.

She looked back at the telephone, ominously silent
now, but for exactly how long?

How long would it be until Detective Mercer came
to haul her off to prison?

Jackson was working in the barn when Jimmy spotted the smoke. "Hey, boss, you'd better come take a
look at this."

Jackson walked out of the barn, his gaze following
the direction Jimmy pointed.

"Sonofabitch." A plume of white smoke rose from
the thick forest covering the west slope of the distant
mountains.

"You know where that is?" Jimmy said.

"Up near Pine Lake."

"Isn't that where Red DeSalvo and his loggers were
working?"

"Yeah." Jackson pulled out his cell phone. "The Forest Service is probably already on it, but we'd better
call it in, just in case."

He pressed the Forest Service number that was on
autodial in his cell address book, reported the fire,
then went to retrieve his binoculars from the pickup
and began to scan the white smoke in the distance. He
glanced up at the sound of a chopper, watched it appear overhead on its way to collect buckets of water
from the lake.

"Looks like they're already on it," Jimmy said.

"Looks that way."

"Maybe we'll get lucky and they'll be able to stop it before it gets too bad." Current forest policy was to let the trees burn and just protect whatever structures might be in danger. It was probably good in some cases, clearing out the underbrush and giving the forest a chance to breathe, but it made for a long, dangerous, smoky summer, and a helluva lot of anxiety and fear.

"We'd better pull the cows out of the upper meadow," Jackson said.

Jimmy nodded, his long black ponytail shifting against the back of his neck. "I'll get the men, saddle some horses and get up there."

Wheel was out of the hospital, but not ready for such strenuous work. The men would have to go on horseback. It was too dry to risk a spark from one of the ATVs, and there was a ban on the use of any machinery between noon and midnight to keep down the fire danger.

Jackson couldn't help wondering if the loggers had any part in starting the blaze, since Red and his crew weren't much good at following rules.

"Saddle Galahad," he said, "and I'll go with you."

"You got it." Jimmy waved over his shoulder as he walked away, and Jackson headed off to retrieve his gear.

At least the fire would get him away from the house. For the past two weeks, he had hardly been out of his study, just sat there staring at the walls as if they held the answer to what had happened between him and Sarah.

He was in love with her. Deeply in love, and God,

it hurt. He could barely eat, couldn't sleep, thought about Sarah and Holly from morning till night. Losing her was killing him, and he didn't even know how it had happened.

From the start, he had tried to keep his distance. He had told himself not to fall for her again, not to let her hurt him the way she had before. But Sarah Allen had gotten into his blood when he was a kid of nineteen. Clearly, he had never gotten over her.

As he grabbed his saddlebags, a blanket and a jacket and headed out the door, Jackson wondered if he ever really would.

Chapter 31

Sitting at the cheap pressboard desk she had purchased at the mercantile then assembled and put in her bedroom, Sarah pushed the button on her laptop, saving the article she had been writing for the newspaper, a story about Tanya Morton, last year's homecoming queen. Tanya had been chosen as a contestant on a reality TV show. Being a local girl, it was big news in Wind Canyon.

She looked out the window, saw a layer of thick smoke spreading across the mountains in the distance. She knew where the fire was—up near the lake where Jackson had taken her and Holly camping. She had seen it on the news. The air in town was smoky and miserable to breathe, and she kept worrying about Jackson, hoping the firefighters would be able to bring the blaze under control and Raintree Ranch would be safe.

She left her desk and walked over to the window on the opposite side of the bedroom, saw Holly playing on the rope swing hanging down from the big sycamore tree out back. Rags sprawled in the grass a few feet away.

The doorbell rang as she walked out of the bedroom. Every time she heard it, a tremor of fear ran down her spine. Was it Mercer? Had he finally come to arrest her?

Relief filtered through her when she opened the door and saw Nan standing on the porch.

"Thought I'd come by and check on you," Nan said with a smile. "See how you're doing." She walked past Sarah into the house, carrying a baking pan covered with foil. "Half a chocolate cake. I couldn't eat it all and I thought Holly might like some." She glanced around. "Where is she?"

"Playing out in back. There isn't much of a yard, but it's better than nothing." Sarah took the cake and set it on the small round dining table. Nan had been to the house several times since Sarah moved in, always smiling, always cheerful. Sarah knew Nan had been worried about her moving into town from the ranch.

"So how's it going?" Nan asked. "You getting used to city life?"

Sarah laughed, thinking of the difference between Wind Canyon and Los Angeles. "I guess so. It's certainly more convenient."

"I suppose."

For the first time, Sarah noticed her friend's puffy, red-rimmed eyes and slightly pale complexion. She frowned. "What's wrong, Nan? You look like you've been crying."

Nan sighed and sank down on the sofa. "Jimmy and I broke up."

Sarah sat down beside her. "But I thought you two were really getting along."

"I thought so, too." She pulled a Kleenex out of her purse and dabbed at her watery eyes. "He can't get past what happened when he was with Annie. She was a terrible wife and a rotten mother. She cheated on him and abandoned him and her boys. He's scared to death it'll happen again."

"You're nothing like Annie Baylor. She was no good when Jimmy married her."

"I know that and you know that. I guess Jim can't see the difference."

Sarah ignored a shot of anger. Didn't the man have enough sense to know what a good thing he had? Then again, she'd given up the best man she'd ever known. Maybe sometimes what seemed like choices weren't really choices at all.

She leaned over and hugged her friend. "I'm sorry, Nan."

"Yeah, me, too."

Sarah blew out a breath and fell back on the sofa. "We're a real pair, aren't we?"

Nan managed a smile. "At least we have each other."

It was true. Nan had turned out to be a very dear friend, one of the best Sarah had ever had.

"I know this isn't the best time to ask," Sarah said, "but there's something I've been wanting to talk to you about."

"What is it?"

"I know how much you love children. I've seen you with Holly and I know what a wonderful mother you would make. If something happened to me...would you...would you be willing to take care of Holly?"

"What are you talking about? Nothing's going to happen to you."

"I know, but just say it did. My grandmother's too old to take on the job of raising a six-year-old. With my mom and dad gone, I don't have anyone I can turn to, and I trust you, Nan. You said you always wanted children. If something happened to me, would you be willing to raise Holly as your own?"

Nan reached over and caught Sarah's hand. "Of course I would. I love Holly. She's the sweetest little girl in the world."

"You're a teacher. I don't think you'd have any trouble getting custody, but I could put something in writing—if you would be willing to agree."

Nan's green eyes glistened with a sheen of tears. "I'm flattered you would ask. And I would be honored to raise your little girl."

Tears welled in Sarah's eyes, too. "Thank you."

"But nothing's going to happen."

She just nodded, thinking of Ed Mercer and praying it was true.

Jackson listened to the hum of a big borate bomber flying overhead. The cattle had all been moved out of the upper pasture, down to a safer meadow to graze, and though three thousand forest acres had burned in the week since the blaze had started, the fire crews were making progress. The winds were cooperating and three choppers and two C-130s had been working to retard the flames.

There was a very good chance that this time the

firefighters were going to be able to whip this thing before it got too far out of control.

Sitting behind the desk in his study, Jackson almost smiled. He'd been right about Red DeSalvo and his crew. They'd been logging during the hottest part of the day. A catalytic converter on one of the trucks had been the cause of the blaze.

It was the third infraction Bannock Brothers had committed, and it looked like the company was going to lose its logging contract, at least in the national forest.

Couldn't happen to a bunch of more deserving guys.

Jackson leaned back in his chair, wishing he could muster the energy to do something productive. Instead, he reached over and poured himself a whiskey.

He rarely drank, but lately…well, it seemed like the only time the ache went away. He wouldn't let it get out of control. He wasn't the type. Still, he tipped the glass back and downed a hefty swallow. A warm numbness spread through him and the feeling of grief that seemed to haunt him faded away a little.

He was holding the glass up to the light, studying the rich amber color and contemplating a second swallow, when a familiar, sexy blonde walked into the study. Interested, dark brown eyes ran over him.

"Livvy said I'd find you in here."

Jackson set the whiskey glass down on the desk and came to his feet. "Hello, Maddie."

He hadn't seen her since the Memorial Day celebration in the park, but in her skintight jeans and a tank that showed her impressive cleavage, Maddie Gallagher was as tall and svelte as she had always been, with miles of gleaming blond hair and legs that went on forever.

Jackson waited for the familiar stirring but it never came. "What can I do for you, Maddie?"

She crossed the room, rounded the corner of the desk and sat down right in front of him. "Jimmy called. He says you've been lonely. He thought maybe I could cheer you up."

She usually could. Leave it to Jimmy to give it a try. Maddie was sexy as hell and he was a man with a strong sexual appetite. She ran a long, manicured finger along his cheek. He hadn't shaved, he realized, thinking it must have been at least a couple of days.

"I appreciate the invitation, Maddie, I really do, but—"

She slid her arms around his neck and pulled him toward her, covered his mouth with her soft, full lips. He tried to enjoy it, should have, but all it made him feel was sad.

He eased her arms from around his neck. "Thanks for trying, Maddie. I guess I'm just not in the mood."

She shrugged her lightly suntanned shoulders. "Things change. I'm willing to wait." She slid off his desk, her breasts spilling toward him. He should take what she offered. Maybe it would help.

"Thanks for thinking of me, Maddie. Maybe next time."

"I think of you too much, Jackson." She flashed him a seductive smile as she headed toward the door of the study. "Next time I won't take no for an answer."

He didn't argue. Sooner or later, he'd have to come back to life again.

And sooner or later, he would.

Just not now, not today.

The image of another woman rose into his mind, beautiful blue eyes and thick dark hair, a body that fit perfectly with his. The memory made him hot and hard in an instant. Clearly he wasn't dead yet.

Determined not to think of Sarah, Jackson tossed back the rest of his whiskey and sat back down in his chair.

Gabriel Raines pulled the throttle back on his twin Aerostar and lined up for touchdown on the airstrip. He set down gently, heard the familiar rub of the tires on the asphalt, taxied to the hangar and turned off the engines.

Half an hour later, he was sitting behind the wheel of the brown Jeep Cherokee he had rented and was on his way down the highway. He wasn't headed for the ranch. Instead he was on the road to Sheep River.

He turned off the road at the outskirts of Wind Canyon, pulled down a narrow paved lane and stopped in front of one of three small houses in a cul-de-sac at the end.

He'd flown all the way to Wyoming to talk to Sarah Allen.

Gabe clenched his jaw. He had ignored the first call he had received. Livvy had been crying when he picked up the phone, but she was a woman and he knew from experience the female gender often went overboard on emotion. It was clear she was worried about Jackson, but Gabe assured her that in time his brother would be just fine. It was only a broken heart, after all. Nothing too serious.

When Jimmy had called, he'd begun to rethink the

situation. Jackson had always been the calm one, the voice of reason among the brothers. Liv and Jim were calling Gabe, not Dev, the hothead of the three. Gabe had a temper, too, but mostly he controlled it.

"I don't know what to do," Jim had said. "Livvy and me...we were hoping you might be able to talk to him, help him figure things out."

And with those words, Gabe had gotten mad.

What the hell had Sarah done to his brother? Jackson was no fool. He'd been with a dozen different women. He rarely got involved, always made it clear from the start that he wasn't looking for a serious relationship, and he was always careful no one got hurt.

That he had fallen so hard for Sarah was frightening.

As Gabe turned off the motor, a fresh shot of anger slid through him. He hadn't forgotten that day in the high school cafeteria. Jackson had been stashing his money for weeks, saving a little bit here and there out of the money he earned to feed the family.

When he'd finally saved enough to go to the prom, he had worked up his courage and asked Sarah to go with him.

Sarah had ridiculed him, laughed at him in front of every kid in the cafeteria. Sarah had hurt him badly that day, but according to Livvy and Jim, not nearly as bad as she had hurt him this time.

Gabe got out of the Jeep, slamming the car door harder than he meant to. As he climbed the front porch steps, he shoved his wraparound sunglasses up on his head, took a deep breath and told himself to go easy.

He had seen the way Sarah looked at Jackson that

day up in Alpine Meadow when they had gone after her little girl.

Like his brother was her storybook hero.

Like he was her man and for her there would never be anyone else.

What had gone wrong?

What could possibly have happened to change things so drastically?

Whatever it was, he meant to find out—today.

The door swung open just then and Sarah's blue eyes widened at the sight of him. Or maybe it was the way his jaw tightened when he saw her. He forced himself to relax, told himself to take things slow and easy, one step at a time.

"I need to talk to you, Sarah."

"Of course." She stepped back. "Come on in."

He started through the door and Sarah must have suddenly realized how odd it was for him to be there.

She grabbed hold of his arm. "Oh, my God—you aren't here because of Jackson! Something hasn't happened to him! There hasn't been an accident or...or..."

Some of his anger lessened at the fear in her face. "No accident. It's nothing like that."

A breath of relief seeped out of her. She swallowed, inhaled deeply, managed to compose herself.

"It's nice to see you, Gabriel." But she looked more wary than pleased. "Would you like something to drink? A glass of iced tea or a beer, maybe?"

He didn't want a goddamn beer. His jaw tightened. "I want to know what you've done to my brother."

Her head shot up. "Wh-what do you mean?"

"I mean that since the two of you broke up, he hasn't been himself. He barely eats. He can't sleep. Livvy is terrified he's going to get sick." He took a step closer, just because he felt like a little intimidation. "My brother's in love with you, Sarah. I want to know why you led him on the way you did. Why you let him believe there was a future for the two of you. He wants to marry you. He wants to be a father to your little girl. Doesn't that mean anything to you?"

Her pretty blue eyes welled with tears he hadn't expected to see. There was a softness in Sarah he had rarely seen in a woman. He thought that must be one of the things that had drawn his brother to her.

"I didn't mean for any of this to happen," she said.

"Couldn't you tell he was falling in love with you? How could you let it go so far?"

She tried to turn away, but Gabe caught her shoulders, forcing her to face him. There was something in her expression, something so sad his chest squeezed.

"There's more going on here, isn't there? Something you're not saying, something you haven't told Jackson."

She tried to turn away, but he wouldn't let her. "Tell me what it is."

She bit her lip. He could feel her start to tremble. Gabe's hold tightened. "Tell me, dammit!"

The tears in her eyes spilled over onto her cheeks. He saw it then, saw what he had been missing, why none of this had made any sense. "My God, you're in love with him!"

Her features crumpled. A sob escaped and fresh tears flooded her eyes. "I love him so much." And then she started crying in earnest.

Every instinct urged him to pull her into his arms and comfort her, tell her everything was going to be okay.

But too much was at stake. His brother's future—Sarah's. Even little Holly's.

"I want to know, Sarah. I'm not leaving until I find out what's going on."

She looked up at him, her face as pale as glass. Her words came out so softly he almost didn't hear them. "I killed him. I killed my husband. I'm the one who shot Andrew."

Stunned silence followed. Somewhere a clock ticked. Of all the things he could have imagined her saying, this wasn't one of them.

"You killed him?"

She nodded, her whole body drawing inward as if she were in pain.

"Did you plan it? Was it murder? Did you shoot him on purpose?"

Disbelief widened her eyes. "No! Oh, God, I would never do something like that!" She swallowed, moistened her trembling lips. "H-he called me downstairs and I—I—"

"Stop right there—don't say another word. This isn't for me to hear. It's Jackson who needs to know." He glanced around. "Where's Holly?"

"She's with...with Nan. I had some work to do. Nan said she'd watch her for a couple of...of hours."

"Get your purse and let's go."

Sarah didn't argue, just woodenly picked up her bag and let him haul her out the door. He urged her around to the passenger side of the Jeep, opened the door and shoved her inside, then went around, climbed in himself and started the engine.

Sarah said nothing as he drove down the lane and turned onto the road into town, nothing as he continued on to the two-lane road headed north then turned onto the private lane leading into Raintree Ranch.

She was shaking when the big sprawling ranch house came into view. And so pale he was a little afraid.

"We're almost there," he said, driving up in front of the house, hoping that Jackson was inside as he had been all week.

Gabe turned off the engine, went around to the passenger side and helped Sarah out of the Jeep. She was silent as he took her arm and guided her through the front door into the living room.

When he walked into the study, he saw Jackson sitting in the chair behind his desk. The computer was on. He caught a glimpse of a cost analysis program but Jackson wasn't looking at the screen. He wasn't looking at much of anything until he saw Sarah.

He jerked as if he had been punched, slowly pushed to his feet. "Sarah…"

Jackson started to move toward her, but she held up a trembling hand. "Please…just stay where you are. I have something…something I need to tell you."

She glanced over at Gabe, who gave her a nod then took his cue and quietly closed the door, slipping off to the kitchen. He needed a strong cup of coffee. He hoped Livvy had a pot on the stove.

For several seconds, Sarah just stood there, soaking up the sight of him. It didn't matter that Jackson needed a shave or that his shirt was wrinkled. It didn't matter that he looked a little thinner than he had before. He was still the handsomest man she had ever seen.

And she was still desperately in love with him.

"Your brother brought me here," she began. "I hoped…hoped I would never have to tell you, but I can't go on like this any longer."

Jackson's dark eyes searched her face. "For God's sake, Sarah, what is it?"

"First, I want you to know that I lied to you the last time I saw you. I said I didn't love you but it wasn't the truth. I love you so very, very much. I've loved you for a long time, but—"

He started to move again, but she shook her head and he stopped. "But sometimes loving someone isn't enough. I never wanted to hurt you, Jackson. I never meant for any of this to happen."

"Sarah…"

"I'm the one who killed Andrew, Jackson. That's the reason I can't marry you. Sooner or later the police will find out. I don't want to bring that down on you. You don't deserve it. You never have."

Jackson stood frozen.

Sarah closed her eyes, steeling herself, determined not to cry. "Now that you know, you can do whatever you feel is right. I've made arrangements for Nan to take Holly, so you don't have to worry about that."

Jackson's jaw tightened, but he still didn't move. "How did it happen? I need to know that, Sarah."

She nodded, utterly resigned and sick at heart. "He came home while I was packing. He was furious. He demanded I come down to the study. I could tell how mad he was. I could hear it in his voice."

"Come down here, Sarah."

"What…what is it you want, Andrew?"

She told him the rest, how Andrew had threatened her, how he'd told her he was going to kill her then take

Holly with him to Rio. Told him everything that had happened that night.

"I had a gun," she said, her voice thick with emotion. "Patt—a friend of mine sent it to me through the mail. She said I should use it to protect myself. She said I should never...never let him hurt me again."

"Go on," Jackson said, his features like granite.

Her heart ached just to look at him. She had known it would be this way, known what he would think, what any man would think. She had tried so hard to protect herself from the awful look in his eyes, but it was there just the same.

She swallowed the tears in her throat and forced herself to continue. "When he started toward me, I pulled the pistol out of my purse. I told him to stay away from me. I told him I wouldn't...wouldn't let him hurt me again." She bit down on her lip to keep it from trembling. "Andrew just laughed. Even the gun wasn't... wasn't enough to frighten him."

"You dare to threaten me? I'm going to kill you for that, Sarah."

"What happened then?" Jackson pressed.

She drew in a shaky breath, forced herself to continue. "I warned him. I told him I'd shoot him if...if he came any closer. He said...he said I didn't have the guts." Her voice broke on the last. Her head was spinning, the whole room seemed off-kilter.

"Finish it," Jackson demanded.

She braced herself, shoved out the words. "Then... then he ran toward me. I don't remember pulling the trigger, just the roar of the gun and the feel of the pistol jerking in my hand."

She knew she was crying, could feel the wetness

rolling down her cheeks. "I knew I should call 911, but Andrew... Andrew was already dead and I was afraid for Holly."

She dashed at the tears on her cheeks. "I kept...kept thinking of my little girl. What would happen to my daughter? Dear God, the trial would take months. I knew they would put her in foster care. I had no money. I couldn't afford a lawyer. If they put me in prison, what would happen...happen to Holly?"

She hadn't seen him move; he was simply there, pulling her against him, holding her tightly in his arms. She felt the shudder that rolled through his tall, lean body.

"Jackson..."

"It's all right." His hand smoothed over her hair. "You were protecting yourself and your child. You did what you had to. Andrew left you no choice."

Sarah clung to him, and she wept.

"We'll find our way through this, Sarah." He pressed his cheek against the top of her head. "Somehow, we will."

For long moments she just stood there in the circle of his arms, her heart aching with love for him, wishing she didn't have to tell him the rest. Finally, she let go of him.

"This isn't going away, Jackson." His gaze searched her face and she forced herself not to reach for him, not to step back into his arms. "Mercer called. They found the gun."

He straightened, seemed to collect himself. "What did you do with it after the shooting?"

"I—I wiped off my fingerprints. That night, after Holly went to sleep, I asked one of the neighbors to watch her while I ran a quick errand. Then I walked down to the end of the pier and tossed it in the ocean."

"How did Mercer find it?"

"He said some divers were working and they...they found the gun in the sand at the base of one of the pilings."

Jackson swore softly.

"Mercer won't...won't give up."

Jackson looked at her hard. "Neither will I."

Everything inside her seemed to cry out with regret. It was happening, exactly as she had feared. "Are you sure, Jackson? Are you sure I'm what you want?"

He moved closer. She felt his lips against her hair. "You've been what I've wanted for the past sixteen years."

Chapter 32

Jackson started things rolling the following day. He and Sarah dropped Holly off at her grandmother's place in Sheep River, then headed for Sarah's newly rented house in town.

He had asked Sarah to move back to the cottage and amazingly, she had agreed.

"I never wanted to move away," she confessed. "I love it on the ranch... I love being with you, Jackson. I just didn't want to drag you into all of this."

But he was in the middle of it now and he was staying. They were going to see this through all the way to the end.

While Sarah went to retrieve the boxes she had saved and stored in the garage, Jackson used his cell phone to call his attorney, Thomas Carson. He finished his brief conversation and closed the phone.

"Carson's going to get back to us with a couple of names." The best criminal attorneys in the L.A. area. "Dev's on it, too."

He had known from the moment Sarah had told him the truth about the shooting what he would have to do.

What both of them would have to do.

They couldn't get on with their lives until the matter of Andrew Hollister's death was resolved. To do that, Sarah needed to come forward with the truth.

"It's funny," she said, slipping into his arms. "Now that you're with me, I'm not afraid anymore." She rested her cheek on his shoulder and God it felt so good just to hold her.

"You did what you had to."

She eased out of his embrace and he immediately felt the loss. "I keep thinking…maybe if I hadn't had the gun…"

"If you hadn't had the gun, your husband likely would have killed you. He would have taken Holly and you know what would have happened if he had." He caught her shoulders. "A man died that day up in Alpine Meadow. Things happen. Sometimes you don't have a choice."

"You weren't the one who killed him."

"No, but I would have if I'd had to. I would have done whatever it took to protect the people I love."

Sarah stared up at him. "I never thought you'd understand. It never occurred to me that I could trust you with such a terrible secret."

"It isn't going to be a secret much longer, and once it's out in the open and all of this is settled, we can get on with our lives." He tipped her chin with his fingers.

"I think we should get married. Holly would be protected. To a certain extent, so would you."

Her lovely blue eyes welled with tears. "I want that. I want to marry you more than anything in the world, but I don't want to start our lives together with this awful shadow hanging over our heads. I can't do it, Jackson. Please don't ask me."

"What about Holly?"

"I talked to Nan sometime back. She'll take Holly if it comes to that. It would be wonderful if you and Livvy would help her."

"You know we will. I'm hoping it isn't going to go that far, but if it does, Holly will have everything she needs—including people who love her."

She nodded, brushed away a tear. "Thank you." She walked into the bedroom to begin packing her clothes. He saw her there next to the bed and for the first time in weeks, allowed his mind to remember how good it had been between them. He imagined her lush body spread open on the quilt, welcoming him, taking him deep inside her. He imagined having her in every way a man could take a woman and make her completely his.

She must have read his thoughts because her gaze grew soft and warm. He could see the heat, the desire rising there, the passion that was so much a part of her.

"I feel empty, Jackson. I need you to fill me, make me believe this is all going to work."

There was nothing he wanted more. He ripped open the snaps on the front of his shirt, tugged it free of his jeans and walked toward her. He hauled her into his arms and kissed her long and deep.

He had never wanted a woman the way he wanted Sarah, never felt such satisfaction with a woman before. He meant to go slowly, to remove each of her garments and kiss the soft pale skin he exposed. He meant to spend the next few hours making slow, languid love to her. But the weeks he'd spent without her had taken their toll.

Once men were warriors and he felt that way now, his groin swelling, his erection throbbing against the fly of his jeans. He wanted to bury himself inside her, plant his seed so deeply she would never think of another man.

The sex was wild and lusty—hot, sweaty, raunchy sex that had nothing to do with love and everything to do with a man claiming his mate.

The second time was different, easy and gentle, the love he felt for her pouring out of him, the love she felt for him washing over him in a soft, sweet wave.

"I wish I could stay in this bed forever," she said with a smile as she lay contentedly beside him.

Jackson chuckled. "I don't know about forever, but I can manage a few more hours." He came up over her, kissed her and began to make love to her again.

The persistent knock at the door finally reached him. It was fierce and determined. Jackson knew in an instant who was there.

And that they had waited too long.

"Sarah Adelaide Allen, you're under arrest for the murder of Andrew Hollister." Detective Ed Mercer stood next to Ben Weber and a female deputy sheriff.

Sarah trembled, lifted her chin and stepped forward. They had dressed hurriedly, Sarah once more in her jeans, sneakers and a blue cotton blouse. Mercer spun her around and clamped a pair of plastic bands around her wrists.

"Is that really necessary?" Jackson asked, doing his best not to grab the man by the front of his coat and bust him right in the mouth. Knowing if he did, he would go straight to jail and if that happened, he wouldn't be any good to Sarah.

"Probably not," Mercer smirked, "but that's the way it's going to be."

Ben Weber looked embarrassed. "I'm sorry it turned out this way, Jackson."

"It was self-defense, Ben. And she was turning herself in. We've just been waiting for a call from her attorney."

The sheriff nodded. "I figured there was more to it. Let me know if there's anything I can do."

Jackson had known Ben Weber for years. There was a great deal of mutual respect between them. If Jackson said Sarah was innocent, Ben would give her the benefit of the doubt. Unfortunately, Ed Mercer and the LAPD weren't going to be quite that cooperative.

"I'll follow you down to the station," Jackson told Sarah. On the way, he would call Carson and Dev. One of them was sure to have a name by now. Sarah needed legal help and she needed it today.

She stopped at the bottom of the steps, turned and looked up at him. "You don't deserve this."

"Neither do you." He caught up with her, walked beside her to the door of the sheriff's car. "I'll pick Holly up at your grandmother's and take her to Nan's, explain what's happened. We'll work things out between us."

Sarah just nodded. Bright tears glistened in her eyes. "I'm so sorry."

Jackson leaned down and kissed her full on the mouth. "Just hang on, all right?"

She nodded. Mercer shoved her head beneath the roof of the patrol car and she settled inside. She didn't look at him again as the car pulled off down the road.

"So where is Sarah now?" Dev asked Jackson over the cell phone.

"Her attorney advised her to waive extradition proceedings. They're transporting her straight to L.A. I haven't left Wyoming yet. At the moment, I'm standing outside her house in town. I need to pack some clothes for Holly. She's still at her grandmother's house. I'm going to pick her up and take her over to Nan Hargrove's for the next few days, till we see what's going to happen. As soon as I get her settled, I'm heading for L.A."

"Morgan Slater is one of the best attorneys in California. He'll do a good job for Sarah."

"I checked him out. He's got one helluva reputation."

"Listen to me, bro. You need to keep your head on straight. You have to believe that Sarah's going to be all right. Hollister was a scumbag and a wife-beater. With Sarah's medical history, self-defense should be a pretty easy sell."

Jackson released a breath. "I hope you're right."

"I'll keep my ears open. I'll let you know if I come up with anything useful."

"Thanks, Dev." Jackson closed the phone and used Sarah's key to open the door to her little rental house. The place seemed forlorn without her. As he crossed the living room and went into her bedroom, he could almost hear her cries of pleasure as he had made love to her there on the bed.

He shook his head and tried to focus his thoughts on what needed to be done. Her luggage was in the closet right where she'd told him to look.

His eyebrows went up when he spotted it and he whistled. *Louis Vuitton.* He almost smiled. Sarah had kept almost nothing Andrew had given her. But what woman could resist expensive designer luggage?

He pulled down two bags made of dark brown fabric with the logo woven into the material, dark brown leather handles and brass trim, and a personal tote to match. He opened them up on the bed. Sarah's initials were imprinted in gold on each piece, which was probably the reason she hadn't tried to sell them on eBay. The bags appeared to be several years old and had seen plenty of use, but they were still in good condition.

He glanced around the bedroom, thinking the luggage was probably the most expensive thing Sarah owned. The thought occurred that if he bought luggage for Sarah, he'd buy something with a soft floral pattern, something feminine and sexy. Undoubtedly Andrew liked the prestige of his wife traveling with world-class, designer bags.

He studied the cases, a thought suddenly niggling at the back of his mind. Andrew expected Sarah to go with him to Rio. He would have insisted she use the Louis Vuitton he had bought her.

He leaned over to examine the first bag, an overnighter, about twenty-four inches. He checked all the pockets and ran his fingers along the inside lining, carefully checking every inch.

He glanced at the tote but Sarah probably would

have carried that on the plane, which meant it would have had to go through airport security. He checked it quickly, not really expecting to find anything.

He moved to the final bag, which was slightly bigger. Sliding his fingers carefully along the interior, he checked the pockets, tested each section of the lining. He was about to give up, when his fingers touched something behind one of the removable zippered pouches. Velcro buzzed as he unfastened the pouch and felt the protrusion.

His adrenaline kicked up as he pulled his pocket-knife out of his jeans and cut into the lining, which had been stitched back together by hand. Reaching in, he carefully removed the item inside.

It was a USB. He rechecked the pocket, felt something more in the lining and pulled out a slip of paper with a row of numbers written on it.

Andrew hadn't wanted to carry the flash drive or the paper himself in case there was a problem, but his wife was another story. Jackson shoved the piece of paper into his pocket, walked over to Sarah's laptop and turned it on. He waited while the machine warmed up, then shoved in the flash drive.

A list of files popped up.

Good ol' Andrew, Jackson thought as he opened the first file and found exactly what he and Sarah had been searching for all along.

There was information on Martin Kozak's illegal operations, a long list detailing the man's every move.

There was information on Vernon Rimmer, the greedy highway inspector, the dates and amounts of the payoffs he had received, and the numbers identifying Rimmer's offshore Cayman Island accounts, the same ones Dev had managed to come up with.

Another file held documentation of Hexel Pharmaceuticals' activities, including the weight of the barrels of toxic waste and the dates they were delivered to the mine. There were numerous other miscellaneous infractions.

A number of other companies were mentioned, other shady deals outlined in glaring detail. None of the company names were familiar, but Jackson figured the FBI would likely know who they were.

The disk held a wealth of information.

If he was lucky, the contents would be valuable enough to exchange for dropping all the charges against Sarah. The only one who was truly interested in seeing her convicted of killing a scumbag like Andrew was Ed Mercer. Jackson had a strong suspicion that this time Mercer was going to be flat out of luck.

He grinned as he closed the files and turned off the computer, pocketed the USB key and grabbed his cell phone. The first call he made was to Morgan Slater, Sarah's attorney. He filled Slater in on his find and Slater agreed to make the call to Richard Kemp at the FBI. They had to handle this very carefully, or it would be Jackson who went to jail for withholding information.

Satisfied things were progressing in the direction he wanted, he walked back to the bedroom, grabbed one of the suitcases and went in to collect some of Holly's things. As soon as he got the little girl settled, he was heading for L.A.

He wasn't coming back until he could bring Sarah home.

Chapter 33

Sarah sat at a table in a room at the district attorney's office. Carolyn Gallegos, Assistant District Attorney, sat across from her, an attractive Hispanic woman in her forties. Richard Kemp of the FBI, in his dark blue suit and power tie, was also there, as well as Sarah's lawyer, Morgan Slater, late forties, salt-and-pepper hair, a man who exuded power and control.

Most importantly, Jackson sat beside her.

The deal was almost finished. The FBI was practically salivating to get their hands on Andrew's files. Amazingly, no one really doubted her story. They knew enough about Andrew's reputation to figure it was probably true. Or maybe they figured no matter the reason she shot him, he deserved it.

At any rate, her heart was gently pulsing with hope and whenever she looked over at Jackson, she saw confidence in the hard lines of his face.

"There's just one last thing, Ms. Allen," Richard Kemp said. "We'll need to know the name of the person who sent you the gun used in the shooting."

Her stomach dropped. Her heart set up a clatter. She had no idea what to say—only what not to say—and that was Patty Gorski's name. Not even the threat of prison could pry out those words.

Jackson reached beneath the table and took hold of her hand.

Morgan Slater must have read her decision in her face because he spoke up before she could form any sort of reply.

"My client isn't certain who sent her the revolver. She belonged to several internet chat groups for battered women. Some of them knew about the beatings she had suffered at the hands of her husband. The package came anonymously, disguised as clothing purchased on the internet. There was a note but it merely said she should use the gun if necessary in order to protect herself."

"Where is that note now?" Carolyn Gallegos asked.

"I burned it months ago," Sarah answered truthfully. "I was afraid of what Andrew would do to me if he found it."

"I see," Ms. Gallegos said. And Sarah thought that maybe she actually did. She was a woman. In her work, she must have dealt with dozens of cases of abuse. She closed the notebook sitting open in front of her. "As far as this office is concerned, the matter is resolved. Special Agent Kemp?"

He flicked a glance at Jackson, but fixed his attention on Sarah's lawyer. "If you can provide us with the USB key, we'll support the district attorney's decision."

Sarah drew in a shaky breath and blinked to keep from crying.

"It's over, Sarah," Morgan Slater said gently, rising to his feet. "I'll take care of whatever paperwork is necessary. You and Mr. Raines are free to leave."

The tears rushed past her defenses and this time she could not will them away. "Thank you. Thank you so much."

Slater smiled. "It was my pleasure." And it seemed as though he meant it. His exorbitant fee aside, clearly he believed she had shot her husband in self-defense and was glad he could help. Maybe there were more people out there than she had imagined who understood what she had been through with Andrew.

She left the district attorney's office and as she descended the wide stone steps leading down to the street, held on to Jackson's hand.

He stopped when they reached the curb. "It's over, Sarah."

"I'll never be able to repay you for what you've done."

He actually grinned. "Oh, I think you will." And the look in his eyes was so hot she laughed.

"Let's get married," he said.

"Now?"

"Anytime you say."

She swallowed past the lump that rose in her throat. "As soon as we get back to the ranch, I'll marry you. I love you, Jackson Raines."

Epilogue

A glorious sun shone down from a sky so vibrant a blue it seemed surreal. It was amazing how quickly a wedding could be put together when the people you love all pitched in to help.

She and Jackson were repeating their vows on a grassy rise behind the ranch house. Chairs had been set up and an arbor perched at the end of a long white runner beneath the leafy branches of a pair of alder trees.

Holly was the flower girl, dropping rose petals as she walked between the rows of white rented chairs. Nan was her bridesmaid, looking radiant in a lavender tea-length gown. Her grandmother sat next to Livvy in the front row, dabbing away happy tears. Since Sarah didn't have a father, she walked down the aisle with Jimmy, while Dev and Gabe stood next to Jackson, acting as his best men.

Nan did an excellent job of ignoring her former beau, which definitely didn't please him. Sarah figured it was only a matter of time until Jimmy realized his feelings for Nan ran deep, and the two of them got back together. But, of course, she couldn't be sure.

She returned her attention to the tall man waiting for her under the white roses entwined in the arbor. In her simply cut cream silk gown trimmed with matching cream lace, she walked toward him. The dress had a narrow skirt that came to just above her knees, and she wore matching cream satin, very high heels.

Jackson looked ruggedly handsome in a black-Western-cut tuxedo and black lizard-skin boots. All of the men in the bridal party wore matching suits, black boots and black cowboy hats, which seemed fitting out here on the ranch.

The service was lovely. Though Sarah barely registered the minister's words, she would never forget her husband's kiss, sweet and tender, yet fierce and utterly possessive.

All of her friends were there: her boss, Smiley Reed, and his girlfriend, Myra Cunningham; Mike Stevens; Jackson's attorney, Thomas Carson; the Whittakers from the ranch next door; Cody and Marilyn Dillon; Sheriff Weber; Fred Wilkins and his wife from the mercantile. There were at least a dozen others, long-time friends of Jackson's. It was amazing how they all managed to get there on such short notice.

Only one person was missing.

Sarah had called her, of course, and told her about the wedding. She had told her best friend everything that had happened and how it had all turned out. That the investigation was finally closed and both of them were safe. They had talked for nearly an hour.

Both of them had cried.

But Patty lived in Chicago and there was no way she could get all the way to Wyoming with only a week's notice. The airfare alone would be staggering.

Sarah felt Jackson's arm around her waist as he led her away from the big tent set up over rows of buffet tables and a dance floor.

"I've got a surprise for you."

She smiled. "A surprise?"

He just grinned and tipped his head toward the house.

Sarah's gaze swung in that direction and she froze. A robust woman with bright red hair in a short, hot-pink dress ran toward her, waving and wobbling on high heels she was clearly not used to wearing. Tears sprang into Sarah's eyes.

Patty Gorski.

"My plane was late taking off," Patty said, fighting to catch her breath. "Jackson sent a car to the airport to pick me up. Thank God it was still waiting when I finally got here."

"Patty! Oh, my God, I can't believe you're really here." Sarah went into the older woman's arms and the two women hugged. "I can't believe you actually came."

"Jackson called me. He sent a ticket and made all the arrangements. He said there wasn't going to be a wedding unless I came."

"Oh, Patty." The women embraced again.

"You're prettier than your picture," Patty said, grinning up at her.

"You're shorter than I thought."

Both of them laughed.

Sarah looked over at Jackson. "This is the best wedding gift you ever could have given me. Thank you so much, Jackson."

He just smiled.

Patty eyed him from top to bottom, leaned over and whispered, "My God, he's gorgeous." She straightened and grinned. "A man like that might be enough to make me contemplate marriage again."

Sarah laughed.

Patty turned serious. "I got the check. It came special delivery yesterday. Oh, my God—half a million dollars!"

"Just remember it's supposed to be an anonymous donation."

"Well, officially it is."

The numbers Jackson had found on the paper in her luggage had turned out to be another account in the Cayman Offshore Corporation. This one belonged to Andrew. With the numbers, they were able to withdraw the money Andrew had intended to take with him to Rio, all he had left of his ill-gotten gains. It seemed only fitting that Patty Gorski's battered women's group get the benefit of the funds.

"Listen, you two," Patty said. "This is your wedding day. I can only stay a couple of hours, then I have to head back home."

"But you've come all this way!"

"I came to meet you and I came to thank you for the money. Besides, Jackson promised to bring you to Chicago. We'll have all the time we need to really get to know each other. Now go on and enjoy yourself."

Sarah looked up at her tall, ruggedly handsome husband. "I'll expect you to keep your word on that," she said with a smile.

Jackson caught her chin, bent and lightly kissed her. "Count on it, darlin'."

Sweeping Patty along with them toward the tent, Sarah made introductions, including Holly, left Patty with Livvy and went with Jackson to cut the wedding cake.

"Come on, Mom," Holly said, grabbing her hand and tugging her toward the white, four-layer cake trimmed with fresh roses. "Everybody's waiting!"

"Well, then, we'd better get it done." Sarah looked around her, at the friends and family she had come to love. "Thank you," she said to Jackson, "for everything."

He gave her a wicked smile. "You can thank me properly later."

Sarah grinned up at him, thinking how happy this man made her, imagining their wedding night.

And planning to do just that.

* * * * *

Also by Delores Fossen

Harlequin Intrigue

Appaloosa Pass Ranch

Lone Wolf Lawman
Taking Aim at the Sheriff
Trouble with a Badge
The Marshal's Justice
Six-Gun Showdown

Sweetwater Ranch

Maverick Sheriff
Cowboy Behind the Badge
Rustling Up Trouble
Kidnapping in Kendall County
The Deputy's Redemption
Reining in Justice
Surrendering to the Sheriff
A Lawman's Justice

HQN Books

The McCord Brothers

Texas on My Mind
Lone Star Nights

And don't miss *Blame It on the Cowboy*,
available October 2016!

SAVIOR IN THE SADDLE

Delores Fossen

To my daughter, Beth

Chapter 1

Austin, Texas

They had found her.

Willa Marks saw the proof of that when the man stepped from the black four-door Ford that had just pulled into her driveway.

He had a badge clipped to his belt.

She pressed her fingers to her mouth to silence the gasp that nearly escaped from her throat and she eased down the blinds that she'd lifted a fraction so she could peek out.

Oh, God.

This couldn't be happening.

Willa hurried away from the window and to the wall next to the door. Her shoulder brushed against the trio of yellow sticky notes that she'd left there, and one of them fluttered to the floor.

Don't Trust the Cops, the note said.

She no longer needed the reminder. At least, Willa didn't think she did. But she'd left it there just in case. It was too important for her to forget something like that again.

"It'll be okay," she whispered to her unborn child, hoping she wasn't lying to the baby and herself.

She slid her hand over her pregnant belly, but she knew her hand wouldn't be much protection if this turned out to be the start of another round in the nightmare that just would not end.

The doorbell rang, the sound knifing through the room, and this time she wasn't able to muffle her gasp. Of course, she'd known they would ring the bell. And they wouldn't stop until she let them inside.

They had found her.

Well, by God, they weren't taking her back into their so-called protective custody. Look where that had gotten her the last two times.

She and her baby had nearly been killed.

There were ten notes around the house to remind her of that, and just in case that wasn't enough, the warning scrolled across the screen saver of her laptop: Don't Trust the Cops.

The doorbell rang again, and it was followed by a heavy knock. "Ms. Marks, I'm Lieutenant Bo Duggan from San Antonio P.D. I know you're in there."

Maybe he had seen her car in the garage. Or perhaps he'd even spotted her when she'd made a quick trip just a half hour earlier to the grocery store.

But how exactly had they found her?

She'd been so careful—using an alias, paying only with cash, leaving no paper trail. She hadn't wanted to dye her hair because of the chemicals, but she hadn't cut it in months and, with it pulled back from her face, she didn't resemble the photos that had been snapped of her four months earlier and splattered all over the news.

Apparently all those safety measures hadn't been enough.

"Lieutenant Bo Duggan," she repeated under her breath, and Willa hurried to grab her PDA from her desk next to the sofa.

There was another knock, and another, but Willa ignored them and scrolled through the pictures and names she'd assembled in case her memory failed her again. She found him. Bo Duggan's photo was there, and she'd added a caption: I Think I Can Trust Him.

It was the word *think* that kicked up her heartbeat an extra notch. But then, in the past four months, there was no one that she trusted completely.

Not even herself.

"We need to talk to you," Lieutenant Duggan said from the other side of the door. "We know you're scared, but there are things we have to ask you—important things."

Willa carried the PDA back to the window and peeked out again. The lieutenant's face matched the picture she had, but he wasn't alone.

There was another man with him.

The second man was tall and lanky. He wore jeans and a crisp, white shirt topped with a buckskin jacket, and he held a saddle-brown Stetson in his left hand. His dress was casual, unlike the lieutenant who had on a dark blue suit.

It was the second man that Willa focused on. Did she know him?

His face wasn't familiar.

He had thick black hair that was slightly long and rumpled, no doubt from the cold December wind that was assaulting them. With that Stetson, jeans and jacket, he looked like a cowboy from the *Texas Monthly* magazine she had on her coffee table.

His skin was deeply tanned, but she shook her head, rethinking that. The skin tone was probably natural. Those high cheekbones and features were Native American.

She frantically scrolled through the pictures again, but she didn't expect to find him. With those unique looks, Willa thought he might be someone she would remember without the prompts, pictures and captions.

"Ms. Marks," the lieutenant tried again. "Please, open the door."

The knocks got harder, and each blow against the thick wood sent her pulse racing out of control. She couldn't call the local cops. There were plenty of notes telling her not to trust them. So maybe she could wait out these two. Eventually Lieutenant Duggan and his Native American partner would get tired of knocking and leave.

She hoped.

Then she could gather her things and go on the run again.

The baby inside her kicked hard, as if protesting that. "Well, I'm not too happy about it, either," Willa mumbled.

She'd lived here at this suburban Austin rental house for two months now, and that was a month longer than the extended-stay hotel where she'd stayed in Houston. Two months hadn't been long enough for her to settle in or to stop being afraid, but she had started to believe she might be able to remain here until after the baby was born. Or at least until Christmas, which was only three days away.

So much for her short-term dreams.

They were as fleeting as her short-term memory had been just weeks ago.

"Willa?" someone called out.

Not the lieutenant. Another look out the blinds, and she realized it was the other man who'd spoken. The man whose picture wasn't in her PDA. But he had said her name as if he knew her.

No, it was more than that.

He said her name as if he knew her *intimately*.

"Willa, it's me, Brandon. Look, I know you're probably still mad at me—I don't blame you. But I've been searching for you all this time so I could tell you how sorry I am about the argument we had."

"Brandon?" She repeated it several times, but it jogged no memory.

Who was he? What did he want? And what argument had they had? Better yet, just how badly did she need to know the answers to those questions?

Willa made sure all four locks on the front door were engaged, though she already knew they were. That was routine these days. The lights were green on the security panel box, meaning it was armed and ready to sound if tripped. Also routine. As were the window locks, gun and the multiple cans of pepper spray she had stashed around the house.

The lieutenant and his partner couldn't get in. Well, not unless they broke down the door or smashed a window, but that could happen if she spoke to them or not.

"Do I know you?" she called out. And Willa prayed that merely asking the question wouldn't turn out to be a deadly mistake.

She watched through the blinds, and she saw the men whispering to each other. Both of them also fired glances all around the yard and street. Not ordinary glances, either. The kind that cops made when they were worried they might be ambushed.

Of course, it was also the kind of glances that criminals made to make sure they weren't being watched.

"You know me," the man, Brandon, assured her. He said it with complete confidence, but there was also a tinge of frustration in his voice. "Willa, open the door. I want to see you."

Willa didn't budge. "How do you know me?"

He hesitated. It wasn't just a pause. But definitely a hesitation. She'd lost so much after everything she'd been through, but she'd gained something, too. Willa had gotten very good at reading people.

Brandon was on edge.

"They told me you had memory loss from a fall you took at the hospital, and that you were in a coma for a while," Brandon finally said. "You still don't remember me after all this time?"

No, but she didn't intend to tell him that.

Truth was, she had no memories—*none*—before the nightmare that had happened four months earlier when she and about three dozen other pregnant women and medical staff had been held hostage at gunpoint for hours on the fourth floor at the San Antonio Maternity Hospital. Questioned. Verbally abused. And worse.

People had died that day, and those who had survived did not come out unscathed.

She was proof of that.

The gunmen had even forced her to help them retrieve some computer files in the lab. Or so she'd been told because part of the hostage standoff had been captured on a hospital surveillance camera.

Willa had no recollection of that, either.

No memories before that fall she'd supposedly taken when one of the gunmen had pushed her down during her attempted escape. No memories before or immediately following the coma she'd supposedly been in when her brain had swollen from a deep concussion.

And what she had remembered since was spotty in too many areas.

The head injury had given her both amnesia and short-term memory loss. That was the last diagnosis she'd received anyway. She hadn't seen a neurologist in nearly a month.

She had made some progress with the short-term memory issues but none with the amnesia itself. She could have indeed met this Brandon, but she knew so few details of her life that anything was possible.

For all practical purposes, Willa's life had begun two months ago when her short-term memory had started to stabilize.

She knew the basics. She was Willa Diane Marks, a computer software designer from San Antonio. Both parents were dead. No living relatives. She wasn't rich, but she'd had more than enough money to decide at the age of thirty-three that she wanted to reduce her hours at the business she'd started and have a child. Since she hadn't been involved in a relationship at the time, she'd used artificial insemination, which had been done at the very hospital where, three months later, she'd been held hostage.

Willa could thank a nurse at the San Antonio Maternity Hospital for filling her in on those few details. And just so she would remember them, Willa had put them in notes in a computer file. Notes she read daily in case she forgot. Heck, there was even a note to remind herself to read the file.

"Well?" Lieutenant Duggan prompted. "Are you going to let us in? Because I have a warrant and I can break down the door if necessary. I don't want to do that, and I don't think you do either. Am I right?"

She dodged the questions. "Brandon, how do you know me?" Willa countered.

More hesitation. More whispered conversation between the men. Finally, Brandon angled his eyes to the window. Right where she was. As if he'd known all along that she was there.

Brandon's gaze met hers. "Willa, I'm your ex-boyfriend."

Whatever she had expected him to say, that wasn't it.

Her heart went to her knees.

The baby stopped kicking and went still. So did Willa. Her breath lodged somewhere between her lungs and her throat, and she forced herself to exhale so she wouldn't get light-headed. She had enough things against her already without adding that.

"My ex-boyfriend?" she challenged. She had been involved with this man, but there was no photo of him in her PDA? No yellow sticky note with his name on her wall? And he darn sure wasn't in her memory. "Prove it."

"Open the door, and I will." It wasn't exactly a promise, but it was close.

Close enough for Willa to put her PDA aside and grab the .38 handgun she kept on top of the foyer table. Before she could change her mind, she undid the locks, paused the security system and opened the front door. There was still a locked screen door between the men and her, but even through the gray mesh, she could see their faces clearly.

Brandon's eyes were a dark earthy brown.

And much to Willa's surprise, she reacted to him. Or rather her body did. There was a deep pull within her.

Attraction, she realized.

She was physically attracted to him. Strange, because it was a new sensation for her. She was certain at one time or another she had been attracted to a man, but she didn't remember this feeling.

"What proof do you have?" Willa immediately asked.

Those rich brown eyes combed over her face, but she couldn't tell what was going through his mind. His gaze dropped to her stomach. Since she was seven months pregnant and huge, it would have been hard not to miss her baby bulge. Then, his attention landed on the .38 Smith & Wesson she had gripped in her hand at her side.

"There's no need for that," Brandon said, his voice mostly calm. There was still that edge to it. "Neither of us will hurt you."

"Forgive me if I don't believe you," she fired back.

"You have reason not to trust us," Lieutenant Duggan volunteered. "We didn't do a good job of protecting you while you were in the hospital recovering from your head injury."

She nearly laughed. "No. You didn't. A gunman got into my room just two days after the hostages were rescued, and he tried to shoot and kill me."

Willa didn't exactly have memories of that incident, either. Thank God. The memory loss was good for some things, and she didn't need that particular nightmare in her head. But she'd read the reports, over and over, and every time she would forget, she would reread them. She needed to remember that the cops hadn't protected her then. Or now.

The lieutenant nodded. "That gunman was caught. His name was Danny Monroe, and later that same morning when he tried to kill a police captain and another hostage, he was shot. He died in surgery. You don't have to worry about him now."

"Maybe not him. But that wasn't the only attempt made on my life," Willa reminded the lieutenant. "Someone tried to break into the safe house where you had me staying after I got out of the hospital."

"You remember that?" Duggan asked.

"No," Willa reluctantly admitted. "But I haven't had any short-term memory problems for the last two months. I remember everything that's happened during that time, and I remember all the notes I've read about the incident."

And that was the truth. *Almost.*

"We're not sure who tried to get into the safe house," the lieutenant admitted, "but it's still under investigation."

"Well, the investigation can continue without my

help." She looked at Brandon who was staring at her. "You said you have proof that you're my ex-boyfriend?"

He nodded and shifted his head against the wind when another cold gust slammed into them. "Can we come in, and I'll show you?"

"You can show me what you have from out there. And you'd better have more than a going-steady ring or a picture from our high school prom."

Even though there was something that made her want to trust, and *believe,* the man. Willa groaned. Hadn't the last four months taught her anything?

Brandon mumbled something she didn't catch, and he reached into his pocket, prompting her to bring up her gun. Lieutenant Duggan's hand went to the butt of his own weapon that was tucked in a shoulder holster inside his jacket.

Brandon held up his hands in a calm-down gesture. "I'm not going for a gun."

But he had one. Willa saw it then. It was in a cowboy-style waist holster that rested low on his hips.

She also spotted the badge clipped to his holster, and she backed up a step.

"You're a cop?" she accused.

Brandon nodded. "Not SAPD though. I'm the sheriff of a small town, Crockett Creek. It's about a half hour from San Antonio."

He was still a lawman. The very people her notes warned her not to trust.

"You didn't remember that Brandon Ruiz is a sheriff?" Lieutenant Duggan asked.

"No," she snapped. "And I think there's a reason for that. You're trying to trick me. You figured if you could convince me that this man, this stranger, is my ex-boyfriend that I would let you in so you could talk me into doing whatever it is that brought you here."

Duggan and Brandon exchanged glances, and it was Brandon who continued. "It's true. We do have things to tell you. Things that could affect your safety—and the baby's." He paused, his gaze heading back in that direction again.

He swallowed hard. And looked away.

So, he couldn't even look her in the eye. Or the belly. He was lying.

"Get off my porch," Willa demanded. "And stay away from me."

"I can't," Brandon said. "I have the proof you want." He took a piece of paper from his pocket.

Willa already had her hand on the door, ready to slam it shut, but that stopped her. "What is that?"

"It's a medical report." Brandon took his time continuing that explanation. "You had an amniocentesis done after the hostage incident."

She had. There were notes about it on her computer. The doctors had been concerned that her injury might have affected the baby, so she'd had the test done to examine the amniotic fluid to make sure all was well.

"What does that have to do with anything?" Willa asked.

Brandon's mouth tightened a little. "We, uh, were able to compare the baby's DNA we got from the amniocentesis results that were on file at the hospital."

Now it was Willa who held up her hand. "Wait just a darn minute. Why were you comparing DNA? I had artificial insemination, and I used an anonymous donor."

"No," Lieutenant Duggan disagreed.

And that one-word denial was all he said for several heart-stopping moments.

"We had the nurse tell you that," the lieutenant explained, "because you were so upset—you were hysterical. The doctors couldn't sedate you because you were in the first trimester of your pregnancy, and they thought you might lose the baby if we couldn't calm you down."

"So, they lied," Brandon added.

Willa moved her hand to her heart to try to steady it. "Lied about what exactly?"

Brandon's gaze came to hers. "There was no artificial insemination, Willa. And that baby you're carrying is *mine*."

Chapter 2

Brandon waited for Willa Marks to grasp what he'd just told her.

It didn't take long. Within seconds, her eyes widened. She went pale, and she inched back farther away from the screen door, no doubt to put some distance between her and them.

She stood there, looking scared, lost and vulnerable in her maternity jeans and dove-gray sweater that seemed to swallow her. She was petite, barely five-three. Hardly big enough to be fighting off bad guys, but she'd had to do too much of that in the past four months.

From the corner of his eye, Brandon saw the lieutenant make another sweeping glance around the yard and street. Brandon did the same. Because it might not be safe for Willa or for them to be standing out here in the open like this.

"You're my baby's father?" Willa questioned. Despite her obvious surprise, there was still a Texas-size dose of suspicion in her expression and her tone.

Her memory might not be in full working gear, but her instincts sure were.

She had a reason to be suspicious.

But Brandon didn't want her suspicions to get her and the baby killed.

"We need to come in," Brandon insisted, and he tried not to make it sound like a question.

He immediately saw the debate in her wide blue eyes. She volleyed glances between Bo Duggan and him before she mumbled something under her breath. She went to the screen door, unlocked it and then stepped back.

She held on to the gun, and Brandon hoped like the devil that he didn't have to wrestle it away from her.

Brandon walked in first, and Bo was right behind him. Bo closed the door, and Brandon immediately felt the warmth from the central heating. But not from their guest.

Willa was glaring at them.

He glanced around. Old habits. He'd been a peace officer for eight years. That was eight years too long to let down his guard. Willa had given no indication that someone was inside holding her hostage, but he needed to make sure that wasn't the case.

The place was small so he didn't have to look too far to take it all in. They were in a living-dining combination area, and there was a modest kitchen through the double doorway near the dining table. In the center of the table was a potted plant that had been decorated with tiny foil Christmas ornaments. No wrapped gifts, and judging from Willa's situation, there probably wouldn't be any.

On the other side of the house, he could see directly into the two bedrooms and the bathroom, with all the doors wide open. Apparently, Willa was trying to minimize the chance that anyone could sneak in through one of the windows without her hearing them.

The place was neat as a pin except for the yellow sticky notes all over the walls and surfaces of the furniture. He spotted one on the hardwood floor and reached down to pick it up.

"Don't trust the cops," he read and passed it to Bo.

Bo glanced at it as well and then looked at her. "I thought you weren't having any more short-term memory loss."

"I'm not. The notes are leftovers from a time when I was having problems. I just haven't gotten around to removing them." Her chin came up, causing her long blondish-brown ponytail to swish. It brushed against her shoulder and settled on the top of her left breast.

Brandon quickly got his attention off that.

Should he go to her, he wondered? Should he try to hug or kiss her? That was something Bo and he hadn't discussed on the ride over, but Brandon wished they had. He knew what he had to say to Willa, what he had to do about her safety situation, but he hadn't given much thought to the personal aspect of this.

Willa held out her hand. "Let me see that DNA report," she insisted.

Brandon walked closer, halving the distance between them and gave it to her.

He watched her read through the report, and with

each line her gaze skirted across, her forehead bunched up even more.

"It could be a lie," she concluded, handing it back to him.

"Why would we lie about that?" Bo questioned.

Willa opened her mouth. Then closed it. She shook her head. "I don't know, but you just admitted you lied four months ago when you had a nurse tell me I was artificially inseminated."

"We did that only because we didn't want you to lose the baby. It worked," Bo insisted. "You settled down, quit asking for Brandon, and you started to heal."

"I asked for him?" She immediately wanted to know.

Brandon let Bo answer. "You did. You wanted to see him because he's your baby's father."

Her accusing gaze came back to Brandon. "Then why weren't you there at the hospital that day, when I was scheduled for my first ultrasound along with some other lab tests?"

"I didn't know about it," Brandon answered.

"SAPD thinks the ultrasound and lab tests were a ploy to get you the hospital that afternoon because the appointment wasn't on the schedule," Bo explained. "We believe the gunmen called you with the bogus appointments because they'd researched the records of several of the pregnant women, and they knew you were a whiz with computers. They thought you could help them access some files."

"I know all of that," she snapped. "It's in my notes." She pointed to Brandon. "That doesn't explain why you weren't there."

Brandon lifted his shoulder, trying to shrug. "We'd had an argument about a month earlier, and you told me to get out, that it was over between us. I was out of the state at the time, and I didn't know you'd been taken hostage until two days after it ended. By then, you were in protective custody at a secret location."

"He asked for your location," Bo continued. "But there had already been an attempt on your life, and we thought it best if no one knew where you were."

And then there had been another breach of security. Another intruder. That had caused Willa to go on the run, leaving the safe house and not telling anyone where she was. It'd taken SAPD all this time to find her.

Without moving her gaze from Brandon's, she walked closer, her steps slow and deliberate. Until she was very close. So close he could take in her scent. There was some kind of floral fragrance in her hair. Roses, maybe.

She reached out and caught onto his arm. Brandon wasn't sure what she had in mind, but he didn't think she was about to launch herself against him for a welcome-home kiss.

No. Her suspicions were getting stronger.

She took his hand and placed it on her stomach. On the baby.

Brandon pulled in his breath before he could stop himself, but he did manage to hold his ground and not move away. He also kept eye contact with her, which was probably stupid.

Willa didn't say a word. She just stared at him.

The moments crawled by and because Brandon didn't know what the hell else to do he just stood there.

"Let me guess," Willa said, her words as slow and deliberate as her steps had been. "We argued about the baby. That's why we broke up. Because you weren't ready to be a father."

Brandon settled for a nod.

"What was I to you—your one-night stand?" she asked. No more of that slow and deliberate tone. She was riled now.

"No," he answered truthfully. "Willa, you weren't a one-night stand."

She studied his eyes. Then she studied him. Her gaze eased down the length of his body. Back up. And then she groaned, turned and sank down on the sofa. She put the gun on the coffee table, something that probably pleased Bo as much as it did him.

They'd made it past step one.

But they had a hell of a long way to go.

"I'll give you two some time alone," Bo said, hitching his thumb to the door. "I'll be in the car. But just don't take too long."

And Brandon knew why. This was not going to be a lengthy romantic welcome-home chat. They were in a hurry.

Bo opened the door, and the wind cut through the room again. The notes on the walls stirred, and two of them went flying through the air. One of them landed near Brandon's boots.

"Take prenatal vitamins," he read aloud and handed her the note. He eased down into the chair across from her. "Just how bad is your memory?"

"Just how much didn't you want this baby?" Willa countered.

So, her memory wasn't up for discussion. He wished she'd taken the baby talk off the table as well.

Brandon knew they had to discuss it, eventually.

That was all part of the plan, but he hadn't counted on having the emotional reaction of touching Willa. And he sure as hell hadn't counted on this gut need to protect her. He'd planned on doing what SAPD wanted and then walking away.

Especially walking away.

He was good at that.

But he'd been in the room with Willa for less than fifteen minutes, and he was already having doubts about this plan. She deserved the truth.

The *whole* truth about why he was there.

"Tell me who you are," she insisted. "Not just your name. I want to know who you really are."

Brandon nodded and gathered his thoughts. "My full name is Brandon Michael Ruiz. Like you, I was born in San Antonio. I'm thirty-six. Never been married. I spent some time in the army before I came back to Texas and made it my home again."

She motioned for him to continue.

"I've been sheriff of Crockett Creek for eight years."

"And your bloodline?"

"My dad was—is," he corrected, "Comanche. My mother was part Irish, part Italian, part German. Guess that makes me a real American, huh?"

Willa ignored his attempt to lighten up the conversation. "How did we meet?"

Thankfully, he didn't have to pause to collect his thoughts. "At a restaurant on the Riverwalk in San Antonio. The place was crowded, and we shared a table."

She stared at him again. "I think you're probably lying about that. I don't know why." She waved him off before he could try to convince her otherwise. "It doesn't matter. It's obvious you don't want to be here so that means the lieutenant brought you to convince me to do something."

Well, he hadn't expected her to give him that kind of opening.

"But first, you're supposed to regain my trust," she continued. "And SAPD's theory is the reason I'll trust you again is that we have a child in common." She moved closer to the edge of the sofa. "But you and I both know how things really are, don't we, Brandon?"

Yeah, he thought, maybe they did, so Brandon stuck with the truth. "I gave up the idea of being a father not long after I got out of the military. Let's just say I didn't think my gene pool was worth passing along to an innocent baby."

She made a sound to indicate she was thinking about that. And he could see the doubt creep back into her eyes. "That probably has something to do with the *was* versus the *is* when you described your father's bloodline, but I don't believe you want to share that secret with me so I won't push."

Surprised, Brandon angled his head to the side and studied her. "Have you been taking deception-training classes since you've been in hiding?"

The corner of her mouth lifted, but the smile didn't make it to her eyes. "When I couldn't remember anything for more than ten minutes, I started relying on other things. Eye contact. Facial signals. My gut instincts," she added in a mumble.

Brandon tried his hand at it. "The way you said the last part—*my gut instincts*—does that mean you don't like what your gut instincts are telling you about me?"

Her glare returned. "Stand up," she said abruptly.

"Excuse me?"

"Stand up. *Please*." That last word was clearly an afterthought.

Brandon did stand, all the while wondering where this would lead. And Willa stood up as well. She went to him, hesitating just a second, before she reached up and caught on to the back of his neck. She pulled him down and touched her mouth to his.

It was a peck, hardly qualifying as a kiss, but it lit a very bad fire inside him that shouldn't be lit. A fire below the belt.

She pulled back and drew her tongue over her bottom lip. Yet something to stoke that blaze that he had to put out.

"Yes," she said, "I think I remember kissing you." Willa shook her head, stared up at him.

Brandon decided to do something to convince her to reconsider that *I think* part. His hand went to her back, and he hauled her to him.

And he kissed her.

Yeah, it was probably stupid, but he didn't keep it a peck or at some wimp level to be merely a test. No. He wanted this to be a kiss she'd remember. So, he pressed his lips against hers, moving over her mouth. Taking in her taste, along with that incredible scent. He got an even better sample of her when his tongue touched hers.

She jerked away from him and stepped back. Way back. Her breath was gusting now. Brandon realized his was, too. And she propped her hands on her hips and stared at him.

"I'm attracted to you," she said in the same tone as if confessing to premeditated murder.

The woman certainly knew how to keep him on his toes. "I'm attracted to you," he echoed.

Her stare turned to another glare. "I hate that I just told you that because it gives you leverage over me. But don't be fooled." Willa walked to the foyer table and grabbed her PDA. "I will never put anything I feel for you over the safety of my baby. That means I'm not going to let you talk me into doing anything I could regret."

Oh, man. Since they kept going back to that, Brandon figured it was time to move on to step two.

At least step two didn't involve kissing her.

"The baby is my priority, too," he clarified. "Yeah, I know. I said I'd dismissed fatherhood, but now that I know a baby's on the way—"

"It's a girl," Willa interrupted. "I'm having a daughter."

It took everything inside him not to react. He nodded. "A daughter," he repeated.

Brandon eased that information aside and got back to work.

Yes, he still wanted to protect Willa. He was sorry for what she'd been through. But the groundwork had been laid. She'd bought the story, and it was time to move on. However, before he could do that, Willa lifted the PDA and a second later, there was a small burst of light.

She took his picture.

She typed in something. Paused. And added something else. Notes about him no doubt.

Don't Trust Brandon Ruiz maybe.

Well, she would have to learn to trust him. At least temporarily.

"You're going to have to leave this place and come with me," he told her. Willa started to object, but Brandon talked right over her. "You don't have a choice. The baby's safety is at stake, and I won't let you endanger my child."

There. That was the gauntlet.

"*Your* child?" she said, mocking him.

"Oh, no, we're not going back to that part about my ambivalence toward fatherhood. We'll do what's best for this baby. And what's best is for you not to be here."

Willa didn't say a word, not even to demand more information. She was no doubt trying to figure out how she could escape. That attempt would probably come when she tried to excuse herself to go to the bathroom. Or to get something from the kitchen.

But that wasn't going to happen.

"We've received an intelligence report that there's going to be another hostage situation," Brandon stated as clearly as he could.

Her bottom lip started to tremble. "Where?" Her voice was all breath.

"We don't know that. Or when. Or who will be involved. All we have is that it'll take place at an undisclosed hospital and that the person responsible has hired two computer techs to break into some files."

She caught her bottom lip between her teeth to stop the trembling. From what he'd been told, Willa didn't have any actual memories of the hostage situation she'd endured, but she had read reports. Heck, she'd probably memorized them and knew she didn't want any other person to go through what she had.

"You could put guards at all the hospitals," Willa suggested.

He shook his head. "Too many of them. We can put them on alert, of course, and warn them of the potential danger, but we're not even sure this attack will happen at a hospital in the state. It could happen anywhere."

She waited a moment. Mumbled something. "How can I help?" she finally asked.

Brandon took a deep breath. Even though he still had to be mindful of her attempted escape, step two had been a success. Now, it was time for the grand finale.

Well, part of it anyway.

The last step wouldn't happen until SAPD was sure this new hostage threat had been squelched.

"We think someone masterminded the situation with the maternity hostages," he continued.

"But you caught the two gunmen and the man who hired them. I read about it."

"Yes, his name was Gavin Cunningham, and last week he committed suicide in prison. In his suicide note he indicated he hadn't worked alone, that someone had helped him set up the entire maternity hostage situation."

The breath rushed from her mouth. "Who helped him?"

"We're not sure. That's where we're hoping you can fill us in."

"I get it," she said almost immediately. "You want me to resume my therapy so I can remember if the gunman who held me said anything about the identity of his boss."

"Yeah."

Among other things.

"But I might not remember," she pointed out. "Or

maybe the gunman didn't say anything to me at all. I could be putting myself out there for no reason."

"You wouldn't be just putting yourself out there, Willa." Brandon tried to keep his voice level and calm. "I'd be with you. You'd be in my protective custody."

She rolled her eyes. "Let me guess—that wasn't your idea. It was Lieutenant Duggan's."

Brandon evaded that. "Bo Duggan lost his wife during that hostage situation. She died after giving birth to their twins. He's, well, eager to solve this case once and for all."

She stayed quiet a moment. Then, she said, "No."

"No?" Brandon challenged. Well, there went his calm and level voice.

"No," she insisted. "I won't go with you into protective custody. And I won't work directly with Lieutenant Duggan, SAPD or even you."

She pointed to her laptop. Don't Trust the Cops was scrolling across the screen in bold white letters on a black background.

She had a reason not to trust cops, or anyone else for that matter. But he had to get her past that because she had no choice. Willa had to trust him.

Even if he didn't deserve that trust.

"I'll restart my therapy on my own," she continued. "I can't take any memory-activating drugs because they might harm the baby, but maybe hypnosis will work if I try it again. I can do the hypnosis sessions here."

Brandon shook his head. "No, you can't."

That got her back on her feet. "Now, just a darn minute. You might be my baby's biological father and my former boyfriend, but that doesn't give you any say in my life."

He got to his feet as well. "This badge does."

She pulled back her shoulders and looked as if he slapped her. "You're pulling rank on me?"

"I don't have a choice, Willa." He'd practiced this on the drive over, but he didn't think practice would make it sound any better than it had when he'd first said it. "We didn't just get intel about another hostage situation. We learned from a deep-cover agent that an assassin has been hired."

Her shoulders went back even farther. "An assassin?"

He nodded and relied on the words he'd rehearsed. "An assassin hired to come after you."

Oh, man. She didn't just pale, every drop of color drained from her face. Willa slipped her PDA into the pocket of her sweater, sank back onto the sofa and buried her face in her hands.

Brandon went in for the kill. He had to tell her the final part of this covert briefing. The detail that would put her back in police custody.

And maybe right back in danger.

"That's how we knew where to find you," Brandon said, hating the sound of his own voice and the words coming out of his mouth.

Words that were unfortunately true.

"We got your address from the intelligence report that the Justice Department agent had intercepted from the assassin." Brandon checked his watch, though he already knew time was running out. "If the intel is right, and we think it is, he plans to kill you tonight."

Chapter 3

Willa was glad she was sitting down.

She didn't speak—she couldn't—and she didn't look at Brandon. Instead, she forced herself to focus on what he'd just told her.

An assassin would come tonight to kill her.

Maybe.

The warning on her screen saver flashed in her head, and it was the reminder she needed to put this in perspective.

"Is it true?" she asked, with her eyes still turned away from Brandon. She wanted to listen for the inflection in his voice.

"It's true, an assassin plans to kill you. We think because his boss doesn't want to risk your memory recovering so you can tell the authorities his identity. But I'm going to protect you," Brandon quickly added.

"Because you'll gather your things and come with me. I've already arranged a place for you."

Her emotions were like a whirlwind inside her, but she thought he might be telling the truth about the assassin. There was some kind of danger anyway. Brandon definitely wasn't lying about that.

Willa wasn't naive enough to believe she'd be able to keep out a professional killer. All the security precautions she had already taken wouldn't be enough, and the last thing she wanted was to go gun to gun with an assassin. The three-hour handgun course was her only training with a firearm, and she was betting the man coming after her would know how to kill with one shot.

She nodded, stood and rubbed her hands on the sides of her jeans. "Give me a minute, please. I need some time to gather my thoughts."

And her things.

She had an emergency bag already packed and stashed beneath her bed, and she'd practiced climbing out the window. She could cut through the backyard and walk to the train station, which was only four blocks away. That's one of the reasons she'd chosen this particular house to rent.

Willa headed for her bedroom, but she didn't get far. Brandon was right behind her. She whirled around, not realizing he was so close, and she knocked right into him. The contact was a reminder of that kiss, and the fact that he was going to be a hard man to shake.

"I can't let you escape," he told her.

"Who said I'm trying to escape?" Willa tossed right back.

He gave her a flat look to indicate he knew what she had in mind. Probably did, too. He was a cop, after all.

"Lieutenant Duggan is watching the back of the house, so you wouldn't get far anyway," Brandon added. "Now, get your things so we can leave."

Willa considered arguing with him, but he looked as stubborn as she was. Not a good DNA legacy to pass on to their daughter. A double dose of bullheadedness.

If he was the baby's father, that is.

She wasn't convinced he'd told her the truth about that, either.

"I'll get my things," she agreed. But that was the only thing she was agreeing to do. She wasn't going with them, and that meant she had to distract Brandon in some way so she could escape.

"What did you type about me on your PDA?" he asked, following her into the bedroom. There was barely enough space for one person, and she was quickly learning that Brandon had a way of monopolizing not just the room but all the air in it.

"Nothing," she lied. And she grabbed the packed overnight bag, put it on the bed and tossed in the PDA. The bag already contained a change of clothes, toiletries, meds, cash, a fake ID that had cost her dearly and a flash drive with duplicate files that were on her computer.

She also had a gun in there.

Willa didn't want to use it, but she would if it came down to protecting her baby.

Because she wanted to buy some time for that escape opportunity, Willa went through the dresser drawer and pretended to look for something to add to the bag. Maybe conversation would help, too. Besides, there was one thing she needed to verify, even though she wasn't sure a chat with Brandon would give her that proof.

"Are you really my baby's father?" she asked.

But he didn't answer. He walked across the room and looked into the drawer to see what she was doing. He likely thought she had a gun and was maybe about to pull it on him. No gun. However, he took the tiny canister of pepper spray from the top of the dresser and cupped it in his hand.

Willa gave him a cynical smile. "You trust me about as much as I trust you. So answer my question. Are you really my baby's father?"

He looked her straight in the eyes.

And nodded.

"The DNA test is real," he said. "The child you're carrying is mine."

Everything inside her went still. Because that didn't sound like a lie.

"We were in love?" she pressed.

"No," he answered just as quickly.

That seemed to be the truth as well. Strange that he wouldn't have said yes and then used that love confession to convince her to cooperate with him.

"All right." For show, she took out several pairs of panties and shoved them into the bag. "So, we weren't in love, and I wasn't your one-night stand. What was I to you?"

"The same thing you are to me now." He didn't wait for her to respond to that puzzling answer. "Finish packing."

She added a bra to the bag and stuffed in a flannel nightgown. Willa lifted the bag and put the strap over her like a messenger bag even though it was a tight fit over her belly. "I have to get some things from the bathroom. Prenatal vitamins," she added, knowing he wouldn't refuse to let her get those.

The bathroom window was small, but she knew she could squeeze through it. She'd have to hurry and hope that Lieutenant Duggan wasn't keeping watch on that particular side of the house. All she needed was two minutes, and she could be out of there. Away from the assassin, and away from the cops—including, perhaps, her baby's father.

And that gave her an idea.

With Brandon right on her heels, she went into the bathroom and took out a cotton swab from the medicine cabinet. It obviously wasn't sterile, but she thought it would give her a clean enough sample. After all, labs got DNA from toothbrushes and baby bottles. Once she had his DNA extracted, she could have it compared to the baby's amniotic fluid. Willa didn't have the fluid itself, but she had her baby's DNA profile in an online storage file that she could retrieve from any computer.

Of course, a comparison would take days. Maybe longer. Still, she would eventually know one way or another.

Her gut was already telling her the test was unnecessary, that Brandon was indeed her baby's father. But her brain wanted to know why her gut trusted this man when it was clear that he wasn't volunteering the whole truth.

"Open your mouth please." She added the *please* hoping it would get him to cooperate.

He did. Brandon swabbed the inside of his left cheek and handed it back to her. "It'll be a match," he promised.

"We'll see."

He glanced at the swab. "You'll want to put that in a plastic bag." And he pulled a small evidence baggie from his jacket pocket.

Willa eyed him and the bag with suspicion, and instead of using his bag that might be contaminated with his DNA or something else, she headed to the kitchen and got a plastic sandwich bag. She sealed up the swab, put it in the overnight case and snapped her fingers.

"Prenatal vitamins," she said as if remembering them. "I wouldn't want to forget those."

She took slow steps, trying to get the timing of this just right. She needed to get to the bathroom just ahead of Brandon so she could slam the door. Lock it.

And escape.

"I also have to use the bathroom," she lied when she was a few steps away. "As in, actually *use* the bathroom. I don't want an audience for that."

She went inside and pushed the door so it would close.

Brandon caught it.

"I don't want an audience," she restated.

"And I don't want you trying to escape. Don't worry. I'll close my eyes. But this door is staying partly open."

Great. Just great. She hadn't wanted to do this, but she was obviously going to have to give him a hit of the pepper spray. She reached into her bag to retrieve it, but he caught her wrist.

Then he grabbed the bag.

"I'll hold this for you. It can't be good for a pregnant woman to carry around this much weight."

"It's not that heavy." Willa glared at him and kept a firm hold on her bag. "Why don't you just back off?"

"Because I can't. Forget about the personal connection we have because of the baby, forget about how you feel or don't feel about me. Just remember, I'm a lawman, and I'm not going to stand by and let that assassin come after you."

She had to tamp down her anger so she could try to reason with him. "The last two times I trusted a lawman, I was nearly killed. You know that. You've read the reports. I've done a lot better on my own."

"But you've never come up against a hired gun like Martin Shore. He's not someone you can get away from without help."

For some reason having the name attached to the assassin made her heart pound even harder. "Martin Shore," she repeated. "How did he even find me?"

"Apparently Shore's boss has been trying to track you through neurologists all over the state. Nearly a dozen doctors have had their files hacked. Including Dr. Betterman, the OB you saw four weeks ago."

She shook her head. "But I didn't use my real name, and I paid him in cash."

"You did, but in your hacked medical record, Dr. Betterman had written your diagnosis of posttraumatic amnesia and post-concussional neurosis resulting in short-term memory loss. He also listed your age, the date of the onset of the symptoms. And that you were in your third trimester of pregnancy and therefore couldn't receive traditional medications."

Oh, God.

There wouldn't have been many patients who fit into all those categories.

Then, Willa remembered something. "I didn't give the doctor my street address. He said he needed to mail me the results from my latest EEG, so I gave him the address of the rental box at a private mail facility all the way across town."

Brandon nodded. "The clerk there was murdered about four hours ago. We're pretty sure after he was tortured before he gave up your physical address to someone who wanted to find you. Because it was about an hour later when a deep-cover agent intercepted the intel about Shore being hired to kill you."

Willa choked back another *Oh, God,* and the tears that threatened to follow. She wouldn't cry. It would only waste time because she knew what she had to do.

"Just let me go," she begged Brandon. "If this is really your child as you say, then please help me get away."

"It *is* my child. And I can't let you leave."

"Swear it," she said, sounding as desperate as she felt. "Swear on my life that the baby is yours."

Brandon put his fingers beneath her chin and lifted it to make direct eye contact. "I swear on your life. On mine. On our baby's life. The child you're carrying is mine."

He sounded so sincere. Looked it, too. Still, there was something, something she couldn't quite put her finger on.

"If you're lying to me—"

But Willa didn't get a chance to finish that threat. There was no warning. No time to get down.

A bullet slammed through the bathroom window.

Chapter 4

Brandon latched on to Willa and pushed her out of the bathroom.

It wasn't a second too soon because there was another shot ripping through what was left of the glass in the small window. He drew his gun and maneuvered her into the living room and then to the kitchen. He wanted her as far away from those shots as he could manage.

Hell.

He hadn't expected the attack to come this soon. He'd hoped to have Willa tucked safely away before Martin Shore tried to kill her. Brandon obviously hadn't succeeded, and Willa might pay the price for his miscalculation.

Brandon used his phone to call for backup from the Austin P.D. He couldn't risk trying to ring Bo because his temporary partner might be trying to conceal his location from the shooter.

Willa grabbed a knife and a can of pepper spray from the counter and covered her pregnant belly with her hand. Neither her hand nor the items would provide the baby with much protection, so Brandon threw open the fridge and positioned her behind the door. That would give her an extra layer. He considered pulling out the fridge and placing her in the space behind it, but if Shore moved to that side of the house, the bullets might make it through the wall.

"You weren't lying," Willa mumbled.

Not about Shore, he wasn't. But he had told her lies all right. Later, much later, he needed to fill her in on the whole truth.

There was another shot, not through the bathroom. There was the sound of more glass shattering, and it seemed to be coming from Willa's bedroom.

Brandon waited. Listening.

Where the hell was Bo? And better yet, where had the lieutenant been when that first shot had been fired? Brandon hoped Shore hadn't managed to injure Bo or worse.

Another sound, not a bullet this time, sent Brandon's heart to his knees. Because this one had come from inside. From Willa's bedroom. It was the sound of footsteps.

The assassin was in her house.

Brandon glanced at Willa. Her eyes were wide, and her breath was gusting. She'd obviously heard the footsteps, too, and she knew the danger was bearing down on them.

He couldn't wait for word from Bo or for backup to arrive. Once Shore made it to the tiny kitchen, he would see them immediately. They would be sitting

ducks, and that meant Brandon had to act fast to keep
Willa alive.

"This way," he mouthed.

Brandon kept his gun ready and aimed at the opening that led from the dining room and into the kitchen.
No doubt that was where Shore was headed. He maneuvered Willa behind him so he could shield her with
his body, and he started to back them out of the room.
It wasn't the best of plans because Shore could double back or even have an accomplice who could come
from the other direction, but Brandon had no choice.

He had to get Willa out of there.

Each step seemed to take minutes, but he led them
across the kitchen and toward the tiny mudroom and
the back door. He wasn't sure what was on the other
side of that door, but hopefully it was a yard with some
kind of cover. He needed to get Willa behind a tree or
something to shelter her from the bullets that would
come at them when Shore realized they were no longer inside.

They made it to the opening of the mudroom where
they heard a plinking noise as if something metal had
been dropped.

Brandon glanced back into the dining room and
soon noticed something he didn't want to see: the small,
dark green oval object on the floor.

A grenade.

"Run!" Brandon shouted.

Willa reacted fast, thank God. With the knife and
pepper spray in her left hand, she pushed her messenger bag out of the way, disengaged the locks and threw
open the door. Brandon had one last look to make sure
Shore wasn't about to gun them down from inside the

house, and changed places with Willa, so he could be in front of her. Either position was a risk because it was possible the grenade was a decoy to get them to run. If so, they were about to run directly into a professional assassin.

They hurried out onto a small porch and down the steps that led into a yard. No trees, something that made Brandon curse. But there was a small storage shed. He grabbed Willa's arm and made a beeline for it.

There was no sign of Bo. No sign of backup, either, but then it'd only been a couple of minutes since he'd made the call requesting help. Bo had likely called, too.

Well, Bo would have if he wasn't lying dead somewhere.

Shore could have managed to take out Bo before he started the attack on the house.

Brandon hated to force Willa to run, but he had no choice. He prayed this exertion wouldn't hurt the baby. Of course, the stress couldn't be good for the child, either. But Brandon also pushed that aside. Right now, he had to keep Willa alive because it was the only way to save the child.

He positioned Willa to the side of the small wooden shed.

Just as the explosion ripped through the yard.

Brandon had considered that the grenade might be a dummy, but it obviously wasn't.

The debris from the blast came right at them.

Brandon tried to keep watch, to make certain Shore hadn't come into the yard for another attack, but it was hard to see anything. The left side of the house was literally a fireball, and bits of wood, the roof and even wads of fire were raining down on them.

His instincts and training were to protect his fellow peace officer, but Brandon couldn't risk taking Willa closer to the house. There could be a secondary explosion, and he needed to put some distance between the burning building and her.

Thankfully, she still had the bag draped across her body, and she used it to shelter her face from the dangerous falling debris.

"Is there a gate on the back fence?" he asked her.

She nodded, tried to speak, but no sound came out. Willa was obviously terrified, and there was nothing he could do to assure her that he could protect her. Shore could have orchestrated this entire attack just to get them out in the open.

And the *open* was where they'd have to go to get to the gate.

Brandon checked the strips of grass and shrubs that made up the side yards. No one was there that he could see. No one was on the porch, either, and it was too much to hope that Shore had blown up with that grenade. No. The man was out there, somewhere, waiting.

"Let's go," he told Willa.

As he'd done in the kitchen, Brandon kept in front of her and backed her toward the gate. The debris continued to fall, and he could hear neighbors shouting for help. What he couldn't hear was Bo or the sound of sirens from backup. Until he had help, he had to do everything within his power to get Willa away from there.

Thick black smoke billowed out from the house, fanning out across the yard, and making it impossible for Brandon to see all the places where Shore could be hiding. He kept his gun aimed. Ready.

He saw the movement just at the edge of the smoke.

It was a man. And it wasn't Bo. Brandon recognized him from intelligence photos.

It was Martin Shore.

The killer was there, coming for them.

Behind him, Willa fumbled with the gate to open it. She'd obviously put some kind of lock on it, and that lock was now a trap.

Brandon protected Willa as best he could, but he couldn't help with the locks. He kept his eyes and gun trained on Shore and was ready to push Willa to the ground if necessary. That wouldn't take her out of the line of fire, but it might shield her long enough until backup arrived. By now, all the neighbors and any-one for blocks around had probably called for help or come out of their residences to see what was going on.

And what was going on was that Shore was about to try to kill them again.

The man kept walking but lifted his gun, aiming it at them.

Willa cursed, but she must have finally gotten the locks to cooperate because she shoved open the gate. In the same motion Brandon pushed her through to the other side.

A bullet slammed into the fence.

The shot came so close to Brandon's head that he swore he could feel it.

He jumped out of the way, staying low and lunged out of the yard to join Willa on the other side. They made it to a sidewalk that was rimmed with a street and then another row of pristine suburban houses. They could try to duck into one of them, but that wouldn't stop Shore. He'd just fire into the place and possibly kill some innocent bystanders.

"We have to run," Brandon told her. He didn't wait for her to do that. He put his left hand on her shoulder to get her moving, away from the fence and away from her burning house.

Running might not even be possible for someone in the last trimester of pregnancy, but he had to get her to cover so he could try to make a stand against Shore.

Brandon headed up the sidewalk toward the cul de sac where a car was parked. That was their best bet.

Until he saw the kids.

There were three of them, all on skates, and probably no more than ten or eleven years old. If he went in that direction, so would Shore's bullets.

"Get down!" Brandon shouted to the boys. Hopefully they and anyone else in the area would do as he'd ordered.

"This way," Willa insisted, turning and leading him in the opposite direction.

She obviously realized the danger to the children, but she also had to know the danger of going past her house again. Shore had probably made it across the yard by now, and if he wasn't already at the gate, he soon would be.

Brandon adjusted his gun, and aimed, and they hurried past Willa's section of the fence. The smoke was thicker now, and the wind was carrying it right in their direction. Willa coughed, but she didn't stop.

He didn't want to think of the risk this might be causing the baby. Brandon only wanted to get her out of there. Their best option was the intersection just ahead. Cars were trickling past, but if he could get Willa to that point, he could position her on the side of the last stretch of fence and perhaps get her out of Shore's line of sight.

Brandon heard the creak of the wooden gate and glanced over his shoulder just as it opened.

Shore came out, and he had his gun ready.

The assassin glanced around and spotted them. Brandon wanted to shoot him then and there, but he couldn't risk a stray shot hitting the children.

Shore obviously didn't feel the same. He re-aimed, pointing the gun directly at Willa.

Brandon grabbed on to her waist and shoved her into the side of the fence.

A bullet flew past them.

God knew where it landed, and Brandon prayed it hadn't gone into one of the houses or a car.

"We can't stop," he told Willa, though he could hear her breathing hard.

They headed up the street toward a parked car, but then Brandon spotted the city bus. It was only about two blocks away and was lumbering in their direction. If he could get Willa on that bus before Shore saw them, they might be able to escape before the man could figure out where to aim more of those deadly shots.

Brandon kept Willa positioned behind him, and he hurried toward the bus. He also pushed back his jacket to reveal his badge.

"Get back inside!" he shouted to an elderly woman who opened her door.

Still hurrying toward the bus, Brandon flagged down the driver and hoped like the devil the man would stop. He didn't take his attention off the intersection where he knew Shore would soon appear.

The assassin wouldn't just give up.

The bus inched closer, and with Willa in tow, Brandon raced toward the vehicle. The seconds clicked off in Brandon's head. He wanted to make sure these seconds weren't their last ones.

The driver slowed even more as he approached them. Probably because he was concerned about the gun Brandon was holding.

"Open up!" Brandon told the middle-aged Hispanic driver. And he flashed his badge again.

The door swung open.

Just as Brandon caught a glimpse of Shore.

The assassin was at the intersection, barely a block away. Willa was still in Shore's kill zone.

Brandon pushed her onto the bus and was relieved that they were the sole passengers.

"I'm Sheriff Ruiz," he said identifying himself. "Drive!" Brandon ordered the man behind the wheel.

He dragged Willa to the bus's floor, praying that Shore hadn't seen him.

But he obviously had.

Because a bullet came crashing through the bus window.

Chapter 5

Willa covered her head with the bag when the glass spewed across the bus.

The nightmare wasn't over.

Shore was still after them, and if he managed to injure the driver, then the bus would almost certainly crash. The crash alone might not be fatal, but it would leave them wide open for another attack.

"Don't stop," Brandon warned the driver, "and stay low in the seat."

The driver was cursing and praying at the same time. Brandon was mumbling something as well, but Willa didn't think she had the breath to utter anything.

Her baby began to kick, hard, but Willa welcomed the movement. It meant her daughter was safe. *For now.* But they weren't out of danger.

The next bullet proved that.

It came through the back window, tearing the glass apart, and it exited through the front. Thankfully, it didn't come near them or the driver, and the driver slammed on the accelerator to get them out of there.

"Shore's on foot," Brandon reminded her. "He won't be able to come after us for long."

Willa held her breath, waiting and trying to brace herself for more bullets. But the shots didn't continue.

Brandon lifted his head and looked out the window. "He's gone," he let her know.

Willa still didn't move. She lay there and prayed the threat was truly over.

"Drive to the nearest police station," Brandon told the driver, and he took out his phone.

While Brandon punched in some numbers, he helped her from the floor and moved her onto one of the seats. He dropped down onto the seat directly across from her.

"Are you okay?" he asked.

Willa nodded, but she doubted he believed her. For one thing, she was still breathing so fast that she was close to hyperventilating, and she was trembling from head to toe. It might be part of Brandon's job to be on the business end of gunfire, but until the hostage situation at the maternity hospital, Willa had never known what it was like to face real danger.

Well, now she knew.

And it couldn't continue.

Somehow, she had to find a safe place for her and her baby. If there was such a thing as a safe place. This was the third attack in four months. Four attacks if she counted being taken hostage at the hospital. Part of her was furious that time after time someone or something had endangered her precious baby. She wanted answers. She wanted justice.

But another part of her only wanted to run and hide.

Willa looked back at the broken glass and damage the bullets had done to the seats. She also looked out at the sidewalk that was zipping by. No sign of Shore, thank God. Maybe they had finally lost him.

She listened while Brandon gave an update to whomever he had called. He also asked about Lieutenant Bo Duggan, and then about Martin Shore. Brandon's forehead bunched up when he apparently got a response.

"We're on our way," Brandon said to the person on the other end of the line, and he snapped his phone shut.

"They got Martin Shore?" she immediately asked.

He shook his head. "But they're looking. Backup arrived, and there are officers fanning out all over the area."

The hopeful tone was tinged with doubt. And Willa knew why. From what Brandon had told her, Martin Shore was a professional killer, and he probably knew how to evade the police. He was no doubt on the run so he could regroup.

And come after her again.

"Bo Duggan was shot," Brandon added, his voice practically a whisper. He closed his eyes a moment but not before she saw the flash of anger mixed with pain. "He's on the way to the hospital."

"I'm sorry." Not that it would probably help, but Willa reached out and touched his arm.

That touch brought his eyes open, and he met her gaze. "So am I. Sorry for the lieutenant and sorry that I didn't get to you sooner so I could stop this attack."

Willa didn't intend to take the blame for this, but it

certainly wasn't Brandon's fault, either. The problem was she didn't know where to place the blame.

"You were trying to talk me into leaving with you and Lieutenant Duggan," she reminded him. She groaned softly. "And I was trying to figure out a way to escape."

He glanced back at the street and shook his head. "I wish to hell you had gotten out of there before Shore arrived."

So had she. But here they were. Seconds after nearly being killed. Willa wondered if she would ever have peace of mind again, or if she would have to stay on the run for the rest of her life. It was possible that she could never give her precious baby a normal life.

"The police station's just around the block," the driver told them.

Willa had to take a deep breath. A police station filled with people she didn't trust. But she couldn't very well jump off the bus. Shore could still be out there. And besides, she didn't even have a house to return to. Other than the meager items in the messenger bag, the only things she had were Brandon and her memory.

Both were somewhat suspect.

"Don't trust the cops," Brandon mumbled, repeating what he'd seen on her computer screen and notes.

"Yes. But as you can see, I had my reasons for that distrust."

"And you still do?" he asked.

It wasn't a simple question, and there seemed to be a Texas-size amount of emotion behind it.

"I think I can trust you," she admitted. "Because I believe you truly are my baby's father."

Other than his word and the DNA results that could

be fake, she had no other reason to believe him. But she did. Willa only hoped that didn't turn out to be another mistake.

The driver took a left turn and she spotted the police station just ahead.

Brandon put his hands on her shoulders and forced eye contact. "Look, when we get inside, I have no idea where they'll take us or what SAPD will tell you when they arrive."

That seemed like some kind of warning and Willa stared at him. "What do you mean?"

He opened his mouth. Closed it. Opened it again. Then, shook his head. He pulled her closer to him and put his mouth right against her ear.

"Shore was hired to kill you," Brandon whispered. "That part is the truth. So is the part about another hospital hostage situation." He paused. "But almost everything else that Bo and I told you is a lie."

It took a moment for that to sink in, but when it did, it felt like a punch. She gasped, a sound of outrage, and she tried to pull back, but Brandon held her in place.

The driver hit his brakes and brought the bus to a stop directly in front of police headquarters. Officers poured out from the building and began to run toward them.

"What do you mean everything else was a lie?" Willa demanded.

Brandon looked her straight in the eyes. "I'm not your ex-boyfriend, Willa. Before today, I'd never laid eyes or anything else on you."

Brandon didn't have time to soothe that look in Willa's eyes. It was a mixture of anger, confusion and hurt.

He also didn't have time to try to justify the lies he'd already told her.

Besides, there was no justification for that.

After SAPD had come to him and explained what was going on with a possible new hostage incident, Brandon had agreed to help them, but the plan had felt wrong from the very beginning.

And look where it'd gotten Willa.

She'd nearly been killed today, and they weren't out of the woods yet. As long as Shore was alive, the threat would be there.

"What do you mean you lied to me?" Willa demanded.

Brandon heard her, barely. That's because several officers ran onto the bus, and the sounds of their voices and footsteps drowned her out. One was plainclothes, in his late thirties with sandy-brown hair, and the other was younger and in a uniform. Both had their weapons drawn.

"I'm Sheriff Brandon Ruiz," he said, showing his badge. He slipped his gun back into his holster. "Any word about Lieutenant Duggan?"

The older officer shook his head. "Nothing yet."

Hell. Bo had to be all right. Brandon barely knew the man, but on the drive from San Antonio, Bo had talked all about his four-month-old twins. He'd also talked about his late wife, who'd died shortly after the maternity hostage incident. If something happened to Bo, those babies would be orphans.

Willa latched on to his arm when Brandon stood. "What do you mean you li—"

Brandon stopped that question by pressing his mouth to hers. The kiss was hard, rough and way out of line, but he didn't want her to say anything in front of the other officers. He wasn't sure how much SAPD wanted him to explain about Willa and what might end up being a second hostage situation.

"We'll talk later," Brandon whispered and hoped his tone was enough of a warning for Willa to stay quiet.

He wouldn't blame her if she refused to cooperate, but he prayed that she would.

"Are you hurt?" the uniform asked them.

Brandon took the overnight bag from Willa and pulled her to her feet so he could check her out. She was riled to the core and confused, but she didn't appear to be injured physically. That was something at least.

"Do you need to see a doctor?" Brandon asked, and he held his breath hoping that she wasn't having contractions or anything.

"No," she answered through clenched teeth. "I only need to talk to you." Her gaze drifted to the police building, and she swallowed hard.

Don't trust the cops was probably racing through her head right now.

"SAPD is sending up some officers," the older cop relayed to Brandon. "They're already on their way. You can wait inside headquarters until they arrive. Plus, we'll need to get your statements on the shooting and the explosion."

"Ms. Marks will need a safe house right away," Brandon informed them. "After what she's been through, she needs to rest."

"I can find a place on my own," Willa insisted right back.

He didn't argue with her, for now, but there was no

way he could let her go off on her own. God knows how he would be able to convince her of that, though.

Brandon led her off the bus, and the officers hurried them to the far side of the building to the patrol entrance, probably because they were still concerned about Shore being at large.

"I'd like to go someplace private," Willa told the officer the moment they were inside. "Because Sheriff Ruiz and I need to talk. It's important, and it can't wait."

The officer volleyed glances between Brandon and her, and the man was no doubt wondering what this was all about. Brandon didn't intend to fill him in, at least not until he'd spoken with the officers from SAPD. Even if those officers had indeed already left their headquarters, they probably wouldn't arrive for at least another forty-five minutes.

"Follow me," the officer finally said. He took them through the maze of squad rooms and stopped outside a break room that had chairs, a sofa and some vending machines. "I hope this'll do," the officer commented. "And while you're talking I'll see about an update on Lieutenant Duggan."

Brandon thanked the man but didn't say anything else until he was out of earshot. Too bad there was no door so he could give them an extra layer of privacy.

They were going to need it.

"Why did you lie?" Willa demanded.

Since this probably wouldn't be a short or quiet conversation, Brandon placed her overnight bag on the floor and pulled her to the side of a vending machine. "Because SAPD convinced me that the fastest way to stop another hostage incident was to get you to trust me."

Her eyes narrowed, but it didn't seem to be simply from anger. "And it worked. Well, partly. I *was* starting to trust you."

"You still can," he promised.

She looked at him as if he'd lost his mind. "You're a liar."

"About some things. It's true, I'd never met you before today." It was a risk because she might slap him, but Brandon placed his hand over her stomach. "But I really am your baby's father."

She blinked and then stared at him, examining his eyes. "You expect me to believe that?"

"It's the truth." And he blew out a long breath. It was actually a relief to tell her the truth. "Nearly ten years ago I was in the military and headed to a dangerous assignment in the Middle East. I was engaged at the time, and my then fiancée convinced me to store some semen in case I was injured. When I got back from the assignment, the engagement was over. And I knew I didn't need what I'd stored, so I signed a donor agreement, and it was sent to a sperm bank."

Willa continued to study him and was no doubt trying to decide if he was telling the truth.

"A sperm bank?" she questioned.

He nodded. "Obviously it was the one you used for your artificial insemination."

"Obviously." But there was still a lot of skepticism in her voice. "Why should I believe you?"

"Because it's true. The DNA test results I gave you are real," he continued. "And it proves I'm the baby's biological father."

Brandon tried not to show what he was feeling. He didn't want Willa to mistake it for dishonesty. But that last word, *father,* had not come easily.

And probably never would.

He kept that to himself.

The staring went on, and on, and finally Willa's shoulders relaxed. A weary breath left her mouth, and she sagged against the wall.

Since she looked ready to drop, Brandon held on to her. Or rather he tried. But Willa pushed him away.

"My sperm donor," she mumbled. She shook her head. "How did SAPD find you?"

"Bo Duggan said they'd been looking at all the angles as to how to approach you, so they kept digging into your background. You aren't close to anyone in your family, so they widened the search. And finally got to your medical records. They traced the donor number for your insemination, and that led them to me."

"They knew you were a cop?" she asked.

"Not at first. But I think that ended up being a bonus for them." It had certainly given the police captain carte blanche to press him into cooperating. "SAPD knew you wouldn't welcome them with open arms, and they were desperate. They need your cooperation."

"They need me to remember," Willa corrected. "To remember what happened during the hostage situation so I can see if it relates to what might happen in another crisis. But I can't remember. I've tried and I can't."

He lifted his shoulder. "That's where I was supposed to come in. They want me to coax you into going through more therapy. You've already made so much progress. You said yourself that your short-term memory problems were over."

"I lied." She huffed and pushed her hair away from her face.

Brandon had to do a double take. "What?"

Willa dodged his gaze. "My memory's not nearly as bad as it was right after my injury, but sometimes I still forget. That's why I put your picture on my PDA." Her gaze snapped back to him and she scowled. "I typed in my PDA that I thought I could trust you. I need to change that."

"No. You don't."

Her scowl melted away, and tears sprang to her eyes. That's when Brandon noticed that she was still trembling. From the attack, no doubt.

Even though it was a risk on many levels, he pulled her to him. Willa fought him, struggling to break the embrace, but Brandon held on.

"That's my baby you're carrying," he reminded her. And in doing so, he reminded himself. "I'm not going to let you go through this alone."

Willa likely had no clue as to what it took for him to say that. She pulled back slightly and, even though she was still blinking away tears, she looked up at him. Her breath broke and she melted against him.

"Nothing bad can happen to this baby," she muttered through the sobs.

"It won't." Though it was a promise that would be hell to keep.

He touched his mouth to her forehead. Just a touch. But he felt the heat spear through him. Brandon definitely didn't want to feel that heat, but he couldn't deny it was there.

What the hell was wrong with him?

He wanted to believe the attraction existed because of the baby. Maybe some kind of primal DNA trigger so he'd feel compelled to protect the unborn child.

Brandon silently cursed.

This attraction didn't have anything to do with the baby. He was attracted to Willa. Plain and simple. And that attraction could cause some big-time problems for both of them.

Thankfully, his phone rang because Brandon was ready for both a distraction and news. After he glanced at his caller ID, he figured he would at least get the latter.

The call was from Sergeant Cash Newsome, a cop in SAPD and someone Brandon had known for years. They'd both been in the army together and had done a tour of duty in the Middle East. Since Cash was also Bo Duggan's right-hand man, Brandon hoped he would have an update about the lieutenant's status.

"I heard you ran into Martin Shore," Cash greeted.

"Literally," Brandon confirmed. "How's Bo?"

"It's good news. He has a non-life-threatening gunshot wound to the shoulder. He'll be out of commission for a day or two, but he'll make a full recovery."

Brandon released the breath he'd been holding. "And what about Martin Shore?"

"Still no sign of him. We haven't given up," Cash quickly added. "We're searching the area, going door to door. We won't stop looking until we find him."

They might get lucky, but Brandon had to be realistic. A hired gun that was gutsy enough to attack in a residential neighborhood in broad daylight probably had made arrangements for an escape. Shore was likely already out of the area.

And planning round two.

"Any idea why Shore came after Willa earlier than intel had indicated?" Brandon asked.

"Our best guess is that he had her house under surveillance and saw Bo and you arrive. He probably thought he should go ahead while he still had her in his sights."

That made sense, and it told him a lot about Shore. The man could and would improvise, and that made him even more dangerous.

"We've arranged a safe house for Willa," Cash continued. "It's local so you won't have to be on the road too long with her. I guess it goes without saying that she'll be in your protective custody."

Yeah. Without saying. Brandon was too deep into this to turn back now.

"Sergeant Harris McCoy and I will be there in about a half hour, and we'll take you to the safe house." Cash paused. "We'd also like Willa to see a therapist who specializes in recovering lost memories."

Brandon glanced at Willa. Even though she probably hadn't heard what Cash had just said, she could no doubt sense Brandon's own hesitation. He was hesitating not because he thought the therapist was a bad idea but because he wasn't sure he'd be able to convince Willa to trust anyone associated with the police.

Including him.

"I'll have to get back to you on that last part," Brandon told Cash.

Willa's left eyebrow lifted.

"Why?" Cash asked. "Have you talked her into co-operating yet?"

"No."

"Try harder. Because we've just gotten an update on what could be our next hostage situation."

"And?" Brandon asked when Cash didn't continue.

"And the news isn't good."

Chapter 6

Two days.

The short timeline kept going through Willa's head, stuck like a broken record, on the entire drive from Austin to the safe house. Two days.

Christmas.

That's when SAPD thought there'd be another hostage situation at a hospital. Or at least that's the information Sergeant Cash Newsome had relayed to Brandon while they were waiting in the break room at the Austin P.D. building. The authorities had two days to stop another nightmare from happening. But while the so-called intel had provided a time, SAPD didn't have a location. Or a motive.

They were counting on Willa to help them.

"Good luck with that," she said to herself. She huffed at that and the so-called safe house as it came into view.

Even if she could completely regain her memory before then, Willa wasn't convinced she actually knew anything that would help.

Two days.

And God knew how many women and babies would have to go through the same kind of hell that she'd gone through for the past four months.

"You okay?" Brandon asked, bringing the car to a stop in the tiny garage of the safe house.

Willa considered lying but decided it was useless. "No."

He matched her heavy sigh with one of his own and hit the button on the automatic garage opener. He waited until the garage door was completely shut before they got out of the nondescript dark blue car that SAPD had provided.

There was a single light on in the laundry room situated just off the garage entrance, but there was enough moonlight filtering through the windows that she didn't have any trouble seeing.

Willa glanced around at the safe house. Well, what there was of it anyway.

It was small, much like her rental place that Shore had blown up on the other side of town. Except this place wasn't in the suburbs. It was in the country, halfway between San Antonio and Austin, and to get to it they'd used a rural road. Their nearest neighbor was more than a mile away.

She walked through the house, taking inventory. Two sparsely decorated bedrooms, one bath and a living-dining-kitchen combo. Though Brandon and she had already eaten dinner at police headquarters, the fridge had been stocked with plastic-wrapped sandwiches, bottled water and juice.

The cramped quarters and limited food options, however, meant nothing to her. The only thing Willa cared about right now was being as far away from Martin Shore as possible.

She watched as Brandon double-locked the door, and then he took out the codes that Sergeant Cash Newsome had given him so he could arm the security system.

"I suppose the windows and both the front and back doors are connected to the system?" she asked.

He nodded. "They are. There's also an alarm that runs around the immediate perimeter of the house in case anyone attempts a break-in. It's supposed to be safe."

She nodded as well. Then swallowed hard. Because no place might be safe enough to protect them from Martin Shore. Or the people who might be planning another hostage situation.

Brandon turned slowly and faced her. "I don't want us to sleep here inside the house."

Willa had thought he was about to tell her to get some rest. Maybe even give her another reassurance that nothing else bad would happen. She hadn't expected that from him. And her breath stalled in her throat.

"Do you trust me?" he asked.

The question hit her almost as hard as his bombshell about not wanting to stay there. She automatically reached for the PDA in her bag. But Willa didn't need to see his picture or the note she'd written to go along with it.

She remembered.

And what she remembered was that she *thought* she could trust him.

"What's this about?" she wanted to know.

Brandon scrubbed his hand over his face. "You know I made several calls after I got off the phone with Sergeant Cash Newsome?"

Yes. He'd stepped to the other side of the room for those calls, and he'd whispered so she couldn't hear. Willa figured he was discussing the therapy appointment that SAPD had made for her. An appointment that was supposed to happen at eight the following morning. Since it was already nine in the evening, that appointment wasn't far off.

"Cash is an old army buddy, and while I trust him, I wanted someone outside of SAPD," Brandon explained. "I contacted another old friend who runs a security company."

"Is that the person who dropped you off the duffel bag?" she asked.

"Yeah." Brandon had that particular bag slung over his shoulder, but he eased it off and set it on an overstuffed fabric chair. "I asked him to bring me some supplies that I might need. I also asked him to see if he's heard anything about a possible leak at SAPD."

Her breath stalled again. Mercy, she hadn't braced herself nearly enough for any of this. "What kind of leak?"

"The worst kind for us. A leak in communication. I don't like the fact that SAPD's intel told them that Shore wouldn't attack you until tonight."

She thought about that a moment, and the conclusion she came to caused her heart rate to spike. "You think someone tipped Shore off?"

Brandon shrugged. "I don't want to believe it, but I also don't want to put blind trust in people I don't really know."

Neither did she. "You don't think Bo Duggan could have done this?"

"Not him. But I don't know how many people in SAPD had access to the information about Shore." He made a sweeping glance around the room. "Or this place."

That didn't steady her heart. Willa slid her hand over her stomach. "So, what should we do?"

Brandon didn't answer immediately, and his forehead bunched up. "My friend sent me several portable security cameras and a monitor. I want to set the cameras up here, inside, but I want us to sleep in the car in the garage."

She instantly thought of the grenade that Shore had tossed into her rental. "Shore could try to blow us up again."

Brandon nodded. "He could. But I'll keep watch on the monitor. And the cameras are motion-activated and will sound if they're triggered. If anyone approaches the house, I can drive us out of here." He reached out, touched her arm and rubbed gently. "This is just a precaution, Willa."

He added the last part as if he expected her to challenge him, but Willa had no intentions of doing that.

She nodded. "I need to go to the bathroom, but once you have the camera set up, we can go back to the car."

It wouldn't be comfortable, but she still might be

able to sleep there. Her fatigue was past the bone-weary stage, and she had no choice but to rest.

Willa took her toiletries from her bag so she could brush her teeth and take her prenatal vitamin. She also used the bathroom and hoped she wouldn't have to make too many treks back into the house because of her pregnancy bladder.

When she came back into the living room, Brandon had lowered all the blinds in the house and was setting up the tiny golf-ball-size camera in the front window. Since it was so small and white, it blended right into the window sill.

"There's a camera in the kitchen," he explained, "and the front bedroom. I'll put the other one just outside the garage door, and then I can monitor all of them with that." He pointed to a GPS-looking device with four split screens.

"We can take turns watching it," she suggested.

"No need. The monitor will beep if any of the cameras are triggered by motion. That means you can get some sleep. Think of the baby," he added before Willa could argue.

"I do, all the time," she mumbled. "Do you?" She instantly regretted that question. Brandon had only recently found out he was going to be a father, and he probably hadn't even come to terms with it yet. Added to that, he had the extra worry about keeping them safe.

Willa waved off the question and reached for her bag.

"I think about the baby," he said, his words soft and slow. He took the bag from her, keeping his attention focused on it and not her.

"It's okay," she assured him. "When the danger has

passed, I don't expect anything from you. In fact, I don't want anything from you."

That was a semi-truth. Her body wanted him. For sex. How ironic. She hadn't had as much of a sexual twinge since she'd gotten pregnant; yet near Brandon, in her last trimester no less, she kept feeling that tug deep within her.

"Good." And that was all he said for several moments. "Honestly, I'm not sure I can give you and this baby what you really need."

His eyes met hers for just a second, before he looked away and put the monitor in the equipment bag. He hoisted it over his other shoulder and headed for the garage door. Willa grabbed the pillow and cover that had been stacked on the sofa and followed him.

This was good, she assured herself. Brandon didn't want to be part of her or their baby's life. That's exactly the way she'd planned things. Heck, it was the reason she'd no doubt used artificial insemination. Because she hadn't wanted a man in her life.

So, why did his confession sting?

She barely knew the man and, other than the fact he was almost certainly the biological father of her baby, that was the only thing that connected them.

Well, except for the attraction.

And the danger.

And this entire bizarre connection she felt with him.

Willa huffed. She was talking herself into falling hard for Brandon, and that could be a fatal mistake.

Since the front seats of the car reclined, Willa got in on the passenger's side and prepared a makeshift bed. Brandon eased the garage door open just a fraction and placed the camera outside. After closing it, he got behind the wheel and started his own preparations. Not for a bed, though, but for security. So that he wouldn't lose them, he put the keys in the ignition, set up the monitor on the dashboard and placed the bags on the backseat.

Willa turned, leaned over and retrieved the PDA from her bag. What she hadn't counted on was Brandon moving at the same time. He turned to adjust his holster, and they practically collided.

And then they froze.

Breath met breath, and Willa got an instant reminder of that attraction. It suddenly raced through her. Hot and wild. As if her huge pregnant belly wasn't a hindrance to anything sexual.

Brandon made a sound, deep within his throat. A sort of rumbling. That sound stirred through her as well. So did his scent. Something manly and woodsy. That scent alerted every part of her body that hadn't already been alerted.

"This can't happen," she whispered.

"Yeah."

But the single word had hardly left his mouth when he dragged her to him and put his lips on hers. His scent had caused a jolt, but the kiss created an avalanche.

Willa found herself sliding her arms around him and pulling him closer. She found herself deepening the kiss. And she found herself getting lost in the steamy maze of passion she immediately knew she couldn't control. She was on fire, and her body was urging her to keep pulling him closer, to keep kissing him, to continue this insanity no matter the cost.

If she'd thought his scent had her hormonal number, his taste was even more potent. That taste drew her in. And so did Brandon's embrace. His kiss was gentle and left her with no doubts that it was exactly what she wanted.

But shouldn't have.

Willa latched on to that thought and kept mentally repeating it. However, she wasn't the one to stop the kiss. It was Brandon. He eased her away from him and glanced at the monitor.

"I have to keep you safe," he said with a lot of regret and heavy breath in his voice.

Since safety was the main reason they were here in the car, Willa had no comeback for that. He did need to keep an eye on the monitor. He needed to protect her because that was the only way to keep her baby safe. Still, it was a battle to get herself to move away from him.

Willa settled into the seat and tried to level her breathing. Her body was still on fire, but her brain just kept reminding her that she had done the right thing by stopping the makeout session—even if it felt wrong.

"Are you sure we weren't lovers?" she asked, trying to keep things light.

"I'm sure." There was no lightness in his voice. It was strained, just like his expression. The need was still in his intense brown eyes. But the corner of his mouth lifted. "Trust me, I would have remembered having sex with you."

Yes. And even with her amnesia, Willa thought she might have remembered, too. Brandon had a unique way of being unforgettable.

Well, maybe.

She glanced down at the PDA cupped in her hand

and scrolled through the photos and information she'd stored there. She remembered everything she'd recorded for the past two weeks. Prior to that, her memory was spotty and prior to that, there were huge gaps. Two weeks wasn't nearly enough time for her to trust herself. So, Willa began making notes. About the attack from Martin Shore. About Brandon.

About everything.

She had to get everything down before she fell asleep, and that wouldn't be long. Despite the fiery kiss and Brandon's closeness, her body would soon have to rest.

"The night can be the worst time for me," she explained to Brandon as she continued to type. "Sometimes, when I wake up, everything in my memory is gone."

And she meant *everything*.

He stayed quiet a moment. "What should I do if that happens?"

"Run," she joked. But then she shook her head. "I'll be confused. I might even try to attack you because I won't know who you are. But just remind me that your picture is in here." She tapped her PDA.

Brandon looked at it, then at her. His gaze lingered a moment on her face, and on a heavy breath, he turned back to the monitor.

"Sleep," he insisted.

She nodded but didn't close her eyes. Willa pulled the covers to her chin, snuggling them around her so she'd stay warm, but she fastened her attention to the monitor. Thanks to the four cameras, every angle of the house and attached garage were covered. Even in the darkness, they would be able to see someone approaching.

Hopefully, it would stay that way, but Willa had a bad feeling that things were about to get a whole lot worse.

Brandon popped another mint in his mouth and wished it were a big gulp of strong coffee. He needed a hit of caffeine badly, but he didn't want to go back inside the house to see if there was any. That would mean either waking Willa or leaving her alone.

He had no plans to do either.

Since the monitor for the security cameras would alert him to any movement around the house, Brandon had managed a couple of catnaps, but with each one, the nightmares had come.

He glanced at Willa who was sleeping soundly in the reclined seat. The covers had shifted, draping down below her left breast. Brandon eased the cover back in place. He noticed her PDA then. It had slipped from her hand and was now on the console between them.

Was there something stored in the PDA that would help the cops stop another hostage situation? Maybe. Maybe it also contained something that would help Willa restore her memory. At least that was the justification he used when he read the first page entry.

Your name is Willa Marks, and you have amnesia and post-concussional neurosis, also called short-term memory loss. Everything you need to know is on this PDA.

There was a list of places where she had cash stored and her doctor's phone number, followed by a list of rules. Well, two rules to be specific.

Number one: don't trust the cops.
Number two: stay in hiding.

Neither was a surprise. Twice Willa had nearly been killed when she'd trusted the cops. If their positions had been reversed, he might have written the same damn memos.

He scrolled down farther to the next entry that Willa had labeled Latest Update.

The man beside me is Sheriff Brandon Ruiz. My baby's father. Use caution. He has secrets.

"Secrets?" he mumbled. Yeah, he had them.

Well, one anyway. But it was a secret that could affect everything.

What the hell was he going to do about Willa and the baby?

She needed help, all right. But she needed someone with less emotional baggage than he had. He certainly didn't fit the bill.

Frustrated with that and the lack of news about the case, Brandon took out his phone and sent a text message to Cash to see if there was an update. The moment he hit the send button, he heard the beep. It was so soft that it was barely audible, but it went through him as if it'd been a shout.

Brandon's gaze flew to the monitor. He checked the feed from all the cameras and didn't see anything out of the ordinary. Well, not at first anyway. He moved closer to the screen, trying to pick through the pitchy darkness of the tiny images.

There.

Beneath the bedroom window.

He spotted the man dressed head to toe in black. His movement had obviously triggered the perimeter security sensor. Brandon watched as the man lifted his hand and bashed something against the glass in the window.

"Willa," Brandon whispered. "We have to get out of here now."

Her eyes flew open, and she gave the seat a quick adjustment so she was in a sitting position. Her attention went straight to the monitor.

"Is it Shore?" she asked.

"I can't tell." But Brandon would put money on the fact that it was the assassin. If not, then it was someone equally dangerous.

"Put on your seat belt," Brandon instructed. He did the same. "And stay down. The second I open the garage door, I'm driving out of here fast."

That was a risk, of course, because Shore could shoot at them, but Brandon knew that was a risk he had to take—especially when he saw the man toss something through the broken bedroom window.

Hell.

It could be another grenade. And if it was, the explosion could easily destroy the garage, or at minimum, the damage from a blast could trap them inside.

Brandon started the car and hit the remote opener clipped to the visor. It seemed to take way too long for the door to lift, and with each passing second, he prayed that Shore wouldn't have time to make it to the front of the garage entrance so he could shoot at them head-on.

As soon as Brandon had clearance to get out of the

garage, he jammed his foot on the accelerator, and the car bolted out into the darkness.

The shot came almost immediately and shattered the back windshield.

"Stay down!" he reminded Willa, though he knew that might not be enough. Bullets could go through seats as easily as they could through glass.

The sound of the second shot drowned out his repeated warning for her to stay down. The bullet tore through what was left of the safety glass, and the shooter quickly followed it up with a third and fourth shot. But that wasn't all. Behind them, there was an explosion, and both the house and the garage burst into fireballs.

Brandon didn't dare risk looking at Willa to make sure she was okay because he had to focus on getting them away from the shooter.

He headed for the road and glanced in the side mirror to see if the gunman was in pursuit. It was impossible to tell, but it was obvious the guy was still in shooting range because yet another bullet tore through the side of the car. Thank God the shots missed the tires or their chances of escape would drop significantly.

The shots stopped, and Brandon continued to tear his way down the country road. He had to slow down to take a sharp curve, but as soon as he could, he sped up again.

He saw the headlights then.

They flared on behind them, and even though Brandon couldn't see their attacker, he figured the guy had hidden his vehicle nearby. He'd probably killed the car lights so that they wouldn't be alerted. The plan might have worked, too, if Brandon hadn't suspected there might be an attack and set up those security cameras.

Beside him, he could hear Willa's heavy breathing, and from the corner of his eye, he could see that she had her hands splayed protectively over her belly.

"He's following us, isn't he?" she asked. Her voice was raspy and thick.

Brandon glanced in the side mirror and saw the headlights. The guy was definitely in pursuit. "Yeah," he confirmed. "Hang on."

He took the next turn faster than he should have, and Brandon fought with the steering wheel to keep his vehicle on the road. He hated putting Willa through this, but there was no other choice. With Willa in the car, he couldn't risk stopping to have a showdown with this SOB. Later though, he hoped he got the chance to beat this guy to dust.

The anger roared through Brandon, and he could feel the dangerous energy course in his blood. With it, came the flashbacks. Like the nightmares, they were always there, ready to rear their ugly heads. He pinned his attention to the road, to the curves, and forced the old demons to remain at bay.

"Where are we going?" she asked. She levered herself up just a fraction to check her side mirror, but Brandon caught onto her shoulder and shoved her back down.

"Once we get to the highway, I'll drive toward San Antonio. Maybe I can lose him on the interstate and if not, maybe the traffic will get him to back off."

Both possibilities were long shots, but they were the only shots that Brandon had.

"Should I call 9-1-1?" Willa asked. But she hadn't said it eagerly, more as a last resort.

It was a last resort they couldn't risk.

"No," he answered. He could have sworn he heard her sigh with relief.

He took another curve, then another, but the vehicle stayed behind them. Too close. And worse, it was gaining. The only good thing about their situation was that the driver wouldn't be able to fire at them while trying to maintain the speed. Still, that didn't mean they were safe.

Brandon reached a straight stretch of the road and was able to go faster. So did the other car, and it closed in. The driver had on his high beams, making it hard for Brandon to see, but he could tell the vehicle was an SUV. It was much larger and faster than the car he was driving, so the SUV quickly ate up the distance between them.

"Hold on," Brandon warned Willa.

Just as the SUV smashed into their rear bumper.

Brandon fought to keep the car on the road, and he didn't let up on the accelerator. He continued to race toward the highway. If his calculations were correct, that was less than a mile away.

The SUV rammed into them again, and the jolt sent them both snapping in their seats. He bit back some profanity and prayed all this jostling around wouldn't hurt the baby or Willa. While he was praying, he added that he could get them safely out of there.

There was another sharp curve, and then the road stretched out again in a straight line. The SUV's driver took advantage of it and slammed into the back of their car again. Brandon kept a tight grip on the steering wheel, somehow managing to keep the car on the road.

Finally, he spotted the highway, and Brandon took the turn on what had to be two wheels. He quickly righted the car and took off.

Despite the late hour, it wasn't long before he spotted another vehicle just ahead of them. Brandon raced toward it and hoped there would be others to deter the SUV driver from another attack.

The SUV stayed close, and Brandon braced himself in case they were rammed again, but the guy stayed back.

Brandon passed the other vehicle but then slowed, hoping to keep the car between them and the SUV.

"Are we losing him?" Willa asked.

"Not just yet."

There were several other vehicles just ahead on the highway, and Brandon got as close to them as possible. The seconds clicked off in his head, and he held his breath until he saw the cluster of lit buildings at an exit. He wouldn't leave the highway just yet, but only a few miles ahead was the exit for the county sheriff's office and the fire department. He would get off the highway there and, if necessary, he'd even pull into the sheriff's parking lot.

Willa sat up just a fraction and glanced in the side mirror. She stared back at the SUV that was now several cars behind them. "Shore came out into the open at the rental house so he could follow us," she reminded him. "Neither the neighborhood street nor the traffic stopped him."

Yeah. Brandon was aware of that. And that was one of the reasons the knot in his gut had tightened to the point of being painful. If that was Shore in the SUV, then why had he backed off? Of course, the answer might be that it wasn't Shore.

That thought caused Brandon to take a deep breath.

Willa shook her head. "I'm past being tired of this. All I want is for my baby to be safe."

Brandon wanted the same thing, but he was aware that the danger was far from being over.

He put on his blinker when he reached the exit for the sheriff's office, and when Willa saw where he was headed, she sat up even farther in her seat.

"I thought you didn't want to involve the cops," she questioned.

"I don't. We can't," he corrected a moment later. He pulled into the well-lit parking lot and stopped in the spot that was closest to the front door.

The SUV slowed to a crawl but didn't turn into the lot. Brandon watched as it crept out of sight.

The driver wouldn't go far. No. He would wait for them to make a move. For now, the only move Brandon intended to do was stay put. He could go into the sheriff's office, of course, as a final resort, but the sheriff would almost certainly contact the San Antonio Police.

He kept watch to make sure the SUV didn't circle back around, and he glanced at Willa to check that she was all right. She wasn't. She was pale and trembling.

Brandon put his arm around her and eased her closer. She welcomed the contact.

He tried to figure out how to word what he had to tell her and decided there was no easy way to spell out their situation. Basically, they were in the worst kind of trouble, and Willa needed to know that.

"Shore—or whoever just attacked us—had to have known how to find us," Brandon explained.

She pulled back, met his gaze. "This means there's a leak?"

He nodded and hated the fear he saw in her eyes. "You were right, Willa. We can't trust the cops."

She made a sound of agreement and blinked back tears. "What about Sergeant Cash Newsome? Can you call him?"

"Maybe." Brandon did trust his old friend and would try to contact him but not now. Not until he could figure out a way to make sure any conversation he had with Cash would be private.

"So what do we do?" Willa asked.

He put his hand over his gun and kept watch around them. "For now, we wait."

Brandon was sure it wouldn't be long before there would be another attempt to kill them.

Chapter 7

The sound of someone talking woke her.

Willa forced open her heavy eyelids and realized it was no longer dark, and they were no longer parked outside the sheriff's office. The car was moving. And judging from the massive buildings around them, they were driving through downtown San Antonio.

She sat up, yawned and looked at the man behind the wheel. She recognized that dark hair and those steamy brown eyes.

"I remember you," she mumbled.

With the phone sandwiched between his shoulder and ear, Brandon glanced at her and nodded. The corner of his mouth lifted into a near smile. Thank God she didn't have to re-create her life and memories this morning. But then Willa remembered something else.

The danger.

That kicked up her heartbeat to an uncomfortable level, and she looked all around them to make certain Shore wasn't still following them. There were plenty of vehicles on the road, but she saw no signs of that SUV.

"We'll be there in a few minutes," Brandon told the person on the other end of the line. "Remember, this stays just between us."

He closed his phone and shoved it back into his pocket. "That was Cash."

Her breath went thin. "You're sure we can trust him?"

"He's given me no reason not to. Not yet anyway," Brandon added in a mumble. "Cash insists there isn't a leak at SAPD. He thinks Shore is tracking us some other way."

"How?"

"Well, it's not my cell phone because I know it has an anti-tracking device." Brandon glanced at her PDA. And her stomach knotted. It was her lifeline. Her security blanket. It had saved her life—literally.

"It's just a possibility," he added.

True, but Shore was finding them somehow, and maybe her PDA had some kind of GPS tracking system.

It made her physically ill to think of what she had to do, but she couldn't let her lifeline put her baby at risk. Willa opened the glove compartment and fished out a pen.

"Don't give me any reason to regret this," she warned Brandon, and Willa waited until he made eye contact with her before she scrawled the words across her palm.

Trust Brandon Ruiz.

He glanced at the sentence and then mumbled some profanity. Profanity he didn't explain as he brought the car to a stop in a hotel parking lot.

"Leave the PDA in the car," he told her and checked their surroundings. "We won't be coming back to this vehicle or the parking lot."

She glanced around as well, and her attention landed on the hotel. "Are we staying here?"

Brandon shook his head, grabbed her overnight bag and opened the door. "In and out. We'll be on foot for a few blocks."

Good. She didn't want to be anywhere near her PDA or the vehicle with the shot-out windows. "But I'll need to find a bathroom soon," she let him know.

Brandon took her request to heart and hurried them from the car into the hotel. They didn't stop in the lobby but went to the back and exited into another parking lot. They walked past two more buildings before entering another hotel. Willa expected them to exit this one as well, but she came to a dead stop when she spotted the sandy-haired man in the lobby.

He was almost certainly a cop.

Willa didn't know who he was, but he did seem familiar. About six feet tall, lanky build and green eyes. Cop's eyes.

Brandon stopped directly in front of the man. "Willa, this is Sergeant Cash Newsome."

She still didn't release the breath she was holding.

Brandon leaned closer to Cash and lowered his voice to a whisper. "If this puts Willa in any more danger, you'll be the one to answer for it."

Cash stiffened, and his friendly expression faded.

"That doesn't sound like something an old friend would say."

Brandon scowled. "Friendship only gets you one shot. If Shore finds us here, then I'm taking Willa into deep hiding where SAPD and their possible leak can't ever find her."

"Think of those women who could become the next hostages," Cash countered.

"I'm thinking of Willa and the baby. Right now, they come first."

That started a staring match between the two men, and Cash hitched his shoulder toward the elevator. He started in that direction. So did Brandon. Willa stayed put, but after glancing down at what she'd written on her hand, she cursed and caught up to the men.

They went to the fifth floor, and Cash directed them into a suite that was nearly the same size as the safe house they'd left hours earlier. There were massive windows revealing the city's skyline, but what snagged Willa's attention was the smell of bacon and eggs that was coming from the silver dome-covered plates on the coffee table. Her stomach growled, and the baby kicked as if sensing it was time to eat as well.

Brandon handed her the bag. "Go ahead to the bathroom and then I'll explain what's going on after you've had some breakfast."

She really did need to use the bathroom, but she didn't budge. "I'd like to hear now."

Cash and Brandon exchanged glances. Cash's expression was laced with skepticism, but Brandon looked as if he were bracing himself for an argument.

"We need your help," Cash insisted.

But she ignored him and stared at Brandon instead. "What do they want you to convince me to do?"

"They want you to see a doctor who might be able to help you recover your memory."

"A psychiatrist who's a friend of mine," Cash supplied. "Her name is Dr. Lenora Farris and she'll be here in about twenty minutes."

"A shrink?" Willa made sure she let her tone convey her displeasure, and she aimed that displeasure at Brandon. "I've already seen therapists."

"She's supposedly different." Brandon turned so that he was between Cash and her. "I thought if you could remember it might help us put an end to the danger. *All* the danger for both you and any other possible hostages. We might also be able to figure out who hired Shore to come after you."

Willa couldn't argue with that, but she still wasn't convinced this would help. Plus, they were in a hotel suite with a cop, and if there was a leak, they could be sitting ducks for another attack.

Brandon put his mouth right against her ear. "I agreed to two hours. That's it. And then we're getting out of here."

Willa still wanted to argue, but then Brandon brushed a kiss on her forehead. That took the fight right out of her. Of course, maybe the fatigue and her full bladder were partly responsible as well. She shifted the bag to her shoulder, huffed and headed for the adjoining bathroom.

She didn't dawdle, but she did take the time to freshen up and change her top. Thankfully, she'd packed a green sweater in her overnight bag.

When she went back into the main room of the suite,

it was obvious she was interrupting a tense discussion—maybe even an argument. Whatever had been going on came to an abrupt halt when Cash and Brandon spotted her.

Brandon scrubbed his hand over his face. "Eat," he told Willa. And he headed to the bathroom, leaving her alone with Cash.

Since her stomach was still growling and she was getting light-headed, Willa sat and helped herself to one of the plates. There was even a glass of milk and a bottle of prenatal vitamins on the tray.

"You don't remember me?" Cash asked. He poured himself a cup of coffee from a gleaming silver carafe and took the chair across from her.

"No. We've met?"

He nodded. "I was the first officer to get to you after the hostage standoff ended."

Without her PDA, she couldn't confirm that, so Willa settled for making a noncommittal sound while she ate her scrambled eggs.

"I found you in the hall outside the hospital lab," he continued. "You'd fallen, or something. You were barely conscious."

That got her attention. Had she known that "barely conscious" part? She didn't think so. Willa was sure she had put in her notes that she regained consciousness not at the maternity hospital but in the medical center after she came out of a coma.

"Did I say anything when you found me?" she asked.

He shrugged. "You were worried about losing the baby."

Well, that was a no-brainer, but she got the feeling

that Cash was withholding something. Or maybe it was just her overactive imagination.

Brandon came out of the bathroom at the same moment there was a knock at the door. The sound sent both men reaching for their weapons, and it was Brandon who went to the door to peek out the viewer.

"It's a woman," he relayed to Cash. "Tall with auburn hair."

"Dr. Farris," Cash supplied. He confirmed that by looking through the viewer as well, and then opened the door to greet their visitor.

Since she wasn't always able to rely on her memory, Willa had gotten accustomed to reading people. There was usually something—a quick unguarded glance, a tightening of the mouth. Some small detail.

But not with Dr. Farris.

Cash made the introductions, but Willa still didn't get any clues when she shook the woman's hand. Dr. Farris seemed friendly enough but, more than anything, she was a blank slate. Maybe because of her psychiatric training.

"Willa," the doctor greeted, and she held on to Willa's hand for several seconds. "I'm here to help you."

Willa didn't try to hide her skepticism. "Others have tried. And failed."

The doctor nodded and calmly whisked a loose curl from her pale ivory face. "But those therapies were used early on after your injury. Sergeant Newsome tells me you've made improvements since then and that you're not having as many issues with your short-term memory."

Willa aimed a scowl at Cash. "And how exactly would you know that?"

Cash shrugged his shoulders. "Lieutenant Bo Duggan. I had a long talk with him before I set all of this up."

Then obviously the lieutenant was recovering. That was something at least, especially since he'd gotten shot while trying to protect her.

Brandon stepped even closer to Willa and caught her hand in his. However, he directed his attention to Dr. Farris. "How do you think you can help Willa?"

"Well, since we obviously can't use any drugs to induce an altered state, I want to use something called Neuro-Linguistic Programming—NLP—that incorporates video hypnosis. I plan to use triggers that might cue in other parts of her brain to unlock the lost memories."

"What kind of triggers?" Willa demanded.

The doctor offered her a calm smile. "Both visual and auditory. By using NLP, I want to re-create the environment of the maternity ward the way it was when the hostage situation started."

Willa felt a chill go over her. "I'm not going back to that hospital."

"You don't have to. In a way, I'm bringing the hospital to you." Dr. Farris extracted a shiny DVD from her purse. "My assistants and I have worked on this for hours so you can replicate the experience."

Willa didn't want to replicate it because her time as a hostage had almost certainly been terrifying. But she couldn't refuse the opportunity to regain her memory simply because she was scared. As Brandon had already pointed out, the information trapped in her mind could ultimately give them the name of the person trying to kill them and it could save those possible Christmas hostages.

"Is this safe?" Brandon asked.

"Absolutely." The doctor didn't hesitate, either. "And if Willa becomes agitated, I'll stop." She looked at Willa then and waited.

Willa went over everything the doctor had just told her. This, whatever this was, wouldn't harm the baby. And she could stop if it got too extreme. There was no way she could refuse, not with her risking so little and with so much at stake for the future hostages.

Willa finally nodded.

Dr. Farris didn't give a sigh of relief. She didn't show any emotion as she went to the large flat-screen TV and inserted the disk in the DVD player.

"You two should wait in the other room," the doctor told Brandon and Cash.

Willa felt as though someone had just taken her security blanket. Not good. Trusting Brandon was one thing but relying on him emotionally just wasn't very smart.

"I'm staying," Brandon insisted.

Cash said the same, and after staring at them, the doctor finally showed some emotion. She made a sound of mild annoyance and turned away from them.

Despite the little lecture Willa had just given herself about not leaning on Brandon, she was thankful that he would be nearby. After all, it was his name and his name only that she'd written on her hand.

"Should I lie down or something?" Willa asked.

Dr. Farris shook her head and started the DVD. "Just stay seated and focus on what you're seeing and hearing."

That sounded simple enough. Well, simple unless her short-term memory decided to take a hike. Since it'd been weeks since that had happened, Willa thought that part of this ordeal might be over, but she'd been wrong before.

The images started to appear on the screen. Someone was holding a video camera and recording their walk through the double automatic doors.

"We know from the exterior surveillance cameras that this is how you entered the building," the doctor explained. "Once you reach the fourth floor, your movements and what happens there are reenactments based on eyewitnesses." She kept her voice at a whisper and lowered the lights so that the only illumination came from the TV.

Willa forced herself to imagine that she was the one walking into the San Antonio Maternity Hospital. The greeting area didn't look familiar, but they quickly went through it and to the elevators. She pretended that it was her hand that pushed the button to take her to the fourth floor.

When *she* stepped into the elevator and the doors closed, Willa heard the music. There was nothing unusual about it, but it seemed familiar. The elevator seemed familiar, too. There were posters of mothers holding their newborns.

She felt her heart speed up a little when the doors swished open and she saw the fourth floor. Again, there was nothing unusual about it, and she guessed wrong about which direction she would take. The camera went to the left, past an empty waiting area. She saw the signs on the wall leading to the lab.

Why was she going there?

Because she was supposed to have some lab tests and then an ultrasound. That wasn't an actual memory, but she'd been told that by the police. Someone had called and told her she needed lab tests, but that had been a ruse to get her to the hospital.

The ruse had worked.

When the camera reached the lab desk, it stopped. Willa glanced around the corridor spread out in front of her and waited. She didn't have to wait long. She saw the ski-mask-wearing man racing toward her. He was armed.

"Don't close your eyes," the doctor insisted when Willa started to do just that.

It was a challenge, but she forced herself to watch as the man came closer and closer to the camera.

"Come with me," the man demanded, and he jammed the gun at her.

Willa didn't want to go with him. She wanted to run out of the hotel suite, far away from the camera and the nightmarish images, but she forced herself to stay put.

The gunman led her into the lab, past the cubicles where the techs drew blood. They went about twenty yards farther to a door with a sign that read: Authorized Personnel Only Beyond This Point. The man pressed in a code to get the door to open and led her into a room with computers and refrigerated storage containers.

They stopped moving, so Willa looked around as far as the camera angle would allow. She took in as many details as she could manage. The glossy gray tile floor. The sterile white walls and ceiling. The way everything was arranged in precise order. The smell.

She froze.

The smell?

Did she really remember that?

Yes, she did. It wasn't the disinfectant odor like the rest of the hospital. This particular area smelled like some kind of lab chemical.

She felt the air-conditioning spill out from the overhead vents. The room was too cold, and she shivered. Willa waited for more sensations to come, and they did. They came at her hard and fast.

Willa gasped and pressed her fingers to her mouth. "Oh, God. I remember."

Chapter 8

Brandon wasn't sure which of them looked more surprised, but he thought he might be the winner. When Dr. Farris had started that DVD, and Willa had started to watch, the last thing he expected was for Willa to remember anything.

But she apparently had.

She kept her gaze fastened to the screen where the hostage situation continued to play out. It seemed like such a simple exercise. Visual cues of a nightmare. But Willa kept repeating those two words as if it were a mantra. Or a warning.

I remember.

"What do you remember?" Dr. Farris asked, taking the words right out of Brandon's mouth.

Willa pressed her fingertips to both sides of her head and began to rock. Brandon went and sat beside her, then put his arm around her.

"It's okay." He tried to assure her, but he had no way of knowing if that was true.

"I remember the gunman taking me into the lab," Willa said. Her voice was barely a whisper, and he could feel her trembling.

Brandon tightened his grip, and her hands dropped to her lap. "What else?" he pressed.

Both the doctor and Cash moved closer, probably hoping they were all finally about to get answers. Brandon wanted those answers, too, but he hated that Willa was having to go through this all over again.

"The gunman took me into a secure area," she continued. "He pressed in some numbers on a key pad."

"Did he have the code written down?" Cash asked.

Willa nodded. "On a piece of paper he took from his pocket. He opened the door and pushed me inside. 'Go to the computer,' he told me. And I did. I went to the one where he pointed. It was on the far side of the room, sitting on a desk."

Cash leaned down so that he'd be eye level with Willa. "What did he want you to do?"

Before Willa could answer, Dr. Farris eased Cash out of the way. "No more questions, please. This will work best if Willa lets the memories come to her. And sometimes, these bits and pieces are all we'll get. To be honest with you, I wasn't sure it would even work this well."

Willa stared up at the doctor. "These aren't bits and pieces," she mumbled, her voice catching. "The gunman wanted me to hack into some secure files." She paused. "I did it because he put a gun to my head and said he would kill me and the baby if I didn't."

Brandon ignored the punch of anger he felt over

what Willa had been through. He also ignored the doctor's no-question warning. "What files?"

"Ones that were being outsourced to the hospital," Willa readily answered. "The files belonged to the San Antonio Police Department, and they were biological samples that were to be used in several active cases. He wanted me to hack into the files and alter the data."

Definitely not bits and pieces. This was the sort of information that could blow this case wide open.

Brandon met Cash's stare. "Is it routine for SAPD to outsource tests to the hospital?"

Cash shook his head. "No. We usually use the Ranger lab in Austin, but there was a fire, and they got backlogged. I heard we were using some local hospitals to do some of the tests, but I didn't know it was this specific hospital."

"Dean Quinlan," Willa said out of the blue. "It was his name on the files. He was listed as the file manager. Do you know him?" she asked Cash.

"Yeah." Cash propped his hands on his hips and mumbled some profanity. "He's one of our CSIs. Well, he used to be anyway. He resigned shortly after the hostage incident to take a job elsewhere."

The doctor turned off the DVD and looked at Willa. "What else do you remember?"

Willa opened her mouth, hesitated, then closed it. "Nothing. That's all."

"You don't remember what specific files the gunman wanted you to hack into?" Cash demanded.

She shook her head. "No. I'm sorry. I remember sitting down at the computer, and I remember seeing Dean Quinlan's name as the file custodian, but that's it. Everything else after that is a blank." She started to tremble again, and Brandon pulled her closer to him.

Cash checked his watch. "I need to talk to Dean Quinlan and anyone else who knew about those files being processed at the maternity hospital. I'll let you know what I find out." He took out his phone and headed into one of the suite's bedrooms.

"Your memory might continue to return," Dr. Farris told her. She paused to take Willa's pulse. "Sometimes, when you recall portions of the traumatic events, other details soon follow."

Willa nodded and pulled in a long breath. While that was good news for the investigation, Brandon knew this would be hell for Willa. After all, the gunman had likely been trying to kill her when she fell and injured her head.

"How are you feeling?" Dr. Farris asked.

"Exhausted." Willa adjusted her position and placed her head against Brandon's shoulder. "Could you give me a few minutes to gather my thoughts?"

Dr. Farris nodded, but she didn't look at all certain about leaving Willa. Finally, though, she walked toward the second bedroom, went inside and shut the door.

The moment the doctor was out of sight, Willa's head swooshed off his shoulder, and she stood. "I remembered some other things," she whispered.

Brandon froze. He didn't think her memory had returned just this instant. No. It had probably come with the other memories, but Willa had been smart not to tell all to the doctor. While Brandon still trusted Cash, he didn't know Dr. Farris and was glad Willa had withheld something that might put her in even more danger.

If that was possible.

"The gunman tried to call Dean Quinlan while we were in that secure area of the lab," Willa continued. "He had Quinlan's name and number written on the back of the paper with the codes he used to get past the door."

"Did he actually speak to Quinlan?" Brandon, too, kept his voice at a whisper and stood so he could be closer to her.

She shook her head. "His cell phone couldn't get a signal in that part of the lab."

Probably because the walls had been reinforced for safety reasons, he thought. Labs and X-ray areas often have metal barriers to stop the harmful rays from getting into other parts of the building.

"The gunman was frustrated because he couldn't seem to read his notes," Willa explained. "He finally showed them to me, and that's when I saw the names of the files I was supposed to access. There were three of them—the first was Baby Martinez."

"That makes sense," Brandon concluded. "Misty Martinez was a San Antonio woman who was murdered, and her newborn was missing. Since Misty had stored the baby's umbilical cord at the maternity hospital, SAPD requested a DNA test so they could identify the biological father, who turned out to be her killer."

Willa's eyes widened. "Please tell me I didn't do anything to that DNA sample that allowed a killer to get away."

"No. The biological father, Gavin Cunningham, was arrested and got a life sentence."

She nodded but didn't relax. "The second name on

the list was Jessie Beecham..." She paused, shook her head. "And Wes-somebody."

"Dunbar," Brandon provided. And he cursed.

Willa blinked. "You know these people?"

"I know *of* them. Jessie Beecham was a wealthy club owner with ties to the mob. He was murdered earlier this year, and the prime suspect was a rival club owner named Wes Dunbar."

SAPD had sent Brandon the initial reports of the investigation because Wes Dunbar had a country estate in Crockett Creek, Brandon's own town. At the time he'd read those reports, Brandon had no idea just how personal that case would become. Of course, the question was did the investigation into Jessie Beecham's murder have anything to do with Willa's situation?

Maybe not.

Maybe the culprit who'd hired Shore was simply someone who was tying up loose ends for the now-dead gunman who'd held her hostage. Maybe an unknown accomplice. What Brandon needed was more information, and that included a case update on Jessie Beecham's murder.

He glanced at the room where Cash had gone to make his call about the former CSI, Dean Quinlan. He looked at the room where the doctor was as well. And he got a really bad feeling about all of this. God knows who Dr. Farris had already told about Willa's regained memory, and Cash's calls and questions would almost certainly alert the wrong people.

"We need to get out of here?" Willa asked, obviously noticing the alarm on his face.

"Yeah." He grabbed her bag and her arm.

Brandon hoped to hell it wasn't too late.

* * *

Willa was beyond tired of being on the run, but she knew Brandon was right to get them out of there. Maybe both Cash and Dr. Farris were on the up-and-up, but that didn't mean someone, including Martin Shore, would get word that she had remembered what had gone on in the lab the day the maternity hostages were taken.

Brandon eased the suite door shut behind them and got them moving to the elevator. He had her bag slung over his shoulder and kept one hand on her and the other within easy reach of his gun. Willa held her breath until they were in the elevator and the doors slid shut. They weren't out of danger yet, not by a long shot, but she wanted to put as much distance as possible between the suite and them.

"What do we do now?" she asked and mentally cursed the fatigue and fog in her head.

She should have already figured that out for herself, but here she was again relying on Brandon. Once they were safely away from the hotel, she had to find some time to come up with a new plan—and a couple of backup ones.

"We need a vehicle and some cash," Brandon answered. "I have to get you to a safe place, and we can't get there on foot with Shore this close and every cop in San Antonio looking for us."

That "safe place" part certainly sounded good to her, but was it even doable?

"I have some cash in the bag," Willa let him know. "About five hundred dollars."

But she would need a lot more than that if she had to go into hiding for any length of time. Which she probably would. That meant making a trip to the banks in Austin or San Antonio, so she could get to one of her safety deposit boxes where she'd stashed more money.

Brandon stopped the elevator on the second floor. "It's too risky to go into the main part of the lobby," he told her.

So, they left the elevator and went into the stairwell. Brandon stopped long enough to look at the emergency exit route map that was on the wall. Willa looked as well and wasn't pleased that the stairs ended so close to the lobby. They would still be in sight of the front desk and entrance. But hopefully not for long. There appeared to be a back exit just off a coffee shop. She prayed the door there wasn't rigged with an alarm.

When they reached the bottom of the stairs, Brandon stopped and peered out through the glass insert in the door. "No sign of Shore or other cops," he relayed to her.

That didn't give her any sense of relief. Shore had gotten the jump on them before, and it could happen again.

They left the meager cover of the stairwell and stepped out into the back part of the lobby, which was just ten or fifteen feet from the coffee shop. They only made it a few steps before Brandon pulled her into a shallow recessed area that led to the ladies' room. He maneuvered her behind him.

"Shhh," he warned.

Her heart went to her knees, and she came up on her tiptoes so she could look over his shoulder. Willa dreaded what she would see.

There were several people milling around in the lobby and two hotel employees behind the check-in desk. She certainly didn't see the apparent threat Brandon thought was there, but she had no intention of leaving their hiding place, either. She stood there waiting with her breath held.

Two of the people in the lobby picked up their suitcases and headed for the front exit.

That's when Willa spotted the man.

He was on the other side of the check-in desk, partly hidden behind a massive plant.

Oh, God.

It was Martin Shore.

He was volleying glances between the elevator and the front door. And she recognized what he held in his hand.

Her PDA.

Willa clamped her teeth over her bottom lip so that her gasp wouldn't be loud enough to draw anyone's attention—especially Shore's. How had he actually found them? Had Cash or Dr. Farris alerted him, or had Shore merely followed her PDA and guessed their location? His presence could be a fishing expedition, but it didn't matter. He was there—so close—and that meant the danger was there again too.

The baby began to kick, hard, and since her belly was pressed against Brandon's back, he no doubt felt it. He glanced over his shoulder at her but then nailed his attention back on Shore.

They couldn't wait long in the alcove without someone noticing them, and it wouldn't be wise to try to hide out in the ladies' room where they would be trapped. Soon, if not already, Cash and the doctor would realize they were missing and would come looking for them. That would no doubt confirm to Shore that they were still in the building. Besides, she didn't want anyone, including Cash and Dr. Farris, to find them. Willa only wanted to get out of there.

"We need to move fast when we get outside," Brandon whispered.

Willa nodded and hoped that *fast* would be fast enough.

Part of her wondered if it was best just to have a showdown with Shore. Here and now. After all, Brandon was a cop. He knew how to take down a killer. But Shore wasn't an ordinary killer. He wouldn't give up without a hard fight, and that would mean bullets flying. Innocent people could be killed. And once again, her precious baby would be in harm's way.

"Now!" Brandon ordered.

He turned, not abruptly though. He kept his movement unhurried. He also kept her in front of him so that he was between Shore and her. Brandon was protecting her yet again.

The dozen or so steps to the exit seemed to take a lifetime, but Willa knew it was only a few seconds. Brandon shoved open the door and got her outside.

The burst of cold air hit her in the face, but she didn't take the time to catch her breath. Brandon got them moving, not across the parking lot where they could easily be seen. He led her toward the back of the hotel, and they hurried past the service and delivery entrances. There were men unloading boxes, but none seemed to pay any attention to them.

Brandon kept watch behind them and then stopped when they reached the corner of the building. There was about ten yards of wide-open space between the hotel and the next building, which was a one-story chain restaurant.

"Let's move," Brandon insisted, and they quickly got across to the back of the restaurant.

They repeated that process for three more buildings, putting some distance between the hotel and them.

Willa heard the sirens, but it only heightened her fear. However, Brandon paused and looked out as if he were considering the possibility of going to the responding officers.

"Please tell me you're not going out there," she whispered.

"Not a chance." He grabbed her arm again and got them moving farther away from the hotel and from those approaching sirens.

"Then where are we going once we get a car?" Willa demanded.

Brandon lifted her hand so she would have a reminder of what she'd written there. "You have to trust me a little longer, Willa. Because I'm taking you to the one place I know where I can keep you safe."

Chapter 9

They were *home*.

Well, they were at *his* home anyway, Willa amended.

It was apparently the one place he knew where he could keep her safe. Maybe he felt that way because of the two dogs. The minute they turned into the gravel driveway that led to the isolated house, two Dobermans came racing toward them. Neither dog looked very welcoming, and they barked and chased the car.

It wasn't exactly a friendly greeting.

The trek to his rural Crockett Creek house hadn't been a friendly one, either. It'd taken them more than an hour to get far enough away from the hotel and to a pay phone he thought might be safe to use. He'd called one of his deputies, Pete Sanchez, a fiftysomething-year-old man who had arrived to pick them up in San Antonio, so he could then drive them out to Brandon's place.

The drive had been long and tedious. Along with bathroom stops to accommodate Willa and the round-about route the deputy had used to get them to the small Texas town, the trip was more than three hours. Willa was beyond exhausted, and that was probably a good thing because the exhaustion numbed some of the fear.

Temporarily, anyway.

The fear returned when she studied the house itself. Despite the barking dogs, it wasn't a fortress, that's for sure. It looked more like, well, a home.

Deputy Sanchez pulled to a stop in front of the porch and steps.

"Are you sure we'll be safe here?" Willa asked, eyeing the cottage-style house.

With the iron-gray sky and the icy drizzle spitting at them, the house was the only spot of color in the winter landscape. It was a cheery shade of yellow and had dark green shutters and door. There were even flower boxes anchored beneath the windows. It wasn't what she expected from a dark and brooding small-town Texas sheriff.

"The place was painted like this when I bought it," Brandon mumbled, probably sensing her surprise. "Wait here," he told her.

Brandon drew his gun, and just like that, the fatigue could no longer numb the fear. Willa sat there on the backseat of the deputy's four-door black Ford and watched as Brandon got out. He didn't say anything to the dogs. He merely lifted his left hand, and they both went silent. The pair followed Brandon up the steps and to the door he then unlocked. However, they didn't go inside. The dogs waited for him on the porch.

"Please, don't let there be anyone in there," Willa

mumbled. But she obviously didn't mumble it softly enough because the deputy eased around in the seat and looked at her.

"Butch and Sundance wouldn't have let anyone inside," Deputy Sanchez drawled. "Brandon's just being extra cautious. If the dogs are alive and kickin', then no one got near the place and remained in one piece."

Even though Willa didn't like the idea of being around attack dogs, it was better than having no outside protection against a professional assassin.

Pete kept the windshield wipers on, and they scraped away at the sleety drizzle, smearing the ice on the glass.

"I'm assuming Brandon doesn't need the dogs for security," she commented. "Because I'd figured Crockett Creek was a safe town."

"Don't worry, it is. I think the dogs help Brandon make sure his privacy stays private. It's probably why he lives all the way out here by himself. This place is a good ten miles outside of town."

That said a lot about the man whose baby she was carrying. A private man. A man she trusted, she reminded herself.

A man she wanted.

Willa quickly tried to push that thought aside, but it flashed right back in her head. She huffed. Her memory was still a mess in parts, and yet she could remember in complete, agonizing detail every twinge of attraction she felt for a man who placed a high value on privacy and keeping secrets.

"So, who takes care of the place and the dogs when he's out of town?" Willa wanted to know. It hadn't occurred to her until now that Brandon might have a girlfriend.

"His neighbor's boy does that for him."

"Neighbor?" she questioned. Not a girlfriend. Though she didn't see a nearby house or any other signs of a neighbor.

"Zach Grange," the deputy provided. "He raised the dogs from pups, and he's about the only one other than Brandon that they trust to get near them. I figure Brandon likes having 'em around. He worked canines for a while in Special Forces, you know."

No, she didn't know. That was another of the secrets he hadn't been ready to volunteer.

Brandon came back out and returned to the car so he could open her door and take her overnight bag. The wet, cold air came right at her, sending a chill straight through her clothes. Brandon thanked his deputy, and the man tipped his Stetson and drove away.

"Will the dogs bite?" she asked, eyeing them as they went up the steps. Even though it was freezing, literally, she didn't hurry because she didn't want to alarm them.

"They won't bite you." And he aimed a glance at both, one that was effective because the two remained docile on the porch as Willa went past them and into the house.

Her first impression was that the place was toasty warm. Thank goodness. And everything was neat and orderly. There were no clothes lying around, no clutter. The living room had been painted a soft cream color that complemented the slate-blue sofa and recliner. He had a flat-screen TV mounted on the wall above the fireplace.

Other than the winter weather outside, there were no signs of Christmas here. Like her place in Austin.

Hard to concentrate on the holidays when their lives were on the line.

"The kitchen's through here," he explained, pointing through a doorway.

Willa looked inside. Neat and orderly there, too.

"The bathroom's over there." He pointed to the first room off the hall that fed off the living room.

"Is it okay if I take a shower?" she asked.

"Of course." He handed Willa her overnight bag and walked into the kitchen. "Then I'll fix us something to eat, and you can get some rest."

All three of those—a shower, food and rest—sounded heavenly, and Willa headed to the bathroom. But then, she stopped.

"I want the truth," she told him, turning back around to face him. "Will Shore come here looking for us?"

Brandon had been about to open the fridge, but his hand paused in midair. He looked at her and then crossed the room toward her.

"He might," Brandon confessed. "The dogs won't let him get close, but he could try to neutralize them."

Neutralize. What a benign word for *kill.*

"I have a security system wired to all the windows and doors," Brandon continued. "It came with the house, and even though I've never had an occasion to use it, I will now that you're here."

"Good." And she heard herself repeat it several times. Because she suddenly felt shaky, Willa placed the bag on the floor and held the door frame to steady herself.

Brandon caught onto her. "Are you okay?"

She managed a nod. "I'm not very good with this whole trying-to-kill-us thing."

"Few people are good at that," he mumbled. He pulled her into his arms. "And you don't want to be around them if they are."

Since that sounded, well, personal, she eased back and met him eye to eye. She'd done that so she could see his expression when she asked him what he meant by that. But the question faded from her mind when she stared at him.

Mercy.

There it was again. That damn attraction. An itch, some people called it. Willa just thought of it as an itchy nuisance. It was clouding her judgment and drawing her to a man she should be questioning. Instead, she was falling for him.

"What?" he asked.

She had no intention of telling him what she was thinking. A man like Brandon would likely turn and run—after he made sure she was safe, that is. He was a natural protector. An alpha male. And she instinctively knew that a pregnant woman falling hard for him would take him right out of his very narrow comfort zone.

Willa shook her head to try to blow off his question, but she found herself leaning in closer to him. Why, why, why couldn't she just back away?

Because she didn't want to.

Because she wanted Brandon.

He reached to brush a strand of hair off her face, but he didn't pull back his hand. His fingers stayed, touching her cheek.

"You've been through a lot," he said as if that explained the coil of heat that was simmering inside her.

She made a sound of agreement and leaned in. Willa

only intended to touch her mouth to his. Just a taste of what her body was begging her to have. But Brandon made a sound of his own.

Not of agreement.

The husky sound rumbled in his throat, and his hand went from her cheek to the back of her neck. He snapped her to him.

And it wasn't just a touch.

Brandon forgot all about the danger. About the fatigue. About all the other things he should be doing. However, he didn't forget about this need inside him. A need that only Willa seemed capable of satisfying.

Why the hell did he want her like this?

He didn't have an answer for that, and it didn't seem to matter to his mouth, or to the rest of his body. He just hauled her as close to him as she could possibly get, and he kissed her as if he had a right to do exactly that.

He didn't have that right, though.

Kisses and caresses would just lead her on. But that still didn't stop him.

He tightened the grip he had on the back of her neck and angled her head so he could deepen the kiss. She tasted like... Willa. It was a taste he'd already sampled, and while there was the whole forbidden-fruit thing going on here, his response seemed about much more than that. He'd had forbidden fruit before, and it'd never tasted this good.

She made that mind-blowing sound of pleasure deep within her throat and pressed as hard against him as he did against her. They pulled away, only to catch their breath and, as if starved for each other, went right back for another round.

Soon, though, the kiss and the body-to-body contact wasn't enough. Soon, certain parts of him started to demand more. That was Brandon's cue to pull away, and he tried. But Willa held on, and he didn't put up much of a fight.

"I'm on fire," she mumbled against his mouth.

That was something he didn't need to hear, but it wasn't something he could forget, either. It was a primal invitation to his overly aroused body, and his instincts were to scoop her up in his arms and haul her off to bed.

That couldn't happen, of course.

Brandon repeated that to himself but still didn't pull away. Instead, he dropped some kisses on her neck and cupped her left breast with his hand.

"Still on fire," she let him know, and she added more of those sounds of silky feminine pleasure.

Willa went after his neck as well and landed a few kisses in one of his very sensitive spots. Too sensitive. More of that, and a trip to the bed would happen whether it should or not.

Brandon forced himself to pull back.

Willa's breath was gusting now, and his wasn't much slower. They stared at each other, too close for him not to consider just jumping right back in. But he didn't. If a simple kiss was leading her on, then this was a dozen steps past that at a time when Willa was most vulnerable. She was pregnant and scared. And he was taking advantage of that and this attraction between them.

She ran her tongue over her bottom lip and made another sound of pleasure. Brandon's body clenched, and he took a huge step back.

"So?" she said. "What happens now?"

No way was he going to answer that. Because a response—any response—could get him in even hotter water.

"Ah," she mumbled when he glanced away. "I guess that means we aren't going to do *that*."

"No," he agreed. "Wrong time, wrong place. Hell… wrong everything." Brandon mumbled some harsher profanity under his breath.

"Wrong man?" she concluded.

"Especially that." He glanced away again and was sorry he'd said anything.

"You have that look again, as if I just poked a stick at a raw wound. You obviously have secrets you don't want to share."

She grabbed his chin and drew his gaze back to hers. "Since you've saved my life more than once in the past twenty-four hours, I would tell you my deepest darkest secret…if I could remember it."

She smiled.

He didn't.

"You don't remember your secrets?" he asked. This was the first time it had occurred to him that she hadn't regained her full memory after watching that DVD in the hotel suite.

Willa shrugged. "I'd like to say yes to that, but there are still blanks." She drew in a quick breath. "On the drive over, I kept trying to piece things together, but I don't remember how I ended up on the floor of that hospital."

Good. Maybe she wouldn't regain those horrific memories. She had remembered what files the gunman had forced her to access, and that had to be enough.

Willa had already had enough stress without recalling an attack that had left her in a coma.

She touched his face again, turning him in her direction. "I sense you're pushing me away. That's probably for the best, if I were in a sane mode right now. I'm not. I'm in pregnancy mode where I need to protect this baby at all costs. I figure you're my best bet for that protection because you have a genetic link."

He stared at her. "Yeah," he settled for saying.

Brandon almost left it at that. Almost. But for some reason he decided that Willa deserved something better. A better explanation. And she certainly deserved something better than him.

"My birth father is a man named Wade Decalley," Brandon heard himself say. "My mother never talked about him much, and a few years ago, I found out why." He paused long enough to gather his breath. "He's a convicted serial killer, and he's spent the last thirteen years on death row."

Brandon realized it was the first time he'd said that out loud. The first time he'd actually told anyone the truth about his father.

Willa didn't blink. Didn't gasp. She merely put her fingers on his arm and rubbed gently. "I'm sorry."

"No need," he practically snapped. "I didn't know about him when I agreed to donate the semen I'd stored for my military tour in the Middle East."

Now she blinked, and she gave him an ah-ha kind of look. "Now, I get it. You don't want to pass on your DNA to a child because of your father."

"But I did anyway. I'm sorry for that, Willa. I'm sorry you didn't get the biological father you thought you were getting for this baby."

The corner of her mouth lifted, but she was also blinking back tears. "I think this baby girl has an amazing biological dad, one who would risk his own life to protect her." Willa leaned in and kissed his cheek. "I don't regret her having your DNA."

"You might," he mumbled.

She huffed, pulled away from him and fluttered her fingers in the direction of the bathroom. "I think I'll grab that shower now."

Brandon hoped it would help her relax, especially after their kissing session and his confession about his family *legacy*. He sure as hell could use something to help him relax, too, but he had too much to do. While he fixed Willa something to eat, he needed to call and try to get some information about Jessie Beecham's murder and the files that the gunman had wanted Willa to tamper with.

That meant contacting Cash.

Brandon took a prepaid cell phone from the kitchen drawer. A phone that couldn't be traced. He'd bought it on impulse, a throwback to his Special Ops days when he had been trained to be prepared for anything. At the time of the purchase, he had figured it would never be used, that he would spend the rest of his life as a sheriff, not doing anything that required a prepaid cell. But he needed to return to his roots in covert ops in order to keep Willa safe.

However, it would have to end there.

Once he had the answers they needed and Martin Shore and the danger had been neutralized, there would be only one thing left for him to do.

The best thing he could do for both Willa and the baby was to get as far away from them as possible.

Chapter 10

Willa sat at the cozy kitchen table and ate the turkey and cheese sandwich Brandon had fixed for her. She wasn't actually hungry, but she forced herself to eat because of the baby.

Brandon's own sandwich lay untouched on the table across from her, and instead of eating, he was pacing while he talked on a cell phone. Since he'd been on the phone when she came out of the shower, she had no idea how long this conversation had been going on. But she did know that he was talking to Cash.

And Brandon obviously wasn't happy about the answers he was hearing.

"Now you think Dr. Farris could be responsible for the leak?" Brandon challenged. He didn't wait for an answer. He went to the laptop sitting on a corner desk and pressed some keys. "Because before we even met the doctor, Martin Shore found us at the safe house that SAPD provided."

He paused, and she could hear the faint sound of Cash's voice on the other end of the line. Unfortunately, she couldn't hear what he was saying.

"You do that," he told Cash. "You dig into Dr. Farris's background, and I'll do the same. If the woman is dirty, I want her arrested."

So did Willa. She cringed because she'd actually been in the room with the person who might want her dead. And she'd trusted the doctor. Well, she'd trusted her enough to watch that DVD that had spurred her memory and almost certainly created more danger.

"Cash thinks the doctor is the leak?" Willa mouthed.

He shook his head and held his hand over the speaker end of the cell. "I think he's grasping at straws. He has no proof."

And they didn't have proof of Cash's innocence, either.

"Good," Brandon said several moments later, removing his hand so he could continue his call to Cash. The printer next to the laptop began to spit out something. "Because I'd like to talk with Dean Quinlan, too. Yes, you can do that. Have him call me at this number."

Dean Quinlan—the former CSI whose name had been on the files at the hospital. Willa didn't think she'd actually met the man, but like Brandon, she wanted to ask him questions about his involvement in all this.

"No, I'm not bringing Willa in," Brandon insisted. "And no, I'm not telling you where we are." He hung up. "Don't worry. Cash didn't send the fax. My deputy did, so Cash doesn't know we're here." He snatched the piece of paper from the printer.

"Recognize him?" Brandon asked, sliding the paper across the table toward her. It was a picture of a brown-haired man with a thin face.

Willa shook her head. "No. Who is he?"

"That's Dean Quinlan."

She took a harder look at the man who seemed to be at the center of everything. Was he the person who'd hired Shore to kill her? He didn't look like a killer, but Dean Quinlan could want her dead because she might be able to prove his involvement in the maternity hostage situation.

"He wants to talk to you?" she asked.

"Yeah. But don't expect Quinlan to confess to anything. Cash questioned him over the phone—Quinlan refused to meet with him—but the man claims he's innocent."

And he might be. But someone was guilty. "What about the actual lab samples at the maternity hospital? Did I tamper with them?" She shook her head, huffed. "Because I only remember hacking into them."

"Cash claims the test results were fine. They did a duplicate set of tests at another site and came up with the same results." He sat down across from her and met her gaze. "Of course, if you managed to tamper with the actual samples, then the duplicate test would give the same results."

Willa put her sandwich back on the plate and tried to recall any other details. But her mind just wouldn't let her go there.

"If I somehow contaminated or corrupted the samples, then how would I prove that?" she wanted to know.

"You can't. But it's possible they could exhume Jessie Beecham's body to get what they need. There were two DNA samples in the files you accessed," Brandon explained. "They were taken from tissue found beneath Beecham's fingernails."

"Jessie Beecham," she repeated. "The club owner with ties to the mob who was found murdered."

Another nod. "But this wasn't a mob hit. Too messy for that. It appears Beecham had been in some kind of physical altercation with his killer before he was struck on the head with a blunt object. His wallet, gun and phone were all missing, so SAPD suspected the motive might be robbery."

Willa gave that some thought. "Or maybe it was meant to look like a robbery?"

"Yeah." And he paused again. "So, SAPD wanted a fast turnaround on the DNA they collected from his fingernails because they wanted a quick arrest. Beecham's allies were making a lot of noise and blaming Beecham's rival. SAPD thought they might have a mob war on their hands. Since the lab in Austin was out of commission thanks to the fire, they sent it to the secure area of the San Antonio Maternity Hospital."

Which had turned out not to be so secure thanks to the gunman, and her. "Who would have known the samples were there?" she immediately asked.

"Anyone in SAPD." Brandon mumbled some frustrated profanity. "Or someone who worked in the hospital lab itself."

In other words, there were too many people involved to narrow it down to one specific suspect. She already didn't trust Dr. Farris, Cash and this Dean Quinlan, but she would possibly have to add many more to her list.

Brandon took the photo from her and stared at it.

"According to Cash, the DNA samples were held in a secure vault, and the handful of hospital staff who had access to that area all had the proper security clearances. They've all checked out and are no longer suspects."

"Well, someone gave the gunman the code to get into the vault area because it was written on the paper he took from his pocket."

"Cash believes the gunman could have gotten the info after the hostage situation started. A lab tech was killed within minutes after the gunmen stormed the hospital. It's possible the gunman threatened to kill the tech, and he coughed up the code."

"And the gunman killed him anyway," Willa supplied. Then she thought of something else. "The gunman tried to call Dean Quinlan."

"Quinlan denies that," Brandon grumbled. "But I don't buy it. Quinlan could have been bought off."

"By whom?"

"By Wes Dunbar, the rival club owner. Jessie Beecham and he were long-time enemies. They could have gotten into an altercation that resulted in Beecham's death." He dropped the picture onto the table. "But the DNA samples didn't prove that. The DNA belonged to a homeless man with a criminal record a mile long."

"So, this homeless man was arrested?" Willa asked.

"He was. And his court-appointed lawyer did a plea bargain. The guy's already in jail for manslaughter."

But he could be innocent. All of this, including the hostage situation itself, could have been orchestrated to put the blame for murder on a homeless man when the real killer was still out there.

It didn't take Willa long to come up with a possible identity for the real killer. "Wes Dunbar, the rival club owner, could have murdered Beecham and then paid off the CSI, Dean Quinlan, to tamper with the evidence."

Brandon nodded and pulled in a hard breath.

So, why was there the threat of another hostage situation? Had someone else decided to do the same thing as Wes Dunbar? If so, Willa's memory wasn't going to be of any help. That caused her to groan. As long as the danger was there, she was anchored to Brandon. Part of her—okay, her body—was all right with that. She wanted to sleep with him, and she was certain that was driving a lot of her other desires.

But it was clear that Brandon wasn't in this for a one-night stand or a happily ever after. She didn't need her memory to feel that he wanted to be out of her life. And that meant solving this case. The sooner that was done, the sooner they could both go back to the way things were before. That's what she wanted.

Willa repeated that.

It still didn't ring true.

She forced herself to focus just on the case. "Any suggestions as to what I should do next?"

Brandon's jaw muscles stirred, but before he could answer, his phone rang. Even though the cell didn't have caller ID, she figured it was Cash. Hopefully, the cop would have information that would help them.

Brandon didn't say a word when he took the call. He merely put the phone to his ear. A moment later, she saw the surprise, and then the concern, go through his eyes.

"Dean Quinlan," he said.

Though the sound of the man's name caused her

heart to race, this was good news. Well, potentially good. Dean was the next step in getting information because even if he was simply trying to cover his guilt, he could still slip up and tell them if Wes Dunbar or someone else hired him to have those DNA samples tampered with.

"A meeting?" Brandon questioned.

Willa waited with her breath held. She didn't relish the idea of seeing this man, but again, it might be the beginning of the end to the danger.

"All right," Brandon said a moment later. "I'll meet you at my office in Crockett Creek." He paused again. "No, I can't be there that soon. I'm at least two hours out."

That was a lie, of course, to try to conceal their real location.

Brandon checked his watch. "I'll meet you there at three o'clock. And, Quinlan, my suggestion is you'd better have answers. The *right answers*. Or I'll find a reason to arrest you."

It seemed as if Brandon was about to hang up, but he stopped. "What do you mean?" he demanded from Dean. "Who's trying to kill you?"

Whatever Dean said, it caused Brandon's jaw muscles to go to work again. He cursed when he slapped the phone shut.

"Someone's trying to kill Dean Quinlan?" Willa asked.

"Yeah." And that's all Brandon said for several moments. "He claims Cash wants him dead. And Quinlan says he has something to prove it."

Chapter 11

Deputy Pete Sanchez parked in front of the back entrance to the Crockett Creek sheriff's office. It was Brandon's usual parking space, but before today, he'd never felt like checking his too-familiar surroundings before he exited. Of course, that had plenty to do with Willa being with him.

Brandon tried to give her a reassuring glance before he got her out of the vehicle and hurried her inside. He'd already apologized a couple of times for having to bring her for what would likely be a high-stress meeting with Dean Quinlan. However, the alternative was leaving her alone at his place, and that wasn't going to happen. Brandon had no intention of letting her out of his sight.

Martin Shore was still out there somewhere. And even though it was Christmas Eve, the holiday season wouldn't stop the hired gun from striking again.

Brandon heard the voices the moment he stepped inside. He was already on full alert, but those voices upped his anxiety. One of the voices belonged to his other deputy, Sheila Gafford, a thirty-year law-enforcement veteran who didn't normally raise her voice. But that's exactly what she was doing now.

"I told you to sit down and wait," Sheila ordered.

"And I told you that I will see the sheriff *now*," the man responded.

Brandon didn't recognize the voice, but he sure as heck recognized anger when he heard it. This guy was outraged about something.

"Wait here with Willa," Brandon told Pete, and he left them in his office while he went to the front of the building. Sheila was there, staring down a tall man wearing a business suit.

The man looked past the deputy and glared when he spotted Brandon making his way toward them.

"A problem?" Brandon asked Sheila.

His deputy rolled her coffee-brown eyes and huffed. "This is Mr. Wes—"

"Dunbar," the visitor interrupted.

Well, Brandon hadn't had to go looking for the devil after all because here was his number one suspect, just a few feet away.

"Are you Sheriff Ruiz?" Wes demanded.

Even though he was rail thin, he had a booming voice, and everything about him screamed money. The suit was high-priced. Haircut, too. And judging from his perfect nails, the man had regular manicures. He didn't look the sort to do his own dirty work, but then Jessie Beecham had likely been killed in the heat of an argument.

"I'm Sheriff Ruiz," Brandon confirmed. "What do you want?"

"To talk to you. I heard about that former maternity hostage, Willa Marks. She's connected to what happened in the hospital that day."

"Yeah? What makes you think that?" Brandon didn't intend to volunteer anything.

"Don't play stupid with me. Protect her all you want. She's not the reason I'm here. But I figure that sewer rat, Dean Quinlan, is dying to get to her, and since I'm dying to get to Quinlan, I figured the fastest way to do that would be through you."

Brandon glanced around to see if Dean was already there. He wasn't. Though he should have been. He was nearly a half hour late. Of course, maybe Wes Dunbar's impromptu visit had something to do with that. However, Brandon spotted an expensive black luxury sedan he didn't recognize. It no doubt belonged to Wes, and the man behind the wheel was probably his driver.

"Why do you want to get to Dean Quinlan?" Brandon asked.

"Simple. He's trying to pin Jessie Beecham's murder on me by claiming I'm the one who hired those idiots to take the maternity hostages."

"Dean told you this?"

"Didn't have to. I hear things, and I don't like what I'm hearing. Jessie's killer is already behind bars, and Jessie's in hell. Case closed."

Maybe closed but not necessarily resolved. "Did you try to kill Willa Marks?" Brandon didn't expect a straight answer, but he figured it wouldn't hurt to ask.

"I have no reason to kill her. As far as I can tell she's not blabbing to the cops that I'm Jessie's killer.

Plus, I heard her head's all messed up. She doesn't remember her own name, much less what happened at the hospital that day."

Brandon wanted to punch that smug look off Wes's face. But while that might give him some temporary satisfaction, it wouldn't help Willa.

"You seem to know a lot about Ms. Marks," Brandon commented. It was a fishing expedition. He wanted to know if Wes was getting his info from anyone in SAPD.

But Wes didn't bite. A dry smile bent his mouth for several short seconds, and he aimed his finger at Brandon. "If Dean Quinlan gets in touch with you, my advice is not to believe a word he says."

"Why would he lie to me?"

"To cover his scrawny butt. I figure he screwed up something. He was a CSI after all. He screwed up something, and then tried to put the blame on anyone but himself." His finger landed against his own chest. "Well, that blame better not come anywhere near me. Got that?"

Wes didn't wait for Brandon's response. He turned and stormed out. Wes climbed into a sleek black limo waiting for him just outside and the driver took off.

"Never known a Christmas Eve like this one," Sheila grumbled. She pushed her dark, gray-threaded hair away from her face. "I swear, the phone's been ringing off the hook. Four messages in the past two hours—all from Dr. Lenora Farris."

Brandon cursed. "What does she want?"

"Same thing as the bozo who just left. She wants to talk to you. Says it's important. Says you're to return her calls ASAP." She lifted her hands in the air. "Don't these people have anything better to do over the holidays than pester us?"

Apparently not. "Did Dean Quinlan show up?"

"Not yet." She checked the clock on the wall. "Guess you want me to wait here until he does?"

"I do. Thanks, Sheila. But keep the door locked. I don't want just anyone waltzing in here unannounced."

The woman complained under her breath, as Brandon had known she would. She obviously didn't like being called into work on her off day, but she would stay. And she would do everything within her power to help him protect Willa. That was all he could ask for at the moment. But once this meeting with Dean was over, Brandon had to figure out his next move. It probably wasn't wise to stay around Crockett Creek now that both Wes and Dean knew he was there.

He walked back to his office where Pete was standing guard in the doorway. Willa was there, too, peeking out, and judging from her expression, she'd heard everything Wes had said.

"He's gone?" she asked.

Brandon nodded and tipped his head to Pete to get him moving as well. Pete went in the direction of the deputies' office on the other side of the reception desk.

Since Willa looked ready to collapse, Brandon pulled her into his arms. "Wes was just blowing smoke," he assured her. But the fact that he felt the need to blow smoke said a lot.

Wes was acting like a guilty man.

Of course, he had the strongest motive of all their suspects. If that had been his DNA underneath Jessie Beecham's fingernails, then Wes could have been convicted of murder. Now, the question was had he killed

Beecham and then orchestrated the hostage situation to cover it up?

If so, then Wes would almost certainly want Willa dead.

Brandon was about to offer Willa more reassurances, but movement stopped him. It hadn't come from the hall but from Willa's middle.

The baby was kicking.

He pulled back slightly and looked down.

"Soccer practice," Willa joked.

There was certainly a lot of movement, much more than he'd expected for an unborn child. And some of the kicks were hard, too. He could actually see the thumps against Willa's top.

Without thinking, Brandon slid his palm over her belly. And he froze. He shouldn't be doing this. This was something a real father should do, and it was far too intimate. More intimate than the hot kissing session they'd shared in his kitchen.

"Amazing, isn't it?" Willa asked.

Brandon made a sound that could have meant anything, and he jerked back his hand. "It must hurt."

"No," she insisted. She stared at him. "It's okay, Brandon. A touch doesn't commit you to anything. Kisses don't, either."

"But sex would," he mumbled before he could stop himself. Hell. What was wrong with him? First he couldn't control his hand, and now he couldn't control his mouth.

"Depends on the sex."

His gaze fired to hers, and he expected to see another of those teasing half smiles. But no smile. She looked dead serious. Then, she huffed.

"Sorry," she whispered. "I guess there's no such thing as no-strings-attached sex when it comes to us."

"No," he agreed.

He wanted to explain that he wasn't the father his baby deserved, but Willa had already heard it. It obviously hadn't sunk in because he still saw the welcoming look in her eyes. For a woman who distrusted nearly everyone, it was a powerful, and touching, burden to place on him.

Brandon heard someone knock. The sound came from the back where Willa and he had entered. He drew his gun, motioned for her to stay put and went to look out the sliver of a reinforced side window.

Thankfully, the man looked exactly like his photograph so Brandon had no trouble recognizing their visitor.

It was Dean Quinlan.

Dean's gaze was slashing all around the parking lot as if he expected someone to jump out and attack. Which might be close to the truth. Brandon didn't see any sign of a weapon, so he opened the door.

"What was Wes Dunbar doing here?" Dean demanded.

Brandon didn't even try to relieve the man's nerves. "Looking for you, I think."

Dean tried to bolt inside, but Brandon stopped and frisked him. He wasn't carrying concealed, but he did have an envelope gripped in his left hand.

Brandon stepped aside so the man could enter, but he kept himself between Dean and his office where he'd left Willa. Even though he was a good six inches shorter than Brandon, Dean tried to look over his shoulder.

"Did you tell Wes that I was coming here?" Dean asked. He continued to glance around, and there were beads of sweat on his forehead despite the chilly winter temperature outside.

"No. Did you?"

Dean looked at him as if he'd lost his mind. "Why would I tell a scumbag like him where I was? He could be the one who wants me dead." He paused. "Well, maybe it's him."

"You got more than one person trying to kill you?" Brandon asked.

"Maybe," Dean repeated and shook his head. "Look, someone's been trying to kill me, and I think it might be the same person who's after Willa Marks. There was a story in the newspaper about someone blowing up her house."

Brandon tried not to curse but failed. He was all for freedom of the press, but the less printed about Willa, the safer she might be.

"Who's trying to kill us?" Brandon heard someone ask. He groaned because it was Willa's voice and he heard her making her way toward them. He shot her a look, warning her to go back to his office.

She ignored him and kept her attention pinned to Dean.

Dean studied her a moment and then handed Brandon the envelope. Brandon didn't put away his weapon, and he handed the envelope to Willa so she could open it.

There was a single black-and-white picture inside.

It was a grainy photo taken in what appeared to be a parking lot, and it took Brandon a moment to figure out that he was looking at a picture of three people.

Wes Dunbar, Dr. Lenora Farris.

And Cash.

Ironically, it was the face of his old friend that was the clearest.

"I've been keeping an eye on Cash and Wes," Dean explained. "I thought one or both of them might be trying to set me up to take the fall for that hostage situation."

"Why would they do that?" Brandon wanted to know.

"Because I think Wes did kill Jessie Beecham, and I think that DNA sample in the lab would have proven it."

Brandon couldn't argue with that. "But why would Cash want to frame you?" He handed the picture to Willa so she could see it as well.

Dean gave Brandon another are-you-out-of-your-mind look. "I've checked on you, and I know you and Cash are old friends. But Cash isn't the man you knew way back when. He's friends with Wes now—did he tell you that?"

No. Cash hadn't. And Brandon wasn't sure he believed Dean. Still, there was the photo.

"That picture proves nothing," Willa said, probably sensing Brandon's conflicting emotions.

"It proves the three of them were together," Dean countered. "And I think they were together for one reason—to figure out how they could cover up the fact that Wes killed his old rival."

Brandon could see one huge flaw in that theory. "Then why involve Dr. Farris? If Wes wanted someone to cover up his crime, he would go to Cash or some other dirty cop."

"You don't know?" But it wasn't really a question, and Dean seemed more than eager to dole out this tidbit. "Dr. Farris and Wes are old friends. But she was also friends with Jessie Beecham. She was having an affair with Jessie around the time he was murdered."

Brandon wanted to kick himself. He'd been so involved in keeping Willa safe that he hadn't given this case the time and work it needed. Hell. Even though this wasn't his specific case, he was a lawman, and he should have done better. If he had, this investigation might already be over and the danger gone.

He glanced at Willa to let her know he was sorry, but he only saw skepticism in her eyes. Brandon had that same skepticism, but what he couldn't doubt was that Dean appeared completely confident that he was telling the truth.

Brandon would check every detail to make sure he was.

"If Dr. Farris was having an affair with Jessie as you say, then why would she want to help the person who possibly murdered him?" Brandon challenged.

"Hey, I didn't say she was in love with the man. She's been going back and forth between Wes and Jessie for years. She might not have been sleeping with Wes at the time of Jessie's death, but from what I've learned about her, she wouldn't want him to be arrested for a murder rap."

Dean wasn't painting a very good picture of Dr. Farris. And Cash must have known her background. Yet he'd brought her to that hotel suite to "help" Willa. Maybe the doctor had really come to see just how much Willa remembered. If so, that meant Dr. Farris could have been the one to alert Martin Shore.

"So, will you help me?" Dean asked. But he wasn't looking at Brandon, he was looking at Willa.

"Help you how?" she asked, wanting to know.

"Tell the cops that I had nothing to do with the hostage situation."

She shook her head. "I can't do that. The gunman—"

Brandon caught her arm to stop her from finishing. He didn't want Dean to know Willa had remembered the gunman trying to call him.

"It's time for you to leave," Brandon told the man.

"No." Dean volleyed glances between the two of them. "Not until she agrees to help me."

"She's not agreeing to anything." Brandon didn't wait for the man to concur. He let go of Willa so he could usher Dean out of the building. Brandon used more force than necessary, and he slammed the door in Dean's face and locked it.

Dean shouted out some profanity and threats, but he must have quickly remembered that only minutes earlier, Wes had been in the area. Brandon watched through the sidelight window as Dean scurried across the back parking lot and climbed into a white compact car.

Brandon turned to Willa to tell her they shouldn't stay put much longer, but she spoke before he could.

"I need access to a computer and the internet," she told him. "I want to search some files and see what I can learn about all the things Dean just told us."

Brandon had a laptop at his house, but now that Wes and God knows who else knew they were in the area, it might not be safe to stay there. At least at the station, he had the two deputies who could back him up in case something went wrong.

"How long will you need?" Brandon asked, checking his watch.

She shook her head. "I'm not sure. I think I remember how to hack into files."

Brandon knew this was illegal, but he didn't care. Right now, he only wanted to get to the truth, and he wanted that truth in the shortest time possible so he could get Willa out of there.

"You can use my office," Brandon told her. "And while you're doing that, I need to make some calls." He had to do some checking on Cash so he could make sure his old friend hadn't betrayed him.

But first things first, he wanted to call the Texas Ranger crime lab in Austin.

After Willa dropped the photo Dean had given them on Brandon's desk, she sat at his computer and started to tap away on the keys. Brandon worked his way through the Ranger organization and contacted Sergeant Egan Caldwell, a Ranger he'd worked with on several cases. It took Brandon nearly fifteen minutes to get through the explanation and his request. He believed there to be a leak in SAPD and he was asking the Rangers to conduct an impartial investigation into the DNA results from Jessie Beecham's murder.

The request and Sergeant Caldwell's agreement would no doubt cause waves. Now, the trick was to prevent those waves from placing Willa in any more danger.

Brandon made several more calls, searching for someplace to take her. He couldn't very well ask SAPD to provide a safe house, but he didn't have many options.

"I think I might have found something," Willa announced.

Brandon was about to hurry to the computer when he heard the knock at the front door.

"We're sure popular today," Sheila called back to Brandon a moment later. "Got two more visitors. Strangers at that. Should I let them in?"

"Not yet." Brandon drew his gun and started for the front, but he soon saw the two people standing on the other side of the reinforced glass door.

It was Cash and Dr. Farris.

Chapter 12

Willa was now certain of one thing. Nearly every one of their suspects knew where Brandon and she were. Martin Shore was the only one yet to make an appearance at Brandon's office, and she prayed he was far away from them.

She watched from the doorway of his office as Brandon "greeted" their latest visitors. Both Dr. Farris and Cash were visibly angry, but so was Brandon. Heck, so was she.

Especially after what she'd just learned about Dr. Farris.

Thank goodness her hacking skills were as sharp as ever. Willa might not remember key incidents of the past two months, but she obviously recalled how to worm her way into someone's personal information.

Now what she needed was some time to dig into the

other suspects' computer files. So far they hadn't had much time to do that.

There hadn't been time for much of anything.

They had both showered and changed their clothes before Pete had arrived to pick them up at Brandon's house. Brandon had replaced his jeans with a clean pair and put on a black shirt and leather jacket. Hardly Christmas colors but neither was Willa's cream-colored sweater. She hadn't had anything else clean to wear, which meant she was either going to have to do laundry soon or buy something new. Heaven knows when she would get the chance to do either.

"Let us in," Cash demanded. "It's freezing out here."

It was, and that probably explained why Cash and the doctor were huddled together. Both had their heads lowered, but the sleet was starting to come down.

"Are you two friends again?" Brandon asked Cash and the doctor, not keeping the sarcasm from his voice. "Because just a few hours ago, you thought Dr. Farris here might be supplying bad guys with information about Willa."

The doctor turned that frosty look at Cash. "No. We're not friends. And we didn't arrive together. I had no idea he was coming here until I saw him pull into the parking lot."

"I'm a cop," Cash reminded her. "I have a right to be here." He aimed his attention at Brandon. "Any reason you wouldn't tell me where you were?"

"Yeah. The reason is Martin Shore and his repeated attempts to kill Willa." Brandon kept a tight grip on his weapon, and he didn't move out of the doorway so the pair could fully enter the station.

"I'm trying to stop another attack," Cash insisted.

"That's why I've spent the past few hours looking for you. I got your address from the state database, but it wasn't in the GPS. I found the farm road and stopped and asked someone where your place was, but the person wouldn't tell me. He said it would be dangerous for me to try to get to your house anyway because you keep attack dogs."

Good. Brandon would thank all his neighbors first chance he got for keeping the location of his house a secret.

"It's cold," the doctor reminded Brandon. She shoved her hands in her pockets and bobbed on her tiptoes in an attempt to keep warm.

"Then if you want to get warm, my suggestion is talk fast so you can leave fast," Brandon told them, and it earned him more glares from the pair.

Dr. Farris looked past Brandon, and the doctor's gaze met Willa's. She grabbed the photo Dean had given them and walked closer. She kept the picture facing toward her in case Brandon wanted to withhold it for some reason. But she wanted them to see, and more than that, Willa wanted an explanation about why the three had been together.

"You shouldn't have left without speaking to me," Dr. Farris warned her. "The therapy session wasn't over, and I needed to debrief you so you could put all that you remembered in perspective."

Willa stopped next to Brandon. "I'd had all the perspective I could handle for one day. Plus, Shore was in the lobby waiting for us when we left. I don't suppose either of you would know why he was there?"

The doctor and Cash exchanged glances again and then shook their heads. "I have no idea why he was there," Cash insisted. "But maybe it's like Brandon suggested on the phone—Shore could have been following your PDA."

"My PDA was several buildings away in a parked car."

Cash shrugged. "Maybe Shore had already followed you by then. Maybe he saw you go into the hotel."

Willa couldn't totally discount that, but she didn't intend to trust Cash, either.

"You need to come back with me," the doctor insisted. "Or at least let me finish the session."

"Willa's not going anywhere with you," Brandon informed her. He took the photo from Willa and put it right in Cash's and the doctor's faces. "Got an explanation for this?"

Well, that got a reaction. The color drained from Dr. Farris's cheeks, and Cash cursed.

"Where did you get that?" Cash demanded.

"A concerned citizen. Now, would you like to tell me what was going on in this meeting?"

"Nothing," the doctor volunteered. "I was duped into being there."

"But Wes and you are old friends," Willa pointed out.

"*Former* friends," the doctor corrected. "I got a call from someone claiming to be Wes's assistant. The person—a man—told me that Wes had proof of who'd killed Jessie Beecham. I went, of course, because I wanted to know who was responsible so I could have the police arrest him. And when I arrived, Cash was there."

"I got a similar call," Cash continued. He stared at the photo. "So did Wes. It didn't take us long to figure out that we'd all been brought there under false pretenses. But we didn't know why someone would want to bring the three of us together." He paused. "Now, we know. It was to get this incriminating photo."

Again, that could be the truth, but Willa was glad Brandon wasn't letting them inside. It did make her wonder, though, if Dean Quinlan had set up the incriminating photo to throw blame off himself.

"Are you sure this meeting wasn't to figure out how to place the blame on the homeless man who's in jail for the murder?" Brandon asked.

Cash opened his mouth to speak, but it took him a few seconds to form the words. The anger tightened and twisted his face. "Brandon, you've got the wrong idea about me. I'm one of the good guys."

"Maybe," Brandon mumbled.

"There's more," Willa started and she glanced at Brandon to make sure it was okay to reveal what she had learned on her computer search. He had no idea what she knew, of course, since there hadn't been time to tell him, but Willa hoped that he would trust her not to spill anything that would only make this worse.

Brandon nodded.

And Willa met the doctor eye to eye. "Dr. Farris, you've come into a rather large sum of money recently."

The doctor placed her hand on her chest, and her mouth dropped open. "How would you know that?" But she shook her head and didn't wait for Willa to answer. "You invaded my privacy. You snooped on me. Well, it doesn't matter. The money was a gift from my grandfather."

"Really?" Willa questioned. "It came in seven different deposits, all just small enough not to alert the IRS. That's not usually the way people give gifts."

Cash and Brandon both gave the doctor a suspicious stare.

Dr. Farris huffed and made an adjustment to the collar of her coat so that it covered the back of her neck. "What? You think that money was some kind of payoff?"

"Was it?" Brandon asked. "Maybe Wes paid you off to keep quiet about him murdering your lover, Jessie Beecham?"

The doctor made a sound of outrage. "I don't have to listen to this. This conversation is over." And with that, she turned and started toward a sleek silver sports car that was parked just up the street.

One down, one to go.

But Cash didn't leave. Instead, his phone rang, and after glancing at the caller ID screen, he took the call. Brandon started to shut the door, but Cash held up his index finger in a wait-a-second gesture. Brandon did wait, but he leaned over and put his mouth to Willa's ear.

"We'll be leaving as soon as I'm done with Cash," he told her.

That didn't surprise Willa, but she had to wonder—where would they go now? Would it be safe enough to return to Brandon's house? Probably not. But then, she wasn't sure it was safe anywhere.

The baby kicked, as if in protest.

Cash ended his call and slapped his phone shut. "You called the Texas Rangers," he said to Brandon in an accusing tone.

"Yeah, I did," Brandon readily admitted. "I want

them to review Jessie Beecham's murder investigation, including the DNA samples."

"Those samples were tested after the hostage incident. They're clean."

"Then you should have no problem with them being tested again."

"You know I do." Cash's jaw was clenched so tightly that Willa was surprised he could manage to speak. "It'll make me look bad in the eyes of my superior officers." He cursed. "Hell, Brandon, you know how this works. Even if those tests hold up—and they will—there'll be questions about how I've handled this case."

Brandon took a step closer. "I need those questions answered. Willa and the baby are in danger, and I thought this was the fastest way to get to the truth."

"You could have come to me!" Cash practically shouted.

Brandon shook his head. "I'm not even sure I can trust you." He held up the picture to remind him of why. "Someone has been leaking info at SAPD, and I want to know who."

"Well, it sure as hell isn't me." Cash groaned and scrubbed his hand over his face. "Come on, we fought together side by side. I deserve the benefit of the doubt."

"No. I can't give you that. Not with Willa's safety at stake. And not until I know for sure who told Martin Shore the location of the safe house where Willa and I were nearly killed."

Cash's gaze flew to Brandon's. "Dr. Farris. She could be the leak."

Willa didn't intend to look so skeptical, but it certainly seemed as if Cash was saying anything to try to save his own skin. "How would Dr. Farris have had access to the information about the safe house?" she asked.

Cash pulled in a hard breath. "She might have gotten it from my computer."

"What?" Brandon snapped.

"I didn't give her the information," Cash quickly defended himself. "But it's possible she got it when I was away from my desk. She showed up about the time we were making the arrangements for the safe house. She said she had the DVD for the therapy and she wanted to get in touch with Willa. I had to leave my desk for a couple of minutes to see someone, and when I came back, Dr. Farris was in my chair, waiting."

"Waiting?" Willa repeated. "Then what makes you think she accessed the location of the safe house?"

"Because it was on my computer screen." Cash continued to explain even over Brandon's loud groan. "I don't remember leaving the file open. In fact, I could have sworn that I closed it."

Brandon got in his face. "And why are you just telling me this now?"

"Because I forgot about it. I haven't exactly been twiddling my thumbs since then. I've been trying to figure out who's after you."

"I don't want your help figuring that out," Willa let him know. She lifted her hand so Cash could see that she'd written Trust Brandon Ruiz on her palm. "Your name isn't on there for a reason. So, please, just leave me alone."

She thought Cash might argue with her. But he merely belted out some more harsh profanity, turned and walked away. Brandon immediately shut and locked the door.

"He's either innocent," Willa mumbled, "or he puts on a good show. Which is it?"

Brandon shook his head. "I wish I knew. But I don't regret calling the Rangers. In fact, I want to fax Sergeant Caldwell this photo that Dean Quinlan gave us and tell him it'd be in the best interest of the case to dig into Dr. Farris's financial records."

All of that was good, but a new investigation might take months to complete. She didn't have months. Her baby would arrive in about sixty days. Maybe it was some kind of early nesting instincts, but Willa wanted to be settled and soon.

But where?

And how?

She thought of the cash she had in several safety deposit boxes in San Antonio and Austin. She either had to get to one of them and start out someplace new, or…

She had to continue to rely on Brandon.

"What?" Brandon asked, probably noticing the renewed concern on her face.

She stared at him and remembered the kisses. The hot attraction. Willa remembered how much she wanted him.

And how much he was trying to keep his emotional distance from her.

That helped with her decision.

She checked the time. It was too late to make it to San Antonio or Austin before the banks closed, and tomorrow was Christmas. It would be the day after before she could get to her cash.

"On the twenty-sixth, I'll need to go to a bank in San Antonio," Willa told him. "You think you can get me there safely?"

He studied her as if trying to figure out what was going on in her head. And he probably would, too. Brandon seemed to be in tune with what she was thinking.

He clutched her shoulders and looked her in the eye. "I'll protect you both until this is over."

Yes, he would. She didn't doubt that. But this would take a heavy emotional toll on both of them. Because the longer she was with him, the more she wanted him. The more she started to spin a fantasy of them being together to raise this child growing inside her.

Rather than start an argument with him, Willa merely nodded, but she would get to the bank the day after Christmas, and she'd go off on her own again.

And her heart would be broken.

But she would have to deal with that later, after she was sure her baby girl was safe.

"I need to pick up some things from my house," Brandon told her. "Let me send this fax, and we'll get out of here."

She turned, ready to go back to his office, but the sound stopped her. It came in an instant with no warning.

A loud blast shook the building.

Willa gasped and automatically ducked down. However, it wasn't a shot. It took her a moment to realize that there had been an explosion.

She looked out the glass door and saw the flames and the debris in the building directly across the street. Oh, God. She knew that sound and recognized the destruction.

A grenade had gone off.

Chapter 13

"Get down!" Brandon yelled, not just to Willa but also to his two deputies who were still in the building.

Brandon pushed Willa to the floor and aimed his gun, but he had nothing to aim at. The diner on the other side of the street was in flames. Since it had closed early because of the holiday, there was no one inside. He couldn't see anyone milling around, either. That was the good news.

But someone or something had caused that explosion.

"You okay, Brandon?" Pete shouted.

"Yeah." Brandon glanced back at Pete who also had his weapon drawn. By his side, Sheila had done the same. "Call the fire department. I don't want that fire spreading to other businesses on Main Street. But tell them not to approach the area until they get an all-clear from one of us."

Brandon heard Sheila pick up the phone and do as he'd asked.

"There's a hired gun after Willa," he told them when Sheila had finished her call. "His name is Martin Shore. He's six-two, stocky build and has a military-style haircut. He's armed and dangerous."

"I don't see anybody," Pete relayed, and with his gun pointed toward the burning diner, he inched closer.

"Look harder," Brandon insisted. He whispered for Willa to stay down, and he levered himself up so he could look as well.

There was still no one visible on the street, but that didn't mean the assassin wasn't there.

Because Brandon had his attention fixed on the burning building, he saw the second explosion at the exact moment that he heard it. The blast tore through the fiery debris and what was left of the diner, and it sent a spray of fire and ashes right at them.

"What the hell is going on out there?" Pete grumbled as he dropped to the floor.

Hell was the appropriate word for what Shore was creating out there. The assassin might be trying to scare them or draw them out, and he was tearing up the town to do it. Of course, Brandon had to consider that the next grenade would be launched at the sheriff's office.

"Help me!" someone yelled.

With her breath gusting, Willa looked back at Brandon. "That's Wes Dunbar."

Yeah. And his shout had come from the front door.

"Let me in!" Wes demanded.

Not a chance. Brandon had no idea if Wes and Shore were partners in crime or if these latest explosions were a result of Wes working alone. And he didn't have time to find out.

"Are we going out there to make sure we don't have any injuries on our hands?" Sheila asked.

That would be standard procedure. It would also be procedure to identify the assailant's location and stop him from doing any more harm.

But Brandon looked down at Willa.

She was shaking and pale, obviously terrified. She had her hands over her belly. He had to try to end this as quickly as possible and get her out of there.

"Call the sheriff over in LaMesa Springs and have him send us some backup," Brandon instructed his deputies.

LaMesa was the town nearest to them, but it was still a good half hour away. By the time backup arrived, it could be too late. Shore might blow up the entire town to get to Willa.

"Sheriff Tanner and his deputy are on their way," Sheila relayed several moments later.

Another blast rattled the windows and sent them all ducking for cover. Outside, Wes banged on the door again and yelled for help.

"The SOB blew up the feed store," Pete spat out.

That did it. Brandon knew this wouldn't end until he stopped it. He got up from the floor despite the fact Willa was trying to pull him back down.

"Martin Shore is a hit man," she reminded him. "The minute you step outside, he'll try to kill you."

That was probably true, but if Shore managed to get close enough to the sheriff's office, he'd kill them all. Or try anyway.

"Brandon, I don't usually argue with what you plan

on doing, but I gotta argue with you now," Pete said. He glanced at Willa. "If this hired gun is after her like you say, then this is where he's headed. It'd be best if Sheila and I go out back and see if we can spot him."

"And maybe kill him," Sheila added.

Pete nodded. "And if he gets through us, at least you'll be here to protect her. I've got no stomach for a pregnant woman being at the mercy of a man who likes to toss grenades. Stay here, boss. And protect that woman and her baby."

Brandon wanted to argue. He wanted it to be him who went out the door and put his life on the line. That was actually his comfort zone. But protecting Willa and the child was also his duty, and they had to come first. Because Pete was right—Shore was almost certainly headed this way.

Brandon finally nodded, giving his deputies the okay.

"We're going out back," Sheila said without hesitation. "If I get a shot at him, I'm taking it."

Good. Because Sheila had solid aim, better than Pete's, and Brandon trusted her to do her job.

"What should we do about the guy yelling out front?" Pete asked.

"Steer clear of him," Brandon warned. "He could be in on this."

Pete nodded, and after Sheila and he put on their heavy jackets, they headed for the back door. Brandon followed them and watched as they made their exit, locking the door behind them. Shore wouldn't be able to get in that way without Brandon hearing him, but the place had eight windows in all. Each had wire mesh running through the glass so that would make it harder for anyone to break in.

Unless Shore bashed through one of them with a grenade.

"Should we stay here or go to your office?" Willa asked.

Brandon glanced around, trying to determine the best place for them to make their stand. Behind the reception desk might be their safest bet. He could see both the front and back doors from that position, and the large reinforced window at the front allowed him to watch what was happening on Main Street. And right now what was happening was the two fires.

He caught the movement from the corner of his eye and automatically shifted his gun in that direction. It had come from the right of the burning diner.

Brandon tried to pick through the thick black smoke to see if it was Shore. But it wasn't. It was a tall man wearing a suit, and Brandon didn't recognize him.

"Over here!" Wes yelled. And the suited man responded by waving. It was Wes's driver.

But what the heck were they still doing in town? Wes had stormed out of his office at least twenty minutes earlier and should have been long gone by now.

"I'm driving over there to get you," the man called out to Wes. He headed for his car.

But he didn't get far.

Something must have alerted him because he swung around and took aim at the other side of the car. In the same motion, he dropped, using the vehicle for cover.

Beneath him, Willa waited, and he could feel her pulse in every part of his body.

They didn't have to wait long.

Brandon saw the movement. So slight. At first, he thought it was a swirl of black smoke. But then he saw the man's hand.

And the gun he carried.

The man stepped out from the cover of the building near Wes's car, and he didn't take aim at the driver who was now on the ground.

He took aim at the window of the sheriff's office.

Right at Brandon.

And he fired.

Brandon pushed her down a split-second before Willa heard something slam into the window of the sheriff's office. She had no doubt that it was a bullet. She also had no doubt about who had fired it.

Martin Shore.

She'd caught just a glimpse of the assassin before Brandon had maneuvered her out of the semi-crouching position and flat on the floor. Well, as flat as she could manage. She was on her side with her hands covering her belly.

There was another thick blast, no doubt from another shot, but she didn't hear the sound of breaking glass. Maybe that meant the reinforced steel webbing was holding the window in place. It probably wouldn't hold for long, especially since Shore fired another shot.

She no longer heard Wes's frantic shouts for them to let him in. Maybe the man had wised up and gotten away from there.

Or maybe Shore had already killed him.

Until this attack, she had thought that maybe Wes had hired Shore to come after her, but after hearing Wes's reaction to the explosion, either he was extremely good at faking fear, or he was an innocent bystander in all of this.

Another bullet slammed into the window, and this time she did hear the glass crashing to the floor. She also felt the cold air start to spill into the building. Brandon didn't return fire. Maybe that's because he would have to fire through the window as well, and he perhaps didn't want to create an opening that Shore could use to shoot at them.

"Let's go," Brandon told her. "But stay down."

She did stay down. He didn't. Brandon rushed them to his office and got her inside, but instead of coming in with her, he stood in the hallway and took aim.

He was right in the line of fire.

There was another shot.

Then, another.

Where were the deputies? Why couldn't they get to Shore and stop him?

Her heart was pounding now, and Willa tried to force herself to calm down. This fear and anxiety might hurt the baby. But she couldn't discount the fact that all of them might die here today. And for what? To cover up what she'd been forced to do while she had been a hostage?

Or was something else going on here?

Brandon had positioned her on the side of his desk, but she could still see out the single window in the center of the wall. Willa kept watch, but she knew that Shore was still at the front because she could hear his shots.

"Stay down," Brandon told her.

And he fired.

That meant Shore had either destroyed the window or was maybe already inside.

She wanted to tell Brandon to get down as well and to be careful, but the movement outside the window caught her attention. It wasn't the deputies. Or Martin Shore.

It was Dean Quinlan.

He didn't appear to be armed, but he had his back pressed to the building next to them. What the heck was he doing out there?

"Brandon," she warned. "Dean's outside."

He stepped back into his office, and his gaze slashed to the window. He didn't take aim at the man but instead kept his gun in the direction of the last shot that had been fired.

She heard the sound of more breaking glass, followed by a heavy thud. Someone was trying to kick in the door.

Oh, God.

Shore was breaking in.

Willa spotted more movement outside the window. It was Pete, the deputy, and he went to Dean and pushed the man to the ground. Pete, too, kept his weapon aimed in the direction of the front of the building. Maybe, just maybe, Pete could get off a shot and stop Shore.

At least that's what she thought until she heard the next bullet.

It didn't come into the building but rather the narrow alley where Dean and Pete were. Pete dropped to the ground as well, but Willa couldn't tell if he'd been hit.

Brandon slammed his door and caught her shoulder to move her deeper into the room, next to a metal filing cabinet. Willa no longer had a clear view of Dean and Pete, but she did see something else.

"That's Wes's driver," she told Brandon.

The man came out from across the street and he had a gun in his hand. He took aim but she couldn't tell who or what he was aiming at.

Pete got back to his feet as well and aimed in the same direction as Wes's driver.

Everything seemed to happen at once. She heard the front door crack and give way. Brandon threw open his own office door and stepped into the hall, ready to kill the intruder.

Willa heard herself call out to him, but her words were drowned out by the sound of the shots. There seemed to be so many of them, all coming from different directions, and the combined blast was deafening.

She closed her eyes for just a second and prayed that Brandon hadn't been hurt.

When she looked out, Brandon was still standing. Thank God. He had his gun pointed toward the front door. So did Wes's driver. And neither man was moving.

"He's down!" Pete shouted.

Did Pete mean Shore? Relief flooded through her, but Willa reminded herself that he could have meant someone else. There had been a lot of shots fired in the past thirty seconds, and there were other people outside, not just Shore.

She waited with her breath held.

"You okay, boss?" Sheila called out.

Brandon glanced at Willa first. "We're okay," he answered.

Willa tried to see what was going on, but everyone

had left the alley. Brandon moved too and went toward the front of the station.

She followed him, terrified of what she might see and that Shore might still be standing out there ready to do what he had been hired to do.

The door was wide open, the wind battering it against the wall, and there were massive gaping holes in what was left of the window. She spotted Wes across the street. He was behind his driver. Or maybe a better word for the man would be *bodyguard* because that's what he seemed to be doing—protecting Wes. He had Wes positioned behind him as Brandon had her.

They inched closer, but Brandon didn't lower his gun.

Willa saw Pete and Dean to the right. Sheila was on the left. Both deputies had their weapons trained as well, but they were definitely converging toward the front door.

She soon realized why.

There was a pool of blood on the small concrete step directly in front of the door, and next to that pool lay Martin Shore.

"I had to shoot him," Wes's driver confessed. "He was about to put a bullet in your deputy."

Brandon stooped down and put his fingers to Shore's neck. Checking for a pulse. But Willa knew he wouldn't find one. Shore's blank eyes were fixed on the dull winter sky, and there was no life left in him.

No life and no breath.

And that meant he couldn't tell them who had hired him to kill her.

This wasn't over.

Chapter 14

Brandon couldn't get his mind to slow down. It was racing with the images and sounds of the latest attack. He could still hear the shots slamming through the glass, and the tremble of Willa's body.

And see the fear on her face.

Those were images that would stay with him for a lifetime.

Once again, she could have easily died, thanks to Martin Shore. And once again, Brandon hadn't been able to prevent her from being at the center of an attack.

His body seemed to be trying to keep up with his racing mind. He put himself on autopilot and tied up what loose ends he could at his office, but he was thankful when the neighboring sheriff, Beck Tanner, and his deputies agreed to take over the investigation so that Brandon could get Willa out of there. That couldn't have happened soon enough. He wanted the baby and her far away from the bullet holes, Martin Shore's dead body and especially away from the person who was responsible for sending Shore after her.

The problem was, Brandon still didn't know who that person was.

Even though Shore was dead and his body was on the way to the county morgue, they didn't know who had hired him.

And might never know.

He certainly couldn't eliminate any of their four suspects. Dean, Wes, Cash and Dr. Farris had all been in the area. And, yes, Wes's man had been the one to shoot and kill Shore, but Wes could have ordered him to do that so he could save his own butt. If Wes thought that Shore was about to be captured and taken into custody, he wouldn't have wanted to risk having the man spill his guts. No. Wes would have told his man to take Shore out.

That thought only caused him and his mind to race more, and when Brandon glanced down at the speedometer, he realized he was going a good twenty miles over the speed limit. Not a bright idea, since the sleet was making the roads slick. Worse, Willa had a white-knuckle grip on the armrest.

"Sorry," he mumbled. And he eased up on the accelerator a bit. Still, he didn't dawdle.

"Don't be. I'm not exactly anxious to be out in the open like this."

Yeah. He knew what she meant. They were literally out in the sticks, nearly eight miles from town and the chaos he'd left there, but Brandon knew that chaos had

a way of following them. That's why he had continued to check his rearview mirror throughout the drive.

"We can't stay at my house tonight," he reminded
her.

And soon, very soon, he'd need to ditch the car since
it was the one Pete had used to pick them up earlier.
Someone could recognize it. Unfortunately, it was the
sheriff department's only vehicle that hadn't been hit
with bullets in the attack.

"So where will we go?" she asked, checking the
side mirror as well.

Brandon had considered several possibilities—including a drive back into Austin or San Antonio. The
problem with that was the icy roads, and it was getting late. The sun was already close to setting, and that
would drop the temperatures even farther. He didn't
want to risk getting into an accident.

Plus, there was no one he truly trusted in either of
those places.

If they went to either city, they would have to check
into a hotel, and while he had the cash stashed at home
to do that, paying with cash might alert a curious desk
clerk who might in turn alert the police. Brandon figured if Wes had heard about the attacks on Willa, then
it had likely been on the news. This latest attack and
Shore's death would be reported as well, and the press
would be able to come up with photos. Their faces
could be plastered on the pages of every newspaper
in the state.

And that brought him back to their temporary sleeping arrangements.

"There's a fishing cabin on the back part of my
property," he told her. He turned onto the road that

led to his house, and he saw the dogs race out to greet them. "There's no electricity, but I do have a generator. We can stay there tonight and then figure out tomorrow where we should go."

"Or you could just drop me off somewhere and put some distance between us." She said it so softly that it took a moment to sink in.

"You think I'd leave you?" He hadn't intended to sound so angry, but damn it, that riled him.

"I think it would be smart for you to do that. Right now, the person who hired Shore is looking for *us*. As in the *two* of us. If we split up, he or she will be looking only for me." She shook her head. "And we both know it's me they're really after."

Brandon brought the car to a stop, not in front of his house, but he parked inside the garage, and he used the remote control to shut the door. While it ground to a close, he turned in the seat to face her. "Let's get something straight. I'm not leaving you." Well, not until he was positive she was safe.

The look in her eyes told him that she understood that last unspoken part.

He cursed and reached for the car door. "Come in with me to get some things."

Because he sure didn't want her waiting in the car alone. It had been chilly before, but it was bitterly cold now, and that along with the possible danger caused them to rush inside. He locked the door and set the security system even though he only planned to be there for a half hour or so.

"Don't turn on the lights, but if you want to wash up, you'd better do it here," Brandon let her know. He tried to take the anger out of his voice but failed. Hell. She had actually thought she could talk him into dumping her so he could save himself. "There won't be any hot water at the cabin."

No hot water. No heat other than the fireplace. No bed, just a single army-style cot. And no comforts of home. It wouldn't be an ideal place to spend what was left of Christmas Eve.

He grabbed his old duffel bag and headed to the linen closet so he could grab some bedding. The place wasn't exactly pitch dark, yet, but he had a little trouble locating the thermal blankets. When he finally got them, he shoved them into the bag and then started for the kitchen.

Willa stepped out in front of him.

"You're mad at me," she said, "but you have to admit I'm sort of like Typhoid Mary right now. There really is no reason for both of us to be in danger."

Oh, yes, there was. Brandon put his hand on her stomach to remind her. He'd intended for it to be a quick touch, but he held it there.

There was just enough light left that he could see her face. Willa stood there looking at him, and her right eyebrow lifted as if questioning him as to what he was about to do.

Brandon had no idea.

He just knew that touching Willa wasn't a good idea. Still, even with the danger and his anger, he didn't stop and didn't pull back. They both seemed to be waiting to see what would happen next.

And what happened next was that he snapped his arm around her, pulled her to him and kissed her. He wasn't gentle. He didn't give her a chance to change her mind and pull away. Brandon just took what was right there in front of him.

Maybe he meant this as some kind of reassurance that he would be there for her. But Brandon cursed himself. This didn't have anything to do with reassurances. He'd been burning to kiss Willa since their last kissing session had ended. He wanted her, and there was no logical explanation for it other than she got him hot.

She curved her hand around the back of his neck and moved as close as she could get. Because of the pregnancy, they weren't exactly body to body, but they were plenty close enough for Brandon to deepen the kiss. He didn't taste the fear or the adrenaline from the attack.

He only tasted Willa.

Man.

That taste went straight through him.

Brandon realized he was trying to get even closer to her when Willa's back hit the wall. That stopped him a moment because he wanted to make sure he wasn't being too rough with her. But Willa merely latched on to a handful of his shirt and pulled him right back to her.

The kiss got even hotter.

They couldn't keep this up. Soon, very soon, their bodies would demand more. They would demand sex. And Brandon knew he had to try to keep a clear head. Plus, having sex with Willa wouldn't be fair since they would no doubt be going their separate ways.

Or would they?

Maybe the scalding kisses were melting his brain because Brandon realized they couldn't entirely go their separate ways.

Hell.

When had that happened?

When had he decided that he would want to see this baby after she was born?

He pulled back again, blinked. And he tried to gather the strength to stop this so he could think. But he saw Willa again. Her mouth was slightly swollen from the hard kisses, and her breath was fast and thin. But that wasn't a "let's stop" look in her eyes.

No way.

Those heavy-lidded eyes were sending out an invitation that his body had no trouble understanding. She wanted to have sex with him and she wanted it now.

Brandon wanted that, too, and there was no amount of willpower that would stop him from taking her mouth again. Willa made a sound of relief. Maybe even victory. And she melted into the kiss.

Her arms went around him, and she fought to get closer. Hard to do but not impossible. Brandon slid his hand between them and shoved up her sweater so he could touch her breasts. She was perfect. Full and round. He'd always been a sucker for a curvy woman, and the pregnancy had obviously left Willa's breasts ripe for the touching.

So, that's what Brandon did.

He shoved down the cups of her bra and circled her nipples with his fingers. Willa obviously approved because she made more of those sounds of pleasure and relief.

Brandon felt no relief. Every touch was like fire to his blood, and he felt that fire course through him. He was already hard and ready for her, but that need skyrocketed when he lowered his head and took her right nipple into his mouth.

"Yes," she mumbled.

That *yes* slammed through him as much as the kisses had done. Maybe more. His body began to demand that he do something about the powder keg that was building inside him.

His mouth went back to hers for a hard, punishing kiss, and he shoved his hand into the waist of her pants and into her panties.

He found her, hot and wet, and he groaned because that wouldn't help any shred of resolve he had left. No. It told him what he already knew.

That he was going to have her.

Here and now.

It didn't have to make sense. It didn't even have to be right. But it would happen.

Brandon scooped Willa up into his arms and headed for the bedroom.

Willa was aware that she was moving, but she didn't care where Brandon was taking her. She only cared about one thing—finally making love with Brandon.

She'd been burning for him since the moment she laid eyes on him. Lust at first sight. But it seemed to be a lot more than just lust. She'd never felt this intensity. Never wanted a man more than her next breath.

However, Brandon seemed to have set a new benchmark.

Even though he hurried to the bedroom, he was gentle when he lay her on the bed. The old-fashioned feather mattress swelled around her, cocooning her in its softness. Brandon followed on top of her, using his forearms to keep his weight from bearing down on her belly. He wasn't soft. He was all sinew and muscle.

All man.

He continued to kiss her, and he set fires wherever his mouth touched her. On her neck. On the tops of her breasts. He kissed her through the fabric of her top. At first. But she wanted his lips and breath on her skin so Willa fought to shove up her top and open her bra.

Brandon took her exactly the way she wanted to be taken.

This foreplay was sweet torture, but the kisses only made her want more.

Since it would almost certainly take some maneuvering for them to have more, Willa turned, shifting their positions so that she was on top. Her sweater had to go so she peeled off both it and her bra and tossed them aside.

In the back of her mind, she considered that she probably didn't look very sexy, but that didn't seem to bother Brandon. He pushed down her stretchy pants, exposing her belly and giving him access to her panties.

He touched her again. Watched her. And while Willa straddled him, she watched him, too. Brandon was lost in the fire, his eyes hot with need. And that need only fueled hers. He had on too many clothes for sex, and she wanted him naked.

His coat came off easily, but she struggled with his holster and gun. Brandon stopped his own attempts to get her out of her pants so he could help. His hands and fingers that had been so clever touching her now seemed rushed and awkward. Willa felt awkward and cursed when she couldn't get his jeans unzipped.

Brandon placed his hand over hers, sliding down the zipper so that Willa could touch him the way he had touched her. Even though the lights were off, she could still see his face. She could see what her touch did to him, and even though she hadn't thought it possible, she burned even hotter for him.

He was clearly ready for sex so Willa saw no reason to wait. She couldn't wait. Her mind and body were racing, pushing her toward the relief that suddenly felt as necessary as life itself.

His hands were rushed again. So was his breath. His breath gusted, his chest pumping as if starved for air. Brandon got her pants and panties off, and he didn't waste even a second of time.

Neither did Willa.

Since she was still straddling him, she was in the perfect position to move this to the next level. She lowered herself, taking him into her body. Inch by inch. Until she had him fully inside her.

The pleasure blurred her vision and sent her heart racing.

Over the past two days, her heart had been doing a lot of racing, but for the first time, it was due to pleasure and not fear. And there was no doubt about it—this was pleasure in its purest form.

She moved. Brandon did, too. He caught her hips to set the rhythm of the strokes inside her. It was too fast. Too frantic. Too intense to last. But Willa wasn't interested in prolonging this. Not this time, anyway. Maybe some other time they could have a long leisurely afternoon of lovemaking. But this time, she needed him too much to want anything but completion.

Brandon didn't try to slow things, either. He continued to take them both to the only place they wanted to go.

Willa locked gazes with him as their bodies found the perfect rhythm and pace to create exactly what they needed. He moved faster. Harder. The grip he had on her hips tightened and everything honed in on that one moment. That one prize that was just seconds within their reach.

"Do something about this," she heard herself mumble.

Brandon did something about it all right. He lifted his hips, pulling her down onto him for one last hard penetrating stroke.

And that was it.

That was all it took.

It was exactly what she needed to go spinning over the edge. Her body closed around him, as he pulled her to him. Close and tight in his arms.

With her heartbeat echoing in her ears and her breath filling the room, she still heard him. She heard what he said at the moment of his surrender.

Brandon whispered her name.

Chapter 15

Even though Brandon's body wanted to stay put with Willa in his arms, the sane and logical part of his brain kicked in. Thank goodness. Because it just wasn't a smart idea for them to linger there and enjoy the moment.

And what a moment.

Later, and probably a lot sooner than he wanted, he would regret this. The timing was all wrong.

Hell.

The sex itself was wrong, too.

He shouldn't have taken Willa as if he had a right to do that. He had no rights. He'd given her no hope of a future, only the pity story of his biological father.

All of that seemed, well, pointless right now. But that was probably because he'd just had the best sex of his life. His body wanted to have her all over again.

His body wanted him to stay inside her and stare up at her beautiful face.

But thankfully, his brain reminded him of the danger.

Brandon eased her off him, and Willa slumped onto the mattress. She was obviously trying to catch her breath, and he wondered if this had been too much for her. He didn't know anything about having sex with a pregnant woman.

"Are you okay?" he asked.

She smiled, maybe to soothe the alarm on his face and in his voice, and she slid her hand around the back of his neck to pull him to her for a kiss. It wasn't a peck. It was the kiss from a woman who was definitely interested in round two. Because that couldn't happen—well, not right now anyway—Brandon ended the mouth-to-mouth contact and got up from the bed so he could dress.

"We have to leave," he reminded her.

Willa groaned, and that sound went right through him. Resisting Willa was next to impossible. Still, he resisted. And Brandon put on his shorts and jeans before his body talked him into getting back in that bed with her.

She got up, too, and the smile didn't leave her face while she dressed. Well, it didn't until she caught him staring at her belly.

"Sorry," she mumbled, quickly pulling on her pants. "Sometimes, I forget just how big I am."

"You're not *big,* you're pregnant. You're supposed to be this size."

And because he thought they both could use it, he slid his hand over her stomach, over the baby, and he kissed her. Like Willa's kiss, it wasn't a peck, either. It turned hot way too fast, but Brandon ended it before it became the start of more mind-blowing foreplay.

"After what just happened, you must know I'm attracted to you," he said against her mouth.

"Even with the pregnant belly?" she questioned.

Especially with the pregnant belly. But since that made him sound like some kind of pervert, Brandon just settled for a nod.

"I need to pack us some food," he hurriedly added. *Keep your mind on the task and get your hands off Willa.* "When we leave tomorrow, there might not be any stores or restaurants open."

He put his holster and jacket back on and headed to the kitchen. Willa could probably use a few minutes alone anyway. To freshen up.

To deal with her regrets.

Brandon was sure she would have them eventually. After all, he might be her baby's father, but he had more baggage than she needed.

He grabbed a plastic bag from beneath the sink and filled it with some granola bars, apples and bottled water. It was hardly the makings of a Christmas dinner, but he hadn't planned on holiday food. If things had been normal, he would have settled for a turkey sandwich while covering the office so that Pete and Sheila could spend the day with their families.

Families.

That word caused him to take a deep breath. Soon, very soon, he had to work out what that meant to him as far as Willa and the baby were concerned.

While he slapped together two turkey sandwiches, Brandon glanced out the kitchen window above the sink. The sun had just set, but he could see and hear the sleet pinging against the glass. It would be a slow, hazardous drive out to the cabin, but there was no way he would make Willa walk the two-plus miles in this weather.

He heard a sound and first thought it was the rustling of the trees in the wind, but he looked closer. Despite the sleet, the oaks near the house were practically still.

An uneasy feeling went through him, and he set the bread aside so he could get a better look. However, he stepped back from the window. Far back and kept in the shadows. And he waited.

Brandon saw it then.

The car.

It was just up the road, probably no more than a hundred yards from the house. There were no headlights, and the car was dark colored. With the clouds covering the moon, he might not have spotted it at all if it hadn't been for the vehicle's parking lights.

His stomach went to his knees.

This couldn't be good. If Sheila, Pete or any of the other townsfolk were coming to see him in this weather, they wouldn't have turned off their headlights. No. There was only one reason to do that.

So the driver could sneak up on them.

"Willa?" Brandon softly called out to her. He tried to keep his voice calm while he kept an eye on the car. It was definitely moving closer, inching along at a snail's pace.

But eventually the driver would arrive at the house.

Brandon was betting whoever that driver was, he or she would be up to no good.

"Yes?" Willa answered.

He heard her footsteps leading out of the bedroom and toward the kitchen. But what he didn't hear were the dogs. If anyone or anything had gotten close to the house, Butch and Sundance would have alerted him. They'd be barking their heads off.

So, why hadn't his dogs sounded the alarm?

Brandon wasn't sure he wanted to know the answer to that.

"Are we ready?" Willa asked, walking into the kitchen. But she froze the moment she saw Brandon. That was probably because he'd drawn his gun. "What's wrong?"

He really hated to tell her this. She'd already been through too much. But he couldn't exactly keep this from her, either. "Someone's out there."

She gasped, hurried to him and followed his gaze out the window. "Who is it?"

Brandon shook his head. "It's my guess that the driver isn't paying a friendly visit."

"Oh, God." And she frantically started looking around the kitchen.

For a moment Brandon thought she might be on the verge of panicking, but he soon realized she was looking for a knife. She found one in the drawer and pulled it out.

"There's a gun on top of the fridge," he let her know. And while he didn't like the idea of Willa being armed, he didn't like the alternative any better.

Besides, things could turn ugly fast, and she might need to defend herself.

She fished around on the fridge and came up with

the Smith & Wesson. It was loaded, and thankfully she treated it that way. She kept it pointed toward the floor.

"Where are the dogs?" she asked.

Brandon had to shake his head again. "I didn't hear any gunshots," he added. Though Willa likely knew that someone could have used a silencer.

It cut at Brandon's heart to think of someone harming his pets, but right now he had to put all his focus on protecting Willa.

"Check the security system panel by the front door and make sure the red light is on," he told Willa. "And stay away from the windows."

She scurried away and Brandon kept watch. The car came even closer but stopped just on the other side of his mailbox. The doors didn't open, and he saw no signs of the driver trying to exit.

It was possible that the person didn't know they were inside. After all, their car was parked in the garage with the door down, and they hadn't turned on any lights. Maybe, just maybe, if he could hide with Willa, the driver would assume the place was empty and leave.

Brandon wasn't sure he wanted that to happen. Part of him wanted to confront this SOB who could be responsible for hiring Shore to come after Willa. But if he could avoid a gunfight with Willa around, then that had to be his first option. No bullets meant Willa and the baby would be safe for another day.

Until the next confrontation.

"The red light is on, and the system is armed," Willa said, coming back into the room. "What do we do now?"

It was risky to stay inside because the person could

try to blow up the house. But it would be an even bigger risk to go outside.

Brandon considered the garage. They could get in the car and wait as they had at the safe house. But that wasn't without risks, either, especially since he would have to disarm the security system for them to go through the mudroom door and into the garage. Plus, there was a door at the back of the garage that led to the yard. He was certain he had locked it, but locks could be easily broken.

"For now, we'll wait here, inside," he whispered.

Brandon moved Willa to the side of the fridge and positioned himself in front of her. They were now out of range of the window, but he could see the back door, and if he peered around the fridge, he could see the front one as well. Thankfully, with the exception of the exterior garage, all the doors and windows were wired with the security system so it should go off if someone tried to break in.

If that happened, they would have to go with Plan B.

He would try to get Willa to the garage so he could take down this person who was hell-bent on trying to kill them.

Behind him, he could hear Willa's shallow breathing, but that, the sleet and the hum of the fridge were the only sounds in the room. Maybe that's why it wasn't hard for him to hear the car door. It was slight, as if someone was trying to ease it shut, but Brandon still heard it.

He braced himself for whatever was going to happen next. At best, the person might just leave or there'd be a knock at the door. Maybe it was someone lost and having car trouble.

But Brandon didn't think this was an "at best" kind of situation.

The seconds crawled by, and Brandon continued to wait. There were no more sounds of car doors. Not even any footsteps.

Still, he didn't relax.

Good thing, too.

The sound of the shot blasted through the house.

Willa choked back a gasp and took aim in case she had to return fire. But Brandon obviously didn't want her to do that because he pushed her even farther back so that she was against the wall.

With him in front of her.

Protecting her, again.

How many more times was he going to have to put himself in danger like this?

If she hadn't been pregnant, if she had only herself to worry about, Willa would have considered making her own stand. She was exhausted and spent from these attacks, and one way or another, she just wanted them to be over. But she couldn't just step out from cover. She had to think of her baby girl.

Brandon took his cell from his pocket and passed it back to her. "Call Pete. His is the first number."

Though her hands were shaking and she was trying to keep a firm hold on the gun, Willa made it to his list of recent calls and pressed the call button. She held her breath and waited for Pete to answer. She also waited for another sound from their attacker.

But nothing.

Not from their attacker. Nor from Pete. He didn't answer the call, and it went to voice mail.

"Pete didn't answer," she whispered, automatically moving on to Sheila's number who was next on the phone list. Willa tried it as well, but there wasn't an answer from Sheila, either.

Something was wrong. Even though it was Christmas Eve, one of them should have answered.

And why hadn't the dogs barked? As frightened as Willa was of them, she wished the Dobermans were there to protect them. They'd need all the help they could get.

"Sheila didn't answer?" Brandon asked, his voice barely audible.

"No. Should I try anyone else?" But as she was asking, she looked at the list of names and numbers. Since this was his prepaid cell, it obviously didn't include his normal list of contacts. With the exception of Cash, there wasn't anyone else, and they obviously couldn't call him.

Or anyone else in SAPD.

There was another shot and, while Willa had thought she was prepared to hear it, the sound still sent a stab of fear through her. Still, she wouldn't let that fear immobilize her. She had a gun, and even though she wasn't sure she knew how to use it, that wouldn't stop her.

"He's shooting at the lock on the front door," Brandon mumbled.

So that explained why there'd been no sound of breaking glass. And there were no indications of the door opening, either. That was something at least. The person hadn't actually managed to get inside.

So, who was out there?

Cash, maybe. Or Wes, Dr. Farris or even Dean. All of them had motive to keep her silent, and it was entirely possible that one or more of them had teamed up against Brandon and her. All four of them potentially had a lot to lose if she ended up testifying about what had gone on in that lab the day of the hostage incident.

Of course, she had to stay alive to be able to testify.

"Call nine-one-one," he instructed. "Ask for help from the county sheriff's office over in Saddle Springs."

God knows how far away that was, but they needed some kind of backup. She quickly pressed in the numbers, and the dispatcher answered on the first ring.

"I'm Willa Marks," she told the dispatcher. And then she realized she didn't have the address. "I'm at Sheriff Brandon Ruiz's residence near Crockett Creek, and we have an intruder. Send someone immediately."

Since she didn't want her voice to give away her location to the person trying to break in, Willa didn't hang up, but she didn't say anything else.

There was another shot, and this one was different from the other two. It sounded as if the bullet had smacked against something metal.

Maybe the lock? Or maybe it was just the brass doorknob.

The emergency dispatcher continued to talk, asking Willa for details about what was going on. Because the questions were coming from the other end of the line, they weren't loud. But they could still be heard. Willa closed the phone and hoped the dispatcher wouldn't have any trouble relaying the request for immediate help.

Willa heard the sound then. A slight creaking noise. She thought it might have come from the hinges on the door, but she prayed she was wrong.

But she wasn't.

Seconds later, she felt the cold winter air slice through the kitchen.

Oh, God.

Someone had opened the front door.

Chapter 16

Brandon didn't take the time to curse himself for staying too long at his house. But he would do that later. Right now though, he apparently had a fight on his hands.

He eased a fraction away from the fridge so he could get a better look at the front door.

It was open.

He didn't see an intruder and didn't hear footsteps so that could mean the person was lurking on the porch. Bullets could easily come through the window and make their way to Willa and the baby.

Who was out there?

Who was doing this to them?

Brandon desperately wanted to know, but he didn't want that knowledge at Willa's expense. Nor did he want to start a gun battle. Right now, his best bet was to wait. To listen. And to try to get off the shot that would put an end to this.

He glanced back at Willa to make sure she was okay. She looked scared but determined, and she still had hold of the gun she'd taken from the top of the fridge. Good. Because he might need her help.

Finally, he heard the footsteps. It was hard to tell because of the wind howling, but he was pretty sure the intruder was still on the porch. For now, anyway. Those footsteps seemed to be leading straight into the house.

Brandon got ready, and took aim at the front door. He wouldn't have but a split second to identify the person and then shoot, and he couldn't risk not getting off the first shot.

He heard another step. Then, another. But he also heard something else.

A car engine.

He tried turning his ear to the sound, but he couldn't figure out if it was coming from the intruder's vehicle or if someone else had just driven up.

Hell.

He hoped this SOB hadn't brought an accomplice.

Brandon spotted the movement in the doorway, and his finger tightened just slightly on the trigger. He was ready. Too ready. Every muscle and nerve in his body was primed for the fight, but the intruder didn't show his face. He stayed there, in the shadows.

Waiting for Brandon to make the first move.

That wouldn't happen. He had Willa in a protected position right now, and he wasn't going to change that unless it was absolutely necessary.

The seconds ticked off again, but there were no more

footsteps. No sounds of a car engine, either. Just the brutal wind and the central heating that had kicked in.

Brandon definitely felt the chill in the air, and behind him, Willa started to shake. Her teeth weren't chattering, yet, but it was close. It hadn't taken but a couple of minutes for the inside temperature to plunge, and with the front door wide open, there was no way the heat could neutralize all that cold air gushing in.

Of course, the intruder was out in the cold, too, and Brandon hoped like the devil that it affected the person's aim and judgment.

There was no movement. No warning. Definitely no footsteps. And even though Brandon was ready for an attack, the sound still surprised him.

A bullet came through the living room window.

The sound blasted through the entire house. So did the shattering glass. The bullet slammed into the kitchen wall by the sink. Not exactly close to Willa and him. A good six feet away. But it was close enough for Brandon to know he had to return fire.

He came out from cover and sent a shot right back through the front window.

Brandon didn't stay in the open. He couldn't. He had to move back into place so that he would be in front of Willa. And once he was there, he waited, praying he'd managed to shoot the intruder.

But there was no indication of that.

Definitely no moan of pain. No body dropping to the porch.

Several seconds later, another shot came roaring into the kitchen. There was no six feet of space this time. The shot came damn close to the fridge.

The third shot came even closer.

"Stay down," he whispered to Willa. Brandon didn't leave cover, but he sent two shots of his own right back at their attacker.

Glass spewed from what was left of the window, but that didn't slow the assault. More bullets came, each of them tearing through his house and coming right at them.

Brandon had no choice but to pull Willa to the floor.

The new position took him out of firing range since there was furniture in between his line of sight and the window. But that same furniture was in the way of the shooter as well. Brandon hoped it would be enough to keep Willa safe.

More bullets came. Four of them. Each were thick blasts that rocketed his adrenaline and put him in fight-or-flight mode. Unfortunately, he needed to take the flight option because of Willa. This person obviously wasn't going to come out in the open so that Brandon would have a clean shot, and this guy wasn't worried about running out of ammunition.

Brandon was.

He couldn't go bullet for bullet in this fight.

"Stay low on the floor," he whispered to Willa. "We're going to the garage."

Yes, it was a risk, but at this point, staying put seemed the biggest risk of all.

Brandon kept himself positioned in front of her, and Willa crawled to the other side of the fridge. He fired another bullet at their attacker and hoped the single shot would buy them a few seconds of time.

It worked.

The person didn't fire any other shots until Willa was near the mudroom door that led out to the garage. Brandon wasn't quite so lucky though. The shot came right at him, and even though he was low on the floor as well, the bullet sliced through the sleeve of his jacket. Well, hopefully it was just the sleeve. He didn't have time to look and see if the bullet had grazed him.

He hurried, trying to get Willa away from the kitchen window. Even though the attacker would have to run from the porch to that particular part of the kitchen, Brandon didn't want to wait around for another attack. He got Willa to her feet and opened the mudroom door so he could get her into the garage.

"What now?" she asked. She was still shivering, and Brandon prayed this stress and all the running around weren't harming the baby.

He glanced at the car and knew he had left the keys in the ignition. He could try to drive them out of there, but since the shooter was out front, that would almost certainly put them right back in the line of fire.

Plus, there was the possibility of a second vehicle. An accomplice who might be blocking the road to prevent them from getting away.

"We're going out back," Brandon whispered.

He tipped his head to the rear door that led into the backyard. Beyond that was a small barn and then the thick woods that made a semicircle around his property. If worse came to worst, there were plenty of hiding places in those woods. However, it would put Willa out there in the freezing night. Thank God she had on her coat, but that probably wouldn't be enough eventually.

No. He had to end this soon.

With his gun still drawn, Brandon unlocked and eased open the door. He peeked out but didn't see any signs of the shooter. He didn't want to wait to give the person time to get around the house, either. Or time to get to Willa and him. It was a good twenty feet to the barn, and the woods were another twenty feet or more beyond that.

"Let's go," he told Willa.

Brandon kept watch all around them. Or at least that's what he tried to do. Hard to cover all the shadows and places a killer could hide and launch a new attack. So, he focused on hurrying to get them to the side of the barn. They reached it.

Just as a bullet came their way.

Hell. The shooter had moved to the backyard and had a visual on them.

Brandon pulled Willa to the ground. The dirt was rock-hard frozen, so he tried to break her fall with his arm.

It wasn't a second too soon because the bullets slammed into the side of the barn. Not one shot but four before the gunman stopped.

Was he moving to a new position?

Brandon glanced out but couldn't see anyone. Worse, the wind was even louder outside so he wasn't even sure he could hear approaching footsteps. All he could do was wait and pray for a safe opening to get Willa into the woods.

"There," Willa whispered. Her voice was frantic enough that Brandon glanced at her to see where her attention and index finger were aimed.

She was pointing at the kitchen door, specifically at the small sidelight window.

He saw the movement. Inside the house.

Brandon shook his head. How the hell had the person gotten inside so quickly? Just seconds earlier, the shots had come from the right exterior side of the house.

Maybe this was an accomplice?

There was no way the county sheriff could have already made it out here.

Brandon's gaze fired all around, in case this was some kind of ploy to distract him. He damn sure didn't want the shooter sneaking up on them.

There was more movement from the sidelight window, and from the corner of his eye, Brandon saw the back door ease open.

With his heart in his throat, he levered himself up a little and took aim.

He didn't fire, just in case this was indeed the county sheriff. Instead, he waited.

Behind him Willa waited, too, and he thought he heard her mumble a prayer. Good. Because they might need divine intervention to get through this.

The door opened all the way, and Brandon saw the hand then. Whoever was in his kitchen was holding a gun.

Brandon watched as the figure stepped onto the porch.

It was a man, and like Brandon, he had his gun ready to fire.

"Brandon?" the man called out.

Hell.

And Willa obviously recognized him, too, because she cursed.

Sergeant Cash Newsome was on the porch.

That barely had time to register in Brandon's mind when the next shot rang out.

* * *

Willa caught just a glimpse of Cash a split second before Brandon dropped back down in front of her. But a glimpse was all she needed to know that Cash was close enough to them to deliver a fatal shot.

If that was his intention.

Brandon fired in the direction of the shooter—still on the right rear of the house. The blast echoed in her ears. Because of her own pounding heartbeat, she was already having trouble hearing, and that certainly didn't help. However, Willa didn't need to hear to know that Brandon and she had to get out of there fast. With the shooter—and now perhaps Cash—they were outgunned. Sure, she had a gun, but she didn't trust her shooting skills against a cop.

"Brandon, Willa, I'm here to help you!" Cash called out.

Thank God Brandon didn't buy that because he began to scoot her toward the back side of the barn.

Away from Cash.

Hopefully, away from the other shooter, too.

There was another shot, but because Brandon was in the way, she couldn't see where this one landed. However, she heard Cash curse. He said something, too, something drowned out by the next shot.

Was this some kind of ploy by Cash to make them think he was innocent, or was he under fire just like them?

Brandon didn't wait to find out.

He got them to the back of the barn, keeping them right at the corner, probably so they could duck around the side if the shooter came at them from either direction. The problem with that was ducking to the side could put them in Cash's sight again.

"We're going to the woods," Brandon whispered. "Stay behind me."

The woods. Well, at least there were plenty of huge trees that could hopefully absorb the bullets—she had no doubts that shooter would continue to fire at them.

Maybe Cash, too.

She got behind Brandon as he asked, and they started to walk backward toward the woods. Willa kept her gun ready and prayed she could do some good with it if it came down to the shooter or them.

The wind howled and slapped at them, and it robbed her of what little breath she had left. Still, she tried to keep walking, hurrying, while she kept watch all around them. Brandon kept watch, too, and he kept volleying his gun between the porch where Cash was and the general area where the shooter had fired the last shot.

Willa felt something soft but solid bump against the lower back part of her leg, and she nearly let out a yelp. She also tried not to trip, especially when Brandon walked right into her.

She risked glancing at what was on the ground and spotted one of the dogs.

Oh, God.

At first, she thought he was dead, but then she saw his chest pumping. The Doberman was taking in quick, shallow breaths.

"Someone drugged him," Brandon mumbled. He turned, caught Willa's arm and practically ran with her to the nearest tree.

They ducked behind it.

"Will your dog be all right?" she asked.

"Maybe." But he didn't sound very hopeful.

Neither was she. Anyone who would try to murder a pregnant woman probably didn't have much value for life in general.

"We'll help him later," Brandon said.

Willa latched on to that thought. There would be a later. They would get out of this safely.

Brandon peered out from behind the tree but immediately popped back into cover. Someone fired a shot, slamming right into the tree where his head had been just seconds earlier. She didn't think it was her imagination that the shooter had moved closer.

"Watch out, Brandon!" Cash shouted.

That sent Willa's heart pumping even more, and she turned, looking all around them, but she didn't see anyone.

There was another shot, but it didn't hit the tree. In fact, she didn't think it had even been fired in their direction.

A moment later, she heard Cash moan.

The man sounded as if he were in pain. And maybe he was. Maybe he had been shot. Of course, it could all be an act to draw them out into the open so he could kill them.

All around them were the sounds of the wind assaulting the trees, and she couldn't pick through that noise and determine what the heck was going on, but she had a horrible gut feeling that things were about to get worse than they already were.

"Should we stay put?" she whispered.

Her voice was beyond shaky, and that must have

been the reason he glanced back at her. "For now." Unlike her, his voice was calm.

Reassuring.

She thought of their short time together. It came like images flying through her mind. She'd only known Brandon for two days. That was it. Under normal circumstances, she would have considered him practically a stranger. But he wasn't. He was the father of her child and the only person she completely trusted.

And she was in love with him.

It was the worst possible time for that to pop into her head. She couldn't tell him, of course. That wasn't such a bad thing. Willa wasn't sure *I love you* was something Brandon would ever want to hear from her.

Maybe it was that particular heartbreaking thought that distracted her. Or maybe she truly didn't hear the sound of the footsteps.

But there had been footsteps. Unheard ones.

Willa had no doubt about that when she felt someone knock the weapon from her hand. She also felt herself being jerked backward.

Into someone's arms.

And before she could even call out, that someone put a gun to her head.

Chapter 17

Brandon sensed the movement behind him and whirled in that direction.

But it was too late.

Someone had Willa.

His breath vanished. His stomach knotted. Hell, his heart nearly stopped. Because this was his worst-case scenario come true. The SOB who had been trying to kill them, now had control of the situation.

Brandon couldn't see the person's face, only the sleeve of a thick coat and the gloved hand that held a gun pressed up against Willa's right temple. The person's body and face were hidden behind the tree.

He made a split-second glance at the porch, the last place he'd seen Cash.

The man was no longer there.

Brandon cursed again. He hadn't seen Cash get

up and leave, but then he hadn't exactly had all his attention focused on the porch, either. He'd known there might be two possible attackers, and he hadn't wanted to watch only Cash and give the second person a chance to sneak up on them.

But that's what had happened.

Or else maybe it was Cash who now had Willa.

Brandon didn't care who it was. He only wanted to get Willa away from that gun.

"Who are you, and what do you want?" Brandon asked the gunman.

The person didn't answer. Didn't move. Neither did Willa. Her entire body seemed frozen in place, and the only movement was from the wind whipping at her hair. Her eyes were wide, her mouth slightly open. She was obviously terrified, and while Brandon wanted to assure her that everything was going to be okay, he knew she wouldn't believe him. He didn't believe it, either.

There were no guarantees that either of them would make it out of this alive.

"Let Willa go," he tried again.

And he would keep on trying because there was no alternative. Somehow, he had to talk the person into dropping that gun, or else he had to use force to take it away. The longer this went on, the higher the chances that Willa would be hurt.

Or worse.

"Willa doesn't remember everything that happened in the hospital lab," Brandon continued. "She has no idea who hired the men who held her hostage."

There was only about eight feet of space between

them, but Brandon inched closer. He had to get within reach of the gun, and lunging for it wouldn't work.

"Think of Willa's baby. My *baby*," he added. Saying those words cut deep into his heart because for the first time, he saw the baby. Not Willa's pregnant stomach. Not the vague images he'd tried to keep pushing away.

Brandon saw what it would be like to hold his child. *His daughter.*

And if this gunman took Willa's life, then his baby wouldn't have a chance. Brandon wouldn't have the opportunity to tell Willa just how much she and this baby meant to him.

"Don't do this," Brandon pleaded. "Please, just let Willa go."

At first he thought his words were useless, that they were having no effect on the person. But then, he saw the slight movement of the trigger finger. The gunman's index finger tensed as if there were some hesitation. Maybe because the gunman hadn't considered just how difficult it was to threaten a woman and her unborn child.

"Let Willa go," Brandon repeated. "And if you need a hostage, take me. Better yet, just leave. Just get back in your car and put an end to this now."

Of course, Brandon couldn't let the person just drive away as if none of this had happened. He would have to stop this once and for all, otherwise the danger would continue. But for now he would say or do whatever it took to get Willa out of the line of fire.

Because Willa was staring at him, he had no trouble seeing when she lifted her left eyebrow. She seemed to be questioning him about what she should do. Maybe she was thinking about trying to drop to the ground so that Brandon could get a clean shot.

But he only shook his head.

If the gunman fired, there wouldn't be time for Willa to move out of the way. It was too big of a risk to take, especially since he seemed to be making progress.

"I can help you," Brandon told the gunman. "I have money inside so you can get away. You can leave now, and no one else will get hurt."

If it was Cash behind that gun, he probably knew that wouldn't happen. But the other three—Wes, Dean and Dr. Farris—they might believe it.

And even Cash might *want* to believe it if he was trying to rationalize a way out of this.

Martin Shore had been a cold-blooded killer, an assassin, but none of the four suspects had likely done a close-kill attempt like this before. Brandon had. During his time in the military, he'd been forced into violent situations. And he knew it wasn't something that most people could stomach.

"Here's what we can do," Brandon continued. It was almost impossible to keep his voice level and calm, especially while looking in Willa's eyes, so he focused on the gunman's trigger finger. "We both put our guns down. We just drop them. Willa and I will get on the ground while you walk away."

The seconds crawled by.

The gunman still didn't utter a sound, but the gloved trigger finger lifted just a fraction. That certainly didn't mean Willa was out of danger, not by a long shot, but he was making progress.

"I want to name our daughter Hannah," Brandon said. It wasn't exactly the first name that came to mind, but it was a name he liked. "She'll be born in February."

The movement on Willa's face caused him to glance at her. She was blinking back tears.

But the gunman didn't have a tearful reaction. The finger went right back on the trigger, and Brandon thought the person was shaking his or her head.

Damn.

He had to say the right thing or do something, and it had to happen now. But what? How could he get through to this would-be killer?

Brandon didn't have a chance to figure that out.

He heard the sound and then saw the movement cut through the darkness. Something came flying through the air.

A small tree branch.

And it smacked right into the back of the gunman's head.

Everything happened fast. Too fast for Brandon to do anything but rely on his instincts to react.

The gunman made a feral sound, part gasp, part outrage. But somehow, the person managed to hang on to the gun.

That didn't stop Brandon.

He latched onto Willa's arm and slung her out of the way. It worked.

Well, it got Willa out of the way.

However, it didn't stop the other things that had already been set in motion.

Their assailant turned. And fired. Not at Willa or Brandon. But at the person who had just delivered that blow with the tree limb.

But before Brandon could take aim and right his

own position, it was already too late. He found himself staring right down the barrel of their attacker's Sig-Sauer.

"Move and you die," the person warned.

The sound of the voice caused Willa's breath to stall in her lungs. She instantly recognized the person who'd just issued Brandon that death threat.

When all of this had first started, she had thought it was Cash or Wes who was holding her at gunpoint. But it wasn't either of the men.

It was Dr. Lenora Farris.

Willa stared up from the ground where Brandon had pushed her out of the way, and she looked around. The gun that Dr. Farris had knocked from her hand minutes earlier was there, on the ground. Willa reached out for it.

"Don't," the doctor warned. It was hardly the caring, empathetic tone she'd used in the hotel suite when she had shown Willa that DVD.

The doctor grabbed Willa again and put her in front of her. She curved her arm around Willa's throat. The position literally made her a human shield. It would make it nearly impossible again for Brandon to fire.

While keeping the gun aimed at Willa's head, the doctor kicked away the gun that Willa had tried to reach. She also used her foot to swat at something else. Something near the tree limb that had hit Dr. Farris in the head.

"Why?" Willa asked, trying to look back at her so she could make eye contact. "You're the one who tried to help me regain my memory."

She gave a weary, hollow laugh and shifted her position so that her back was against the tree. "I didn't want to help you. I was there to find out how much you knew. How much you remembered." The doctor glanced at her. "You remembered too much, Willa."

"Obviously not. Because I don't have a clue why you're doing this."

"Dr. Farris is doing it because she's trying to cover up her guilt," someone snarled.

It was Cash, and he was on the ground to the doctor's left. He sounded as if he was in pain, but it was too dark for Willa to see if he'd been hurt. Though he probably had been. After all, Cash was the one who had tried to hit the doctor with the tree limb, and she had fired in that direction. It was also likely his gun the doctor had kicked out of reach.

But Brandon was still armed. And maybe that's why the doctor turned the gun back on Willa. "Sheriff Ruiz, do as I say, if you want her to live."

Dr. Farris shot a glance Cash's way and what she saw must not have alarmed her enough to finish him off. Instead, she kept her attention nailed to Brandon.

"She put a tracking device on your car," Cash continued. Yes, he was definitely hurt, and he paused to pull in his breath between each word.

God, was he dying? Willa prayed not.

"Why don't you want Willa to remember?" Brandon asked. He stepped closer.

The doctor shook her head and thrust her gun at Willa's stomach. "Stay put and drop your gun," she warned Brandon. "I'm calling the shots here."

"Yeah," Cash agreed. "She's calling the shots because she's a killer. I didn't trust her when I saw that photo Dean had given you. She set me up with that picture. She called, said she had evidence about the case, but I'm guessing she did that so she could get something incriminating in case she needed a fall guy."

If so, then all of this had obviously been premeditated.

"That's why I followed her when she started driving out here toward your place," Cash added. "I figured she'd try to kill you."

Too bad Cash hadn't been able to stop her.

"Put. Down. Your. Gun." Dr. Farris's teeth were clenched when she threatened Brandon.

Willa didn't want him to drop the gun so she tried to help. It was obvious the doctor was far from being calm and in control. Her hands were shaking, and she looked to be on the verge of killing them all.

"The gunman in the lab wanted me to tamper with some DNA files," Willa said. It worked. The doctor went still. "It was the DNA taken from beneath Jessie Beecham's fingernails the night he was murdered."

That last part was a guess. But it was obviously a good one because Dr. Farris groaned softly. "You do remember," she mumbled. Now, there was sadness, maybe even regret, in her voice. "The DNA would have sent me to jail for murder. Because it was my skin tissue beneath Jessie's nails. He scratched me, and I didn't have time to clean him up."

"You killed Jessie Beecham," Willa mumbled. The next question was why, but Willa didn't get a chance to ask her that.

A weary sigh left the doctor's mouth, and she loosened the grip she had around Willa's neck. Since she wasn't watching Cash, Willa hoped the man wasn't so injured that he was unable to do something to help.

Without warning, the doctor pulled the trigger.

The sound blasted through the night, and Willa braced herself to die.

But the bullet slammed into the ground next to her. In the same motion, she swung the gun back to Brandon. "Put down your weapon, or I'll kill you both right now."

Brandon stared at the woman. And then he shook his head and cursed.

He dropped the gun.

Willa's heart dropped with it.

That gun was the only thing protecting them, but Brandon had had no choice. Willa didn't know the doctor very well, but she could tell from the woman's tone that she wasn't bluffing. Of course, Dr. Farris intended to kill them anyway so this would only give them a few more seconds at best.

"I won't go to jail for killing Jessie," the doctor said in an almost whisper. "The man was scum and deserved to die."

Maybe. But now, the doctor was apparently willing to keep on killing.

"I'm sorry," Dr. Farris added.

Everything happened fast. Practically a blur. Dr. Farris lifted her hand, aimed her gun back at Cash. She fired. Two shots. Both slammed into something.

Cash, probably.

The doctor didn't waste even a second. She took aim at Brandon. She was going to fire. Willa had no doubt about that. The doctor was going to shoot Brandon at point-blank range, and he was helpless, standing there, because he couldn't risk coming at the doctor and hurting Willa.

But Willa could do something.

Yes, it was a risk. Anything was at this point. But she couldn't just stand there and let Brandon die.

Willa gathered the air into her lungs and let out the loudest yell she could manage. She threw all of her weight to the left, away from the doctor. The jarring motion worked because Dr. Farris's arm snapped back, releasing the grip she had on Willa's neck. At first, Willa wasn't sure why that had happened.

Then, she saw Brandon.

He had lunged across the space that separated him from the doctor. He was obviously trying to tackle her before she got off another shot.

But he was too late.

The blast, loud and thick, tore through the night.

Everything seemed to freeze, and the images clicked through her head as if someone was snapping pictures. Willa saw Brandon slam into Dr. Farris, and they both flew backward, tumbling onto the ground.

Then, Willa saw the blood.

It was everywhere. On Brandon. On Dr. Farris. Even in the evening light, she could see it on both their clothes.

"Brandon!" Willa called out. He had to be all right. He just had to be. She couldn't lose him.

She scrambled across the yard toward the scuffle. Brandon had the doctor in a fierce grip, his left hand locked around her arm, and his right hand gripped her weapon. And she was fighting back. Though not with much strength.

Willa soon saw why.

Behind Brandon and Dr. Farris, Cash was sitting up, and there was blood all over the front of his shirt. No doubt where Dr. Farris had shot him. He had a gun. The gun that the doctor had knocked from Willa's hand. And judging from the angle of the barrel, he had fired directly at Dr. Farris.

But Brandon had also been in that line of fire.

For one terrifying moment, Willa thought Cash might fire again. At her or at Brandon. But he simply gave a satisfied nod before he collapsed, the gun falling to his side.

Cash might be dead. That registered in Willa's mind. But she couldn't go to him until she helped Brandon. She couldn't let Dr. Farris use that gun to kill him.

Willa reached out to latch on to the doctor's arm so she could help drag the woman away from Brandon. But the arm she held was limp and lifeless.

Willa's gaze flew to Brandon. To his face. To his body. Yes, there was blood. But when he stood, she realized he hadn't been shot. Dr. Farris had been. Cash's bullet had taken out a killer.

And Brandon was safe.

He was safe.

The tears came, burning hot in her eyes, and Willa made it to him in one step. Brandon pulled her warm and deep into his arms and held on.

Chapter 18

Brandon glanced at his watch. It was still five minutes until midnight. Five minutes until it was officially Christmas Day.

Not that they would go anywhere to celebrate.

He didn't intend to leave the hospital until Cash was out of surgery. After all, Cash had probably saved their lives, and Brandon wanted to thank his old friend. However, that didn't mean Willa had to be stuck in an uncomfortable chair in the waiting room.

"Sheila said she could drive you to her place here in town so you can get some sleep," Brandon reminded Willa. It'd been a generous offer from his deputy, but both Sheila and Pete were probably reeling from everything that had happened.

Brandon certainly was.

Judging from Willa's too-pale face and trembling hands, she was as well.

"No thanks," she answered. "I'd rather wait here with you until the doctor gives us an update on Cash."

Since Cash had already been in surgery for hours, Brandon had no idea how much longer their wait would be. So he slipped his arm around her and eased her head onto his shoulder. Maybe she would at least grab a nap.

Or not.

Her head came right back up, and her eyes met his. "Dr. Farris deserved what she got."

"Yeah." Brandon didn't dispute that. The woman had tried to commit premeditated murder, and from what he'd been able to figure out from the notes and emails that SAPD had found on the doctor's computer, she'd taken plenty of steps to do just that.

Thank God she hadn't succeeded.

But not for lack of trying.

In addition to hiring Martin Shore to find and kill Willa, she had spied on Cash's computer to find the location of the safe house where Willa and he had been attacked. Cash had been right about that. He'd also been right about the doctor planting a tracking device on Brandon's vehicle. And to ensure that Brandon's deputies wouldn't respond to his call for backup, the doctor had planted a jammer at the sheriff's office where the deputies were wrapping up Shore's last attack and death. The jammer had prevented their cell phones from ringing. She had even drugged his dogs so they wouldn't alert anyone that she was on his property.

Dr. Farris had been thorough. And in doing so, she had created plenty of future nightmares. Brandon would never forget how close he had come to losing Willa and the baby.

Brandon heard the footsteps in the corridor and got to his feet. He also tried to brace himself for the worst. Cash had not only taken three bullets, he'd lost a lot of blood.

But it wasn't the doctor. It was Pete.

"Merry Christmas," the deputy greeted, though it wasn't very cheery. The fatigue was heavy in Pete's weathered eyes.

"Merry Christmas," Brandon and Willa mumbled back.

"SAPD just called," Pete explained. "They tried your cell first, but the call couldn't go through in here."

Brandon was aware of that. Because the waiting room was right next to radiology, the walls had been reinforced with steel, making reception poor at best. Still, he figured his deputies would keep him informed, and they had. During Cash's three hours of surgery, either Pete or Sheila had paid them a visit at least every half hour.

"SAPD found more stuff on Dr. Farris's computer," Pete continued. He shook his head. "That woman was something else. One of the gunmen who took the maternity hostages was her patient, so she learned about the hostage situation before it even happened. But she didn't lift a finger to stop it."

That sent a coil of anger through Brandon. Willa had gone through hell and nearly died while a hostage, and it could have been stopped before it even started.

Of course, if it had, he might never have met Willa and known about the baby.

Ironic that Willa was here in his arms because of Dr. Farris and those hostage-taking gunmen.

"So, if she knew the gunmen, was she also the one who hired them?" Willa asked.

"I guess you could say she just paid them to do something extra. Their boss had already hired them to tamper with some evidence, and Dr. Farris just paid them on the side to do the same for her. She had her DNA replaced with tissue from the homeless man who was arrested for Jessie Beecham's murder."

"A murder that Dr. Farris committed," Willa mumbled. "Yes. That woman was indeed something else."

Brandon agreed. But this might not be over. "What about the other hostage situation, the one that's supposed to happen today?"

"It was a lie," Pete insisted. "Well, according to the notes SAPD found, it was. She hired Shore to kill Willa and to also get out the word that there'd be another set of hostages taken. But the story was just a ruse to draw Willa out of hiding."

Brandon cursed. The ruse had worked.

"There won't be any other hostages," Willa said. And she repeated it. The breath just swooshed out of her, and when she looked at Brandon, he saw her smile. It was, well, amazing and it lit up her entire face.

Suddenly, it felt like Christmas morning.

"Y'all need me to bring you anything?" Pete asked.

Willa shook her head, but she didn't take her eyes off Brandon. "It's really over. No more danger. No more hostages. I'm free."

"The danger and hostage parts are true. But what about your memory?" Pete asked.

She paused a moment, as if going through her thoughts. "Everything seems to be there. I'm free,"

Willa repeated. "For the first time in months, I'm really free."

Yeah. And that hit him like a sucker punch.

Brandon was sure he wasn't smiling, and that warm
Christmas glow faded as quickly as it'd come.

Willa was indeed free, and that meant she could and
probably would be leaving soon. Of course, that left
Brandon with a huge question.

Was he going to let her go?

It took him about a split second to come up with
the answer to that.

No. He wasn't going to let her go.

Well, not without a fight anyway.

"I know I said I might not make a good father,"
Brandon heard himself blurt out. Not the best start he
could have had for what would be the most important
next few minutes of his life.

"But I'd like to try," Brandon added.

Willa blinked. Stared at him.

"Uh, I should probably go," Pete mumbled. And he
didn't wait for either of them to acknowledge his exit.
Being the smart man that he was, Pete left Brandon to
fumble around with what he wanted to say to Willa.

"I'd like to try to be a good father," Brandon
amended. He shook his head. That still wasn't right.
"I'll do everything within my power to be a good father."

"To Hannah," she supplied, making it sound like
more of a question than clarification.

"Hannah." He huffed. And then cursed when Willa
looked hurt from that huff. "No. I didn't mean it that
way. I used the name, Hannah, to make the baby more
personal to Dr. Farris, so she wouldn't shoot you. It's

a hostage negotiation technique to personalize the crisis situation."

Great. Now, he was babbling.

"But I do like the name Hannah," he added when Willa just stared at him.

Still babbling.

So, Brandon changed tactics. He cradled the back of Willa's neck and pulled her closer. He kissed her. Really kissed her. He put his mouth to hers and took in the softness of her lips. Her taste. That taste soothed him, fired his blood and reminded him just what was at stake here.

Everything was at stake.

"I'm in love with you," he said against her mouth.

He braced himself for her shock and expected her to pull back and stare at him some more. After all, he'd given her no indication of that love. Hell, he hadn't realized himself until he saw Dr. Farris point the gun at her. Then, in that moment, he knew this wasn't about protecting Willa and the baby.

It was about loving them.

Willa didn't pull back, but he felt her smile form on her lips. "You love me?"

Well, this answer was easy. "I do."

"Good." And she kissed him long and hard and stopped only when both of them remembered they needed to breathe. "Because I'm in love with you, too."

The breath he'd just taken stalled in his throat. His entire body seemed to stop, so he could grasp what she'd just said.

"You love me?" he clarified.

"God, yes. I thought that was way too obvious."

Now, it was his turn to smile against her mouth.

But Brandon did ease back because he wanted to see her face. Her eyes. That incredible smile. Willa took his breath away again, and he didn't care if he ever got it back.

Maybe it was because he was totally lost in the moment that he didn't hear the footsteps until they stopped right next to him.

Brandon caught the movement out of the corner of his eye and automatically reached for his weapon. But no weapon was necessary. It was Dr. Ross Jenkins, the surgeon who had been operating on Cash.

Both Brandon and Willa got to their feet, and Brandon tried to interpret the surgeon's poker face. He couldn't. He could only stand there and wait.

"Sergeant Newsome took three bullets to the chest cavity. He's lucky. Damn lucky. Other than a collapsed lung and some broken ribs, he should be fine."

The relief was instant, and Brandon grabbed Willa and hauled her into his arms for a celebratory kiss. Cash was going to be all right. Dr. Farris hadn't succeeded in any part of her plan to kill all three of them.

"I'll keep him sedated most of the day," the doctor continued. "No visitors until tomorrow. So, you two might as well go home." His attention dropped to Willa's belly. "Do I need to call in the OB?"

"No," Willa quickly answered. "No contractions. And Hannah's kicking like crazy. She's fine."

The doctor nodded, pulled on his surgical cap and ambled away.

Willa smiled again, but there were tears in her eyes. "Cash is going to be okay," she mumbled.

Brandon understood those tears. They were of the happy variety. And even though the timing wasn't the best, he decided to see if there was another level of happy to be had here.

But before he could utter a word, Willa pulled back her shoulders and stared at him. "Are you going to ask me to marry you?"

He had been about to do just that, but Brandon hadn't expected her to jump the gun. And he couldn't tell if it was a question she wanted him to ask. The tears were still there in her eyes, but she was no longer smiling.

She was waiting.

It was a risk because if she said no, she might feel too awkward to hang around. She might say they needed space, time or some other thing that Brandon was sure he didn't want.

He wanted Willa.

He wanted their daughter.

And he had never been so sure of anything in his entire life.

To increase her chances of saying yes, he snapped her back to him for a kiss. He made it long, French and hopefully as mind numbing as he could manage. Willa added some mind numbing moves of her own and pressed herself against him. Hard against him. In such a way that reminded him that he could spend at least part of Christmas Day making love to her.

But first, he needed to ask the question.

And get the answer.

He caught her shoulders and looked her straight in the eyes. "Willa, will you—"

"Yes," she interrupted. She grabbed a handful of his shirt and dragged him right back to her.

But Brandon wasn't sure exactly what question she

was answering. "Yes?" he quizzed. He stepped back a little so he could keep a clear head.

Her smile returned. So did the kiss. "Yes, I'll marry you, Brandon. I'll be your wife. Your lover. The mother of your children. Yes to all of it."

That was the only answer he wanted.

So, Brandon pulled her to him and kissed the start of their new life together.

* * * * *

We hope you enjoyed reading
AGAINST THE WIND
by *New York Times* bestselling author
KAT MARTIN
and
SAVIOR IN THE SADDLE
by *USA TODAY* bestselling author
DELORES FOSSEN

Both were originally MIRA Books and
Harlequin® Intrigue stories!

You crave excitement!
Harlequin® Intrigue stories deal in serious
romantic suspense, keeping you on the edge
of your seat as resourceful, true-to-life women
and strong, fearless men fight for survival.

Look for six *new* romances every month from
Harlequin Intrigue!

Available wherever books and ebooks are sold.

The door at the end of the train car opened and a man
stepped through. Becca's pulse leaped. She reached out
and gripped Quentin's leg. "Speak of the devil. He's
headed this way. We need to hide. Right now." She shrank
against Quentin's side, trying to get out of sight of the
man heading directly toward them.

"Kiss me," Quentin urged.

"What?" She shot a glance at him. She'd wanted to
kiss him all day long and wondered if he'd ever try to kiss
her again. "Now?"

"Yes, now. Hurry." He swept the cap off her head,
ruffled her hair, finger-combing it to let it fall around
her shoulders in long, wavy curls. Then he gripped her
arms and pulled her against him, pressing his lips to hers.
Using her hair as a curtain to hide both of their faces,
Quentin prolonged the kiss until Ivan passed them and
walked through to the next car.

When the threat was gone, Quentin still did not let go of Becca. Instead, he pulled her across his lap and deepened the kiss.

Becca wrapped her arms around his neck. If Ivan came back that way, she never knew. All she knew was that if she died that moment, she'd die a happy woman. Quentin's kiss was that good.

The train lurched, throwing them out of the hold they had on each other. Becca lifted her head and stared around the interior of the train car. For the length of that soul-defining kiss, she'd forgotten about Ivan and the threat of starting a gunfight on a train full of people. Heat surged through her and settled low in her belly, and a profound ache radiated inside her chest. She wanted to kiss Quentin and keep kissing him. More than that, she wanted to make love to him and wake up beside him every day.

But she realized how impossible that would be. They were two very different people who worked in highly dangerous jobs, based out of different parts of the country. Nothing about a relationship with Quentin would work. She had to remind herself that he was a ladies' man—a navy guy with a female conquest in every port.

Don't miss A NAVY SEAL TO DIE FOR,
available October 2016 wherever
Harlequin® Intrigue books and ebooks are sold.

www.Harlequin.com

INTRIGUE

EDGE-OF-YOUR-SEAT INTRIGUE, FEARLESS ROMANCE.

Save $1.00

on the purchase of

ANY Harlequin® Intrigue book.

Available wherever books are sold, including most bookstores, supermarkets, drugstores and discount stores.

Save $1.00

on the purchase of any Harlequin® Intrigue book.

Coupon valid until November 30, 2016. Redeemable at participating outlets in the U.S. and Canada only. Not redeemable at Barnes & Noble stores.
Limit one coupon per customer.

52614271

5 65373 00076 2 (8100)0 12218

® and ™ are trademarks owned and used by the trademark owner and/or its licensee.
© 2016 Harlequin Enterprises Limited

NYTCOUP0916